Dear Reader,

Welcome to another month of exciting romances from *Scarlet*. From your letters to date, for which I thank you, it seems as though you are enjoying my monthly choice of new novels.

I wonder, have *you* ever thought of writing a romance? We are always looking for talented new authors here at *Scarlet*. Do you think you could produce 100,000 words of page-turning storytelling which readers such as yourself would enjoy? Don't worry if you're not a professional author, as we're happy to help and advise you if your work shows promise. If you *are* interested in trying your hand at writing for *Scarlet*, why not write to me at Robinson Publishing (enclosing a stamped addressed envelope) and I shall be happy to send you a set of our guidelines?

Keep those letters (and manuscripts!) pouring in!

Till next month,
All best wishes,

Sally Cooper

SALLY COOPER,
Editor-in-Chief – *Scarlet*

About the Author

Danielle Shaw was born in Watford, England. She studied fashion and design at the London College of Fashion and then joined The Royal Opera House, Covent Garden.

Later, Danielle moved to Geneva, where she met her Swedish husband, and worked in various kindergartens. She later returned to the UK and set up her own school.

Danielle is interested in reading, music, theatre, the local countryside and gardening. She also likes to exercise and swims three times a week. 'Above all, though,' says Danielle, 'I much prefer to write!'

Other *Scarlet* titles available this month:

MASTER OF THE HOUSE – Margaret Callaghan
NO GENTLEMAN – Andrea Young
NOBODY'S BABY – Elizabeth Smith

DANIELLE SHAW

SATIN AND LACE

Enquiries to:
Robinson Publishing Ltd
7 Kensington Church Court
London W8 4SP

First published in the UK by Scarlet, 1997

A copy of the British Library Cataloguing in
Publication data is available from the British Library

ISBN 1-85487-930-8

Printed and bound in the EC

10 9 8 7 6 5 4 3 2 1

CHAPTER 1

Sally Palmer breathed a sigh of relief, slipped the gear lever into neutral and waited patiently. To everyone else the busy contraflow with its maze of traffic lights, on the outskirts of Thornhampton, was a nightmare. To Sally it was a chance for quiet reflection. On Fridays it gave her time to plan her weekends and on Mondays it was a brief respite before facing the imminent disasters she would find the moment she stepped into her office at Barrington's.

The chirpy DJ on the radio was telling listeners about the weekend he'd spent with Auntie Nellie or some such relation. Sally never believed him but it made her smile nonetheless. Heaven knows her own weekend hadn't been too much to smile about. One blink and she'd missed it and the list of outstanding jobs she'd planned to tackle remained unfinished.

Monday had begun disastrously too. First she'd dropped a bottle of shampoo in the shower, spilling its entire contents, then she'd snagged her tights and caught her zip in the lining of her skirt. Downstairs she hadn't fared any better – armed with a pair of scissors she found herself in unsuccessful combat with a milk carton whilst studying the calendar. Why were there red circles for this

1

week? Before Richard left – or, more to the point, before she'd told him to leave, red circles meant that time of the month. But for the past fifteen months, red circles hadn't been necessary. Sally pondered the date. 'Not to worry,' she sighed, mopping up spilt milk, 'it will probably come to me later. I can check in my diary at work.'

Locking the house, she was relieved to close the door on every vestige of Monday morning chaos and chose to ignore the last-minute ringing of the telephone. It was probably her sister wanting a babysitter. Jackie had the knack of ringing as she was leaving for the office, knowing too well Sally would be pressed for time and therefore reluctant to say no.

'Sorry, Jackie! This time you'll have to wait, your big sister's got a job to go to.'

'Pardon?' a puzzled voice enquired.

Sally turned to find the postman. 'Oh! I'm sorry, I didn't realize you were there. I was talking to myself.'

'You can get locked away for that,' he grinned, handing her a bundle of letters.

'In that case, they should have come for me years ago. I'm always doing it.' She smiled, thanked the postman and dropped her mail onto the passenger seat of her car.

Now with the traffic having ground to a halt, she was able to examine the assortment of post. There was a postcard from Nicola in Australia, a variety of bills and wonderful cream vellum from Laura. Laura, with her distinctive italic script, no doubt with news of her latest business venture. She couldn't wait to open it. Slowly she slid her finger into the fold of the envelope, only to have thoughts of Laura jarred by the deafening sound of a car's horn. The lights had changed and traffic was

2

moving forward. In her rearview mirror, Sally caught sight of a pimply faced youth, mouthing obscenities. His gesticulating fingers were most definitely not extended in friendly greeting.

In the staff carpark, Sally recognized the usual assortment of vehicles, all belonging to people like herself who preferred to arrive at least half an hour before opening. Like the traffic jams this half-hour gave her a chance to prepare for the day ahead. As personnel officer of Barrington's department store, with its ever increasing staff problems, she had lately begun to feel in constant need of being prepared. George Fry was already busily at work outside her office.

'Morning, Mrs Palmer. I shan't be much longer, just finishing the sign.'

'The sign?' Sally was puzzled. She studied George's open toolbag propped against the wall, along with the nameplate that had once graced her office door. 'Oh! Am I to be moved out of my office, George? Mr Barrington never said.'

'No, it's your new title see.' George held up the shiny new nameplate. Embossed in gold lettering was MRS S. PALMER – HUMAN RESOURCES MANAGER.

Sally groaned. 'Oh no! What a hideous title. What's wrong with "Personnel Manager"? Is this Mr Barrington's idea?'

'Not sure Mrs P.,' George said, picking up a screwdriver, 'but if you ask me it's a bloody stupid idea – begging your pardon that is.'

For a moment the oldest member of the maintenance department looked a trifle embarrassed and shifted uneasily.

3

'Don't worry, George,' Sally assured him, 'I think it's a stupid idea too. I suppose I should be grateful it's only my old sign they're getting rid of and not me.'

'Oh, you don't have to worry about that Mrs P. Only last week Mr Barrington was saying what a valuable member of staff you are.'

'I can't think how he knows, he's hardly ever in the store these days.' Sally placed her briefcase and post on her desk. Calling through to George, who had now completed his task and was gathering up his tools, she continued: 'You've been with the firm a long time, George. What do you think of the rumours that Mr Barrington is going to retire?'

'It's all right for some, Mrs P.,' said George. 'Don't I wish I could have retired at forty-five! As for the rumours, well I don't know.' George scratched his bald head thoughtfully. 'I can't see it myself, but as you know Mr and Mrs B. don't have any kiddies to hand this lot on to. Perhaps they're going to sell up and travel the world together.'

Sally had her own thoughts on this statement, but they were not for the likes of George Fry.

'Of course you could always ask him yourself, I hear he's coming in this week sometime.' George buffed the newly fixed door plate with the sleeve of his khaki overall, and seeing his information had met with a negative response, nodded and walked back down the corridor.

Sally had not heard George's parting comment; she was too busy studying the official brown envelope tucked between the postcard from Nicola and the letter from Laura. She remembered now why she'd circled this week on the calendar. In the confusion of spilt shampoo, snagged tights, broken zips and stabbed fingers she'd

4

completely forgotten. The envelope contained confirmation of her decree absolute. After nine years she was no longer the wife of Richard Anthony Palmer.

Swallowing hard, she buzzed through to her assistant for a coffee.

'Make it strong and black please, and could you ask George Fry to save my old nameplate, I'd like to keep it as a souvenir.'

'You're not thinking of leaving?' Melanie enquired, coming in with a tray of coffee.

'Leaving?'

'Well, you asked for your old nameplate as a souvenir. I managed to get hold of George – he'll drop by with it later.'

'Coming face to face with that sign, Melanie, I admit I felt like leaving. For a start it sounds anything but human . . . but I've been with Barrington's so long, what else could I do? Besides –' she picked up the envelope containing her decree absolute – 'I need this job more than ever now . . . it appears I'm no longer married.'

'Oh Sally, I'm sorry. It hardly seems five minutes since you . . .'

'Started divorce proceedings? Yes, I know.' Sally breathed deeply. 'Well, this won't do, will it? Me sitting here feeling sorry for myself. Looking at this pile of memos from Saturday, it would appear I'm not the only one at Barrington's who has problems!'

She studied the yellow slips of paper. Customer complaints about staff service – or lack of it, supervisory complaints against late timekeepers and Miss Kettle in Kitchenware with yet another incident of sexual harassment. Sally checked in her diary and planned her day accordingly. By midday, pleased with

5

her progress, she opted for an early lunch and made a mental note to stop at Hosiery to buy some new tights.

Later that evening whilst adding bay leaves to a bolognese sauce, Sally's attention was disturbed by the telephone. Recalling the morning call she'd deliberately avoided, she assumed it could only be her sister.

'Perfect timing as ever,' she murmured, picking up the receiver.

Hearing a baby cry in the distance, she sighed, 'Hello, Jackie,' and waited for the usual request.

'Hello, Sal . . . it's not Jackie . . . it's Richard.'

Sally's blood ran cold. Richard! All day she'd forced herself not to think of him. What on earth did he want?

'Sally . . . are you there?'

'Yes I'm here.'

'. . . I'm just ringing to see if you got your letter.'

'The letter?'

'The letter . . . about the decree absolute.'

'Yes . . . Yes, I've got it. It came this morning.'

'And that's all right then is it?'

'All right? . . . I don't understand.'

'I mean it's what *you* want, isn't it?' Richard hesitated, waiting for her reply.

'Of course it's what I want! After all, you got what you wanted, didn't you!' She stopped herself from mentioning the slip of a girl Richard had picked up at the office party. The same office junior she'd tried to pretend didn't exist until Richard dropped the bombshell – he was going to become a father!

'Oh, don't be like that, Sally. I thought we were friends. I mean we still have to talk about the house and things.'

'As far as I'm concerned,' she replied coolly, 'there is nothing further to discuss, Richard. The solicitors have sorted out our finances and I thought it was agreed I should stay on here at the house. After all, it's me who's been paying the mortgage for years!'

'But . . .!' Richard got no further.

A baby began screaming and Sally heard a young woman's voice say, 'Here's her bottle. You give it to her, I'm going to bed!'

As she replaced the receiver, Sally noticed her hands were trembling. Looking at her watch, she saw it was only eight o'clock. Well, she for one was not going to bed at eight in the evening! With anger mounting in her breast, she strode back to the kitchen and, setting the timer for an hour, decided to give both the bolognese sauce and herself ample time to simmer.

Snatching at the list of outstanding jobs with one hand, she picked up her glass of wine with the other and determinedly climbed the stairs to her bedroom. It was as good a place as any to begin. Surveying the chaos left from the morning, she threw the snagged tights into the bin and felt tears of anger fill her eyes.

'What *I* want! What *I* want! The bastard, how dare he!'

Taking a gulp of wine, she placed the glass on the dressing table and flinging the contents of her undies drawer onto the bed, gave a brittle laugh. 'What I want, by the looks of it . . . is a new set of underwear!'

Against the newness of the broderie anglaise duvet, the sets of white undies looked tired and jaded. 'Just like me,' she mused, catching sight of her face in the mirror as she ran her hands through her dishevelled hair.

'Well, Sally Palmer, tomorrow you are going to treat yourself to the prettiest sets of underwear Barrington's have in stock.'

Roz Hughes, departmental manageress, placed several exquisite sets of matching satin and lace lingerie on the counter for Sally's benefit.

'These are the very latest we've had in for Christmas. Mind you, they're also the most expensive. I always boost the department's sales by stocking such frippery at this time of year.' Roz laughed wickedly.

'You know, Sally, it gives me enormous pleasure standing here behind this counter, like a beast in its lair waiting to pounce.'

Sally looked up from where her fingers had been caressing smooth pleated satin, inset with gossamer lace panels. 'Sorry, Roz, I'm afraid you've lost me. Waiting to pounce on what?'

'On the guilt-ridden bastards who come in for late night Christmas shopping, having first drunk themselves witless at office parties.'

Roz looked round quickly to make sure no one else was within earshot before peering over her thick horn-rimmed glasses. 'You know, you can always tell the really guilty ones, those who've had their hands up the skirt of young Sharon or Tracey in the typing pool; they're the ones who spend the most . . . or at least they're the ones I encourage to spend the most!'

'Roz, you're quite dreadful. I don't know how you get away with it, one of these days someone will hear you. What if Mr Barrington . . .'

'Hugh Barrington, my dear Sally, already knows me to be an outrageous old woman. You're forgetting I joined Barrington's when his father was alive and he was then known as young Master Hugh. Take it from me, behind that cool exterior and exquisite tailoring, there's quite a sense of humour.'

Sally found it hard to think of Hugh Barrington with a sense of humour. Polite yes, even charming maybe, but humorous no. Still, as her own contact with HB was strictly on a business level, dealing with Barrington's personnel problems – or was that human resource problems now – humour never really entered into it.

'I expect,' said Roz, putting another delightful lace confection on the counter, 'you've already seen the "boss man" today. They tell me he's doing his rounds.'

Sally was stunned; no one else had mentioned seeing Hugh Barrington in the store. Tall, good looking and immaculately tailored (complemented by handmade shirts, silk ties and the ever present red rose in his lapel), "the boss man", as Roz called him, could hardly be missed.

'Well no, I had no idea, perhaps I'd better get back to my office just in case he wants to see me.'

'Oh no you don't! Not yet, Sally, not after you've made me get this little lot out for you.' Roz's gaze encompassed the contents of the counter. 'You've still got half an hour left of your lunch hour, and from what you were telling me earlier, you are in desperate need of some new undies. Now, are you going to try some of these on, or do you want me to measure you, just in case?'

'Wonderful as you are at your job Roz,' Sally said, picking up an assortment of lingerie, 'even you would find it difficult to measure me as anything other than a

34B. You can tell me something though, did Richard ever come in here to buy underwear?'

Roz shook her head. 'No, why do you ask?'

'Well, as it would appear he got more than his hand up Sharon's skirt, I wondered what he would have bought me.'

'Ouch!' Grimaced Roz, remembering their earlier conversation. 'Sorry, Sally, me and my big mouth again, I was forgetting.'

'Don't worry about it, I certainly don't intend to anymore. I decided last night I'm beginning a new chapter in my life. Don't they say life begins at forty? Well in my case it's beginning at thirty-three and a bit, and this,' she said, dangling a white satin and lace bra set in the air, 'is just a start! You don't have these in black, do you?'

Unaware that Hugh Barrington was in the next department, discussing millinery with Edith Hawtin, Sally said boldly to Roz, 'Right, Mrs Hughes, wrap them up I'll take the lot, including the black!'

For once Roz was almost speechless. 'Including the black? Goodness, Sally, what have you been keeping from me?'

'Nothing,' she replied, wistfully running her index finger along the pleated satin of a bra cup, 'but who knows . . .?'

'Do I take it you're planning a little holiday, Mrs Palmer?'

Sally turned to face the tall, upright frame of Hugh Barrington.

'Why . . . have you heard that I am, Mr Barrington?'

'Well . . . no, but in my experience when married women buy themselves pretty lingerie . . . they're

10

planning a romantic weekend away with their husbands.'

Sally felt the colour rise in her face and the palms of her hands go clammy. All she wanted to do was escape, but how?

Quickly she glanced at her watch. 'Roz, look, don't worry about wrapping them up now. I'll fetch them later. I've just remembered I said I'd go and see Miss Kettle in Kitchenware.'

Hugh Barrington coughed as he watched Sally hurry away.

'Oh dear, Mrs Hughes, do I take it from Mrs Palmer's rapid departure that I have committed a *faux pas*?'

'You most certainly have, Mr Barrington, and if I might be permitted to say so, a most unusual one on your part.'

'Quite so,' he acknowledged, 'and there was me thinking I had a way with the fairer sex.'

Roz discerned the faintest twinkle in his eye. A few years ago Hugh Barrington had had quite a reputation with the ladies and Roz had seen them come and go. That was until he'd married Serena Summers and from then on he'd been the soul of discretion. To everyone else Hugh and Serena Barrington appeared the perfect couple, though Roz knew otherwise.

'Mrs Hughes?'

'I'm sorry, I was miles away . . .'

'Well, are you going to tell me what I said to cause Mrs Palmer to rush off like that?'

Roz was uneasy. It didn't seem right to discuss Sally's personal life with her boss; on the other hand, it wouldn't take long before the news became common knowledge.

'Mrs Palmer received notification of her decree absolute yesterday.'

'Oh dear!' Hugh Barrington's face was grave as he fingered the red rose in his lapel. 'How stupid of me, how utterly stupid. You know I could have sworn I saw them only recently, I thought they were together again.'

'So did we, but it would appear it was Sally's way of trying to be reasonable . . . to prevent any unpleasantness over financial matters. I gather Richard can get quite nasty at times.'

Hugh cast a quizzical eye in Roz's direction, waiting for more information, but none was forthcoming. 'Oh, I see,' he nodded, 'and am I right in thinking there are no children?'

Roz laughed sardonically. 'Yes, that's right. Richard told Sally years ago he didn't want any, that's why she committed herself so totally to her work in personnel.'

'And an excellent job she's made of it too. Look, I really think I should go and apologize. Can you wrap these now, and I'll take them to her office?'

Roz hesitated, picked up the sets of underwear and wrapped them carefully in tissue paper. 'Do you think that's wise?'

'Wise? I'm not quite sure what you mean.'

'Well, if Sally got embarrassed about you discussing her underwear, don't you think it's going to make matters worse by you delivering it?'

'Surely not! Good gracious, I've been looking at and discussing underwear with *you*, Mrs Hughes, since the days of knickers, brassieres and corsets. Now that it's all bras and briefs, I thought you ladies were far more broadminded.'

'Me, perhaps, Mr Barrington, but don't forget I'm not Sally Palmer!'

There was little chance of Hugh forgetting that, as he strode purposefully towards Sally's office. No two women could have been more different. Roz Hughes, tall and thin like a stick insect, with her steel grey hair pulled back into a bun at the nape of her neck, looked every inch the strict schoolmistress of years gone by. While Sally Palmer was petite, soft and rounded, with such expressive deep blue eyes, hidden beneath a long fringe of warm brown hair.

Hugh knew Roz was almost at retirement age – and that Sally had to be in her early thirties. It was funny really, other than thinking of her in her professional capacity as personnel manager, he'd never given much thought to her as a member of the opposite sex. But then years ago, on the advice of his father, Hugh Barrington had made a golden rule: female members of Barrington's work force must remain, at all times, strictly employees.

Hugh studied the new sign on the office door, knocked and entered. Inside there was no sign of Sally. Placing the burgundy and gold bag containing the lingerie on her desk, he was about to leave when a series of prints on the wall caught his eye. A fine arts enthusiast, he stooped to get a better look, then decided to view them from Sally's chair. The pictures had obviously been hung with that purpose in mind.

It was here Sally found him, having gone not to Kitchenware but to the staff cloakroom, to sponge her face. She needed to cool down following her embarrassing encounter. Opening her office door, Hugh Barrington was the last person she expected to find.

Hugh stood up sharply. 'Mrs Palmer, I do apologize. I have no right to be sitting here. Mrs Hughes sent your –' He motioned to the bag – 'but I'm afraid I couldn't help but admire your prints. It seemed the best place to view them was from behind your desk.'

Sally, attempting to regain her composure, was relieved to be drawn into conversation on anything other than underwear.

'Oh yes, the pictures. A friend sends them to me; she has a small arts and crafts gallery. In fact, I had a letter from her only yesterday. She's thinking of expanding and wondered if I could help her.'

'You don't mean to say you intend leaving Barrington's?' There was a note of genuine concern in Hugh's voice.

'No! No!' Sally assured him. 'Laura knows I enjoy going to art and craft fairs; she's just asked me to look out for suitable artists, who might like to exhibit at "Laura's Lair".'

'Laura's Lair?'

'That's what she calls the gallery.'

'Does she indeed? Well, I must say if I was passing by and saw that sign, I'd think it was a den of iniquity and intrigue.'

'Exactly,' said Sally smiling. 'That's the whole idea of it. It draws people inside – and once inside, Laura . . .'

'Go on.'

'I was going to say pounces; she has quite a way with her, you see. But Mrs Hughes has already used that expression today and it doesn't seem as appropriate somehow . . . not in Laura's case.'

'Probably not,' replied Hugh. 'I should imagine Mrs Hughes is an entirely different kettle of fish from your friend Laura. By the way, how did you get on in Kitchenware?'

14

'Kitchenware?'

'Yes, I thought you said you were going to see Miss Kettle.'

'Oh yes!' Sally remembered her earlier excuse for leaving Roz.

'It's all been sorted out. A minor case of sexual harassment. I'm confident there won't be further trouble.'

'Good! We don't really want to find Barrington's splashed across the pages of the Thornhampton Gazette do we?'

'You can rest assured I'll do my best to avoid it, Mr Barrington.'

'I know you will, Mrs Palmer, which is why I've come to see you. As you are so good at sorting things out, I was wondering if you could help my secretary with a small retirement party for Edith Hawtin. She's been with us for years and my wife and I thought it would be a nice gesture. We were thinking of a small get-together one evening after the store closes, heads of departments, the old stalwarts, that sort of thing. What do you think?'

'I think it's a lovely idea, but where would you hold it – the staff restaurant?'

'Good heavens no! Miss Hawtin deserves better than that. I thought in the suite behind my office.'

From the blank look on Sally's face, Hugh realized she was in ignorance. 'You mean to say you've never seen it? My late father had it converted during the war and he used to stay there occasionally. Look, pop along with some ideas for the party on Friday – about four o'clock – and I'll show you.'

CHAPTER 2

By Friday morning Sally had almost forgotten Richard and her disastrous start to the week, and the house no longer resembled the aftermath of a church jumble sale. During the evenings, full of renewed energy, she'd turned out drawers and cupboards, filling bags for the tip and boxes for the charity shop.

'I can't believe how good I feel,' she told Roz over lunch in the staff restaurant. 'I wouldn't have thought getting rid of so much rubbish could make you feel so elated.'

'I suppose having disposed of Richard you can now discard that part of your life too. I must say, you're looking so much better than you did on Tuesday. How's the new lingerie?'

'Wonderful! You know it's a treat to get up in the mornings and put on such pretty things. I feel almost brazen.'

Roz laughed. 'Brazen is a word I'd never use to describe you, Sally, but I would use it for her.' She pointed her fork discreetly in the direction of Michelle Kettle. 'Do you know one of these days that young woman's going to come unstuck.'

Sally remembered her earlier visit to Kitchenware to investigate Michelle's complaint of sexual harassment directed at Mr Knowles of Lighting. Today, standing in close proximity to Lez Knowles, Michelle appeared not to mind his wandering hands.

'What's Lez having today, I wonder?' Roz enquired sarcastically. 'Grope and chips!' She stabbed at the food on her plate. 'God! This fish pie is disgusting. I shall have to complain to the boss man.'

'That reminds me,' said Sally, 'I've an appointment with him this afternoon; he wants to discuss Edith's leaving do. I'd better get a move on if I'm to be ready for the weekend.'

'Mmn. That sounds interesting. Are you doing anything exciting then?'

Sally recognized the suspicious tone in Roz's voice. 'Hardly,' she murmured, finishing her coffee. 'If you think I've made illicit plans for prancing about in my black undies, Roz, I'm going to have to disappoint you. I shall be saving those for a special occasion.'

'Like Edith's party perhaps?' Roz teased. 'Well, I jolly well hope I get an invitation.'

'Of course. Mr Barrington said I was to invite all the oldies!'

'I asked for that, didn't I? Serves me right for being nosy. You're right though, a couple more years and it will be *my* retirement party you'll be planning. Well, I'd better let you go. What time's your appointment?'

'Four o'clock.'

'Ooh! Lucky you, it will be tea and cakes then. Just remember one thing though: don't touch the éclairs!'

17

Sally was puzzled but, with so much still to do, there was no time to ask for an explanation. Leaving the restaurant she paused momentarily by the table where Michelle Kettle and Lez Knowles were having lunch. Lez was feeding Michelle chips with his fingers, completely oblivious to the disapproving looks of neighbouring diners. Sally made a mental note of this as Michelle's scarlet painted mouth opened seductively to accept yet another ketchup covered chip.

Outside Hugh's office, Sally chatted with his long serving secretary. Anyone expecting to find a dolly-bird gracing the MD's outer office was in for a surprise. Not for Hugh Barrington was there a long-legged blonde but instead the short squat figure of Muriel Baxter.

Of florid complexion, a short haircut of the pudding-basin variety and owl-like eyes, Muriel peered defensively across her desk at anyone who dared to attempt to see Hugh Barrington without prior appointment. A mere five foot two, in twinset, pearls and box-pleated skirt, she organized Hugh's office like a regimental sergeant major.

'Mrs Palmer, Mr Barrington won't keep you a moment, he's just taking a call from his wife. Do sit down and tell me what you're planning for Edith Hawtin's farewell. You know I'm really going to miss her, we've both been here so long. I'm extremely envious of her going off on that wonderful cruise with her sister. I was only saying to Mr Barri –'

The door to the inner office opened and the immaculately dressed man himself extended a smile in Sally's direction. 'Mrs Palmer, so sorry to have kept you, do come in.' Closing the door he turned in Muriel's direction. 'Tea for two, Mrs Baxter, please.'

Helping Sally to a chair, he said softly, 'I do hope she hasn't been boring you with details of Miss Hawtin's cruise.'

'Not exactly, but I think she was just about to.'

'It's a pity I can't send Muriel with her,' Hugh grinned.

Not knowing how to reply, Sally remained silent.

'Don't look so shocked, Mrs Palmer. Muriel Baxter is a wonderful secretary, but I'm afraid I don't share her enthusiasm for cruises. I prefer dry land pursuits myself – golf, tennis and walking.'

Sally followed his gaze to an array of recent golf and tennis photos, where with not a hint of Savile Row tailoring, her boss looked tanned and relaxed. What was it George Fry had said about him? Well, if he *was* forty-five, he certainly didn't look it.

'Mind you,' Hugh continued, 'my wife's not averse to life on the ocean waves. She dragged me along once, but I vowed never again. Luckily her sister's only too happy to go with her now.'

Hugh studied the list Sally had compiled for Edith Hawtin's farewell and nodded approvingly. 'That looks about right, I think. A presentation in the staff restaurant at lunchtime and a small gathering of her close friends and colleagues here after the store closes. Perfect.'

Muriel Baxter entered, pushing a polished brass trolley on which rested a fine Wedgwood tea service and a two-tier cake stand, containing a selection of cream cakes.

19

'Will you be wanting me to pour, Mr Barrington?'

'No thank you, Mrs Baxter. I'm sure Mrs Palmer and I are quite capable. That will be all.' Hugh's tone was firm and clipped and Muriel left the room downcast.

'Oh dear!' remarked Sally. 'Is she offended?'

'Quite possibly. Muriel is a great one for ritual, but I'm sure we can manage perfectly well on our own. Now, if you don't mind wheeling that contraption, perhaps you'd care to follow me.'

With that he opened large double doors in what Sally had formerly taken to be panelling and led her into a large sitting room.

'Why, this is amazing, who would have thought it . . .?' Sally ground to a halt with the trolley and stared about her.

'Yes, it is rather novel, isn't it. It was originally my grandfather's idea and my father added to it during the war. Spending so much time here – often days at a time – he filled it with many of his prized possessions. He felt they'd be safer. You know, every day he used to defy the bombs to fall on Barrington's?'

'Well it must have worked,' Sally said, 'but aren't you frightened something will get damaged?' She studied the antique furnishings. 'And the carpet – what if something gets spilt?'

'I appreciate your concern, but as we're only going to have the oldies in here for a few drinks and canapés, I think we can trust them not to throw their food about like the youngsters, don't you?'

He was referring to last year's staff Christmas party when things had got out of hand. For a fleeting moment, Sally was reminded of another office party that had similarly got out of hand. The one that resulted in her divorcing Richard.

Hugh did not wait for her reply, but continued good humouredly, 'Don't worry about the carpet. I'm sure it will be all right. Besides, I think my wife would be pleased to see the whole room ruined. Given half the chance she'd like to get rid of all this.' He waved his arm to encompass the whole area with its red and gold Regency-striped settees, gold carpet and red drapes, tied back with enormous tassels. 'Serena thinks it looks too much like a bordello. Of course I wouldn't know, but I bet my grandfather did!'

Sally followed his gaze to a portrait on the wall. There was a certain presence about the sitter, who, though elderly, had maintained his dark good looks and distinctive glint of eye.

'The first Hugh Barrington and founder of the store on this very site,' Hugh explained. 'Now can I tempt you?'

For a brief moment Sally wondered what Hugh Barrington had in mind, then relieved, realized he was referring to the plate of cream cakes.

Pouring the tea, her eyes alighted on two small chocolate éclairs set daintily between milles feuilles and fresh fruit tartlets. What was it Roz had warned? *Don't have the chocolate éclairs.*

Playing safe she declined the cakes, preferring to take just tea.

'Then you won't object if I take the éclairs for Stanley?'

Sally watched wide-eyed as Hugh walked to a cabinet, removed a plastic container and carefully placed the éclairs inside.

21

'Stanley is my dog. Poor old chap, he's on his last legs really and he has a thing about chocolate éclairs. But don't go telling Mrs Baxter; she thinks it's me who eats them all!'

Sally smiled and sipped her tea. Something Roz said sprang to mind. Something – when she was buying her new underwear – about Hugh Barrington having a sense of humour. He certainly had something Sally thought, something that made her hands shake as he'd watched her pour the tea. At the time, she'd felt strangely uneasy and turned her attention to the list of retirement presents.

'It's the usual, I'm afraid,' Sally added, 'clocks, sets of luggage, teasets and decanters. I've been trying to think of something all week that's different.'

'Well, whatever you do, don't buy her a camera!' Hugh handed the list back to Sally with a smile.

'I've lost count of the times she's tried to show me umpteen photos of her cats and numerous holidays. Now that is one time when Mrs Baxter does have her uses. Speaking of whom, Mrs Palmer, if you'll excuse me, I had better take a look at the letters to sign before the weekend.' Hugh rose and escorted Sally back through to his office.

'Don't forget Stanley's éclairs,' she said softly, as Muriel Baxter came into view with a pile of letters. 'I hope he enjoys them.'

'Thank you, I'd almost forgotten and if you can think of anything more suitable for Miss Hawtin, I'd be extremely grateful.'

'I'll try,' Sally called. 'Have a nice weekend, Mr Barrington.'

'She's such a lovely person, isn't she?' Muriel announced, wheeling the trolley away. 'I take it she didn't touch the cakes, Mr Barrington, and you had your chocolate éclairs? Were they nice?'

'Yes . . . lovely,' Hugh said deliberately.

His reply suited both Muriel's questions, though she was probably unaware of it. Her thoughts were on chocolate éclairs. Muriel Baxter was trying to fathom why she put on pounds simply by looking at cream cakes and her boss, who ate lots of them, never put on an ounce!

Sally handed Hugh the exquisitely gift-wrapped parcel, in Barrington's colours of bugundy and gold, to present to Edith Hawtin. 'I know you said not a camera,' she whispered, 'but I'm sure you will be quite safe. She's hardly likely to invade your office with this after her retirement. Besides, her sister said it was just what she wanted.'

Later, in the suite behind Hugh's office, Edith was discussing her forthcoming cruise with Muriel Baxter for the umpteenth time and asking George Fry for advice on her new camcorder.

Serena Barrington, stunningly tall, blonde and elegant in black, walked to where Roz and Sally were standing by the window, admiring the October night skyline of Thornhampton.

'Hugh tells me the camcorder was your idea, Mrs Palmer. It was obviously the right choice as dear Edith hasn't stopped talking about it all evening.'

'That and her cruise,' Roz remarked sardonically.

'Don't you like cruises, Mrs Hughes? Personally I think they're wonderful, all those exotic ports of call, blue skies and open seas and such interesting people on board too.' Serena looked across the room in her husband's direction. 'Hugh of course loathes them and refuses to go anymore. In fact, he's refusing to go anywhere at the moment because of Stanley.' Her voice carried a note of extreme displeasure.

Sally's attention was drawn at the mention of the name.

'Who's Stanley?' Roz enquired.

'Hugh's damned dog,' Serena hissed. 'You know we are supposed to go away with my sister and her husband for a long weekend, but Hugh won't leave Stanley! It's such a nuisance.'

'Surely you could leave him in kennels?'

Serena turned to face Roz. '*Exactly*, Mrs Hughes, my sentiments entirely, but Hugh won't hear of it, says it's not fair on Stanley.'

Quite why she said it she didn't know, but Sally, remembering the incident with the éclairs said, 'I'll look after Stanley if you like.'

Serena Barrington was clearly overjoyed by Sally's offer and accepted gracefully, unable to believe her luck. She couldn't wait to tell her husband, but not during Edith's little retirement do, just in case . . .

Sitting at her dressing table later that evening, Serena brushed her sleek blonde hair from her face and pinned it to the top of her head like a halo. Then adjusting the triple mirror, so she could view Hugh's reaction to her news as he lay in bed reading, she unscrewed a jar of cleansing cream.

'Hugh darling, you'll never guess, Sally has offered to have Stanley so we can go to Devon with Vivienne and Charles after all.' Serena placed a large blob of cream on her nose, throat, cheeks and forehead and waited for the reaction. None was forthcoming. 'Hugh, did you hear what I said?'

Hugh peered at her over his reading glasses. 'Well I did, but I'm afraid I'm not quite with you. I didn't think we knew any Sallys.'

'Hugh Barrington, you mean to say you work with people for years and never get to know their Christian names. Sally – Sally Palmer!'

This at least drew some response and Serena breathed a sigh of relief and massaged the cream into her neck and throat with long upward strokes.

'Serena, you don't mean to say you've had the cheek to ask Mrs Palmer to look after Stanley? Good heavens! The woman's a personnel officer, not a kennel maid!'

'It's human resources now, darling – or so Gareth tells me. Don't forget you've got to move with the times, Hugh.'

'Well, I for one am quite happy to leave things as they are. I don't believe in using people's Christian names in a working environment. I'm convinced the customers prefer it that way too. Can you honestly say, Serena, that you would prefer to be served by Hilda in Haberdashery or Clarice in Carpets?'

'Hugh, darling, sometimes you sound just like your father and for your information I doubt very much if you would find many Hildas or Clarices anywhere these days.'

25

'Don't be so pedantic. Anyway, I understand perfectly well what you're trying to do. You are trying to draw attention away from the all-important problem of Stanley and Mrs Palmer.'

'But that's just it, Hugh, can't you see there is no problem?'

'But . . .'

Serena, wiping off cleansing cream with moist cottonwool, turned to face her husband. 'No! I won't let you interrupt, Hugh. You must hear me out. Sally – or Mrs Palmer if you prefer – has offered to look after Stanley and that's the truth. You can ask Roz – that's Mrs Hughes to you – if you don't believe me!'

Returning to his book, Hugh could only stare blankly at the pages. Yes, he did believe his wife, but quite how the subject of Stanley and the proposed weekend in Devon had come to be a topic of conversation at Edith Hawtin's retirement party puzzled him. But then, having been married to Serena for twenty-three years and working alongside a numerous assortment of women for far longer, he supposed one should never be surprised by 'girl talk', as his brother-in-law Charles called it. Hugh switched off his bedside light.

Serena added quietly, 'Well, I think it was a very kind gesture on Sally's part and so does Vivienne. I telephoned her when we came back – when you were busy seeing to Stanley!'

Hugh, refusing to be drawn on the subject of his dog at this time of night, listened for the finishing touches of Serena's beauty routine. With the final squeezing of the handcream bottle he could almost count the seconds before she got into bed and switched off her own bedside light. It was on such occasions he gave thanks for their decision to have twin beds.

Serena stood outside Sally's front door, waiting for Hugh and Stanley to follow her up the garden path.

'The door looks as if it could do with a coat of paint, Hugh. I thought you paid your staff decent wages. Paint's not that expensive surely?'

'Serena, please! Don't forget Mrs Palmer's husband left some time ago. It probably isn't a question of money but a question of time. Working fulltime doesn't exactly give you plenty of spare time for DIY; neither does looking after other people's dogs!'

'At least the house looks clean and the garden's pretty, even for this time of year.' Serena turned round just as Sally came to the door.

'I was just saying to Hugh how pretty your front garden looks.'

'Thank you. It's one of my hobbies. Won't you come in?'

'It's probably better if I wait in the car as it will take Hugh some time to explain about Stanley's diet and things. Thanks ever so much, Sally, you're a real poppet. Try not to be too long, Hugh.'

Sally watched Serena, in stylishly cut chocolate-brown trousers and knitted silk sweater, float down the garden path like a model on a catwalk, her elegant cashmere and camel coat swinging nonchalantly from her shoulders. At the gate she turned and blew a kiss. 'Bye bye, Stanley, be a good dog.'

'Did you say it was a walking holiday?' Sally enquired.

'You could say that. Charles and I do the walking, Serena and her sister do the talking.' Hugh shrugged his shoulders as Serena, who was dressed for anything but walking, poured herself into the car.

Taking Stanley's basket and the box of dog-food, Sally led Hugh and the dog into the hall. 'Where do you think he'd like to have his basket? I only have a gas fire in the lounge but he's welcome to sleep there.'

'Good gracious, no! The kitchen will do perfectly. Look, Mrs Palmer, I know you've assured me you really don't mind having Stanley for the weekend, but he's a very old dog and his . . . er . . . bladder doesn't function terribly well – it's his kidneys. I still don't think it's right imposing on you like this.'

'Nonsense, I'm sure he'll be no bother, will you, Stanley?' Sally knelt down and put an arm round the elderly black labrador, who sat with soulful eyes gazing up at his master.

The dog sensed a female who cared – unlike Serena – and lifted a large paw and rested it on Sally's knee.

'There you are. You see, nothing to worry about. We're the best of friends already. Now off you go and enjoy yourselves. Stanley and I will have lots of walks and . . .'

'Don't worry about taking him for walks. I'm sure you'll have enough to do. You look as if you're going to be busy.' Hugh noticed the paint and polyfilla on the dresser.

'Oh that! Well, that's been there for ages. I try to do a few jobs each weekend. Richard, my hus . . . my ex-husband, liked to think he was a dab hand at DIY. Actually he wasn't too bad really. It's just that he

28

never finished one job before starting another. I used to joke that we should call this place "Halfway House".'

' "Halfway House"?'

'Yes, because the jobs were only halfway finished before Richard began another!'

Hugh smiled and looked down at Sally, who was still holding Stanley's paw. 'Right old chap, here's where I leave you, be good, won't you?'

At that, Stanley struggled to a standing position and walked towards the back door. 'Oh dear,' said Hugh, 'I said the wrong thing there. Normally if I say "be good" he takes it as a sign that he has to go in the garden or wherever.'

Opening the back door Sally watched Stanley amble onto the patio and head straight for the bay tree, in its terracotta pot. Seeing her look of concern, Hugh enquired jokingly, 'I hope the bay tree is for ornamental purposes and not culinary.'

Sally hesitated, then responded, with a laugh in her voice, 'I do sometimes use the leaves in cooking, but if I take them from the top branches in future, there won't be a problem, will there?'

Hugh, seeing that she was smiling, thanked her profusely, patted Stanley on the head and left.

In Devon, Hugh and Charles returned from their evening stroll to the village inn. Vivienne and Serena – each with a motive – had insisted on it, choosing to remain at the cottage. Vivienne was concerned. Their son Gareth seemed not the least bit interested in joining his father's legal practice, and Serena was hoping to

29

persuade her sister to join her on a skiing trip in the New Year.

'I'm sure Charles won't mind,' Vivienne was saying as the two men came through the door.

'What won't I mind?' Charles enquired suspiciously.

'Nothing, dear, it's just girl talk. Now who wants a brandy and coffee before we turn in for the night?'

'Tea for me, please, Vivienne.'

'Oh Hugh, you Philistine, you can't have tea with brandy.' Serena was frowning at her husband.

'Philistine I may be, Serena, but I'd prefer tea and no brandy –'

'Speaking of turning in,' Charles interrupted, 'Hugh, old chap, you don't mind if Vivienne and I have the twin room and you and Serena have the double? It's just that we have to have twin beds because of my persistent snoring. If I end up in a bed with Vivienne, I wake up in the morning black and blue, from where she's been kicking me all night.'

Hugh looked at Serena where she reclined on a cushion by the fire. The flames played delicately against her face and cast golden lights into her hair. 'No, not at all, if it's okay with Serena.'

Serena stretched her long body sensuously, nodded and got up. 'I'll go and make your tea, darling,' she whispered, kissing his cheek.

Mellowed by good food, wine and a sense of wellbeing, Hugh lay beside his wife waiting for sleep to claim him. His peace was shattered when Serena propped herself up upon one elbow and smiled down at him.

'Hugh,' she murmured softly, 'you have kept your promise, haven't you?'

30

'Yes, of course . . . have you?'

'Yes, my darling, I have – so it's all right then?' Serena ran her scarlet nails down Hugh's chest and entwined her long legs around his.

But Hugh, thinking suddenly of Sally Palmer's beautiful eyes, had never felt less like making loving with his wife. He wondered if he'd ever be able to face sex with Serena again . . . and acknowledged with brutal honesty that she no longer held any appeal for him. 'Sorry, Serena,' he muttered apologetically, 'I'm exhausted,' and he turned onto his side with a weary sigh.

Serena, not attempting to hide her displeasure, sat up, reached for a glossy magazine, and angrily began to flip noisily through its pages.

Hugh blocked the sound out by remembering Sally's musical voice and, to Serena's chagrin, was soon sleeping soundly.

Years ago, when Hugh realized he couldn't father children and had had problems coming to terms with his infertility, Serena had boldly made her suggestion. She proposed Hugh took a mistress. Her stipulations to the unusual arrangement however, were few. That Hugh never divulged the woman's name, that he never chose a member of Barrington's staff and last but not least, he never had unprotected sex. Of the first and second, she was confident, and tonight's declaration assured her of the third.

When Serena began to holiday 'alone' or take her sister along for company, she in turn had agreed to similar conditions. Together Hugh and Serena were discreet and to their knowledge no one was ever hurt. The arrangement had suited them both admirably . . . until now.

Loading the luggage into the car for their return to Thornhampton, Serena reminded Hugh about the local craft centre.

'Don't forget, Hugh, we must stop and buy Sally something for looking after Stanley. Though God knows,' she said as an aside to her sister, 'what one buys someone who's daft enough to take on an incontinent dog for a weekend!'

At that moment, back at Sally's, Stanley and Sally had returned from their walk, and Stanley now gazed adoringly at Sally as she placed his rug on the settee and helped him climb up. Yawning, she patted him.

'He'll be back soon, Stanley. You'll be pleased to see him and I'll be sorry to see you go. We've had a great time together, haven't we?'

The dog placed a paw on her knee as if in agreement and she in turn stroked him behind the ear.

Hugh found them both fast asleep, when he came in by the back door. Sensing his master's presence, Stanley stirred and wagged his tail. Sally awoke to find Hugh staring down at her with a look she found strangely disconcerting.

'Sorry to startle you but I couldn't get any reply. I saw you both through the window . . . I did knock and ring the doorbell but it didn't appear to be working.'

'No,' she said sleepily, 'the battery went yesterday. Something else for my list but not to worry, I'll get there in the end, I normally do.'

'That's why you're so good at your job. How's he been, any problems?'

'None whatsoever, he's been marvellous, I've enjoyed having him.'

Hugh was on his knees patting the dog when Serena, stunning as ever, appeared at the back door. This time Stanley did not wag his tail. She threw the dog and her husband a look of disdain. 'Hugh, you've been ages. Surely it doesn't take that long to collect a dog and its basket!'

Following them to the car Sally said goodbye and gave Stanley a farewell hug. 'Don't forget, I'll have him any time, he's no trouble.'

Serena snorted, then reached for her Gucci travel bag. 'Oh, by the way, Sally, these are for you. I got the biggest box – as, unlike me, you're obviously not watching your figure.' Kissing the air on both sides of Sally's cheeks, Serena handed her a large box of clotted cream fudge.

CHAPTER 3

Donald Hughes held the car door open for Sally and grinned. 'I hope you two ladies are all prepared for an exciting evening!'

Roz groaned from the front seat. 'I'm not sure which is worse, Donald, an evening spent with you watching football on television, or an evening viewing Edith Hawtin's holiday videos.'

'I'm afraid Roz is blaming me for this, Donald; it was my idea to buy the camcorder in the first place.' Sally stepped down onto the pavement.

'Yes,' sighed Roz. 'It's the choice of two evils: Donald with his lager or Edith's sister with her pea-pod wine.'

'What!' Sally exclaimed. 'You're joking?'

'Never been more serious. Pea-pod, dandelion, parsnip, the lot.'

Sally turned in Donald's direction. 'You know, I think I've suddenly developed an interest in the European cup.'

Roz grabbed hold of Sally's arm. 'No way, José, you're coming with me, you got us into this. Anyway, it won't be that bad. Lillian – Edith's sister – is

34

a bloody good cook, so there's bound to be plenty of tasty morsels to go with the dreadful booze.'

Roz turned and kissed Donald goodbye and Sally was touched by their show of affection. They were such an amazing couple, like chalk and cheese really. The tall, brusque extrovert Roz, head of lingerie at Barrington's, whose tape measure and expert hands had fitted breasts and hips of every size and description, and Donald, who dealt with figures of a different kind.

'What time do you want me to come and fetch you, dear?'

'I'll ring you,' Roz replied. 'It depends how quickly Sally and I can make our getaway.'

'Don't try and escape too soon then. I would like to see the whole match if possible.'

'I'll try.' Roz blew him a kiss and waved goodbye.

'You know, you are very lucky, Roz. Donald's so sweet.'

'I do know, my dear, and would you believe my mother said it would never last. She told me accountants were boring.' Roz gave Sally a knowing wink. 'You can take it from me they definitely aren't! In fact, Donald's quite a – Hey! Isn't that the boss man's car? Christ! You don't mean to say our Edith's invited Hugh and Serena too? And there was me, not having to drive for once, hoping to get rat-arsed on Lillian's pea-pod *nouveau*!'

Sally ignored the departure from Roz's refined 'Barrington speak' into the vernacular. She was more concerned about Hugh and Serena Barrington. An evening spent watching Edith's videos of cats and cruises was hardly their scene.

The midnight-blue Jaguar purred to a halt at the kerbside but only Hugh emerged. 'Good evening, ladies, what a pleasant surprise. Do you think we are in for an entertaining evening?'

Sally sensed Hugh's remark was aimed in her direction. She was the one who'd assured him he would be quite safe from the camcorder. Should she apologize now or later, she wondered, but suddenly the door opened, and in the brightly lit hallway stood Edith Hawtin, newly tanned, wearing a flowing Hawaiian print dress.

'Edith, how charming you look, such amazing colours. You've obviously both had a wonderful time.' Hugh bent to kiss Edith's cheek and at the same time shot a cheeky wink in Sally's direction.

She turned to see if Roz had noticed too, but she was busy handing her coat to Lillian, who then ushered them through to the sitting room – the setting for the night's viewing.

'I'm so sorry, Mrs Barrington couldn't join us,' Edith said, handing Hugh a glass of straw coloured wine.

'Yes, such a shame, she was so looking forward to it. Prior arrangements, I'm afraid, but she sends her love to everyone.' Hugh took a sip of his wine and turned away. Sally thought he was going to choke.

'That's what you get for lying through your teeth,' Roz whispered.

'Still, you have to admit he's a damned good actor, he should be on the stage. Can you just see the snooty Serena wanting to join this lot?' Roz looked about the room at the weird assortment of Barrington's old stalwarts and Edith and Lillian's friends from the Parish Council.

In her mind's eye, Sally could only see Serena kissing the air as she'd handed over the box of fudge. The memory of it still made her seethe.

'Are you all sitting comfortably and do you all have a glass of wine before we begin?' Edith studied her guests who nodded and murmured politely. 'Right, Lillian, you may switch off the lights. By the way, everyone, we'll be having refreshments in the conservatory at half-time.'

In the dimly lit room Sally noticed Hugh lean sideways and pour the contents of his glass into the aspidistra. Sensing his action had been witnessed, he caught Sally's gaze across the room. All other eyes were on the video screen.

Several films and numerous bottles later Roz and Sally found themselves alone at one end of the conservatory. Hugh was talking to George Fry and Muriel Baxter, Lillian and Edith were in animated conversation with a group of ladies from the WI.

'Do you know, Sally, I think the boss man's a brick coming here tonight, which is more than his lady wife would do. Prior engagements indeed. We all know what Serena Barrington's prior arrangements are!' Roz took a gulp of wine and refilled her glass from a bottle on the table.

'I don't know what you mean.'

'Oh come on, Sally, you must have heard about Serena and her –'

'Roz, I think you should keep your voice down, someone might hear. I thought Hugh and Serena were happily married?'

'They are, they are,' Roz insisted in a slurred tone of voice, 'but there's happily married and happily married, isn't there?'

Sally was becoming confused but Roz continued, 'I just think it's a shame there're no kids. I can just imagine him with children. I know he's got his nephew Gareth, but it's not quite the same, is it? If he'd had a son at least they could play golf together whilst Serena was involved with her "prior engagements".'

Sally thought of her own childless marriage to Richard. 'Not everyone wants children, you know. Perhaps Hugh and Serena didn't want –'

'That's just where you're wrong, Sally.' Roz reached over and refilled both their glasses. 'They did want . . . but the problem, would you believe, is in his department. Serena told me once when I was fitting her for a bra.' Roz eyed Hugh lasciviously. 'You wouldn't think such a fine figure of a man could fire only blanks, would you?'

'Roz! I don't believe Serena would tell anyone that; besides it's not always the man who is infertile –'

'Don't you? Well, she did and he is. I'll tell you something else she told me.' Roz held a finger to her lips and pulled Sally closer. 'Serena Barrington had a child, before she and Hugh were married. She gave it up for adoption. Of course I've never told anyone else.'

'And I wish you hadn't told me. It doesn't seem fair on Mr Barri –'

'Oh! You don't have to worry about him. He's taken solace elsewhere over the years, has our Mr Barrington. Mind you, not to the extent of his wife, and probably not for some time. He's the very soul of discretion.'

Sally, shocked by such revelations, gulped at her wine.

'Don't look so amazed, Sally, it goes on all the time in those sorts of circles. You'd be surprised what people tell me while I'm doing a fitting. I understand Hugh and Serena came to some sort of arrangement.'

Sally looked across the room and caught Hugh's eye. He raised his glass in her direction, smiled and walked away to the table laden with the tasty morsels Roz had described earlier. This time Roz saw him too.

'Here's to Hugh Barrington the third.' She clinked her glass loudly against Sally's. 'God, he's such a virile looking bastard, couldn't you just . . .'

'No, I couldn't! Quite frankly Roz, for the past eighteen months I've been enjoying the respite from the poking and prodding of a man who was only interested in satisfying his own lusts.'

'You don't mean you and Hugh Barri –?'

Sally's face, that had been full of anger, creased into laughter. 'No, of course I don't stupid, I mean Richard!'

The two women exploded into giggles. Then, on a more serious note, Roz took hold of Sally's hand. 'Oh, Sally! I'm sorry I thought you and Richard had been really happy. Why, I even remarked to Donald on one occasion that I thought you two were like us at that age – having a truly wild time together.'

Muriel Baxter passed by, carrying her plate piled high. Sally sighed. It was topped with smoked salmon, asparagus canapés and mini scotch eggs.

'I suppose you could say we started out with smoked salmon and fillet steak and ended up with sausage and mash, if you get my drift.'

'Only too well, dear,' Roz said, patting her hand in motherly fashion.

'I was going to offer you some canapés but as you appear to be talking about fillet steak and sausage and mash, I doubt whether I can be of any use.'

Sally and Roz spun round to find Hugh Barrington standing behind them. How long had he been there? Sally felt herself flush scarlet and Roz downed her glass in one gulp.

Hugh offered the plate of canapés but both women declined. 'Perhaps a refill,' he suggested, looking at their empty glasses.

Sally shook her head, whilst Roz fought hard for something to say.

'I think we've had more than enough already, thank you, but do have one yourself, Mr Barrington.' She picked up the bottle.

Hugh declined. 'Like you I've had more than enough, I rationed myself to one glass' – here he looked at Sally – 'don't forget I'm driving.'

'Speaking of which, I'd better ring Donald to come and fetch us. I expect the match has finished by now.'

'Apparently not. George tells me they're into extra time.'

Roz groaned, 'Oh no! I don't think I could stand it here any longer. Especially as I heard Muriel asking for a repeat showing.'

'Then perhaps you'll allow me to take you both home,' he suggested and they gratefully went for their coats.

Edith Hawtin stood in the hallway to wave them goodbye. 'It's so kind of you, Mr Barrington, to take Sally and Roz home. You're sure it's not too far out of your way? We could always ring for a taxi.'

'Nonsense,' Hugh insisted politely, 'it will be my pleasure,' and he found himself escorting a somewhat unsteady Roz and a subdued Sally to his car.

Relieved to see Roz climb in the front passenger seat, Sally turned to Hugh. 'Perhaps you can drop me first; that is, if Roz doesn't mind.'

Roz didn't mind at all, if it meant sitting in the luxury of leather upholstery for another twenty minutes, and even hoped some of the neighbours would still be up to see her travel home in style. Her sex life with Donald might never have been boring but his choice of car – like his job – was.

Despite her protestations, Hugh walked Sally to her front door.

'I'd prefer to know you were safely indoors,' he said, watching her take her key from her handbag. 'By the way, how's the bay tree?'

'Surviving, thank you. How's Stanley?'

'Oh, he's surviving too. The vet has suggested a course of injections, which might help. As long as he's not suffering, I don't have to consider the final option of putting him down. I'm hoping when the time comes, he'll just go in his sleep.'

Sally nodded and thanking Hugh politely for the lift, waved goodbye to Roz. As the car turned in the cul de sac, Roz's attention was caught by a familiar figure, but Sally had already gone inside, and appeared not to have noticed.

In her bedroom Sally slipped off her shoes, hung up her suit and sat facing her reflection in the dressing-table mirror. For a brief moment she didn't know whether to laugh or cry. Roz had certainly made her

41

laugh tonight but there had also been an air of melancholy to the evening. With talk of childless marriages and Hugh and Serena's 'arrangements', Sally thought of the 'what ifs' and the 'if onlys' in relation to her own marriage to Richard.

If she and Richard had had a child, would things have been any different? Concluding it was too late to be having a post mortem, she went in search of some paracetamol. She was feeling decidedly woozy and her head ached like mad. She only hoped Roz was behaving herself in Hugh's company. Would he be taking home Roz the efficient store consultant or Roz the motherly comedienne?

Halfway to the bathroom she heard the doorbell. Had she left something in the car, her scarf perhaps? Alarmed, she reached for her bath robe and going downstairs hoped it would be Roz and not Hugh waiting on the doorstep. The silhouette behind the stained glass panel was that of a man.

'Hello, Sal.'

'Richard! What are you doing here?'

'I've just called to say hello. Aren't you going to ask me in?'

'No, it's much too late and I've got a headache.'

'Well, that wasn't what I came for – but now I come to think of it . . .' Looking her up and down, Richard's eyes caught sight of the delicately pleated satin and lace bra, where her robe gaped open.

'Well, well, do I detect some new undies? You do look nice.' He reached towards the loosely tied sash and slipped unsteadily.

Smelling alcohol on his breath, Sally stepped back into the hall and retied her bath robe.

'How dare you, Richard! What do you mean by coming here at this time of night. I do believe you're drunk!'

'No, Sal, not drunk. I've just had a little drink or two to drown my sorrows. I've a slight cash-flow problem, you see, and I thought you might be able to help me out . . . for old time's sake, shall we say?'

'Old time's sake! You've had more than enough from me for old time's sake, Richard, I don't know how you've got the nerve to even ask!'

'Well, I need some money, Sally, and as you've got yourself some rich new friends – lifts home in expensive cars, eh? – I thought you wouldn't mind giving me a few hundred quid. Or perhaps you can ask your sugar daddy to lend you some. Was it him who paid for your satin and lace?' Richard's hand reached into her robe and made a grab at her breast.

Sally pushed him away angrily. 'Get out! Just get out, Richard! Next time if you want to talk, ring beforehand. But if you think I'm giving you money, you've another think coming. You've had more than enough out of me over the years.'

'We'll see about that, Sal,' Richard said arrogantly, rubbing his shoulder where he'd fallen against the doorframe. 'I was only asking for a few hundred – still if you'd prefer, we can always sell this house.'

'Go to hell!' yelled Sally, slamming the door in his face.

Quite how long she sat with her back against the door, Sally didn't know. She was only aware of her beating heart and silent tears pouring down her face. From

43

outside, the streetlight cast rose-coloured hues through the stained-glass panel, bathing her robe in a delicate pink. Attempting to trace the filigree shadows with her fingers she realized she was shaking.

'The bastard! The bastard!' she cried angrily. 'How dare he? I will not sell this house!'

Suddenly and without warning, the rosy shapes became obliterated by a figure at the front door and she felt her whole being frozen to the spot. Richard! Whatever she did, she must not panic. She wouldn't even answer the door. He was so drunk anyway and with luck would go away.

The doorbell rang incessantly until her nerves began to jangle. It was obvious he wouldn't go without speaking to her now. Bracing herself, she half-opened the door and screamed angrily. 'Look, Richard! I thought I told you to go to hell! Just get out . . .!'

'Sally, my dear, are you all right? Roz said she thought she saw your ex-husband loitering in the shadows . . .'

Slowly the door was pushed open and finding herself confronted in the hallway by Hugh Barrington, Sally slumped to the bottom of the stairs, where she buried her head in her hands and sobbed uncontrollably.

'I'm sorry . . . I thought . . . you were Richard . . . he wanted . . .'

'It's all right,' Hugh's voice whispered reassuringly, 'I understand.' Hugh sat on the stairs and took her gently in his arms. She shivered and felt herself warmed by his embrace. 'It's all right, Sally,' he repeated, 'he's gone. Richard's gone.'

'Are you sure?'

'Positive. I saw him go when I pulled into the close.'

'But why did you come back?'

'Roz was concerned, she said she thought she saw Richard but wasn't quite sure. Initially, I thought it might have been Lillian's wine giving her hallucinations – but just to be on the safe side, I thought I'd come by and check. I would have been earlier but Donald wanted to give me a blow by blow account of the football match.'

Sally smiled weakly. 'Thank you, it was very kind of you.'

'There, that's better. Now, would you like to borrow my handkerchief? Isn't that what we men are supposed to do when we rescue damsels in distress?' Hugh passed her a crisp white handkerchief from his pocket but made no attempt to release her from his grasp.

'You know,' he said presently, 'if you don't mind my saying so, this hallway is freezing. Is there nowhere warmer we could sit?'

Sally withdrew from his embrace and led him through to the lounge where she lit the gas fire. 'Excuse the muddle,' she explained, moving papers from the settee, 'I've been preparing for a seminar. Would you like a cup of coffee?'

'You're sure you don't need a brandy after tonight's upset?'

'Oh no! I've had far too much tonight already; besides, I don't have any brandy. I could offer you a whisky.'

'Heavens no! Actually I'd much prefer a cup of tea.'

Sally looked surprised.

Hugh continued, 'At this time of night I sometimes prefer tea to coffee and besides, Lillian's wine was enough to destroy anyone's stomach.'

'But you didn't drink it!'

'So you did see me pour my glass into the aspidistra! I wasn't quite sure at the time. I just felt someone's eyes were watching me. Thanks for keeping mum.'

'I was hardly likely to tell, was I? I only wish I'd done the same. I'm afraid Roz and I got carried away.'

'So I noticed.'

Not wishing to be reminded of what happened when she and Roz had got carried away, it seemed the ideal time to put the kettle on.

'Assam, Earl Grey, Fennel or Jasmine?'

'Earl Grey would be perfect. I prefer to leave the vegetables and fruit to Lillian Hawtin. My God! I expect there'll be some sore heads tomorrow. Did you see Muriel? I never realized she could eat and drink so much. What's wrong? You look as if you've seen a ghost.'

'Oh dear!' Sally stopped stirring her tea and let the slice of lemon float slowly to the surface. 'I've just noticed your shirt.'

'My shirt?'

'You've got make-up on your shirt! When you first arrived and gave me your handkerchief, I must have . . . Whatever will Mrs Barrington say?'

'Well, as she's away, probably nothing. As for Mrs Burt . . .'

'Who's Mrs Burt?'

'Our daily help. She does the laundry.'

Sally froze. She couldn't risk Mrs Burt telling Serena that Hugh had come home with make-up on his shirt! Even if, as Roz insisted, the two of them did have an arrangement. No, she definitely couldn't allow that.

'You must let me wash it . . .!'

46

'But, Sally that's not necessary, I have heaps of shirts.'

'Mr Barrington, I insist. For my sake please . . . if I wash it and tumble dry it straightaway I can air it by the fire. It won't take long.'

Hugh studied the deep blue, tear-stained eyes pleading with him beneath a tousled fringe. 'All-right,' he conceded, 'but I can assure you it really isn't necessary.'

Removing his jacket, Hugh laid it across the settee. Sally caught sight of the lapel.

'Perhaps I should sponge that too,' she said anxiously. 'I can see traces of blusher.'

'You don't want my trousers as well?' he joked.

Reaching for the jacket, Sally panicked. Hugh was unbuttoning his shirt and she suddenly realized that before too long her boss would be sitting on her settee, naked from the waist up!

'No wait!' she cried, dashing to the door. 'Wait just a moment, I'll get you something to slip on!'

Hugh smiled to himself, hearing her anxious footsteps scurry away up the stairs. Flushed, she reappeared carrying a knee-length cotton kimono. 'I'm afraid this is all I could find, Mr Barrington. Richard took all his clothes with him.'

Turning his back, Hugh removed his shirt and donned the kimono.

'There, how do I look?' he enquired. 'Probably not as fetching as Edith in her Hawaiian print.'

Sally suppressed an embarrassed giggle as their eyes met.

'Now that I'm wearing your clothes and you are about to do my laundry, don't you think you could call me Hugh. I'd much prefer it?'

47

Sally nodded and took the shirt and jacket to the kitchen.

Aware of running water and the sound of scrubbing, Hugh settled back to read the notes for her forthcoming seminar on Human Resource Management, and some time later she appeared with his shirt neatly rolled in a clean white towel. Bemused, Hugh watched her kneeling on the carpet, patting at the roll of towel with her hands. It reminded him of a Swedish massage he'd had years ago.

'What are you doing?'

'Drying your shirt. This is one of the best ways of removing the surplus moisture. It's an idea I picked up at university. It's great for drying tights and underclothes if you need them in a hurry.' She blushed at what she'd just said, then added, 'I suppose you've never had to.'

He smiled. 'Not exactly, as I don't wear tights and I don't think it's a method I've ever seen Mrs Burt use either. I shall have to tell her about it – but then she never seems to be in a hurry. Come to think of it . . . neither am I.'

With that Hugh knelt beside her, ran a hand softly through her hair and took her in his arms. 'Sally,' he murmured, 'my darling Sally.'

With the warmth of the fire at her back, Sally felt Hugh's lips brush gently across her eyes and cheeks, before resting fully on her mouth. Then, very slowly, he lowered her gently to the floor.

Confused by the wine, her headache and the evening's revelations, Sally struggled with the jumble of thoughts flashing through her head. What was it Roz had said earlier, when referring to Hugh Barrington?

'Couldn't you just . . .?' At the time she'd said a definite no, with thoughts of Richard still fresh in her memory. But these were not Richard's lips kissing her throat, nor were they Richard's hands caressing her body. This was Hugh Barrington and his touch was electric . . . but he was also her boss!

Frantically freeing herself from his embrace, Sally became aware of the damp towel at her neck. She shifted uncomfortably and sat up.

'No!' she cried. 'No! We musn't – you're my boss. It's not right – not here.' Her words poured out in an incomprehensible babble.

Making no attempt to draw her back into his arms, Hugh studied her thoughtfully and in silence. Unable to face his penetrating gaze, Sally turned away, holding her robe closely against her breasts. The kimono she'd loaned him lay in a crumpled heap by the settee.

'You know,' he said, reaching for it, 'I think this probably looks better on you. Perhaps I'd better get my jacket.'

'I'll iron your shirt,' she said hurriedly.

'There's no need, I can take it as it is . . .'

But she'd already disappeared, using the kitchen as sanctuary and the ironing board as defence against any further advances. In the yellowing fluorescent light, the kitchen took on a seedy appearance. Hugh recalled Sally's comments – the weekend she'd looked after Stanley – about all the jobs Richard had started and never finished. There was evidence of them every-where.

As Sally's hands, pale and trembling, painstakingly ironed the cream lawn shirt, Hugh turned his attention to the stripped paintwork, half-finished kitchen cupboards and kitchen door; the lounge with its threadbare carpet and ancient gas fire hadn't been much better. It was hardly the setting for seduction, yet he knew he paid Sally a generous wage. What was it she had said earlier, when he'd first arrived, something about Richard wanting money? Was that where Sally's money had gone, on her no-good ex-husband? Hugh felt a sudden surge of anger but then became aware of Sally offering him his shirt. Quickly, before she had a chance to pull away, he took hold of her hand.

'Sally, listen to me, I've got a proposition to make to you. You told me earlier why Richard had called, the fact that he wanted money. Perhaps I can help . . .'

'You mean a loan?'

'Not exactly, I thought you and I . . . perhaps we could spend a weekend together, somewhere nice and –'

Sally's eyes widened in horror as she stared up into his face. 'You mean . . . you mean you want to pay me like some common whore, to be one of your "little arrangements"? Isn't that what you and your wife call them? No! No, I don't think so, Mr Barrington. I prefer to earn my living as a personnel manager, or should that be Human Resources Manager? By the way, you never did tell me whose bloody stupid idea it was to change my title! Thank you for your help earlier, I'm very grateful to you, but now if you don't mind –' she wrenched her hand from his grasp – 'I think you'd better leave!'

'Sally please . . .!' Hugh stopped himself, sensing the futility in attempting further rational conversation. He was tired, Sally looked totally drained and it was almost two o'clock in the morning.

Buttoning the still warm shirt, Hugh Barrington slipped on his jacket. He had a busy day ahead and in less than seven hours was due to attend an important business meeting. In silence, Sally held the door for him, where he embraced her gently, kissing her on the forehead.

'Forget about everything for the moment, please. Get a good night's sleep – or what's left of it. I'll see you later at the office.'

Closing the door, she heard the car purr away into the stillness of early morning and biting on her hand to hold back fresh tears, reached into her pocket. Slowly, she brought out the white Egyptian cotton handkerchief, exquisitely monogrammed with the letters HB in one corner.

'Oh Hugh,' she whispered, clasping the handkerchief to her breast, 'whatever must you think of me?'

Hard as she tried, she couldn't dispel from her exhausted mind how she'd warmed to his caress and how wonderful it felt when his lips met hers. How they'd almost . . . But she'd drawn away, saying . . . Goodness! What had she said? She remembered saying 'no', but, closing her eyes, she struggled to think of her exact words. Something like, 'I can't – we musn't – not here.'

The last two words haunted her most. 'Not here.' Why had she said that? In her heart of hearts she knew. It meant she'd been willing to . . . She shivered. Was that the reason Hugh Barrington felt he could buy her services? Climbing the stairs, her mind in turmoil, Sally wondered how she could ever face him again.

CHAPTER 4

Muriel Baxter, her eyes more heavily lidded than usual, sat nursing her aching head whilst Hugh raged about the office like a bear with a sore one. At twelve thirty Roz and Sally faced each other over a frugal luncheon. Their conversation was subdued.

'Christ! I felt awful this morning, how about you? You know last night as I lay in bed, not only did I keep seeing the films of Edith's cruise, but I felt as if I was on the same bloody boat with her . . . the way the mattress kept rolling. And I know it wasn't Donald making the bed go up and down as for once I really did have the proverbial headache. Sally, you're very quiet, are you okay?'

Sally stirred her coffee absentmindedly. 'Shouldn't it be ship?'

'Ship?'

'Yes, ship. Aren't cruise liners called ships and not boats?'

Roz stared at Sally's blank expression. 'I don't know and I don't bloody care. All I care about at the moment is my head and you. God! I know I feel awful but you most certainly look it. Here I am rabbiting on about boats – oh, all right, *ships* – and you haven't even told me what happened last night.'

Sally's face filled with alarm. 'Last night?'

'Yes, I can see from the look on your face, he turned up. I was right, wasn't I? It was Richard I saw lurking in the shadows?'

Sally breathed a sigh of relief; for one awful moment she thought Roz was talking about Hugh.

'Oh, yes . . . it was Richard.'

'Well, aren't you going to tell me what he wanted . . . or is it too personal?'

'No, it's all right. He just wanted some money and . . . tried to make a pass at me.'

'He did what! He didn't hurt you, did he?'

'No, he was too drunk. I just pushed him away and slammed the door in his face.'

'The bastard – and did he come back?'

Sally wanted desperately to say to Roz, 'No, he didn't come back but Hugh Barrington did and I made a complete fool of myself.' Despite the fact she and Roz had been friends and confidantes for years, it was too intimate to share. It was a burden she had to carry alone.

'Oh, Sally. You poor thing, no wonder you look so ashen. You know I nearly sent Donald round – but with the match going into extra time, he would have been over the limit. It would have been just his luck to have been stopped by the boys in blue and breathalysed.'

Sally, glad of Donald imbibing an extra lager or two, was anxious to change the subject. Roz on the other hand wasn't so keen.

'Look, if it happens again, promise me you'll ring. Any time night or day and one of us will be round.'

Nodding and offering up a silent prayer, Sally thought, please God don't let Richard call again unannounced. Yet, in her heart of hearts she knew he would. She also knew the subject of the house and money would be his reason for doing so.

She looked at her watch. Another four and a half hours to go before she could leave the office. Hugh had mentioned a business meeting when he'd left; now, presumably with that out of the way, he might come and seek her out. Approaching her office she thought for one awful moment she might find him waiting.

'Yes, Mrs Baxter, I'll tell her as soon as she returns from lunch.' Sally heard Melanie's efficient voice and hovering in the doorway waited for her assistant to put down the phone.

'That was Mr Barrington's secretary. Mr B. wants to see you at four o'clock in his office.'

Remembering a previous meeting in Hugh's office at the same time, Sally clenched her fists and felt her nails digging into her palms. She couldn't face Hugh this afternoon, she just couldn't. Her gaze rested on her nameplate: HUMAN RESOURCES MANAGER. Where were her resources now? What excuse could she give Hugh Barrington?

Melanie handed her an envelope. 'I've managed to get you a room in the annexe, here's the confirmation.'

Sally stared blankly. 'The annexe?'

'Accommodation for your course. You asked if there was a female only annexe, remember?'

'Oh yes, how stupid of me, I quite forgot. And is there?'

'Yes, and by all accounts, you were allocated the last available room. It's obviously a very popular idea.'

Sally opened the envelope from the conference centre. The delegates would be of mixed sex but at least she wouldn't have to worry about unwanted male visitors knocking on her door after midnight.

'Lucky you, escaping for a week. Muriel Baxter says H.B. is in a foul mood and wants all sorts of things arranged with the run up to Christmas. I gather she's nursing a sore head after last night's gathering at Edith Hawtin's. By the way, weren't you there too?'

'Yes,' Sally replied lamely, 'it was quite a night!' She retreated to her office but emerged again at a quarter to four. 'I think I'll just pop out for five minutes' fresh air. My head is splitting,' she lied.

'Don't forget your appointment with Mr Barr –' Melanie's voice trailed in pursuit.

Sally had every intention of forgetting and, hurrying to her car, she looked furtively behind her. Thank goodness Hugh's office commanded a better view than the staff carpark! Once home she telephoned Muriel Baxter. Using her headache as the excuse for not keeping her appointment, she announced she was going to bed.

Later, with her house in darkness, there was no one to hear the persistent ringing of her phone or answer the relentless call of the doorbell.

'It's very good of you to offer to look after the children like this, Sally. A lovely surprise and so unexpected.

Dave and I really appreciate it.' Jackie hugged her sister, fetched her coat and called to her husband that she was ready.

'Don't forget I'm going to be away all next week, so I thought I'd give you both a chance to paint the town red. Stay out as late as you like, I'll curl up in the spare room and see you in the morning.'

Sally waved them goodbye with a sigh of relief. It hadn't taken too much persuasion to convince her sister and brother-in-law they needed a night off from their children, but she nevertheless felt guilty for using them. Here at least she was safe from Hugh and Richard.

Upstairs, the bathroom, covered in damp towels and dirty clothing from the children's baths and their parents' showers, brought Sally back to earth with a bump, completely dispelling any earlier paranoid thoughts of Hugh and Richard hammering on Jackie's door, trying to find her.

'This is judgement on you, Sally Palmer,' she whispered, 'and as punishment for your deception, you can jolly well stay here tomorrow and help tidy this place up.'

Exhausted by her labours and overwhelmed by the constant chaos of her sister's house, Sally returned home to the welcome solitude of her own. There, stretching luxuriously in the shower she sighed with pleasure as needles of hot water stung her body, washing away all traces of disinfectant, lavendar polish and what she called *eau famille*

Feeding and changing her youngest nephew during the weekend had been a welcome experience for her, but it also left her wondering how Richard was coping with fatherhood. Now totally saddened and confused, she swathed herself in pink towels, sprayed herself with her favourite scent of patchouli and jasmine and concluded it was just as well she was going away. At Rosebay Hall Conference Centre she would be able to channel her emotions in other directions.

Showered, refreshed and with her bag packed, Sally gathered her papers and was on the road to Rosebay Hall half an hour before Hugh walked up to her front gate with Stanley. The dog wagged his tail and looked up expectantly. Nonplussed by Sally's absence he ambled round to the back door, closely followed by Hugh, and once again began to head for the bay tree.

'Well, old chap,' Hugh sighed, 'perhaps it's just as well she's not at home to see that. We'll have to try again later.'

'*The Role and Main Functions of H.R. in a Retail Environment*' – *discuss*. Sally's eyes swam as she studied the title on the blank sheet of paper.

'Seven hundred and fifty words,' she sighed dejectedly. 'How on earth am I going to think of seven hundred and fifty words, when at the moment I can't even think of seventy! If it wasn't for the fact that tomorrow's the last day, I'd leave now, except I need my certificate for expenses.'

Thinking of how she would have to produce evidence of attending the course directed her attention towards Hugh. Hopefully by now he would have forgotten her non-appearance last Friday and with luck would probably absent himself from the store for a while, leaving the assistant manager in charge.

Sally doodled on the paper with her fountain pen, drawing faces in the 'o's and changing the 'H.R.' into 'H.B.'. From there she found herself scribbling 'Hugh Barrington' in mock itallic script, attempting to copy Laura's stylish handwriting.

Laura! That was it! Why hadn't she thought of Laura before?

Remembering Laura's last letter, Sally was overcome with guilt. She had tracked down two wonderful local artists but as yet hadn't even told Laura of their existence. Screwing up the sheet of paper covered in childish scribblings, she tossed it into the bin. The HR project was thus dismissed; she would write to Laura instead.

That done, the letter was sealed with firm resolve, before she changed her mind and altered its contents. With an air of contentment she propped it against her briefcase and walked to the window. She needed some fresh air, if only to disperse the multitude of thoughts racing in her head.

Peering from the window Sally was overcome with a desire to escape the claustrophobic heat of her room. 'Yes it is late,' she murmured to her reflection in the mirror, 'but the grounds are well lit and I can't possibly get lost if I keep to the main pathway.'

Rosebay Hall, once the home of landed gentry, was set in twenty-seven acres of landscaped gardens. The steps from the main entrance led down to a circular driveway, bordered on all sides by broadleaf trees. At the rear of the hall, sunken gardens and gravel paths led to the newly constructed accommodation blocks.

Tying the belt of her coat against the cold, Sally ventured past the shelter of the trees. There a penetrating north-east wind tossed at her hair and stung her eyes. She breathed in deeply, closing her eyes as she did so and listened. Across the valley the wind whistled and moaned as it spiralled its way up the hill to the conference centre. Sally revelled in its wildness, it was wonderful to feel so free. Freedom: was that what she wanted? Freedom from Barrington's and its H.R. problems? Had she just imagined it, or had things got worse since her job title had changed?

She gave a wry laugh which was caught and tossed by the wind. Freedom! Freedom was one thing, but it didn't pay the bills! No, unless Laura came up with an alternative solution – or she won the lottery – she was stuck with H.R. for years to come. Standing on the brow of a hill, she watched a convoy of cars head back to the hall. Conference delegates returning from sampling the local brew.

For a brief moment, she heard their jovial voices plucked by the wind and smelt the faint aroma of cigars as car doors slammed. When all was quiet she continued her walk. Down in the valley a distant church clock chimed. Counting eleven muted notes, Sally drew up sharply. Eleven o'clock! What time did they shut the main doors?

Only the dimmest of lights shone through the main glazed doorway and Sally watched in horror as the duty receptionist disappeared from her view.

'Please don't go off duty yet,' she cried as she ran back, her legs aching and her breath rasping in the cold night air.

Clutching her side, and reaching the shelter of familiar trees, she leant against the trunk of a gnarled oak, where a roosting bird flapped noisily out of the beech thicket. With an agitated squawk it flew into the night, leaving behind the sound of footsteps snapping on dead twigs. Trying to still her thumping heart, Sally realized only too late it was not her presence that had disturbed the frightened bird. Alarmed, she found herself frozen to the spot and felt a man's hand on her shoulder.

Her muffled scream was heard by no one and struggling with her assailant Sally found herself being dragged into the bushes. Terrified, she attempted to lash out in all directions and finding her arms pinioned and her mouth smothered, used the only weapon she had – her stout walking shoes. With a hefty kick, she landed a blow at what she considered to be shin height.

'My God, Sally! What are you trying to do, cripple me?'

Free from his clutches, Sally turned in amazement to face Hugh Barrington. He was rubbing his left shin briskly.

'Hugh! What the . . . I thought you were a . . .'

'It's perfectly clear what you thought, Sally, and if you'd only answered my calls I wouldn't have had to resort to SAS tactics. Why the hell haven't you rung? Muriel tells me she's left numerous messages at reception. I would have thought from the fees this place charges, the staff aren't totally incapable of passing on a message.'

Sally said nothing, her attention was on the pain showing visibly in Hugh's face as he rubbed his shin.

He continued: 'Anyway, I understand from the receptionist on duty that you received all your messages.'

'You mean to say you've been up to the hall?' she enquired lamely, horrified to discover she'd been found out. All week she had chosen to ignore Muriel Baxter's urgent pleas to ring her boss.

Standing upright, Hugh said angrily, 'Don't you realize Melanie and Muriel have been worried stiff about you? Especially since you reported in sick last Friday . . . not to mention how I've felt about you this past week.'

'You? But I don't understand . . .'

'Don't you? Well you should! After what happened between us last Thursday, you could at least have given me chance to apologize and explain. When you didn't turn up on Friday and I went to your house . . .'

'You went to my house?' Sally stared at Hugh in disbelief.

'Yes, I took Stanley with me – thought he might pave the way to peace. He was disappointed you weren't at home and by the way I'm afraid he – er – savaged the bay tree again.'

Hugh was aware of her smiling in the semi-gloom. 'Well, it's nice to see you smile,' he said. 'A few moments ago . . . if looks could kill.'

'How is Stanley?'

'As well as can be expected in the circumstances. Speaking of which, I'd better get a move on. Serena has a habit of neglecting him if I'm not around. So my guess is he hasn't been fed this evening, let alone been taken for a walk.'

'But what are you doing here then?'

'My dear Sally, I thought that I'd already made that perfectly clear. I came to see you.'

Sally shivered as a gust of wind sent fallen leaves scurrying across the driveway and dead beech leaves crackled in the hedgerow.

'You mean to say you came all this way just to see me? But it's a hundred and twenty miles!'

'Exactly and now I've got to drive a hundred and twenty miles back again!'

'And have you eaten?'

'Not in the proper sense,' Hugh snorted. 'Greasy spoon cafés and chips with everything hardly fall into my category of culinary delights.'

Sally hesitated. 'They give us hospitality trays in our rooms, tea, coffee and biscuits – and I have some fruit – if you'd like it.'

'I wouldn't say no to a cup of something hot.'

Allowing Hugh to take her arm, Sally led the way to the accommodation block along the gravel walkway. 'I just hope the side door is still open,' she whispered.

Casting a sidelong look at Hugh, she studied the set of his jaw and noticed how the combined light from the moon and mock Georgian lampposts accentuated the silver streaks at his temples. There was no doubt about it, Serena had landed herself quite a catch when she'd married Hugh Barrington. Fertile or not he was the epitome of an attractive and desirable male and they were thin on the ground when Sally had reached what her aunts had called 'marriageable age'.

Listening to the rhythmic crunch of their footsteps on gravel, Hugh dispensed with further conversation, preferring to wait until he and Sally were indoors. Even then he was unsure how to handle the situation. The uncertainty of this meeting had bothered him for days.

Not surprisingly, Hugh's irrational behaviour had been monitored closely by Muriel Baxter, who had announced in confidence, when she'd rung Edith Hawtin, that Mr B's behaviour was quite out of character. Between them the two women concluded he was working too hard and hoped the forthcoming Christmas holiday would give him a chance to unwind. Perhaps too, she confided, there was also more than the merest hint of truth in the rumours that Hugh Barrington was seriously considering early retirement.

Sally stood at the door and pushed but it remained tightly closed.

'Oh no!' she groaned, 'this can't be locked too. It has to remain open, it's a fire door.'

'Open – yes,' confirmed Hugh, trying the door for himself, 'but from the inside only. You can't go round leaving doors like this unlocked at night, you never know who's going to be lurking in the bushes.'

He cast a wry glance in Sally's direction, as only minutes earlier he'd given her quite a shock by doing exactly that. Missing the significance of his comment she had her nose pressed up against the glass and was gesticulating to someone at the far end of the corridor. Presently a Muriel Baxter lookalike confronted her through the glass.

Recognizing her from the course, Sally mouthed, 'I appear to be locked out, can you open the door please?' and pointed to the doorcatch.

With a hefty push the woman raised the bar and the door opened.

'Gosh, thank you very much, we thought we were locked out.' Relieved, she walked through the door into the enveloping warmth of heating – set far too high for comfort – and the smell of newly lain carpet.

'We?' The woman enquired.

Sally gestured to Hugh as he followed her inside. Without saying a word the other 'Muriel' shot Sally a look of contempt, strode down the corridor to her room, and slammed the door. Reaching for her own key, Sally stopped abruptly. 'Oh my goodness! I've just realized the significance behind that withering look. This is the women only wing!'

'Well, perhaps you can lend me your kimono again and I'll pretend to be your sister!'

'I don't find that amusing,' Sally remarked, opening her door.

'I apologize and stand duly corrected, Sally. Does that mean I won't get that cup of tea?'

Catching the glimmer of a smile in Hugh's expression she proceeded to fill the kettle. 'No Earl Grey I'm afraid and it's that awful UHT milk. Or would you prefer it black?'

Sally watched as Hugh deftly peeled back the corner of the tiny milk container and poured it into his cup. 'I've an apple and banana if you're hungry,' she added.

Hugh shook his head and sipped his tea. 'Thank you – no – but if those are digestive biscuits in that packet . . .'

'Of course, please help yourself. By the way, how's your leg? I'm sorry I kicked you so hard.'

'I suppose I did ask for it, frightening you like that. I'd been waiting there for so long – I saw you go, you see – and was beginning to get desperate.'

Hugh lifted the leg of his trouser to examine the lower part of his shin. A thin streak of blood dribbled down his leg.

Sally stared in horror. 'Did I really do that . . .?'

'Perhaps the England Manager should have you in the squad. Ever thought of changing your job . . .?'

'As a matter of fact I have,' she broke in. 'Only this evening . . .'

Taken aback, Hugh dropped the leg of his trousers. 'Are you serious, Sally? You mean you want to leave Barrington's?'

She shrugged, reached for a tissue, walked to the bathroom and ran it under the tap. 'I really don't know. After a week spent involved with Human Resources of every description, I don't know what I want. She held out the moistened tissue. 'You'd better use this to clean your leg.'

Hugh looked disappointed and declined to take it. 'You mean you won't be my Florence Nightingale, Sally?'

Feeling the colour rise in her cheeks, Sally found herself kneeling on the floor as Hugh raised the fine wool and worsted cloth to reveal his damaged skin. Even for this time of year, she noticed, he was tanned and healthy looking. Hugh flinched visibly as she dabbed gingerly at the streak of blood.

'I'm so sorry about this,' she reiterated. 'I'm afraid you're going to have an awful bruise. It's a shame I haven't got some antiseptic to put on it. Perhaps they'll have some at reception . . .'

'Oh, no you don't, sadist!' he shouted just as a loud knock came upon the door.

65

'Mrs Palmer! Mrs Palmer! Will you open the door please!'

The night porter stood illuminated in the doorway.

'Mrs Palmer, we've had complaints you are entertaining a man in your room. And as you yourself requested a room in this section, you must be fully aware you are contravening Rosebay's strict rules and regulations.'

Sally's mouth gaped open. 'But I'm not entertaining . . .'

Hugh rose and strode to the door, shaking the leg of his trousers as he did so. He towered above the short, square figure and with a voice that commanded authority, announced, 'How dare you insinuate Mrs Palmer is "entertaining" me in her room. Mrs Palmer happens to be my employee and I have just driven one hundred and twenty miles to discuss an important business matter with her.'

Timid piggy eyes squinted up at Hugh through thick glasses. The porter shifted uneasily. 'Well in that case,' he sniffed, 'I'm prepared to ignore it and won't report it – but . . .'

'I was about to leave anyway.'

The porter, casting a suspicious look in Sally's direction continued, 'Well, in that case sir, perhaps you'd be so good as to leave through the main door so I can see you off the premises.' He turned and walked away with amazingly light steps for one so heavily built.

Sally's face blazed with anger as she picked up the blood-stained tissue and threw it in the bin. 'How dare he! What an odious little man!

'He's only doing his job.'

'Yes – well, but as you said, if you've come all this way to discuss Barrington's business with me . . .'

'That's just it; it wasn't Barrington's business I came for, Sally. I wanted to talk about us. I've already said I wanted to apologize for my behaviour last Thursday . . .'

'Yes, you did,' she said quickly as Hugh walked towards her, 'and I accept your apology but I'd really rather forget all about it.'

Hugh took her in his arms and kissed her tenderly. 'Would you, Sally? Would you really prefer to forget about it? Somehow I don't think you're being entirely honest with yourself.'

She made no attempt at a reply as Hugh released her from his embrace and moved slowly to the door. 'For my part,' he added, 'I prefer not to forget it. Let's talk again next week.'

Long after he'd gone, the fragrance of his aftershave lingered in the air and Sally was left to contemplate the significance of his parting comment.

'A hundred and twenty miles?' she asked herself. 'Why come a hundred and twenty miles just to apologize?' Heaven knows she felt bad enough about last Thursday but now one week on she'd only added to her humiliation by greeting Hugh Barrington the third with a hefty kick on the shin. She was in no doubt, for the same offence, Hugh's illustrious ancestors would probably have had her banished to the colonies!

Watching the seconds slip by relentlessly, Sally waited for the double zeros to herald the approach of midnight and another day ahead. In the semi-gloom the luminous 'oo' – 'oo's' peered eerily, like eyes, in her direction. She smiled to herself, remembering last weekend's attempt to teach her eldest nephew his numbers and the time, using the digital clock. Jack had been enthralled and excited by his newfound knowledge and proudly announced to his parents at breakfast that he was still awake when they'd arrived home at 'ooh ooh' o'clock.

Poor Jack, unable to comprehend his parent's ribald laughter, had sought solace in Sally's arms and cried tears of anguish when the time came for her to depart.

'Promise me you'll come for Christmas,' he sobbed, 'because you're the only one that plays with me. Daddy's always too busy and mummy's always seeing to the baby.'

Christmas, thought Sally. She hardly dared think of Christmas.

CHAPTER 5

Clutching Laura's letter, Sally's spirits rose. It was the answer to her prayers. She no longer need fear the daily confrontations with Hugh Barrington.

Hugh looked at her across the desk. 'Well, you look exceedingly pleased with yourself,' he announced. 'Have you won the lottery or been left a fortune?'

'Not exactly, but I've been offered another job.'

If Sally was expecting Hugh to look disappointed and plead with her to reconsider, then she was very much mistaken.

'Well, naturally Barrington's will be sorry to see you go, but if you've had a better offer . . . How soon do you intend to leave?'

'My contract states three months' notice. I was wondering if . . .'

'How would the end of December suit you?'

Sally stared in amazement. Hugh seemed positively delighted she was leaving!

'What about my replacement?'

'No problem at all,' he continued brightly, 'my nephew Gareth has been pestering me for ages to join Barrington's. I think you've met him a couple of times.

He has a degree in law but doesn't want to join his father's firm. I'll get him to stand in for you until we find a proper replacement.'

Stunned, Sally left the office and went to find Roz. How would Roz react when told of her decision to join Laura at 'Laura's Lair'.

'Leaving Barrington's to work in an arty farty craft shop. My God, Sally, you must be mad! Can you really afford to?' Roz asked incredulously.

'No, not exactly, but I'll be living in the flat above the gallery, Laura won't be charging me any rent . . .'

'I bet she won't be paying you much in wages, either.'

Sally shrugged. 'No, but it will be enough to cover my needs.'

'But what about your house?'

'I'm putting it on the market.'

'What!'

'Richard wants his share. He needs the money.'

'Hard bloody luck, he should have thought of that when he went off with Tarty Tracy.'

'Actually it was Sharon.'

'Hmph! Shifty Sharon then. Sally Palmer, you are a bloody fool! What on earth made you give in to Richard's demands?'

Sally sighed. 'I don't know,' she lied. 'But Sharon is pregnant again and . . .'

'Well, that's Richard's fault, not yours. You should tell him to tie a knot in it!'

Unable to cope with Roz's verbal salvo, Sally stood up. 'I'd better go,' she said dejectedly. 'I've been asked to sort through some files on H.R. for Mr Barrington's nephew.'

'Oh, you mean "Gareth the Golden",' Roz sniggered. 'Well, all I can say is, when you start showing him around, make sure our Miss Kettle stays away from him. Otherwise she'll have her hand in his trousers before you can say Father Christmas!'

Sally hurried away. She couldn't cope with Roz in her present mood, she just hoped the customers weren't on the receiving end of such forthright dialogue.

On Christmas Eve an air of festivity filled the store. Garlands and bows decorated every department and last minute shoppers arrived en masse. A constant opening of doors heralded refreshing bursts of air to harassed shop assistants and the sound of carols drifted in from the market square, competing with the current Christmas CD and a cacophony of chiming tree decorations in the store itself.

'Merry Christmas, Mrs Palmer.'

Michelle Kettle, wearing mock reindeer antlers, waved excitedly across a display of novelty bottle openers and oven gloves. Sally acknowledged her greeting with a gracious smile.

'Merry Christmas, Michelle.'

'Is it true you're leaving?'

Sally nodded to the questioning antlers and moved on. She had no intention of discussing her plans in public and couldn't wait for the store to close. Alone in her office she tidied her desk and studied the pictures on the walls. Should she take them down now or after Christmas?

'Moving things out already, Sally?'

Unaware she was being watched, Sally dropped the wildflower print she'd been holding. It shattered on the floor, scattering tiny shards of glass.

Hugh rushed forward to help pick up the pieces. 'Oh, I'm sorry, I didn't mean to startle you.'

Finding herself on her knees facing him, Sally was aware of his penetrating gaze. She winced as a splinter of glass pierced her finger and oozed forth droplets of blood. Hugh took his handkerchief from his pocket.

'I think this exchange of handkerchiefs is becoming quite ridiculous,' he murmured, wrapping the pristine white cotton round the offending finger. 'Now you'll just have to let me hold that in place until the bleeding stops.'

'Sally, are you coming . . . Oh!'

Roz stood in the doorway, her bun adorned with tinsel and a sprig of mistletoe wedged between her ears and the frames of her glasses.

'Mrs Hughes, how delightfully festive you look. Have you come for Mrs Palmer? I'm afraid she's had a slight accident and cut her finger. Do you think you could go and find a plaster?'

'No, it's all right, I'm sure I don't need one, I'll just . . .' Sally felt Hugh squeeze her hand gently as he threw Roz a look of command.

With mistletoe and tinsel bobbing, Roz turned on her heels in obeyance.

'Sally!' Hugh urged. 'There isn't much time before she comes back. Look, I'll give you the number of my mobile phone. Promise you'll ring me over Christmas.'

Sally hesitated, for what to Hugh seemed like an eternity. 'What about your wife, won't she think it strange if I call you?'

'No, Serena never answers my mobile and I always carry it with me when I take Stanley for a walk – morning and evening. Ring me then.'

Roz's footsteps clicked down the corridor as she returned carrying a box of plasters.

Removing the handkerchief, Hugh watched as Roz fixed the plaster in position. With her back towards him, she was unaware of the small white card being placed under the flowerpot. Hugh gesticulated to Sally, who in a daze merely nodded.

'A perfect job, Mrs Hughes, I'm sure I couldn't have done it better myself. Now I'd better wish you both a Merry Christmas and be on my way.' With that he plucked the sprig of mistletoe from Roz's glasses and kissed her. 'Give my regards to Donald, won't you?'

'Well I never,' gasped Roz after he'd gone. 'In all the years I've worked here, he's never done that before. He must be in a good mood!'

Roz touched her cheek. 'Pity you didn't have any mistletoe, Sally, that was quite something, I can tell you. If only I was twenty years younger.

Sally didn't need to be told; she already knew how it felt to have Hugh Barrington's lips on hers. She also knew what it was like to be held in his embrace. The thought of it caused her heart to beat and her stomach to churn. Should she ring him though, as he'd insisted? That was the million dollar question.

Watching Roz press the button for the staff lift, Sally turned sharply. 'Hold the lift for me,' she begged. 'I've forgotten something I need for the Christmas holiday.'

All the way down to the staff entrance Sally kept her hand in her pocket, clutching the slip of white card Hugh had left behind.

'Don't forget to ring . . .' Roz called to her across the carpark. 'To let me know if you can join us for supper on Boxing Night.'

'No, I won't forget to ring,' Sally replied, thought-fully.

On Boxing Day afternoon, Sally found herself in Thorn-hampton Park with her two nephews. Jack's brightly mittened hands clutched a bag of bread for the ducks and Sam's rosy-cheeked face beamed out from a quilted snow suit. Parking the buggy, she lifted Jack onto a bench and helped him tear bread into duck-sized bites.

'We'll sit here and feed them; it's too dangerous to stand at the edge of the lake.'

'How much longer can we stay?' asked Jack.

'Mummy wants us home at four o'clock for tea.'

Jack scrutinized the face of his new watch and grinned. 'Good, that means we can stay for a whole hour. When the little hand is on four and the big hand is at twelve . . .'

Sally was beginning to wonder if it had been such a good idea to buy Jack the watch. Ever since Christmas morning, almost every question he'd asked had been related to time. She concluded that was why Jackie had suggested this trip to the park, insisting she and Dave would stay behind to clear away the debris from lunch.

'You go and get some fresh air, Sally,' Jackie had urged, 'cooped up in that office every day, you probably need it.'

As yet Sally hadn't told them of her decision to leave Barrington's and when Dave had thrust a whole baguette at her, the moment seemed somehow inappropriate.

Sam, who had been blowing bubbles at the ducks through berry red lips, suddenly stopped. His eyes widened with pleasure and he gurgled merrily, 'Bow wow, bow wow.'

'No Sam,' Sally corrected. 'Ducks go quack, not bow wow.'

'But he's not looking at the ducks, he's seen a dog,' explained Jack, sending a large chunk of bread skimming across the water.

Startled, Sally looked up. The approaching dog, sniffing at a piece of bread that had missed its target, looked familiar. 'Stanley?'

Recognition dawned in the rheumy old eyes as the animal lolloped towards her, his tail wagging furiously.

Hugh sat down on the bench. 'Well, this is a coincidence. What's this, the feeding of the five thousand?'

Sally studied the piles of bread at her feet. 'We were hoping to feed the ducks, but they seem to be a bit thin on the ground.'

'Not like the bread!' Hugh teased. 'Well, the ducks are probably like the rest of Thornhampton, sleeping off a huge lunch.' He looked behind him. 'We appear to be the only mortals in need of fresh air and exercise.'

'I thought you exercised Stanley in the mornings and evenings.'

'Ah yes, I usually do. Why, did you try ringing me?' He looked disappointed when Sally shook her head. 'But I've come out to escape "The Sound of Music".

75

My sister-in-law and her husband are spending the day with us and Christmas wouldn't be Christmas for Vivienne without Julie Andrews, edelweiss *et al.* Is that what you are doing, Sally – escaping?'

'Not exactly, I got the distinct impression my sister and her husband wanted me and the boys out of the house.' Sally motioned to the now sleeping Sam, and Jack, who was once more studying his watch.

Hugh raised a quizzical eyebrow. 'I can't imagine anyone not wanting you around.'

'Can't you, Hugh? Well, you obviously don't want me at Barrington's! In fact you seemed positively delighted when I handed in my notice.'

'Of course I was,' said Hugh quietly, checking that Jack wasn't within earshot, 'but that doesn't mean I don't want you around. Can't you see Sally, that by resigning, you're making things so much easier for us?'

'Easier – how? I don't understand.'

'Well, if you're no longer a Barrington's employee, it makes it easier for us to meet. Isn't that why you resigned?'

'No, it isn't,' Sally said defiantly. 'I did it to avoid seeing you!' She rose to her feet. 'Come along, Jack, time to go home.'

'But it's not four o'clock yet,' Jack reminded her

'You're right, Jack, it's not,' said Hugh, anxious for an ally. 'That looks like a pretty super watch you've got there.'

Proudly, Jack extended his timepiece in Hugh's direction. 'Auntie Sally bought it for me for Christmas. Do you have a watch?'

Hugh turned back his sleeve to display the slim gold-strapped Rolex.

'Oh,' said Jack disappointedly. 'It hasn't any colours. Mine's red, blue and green, you see.'

'Yes I do,' said Hugh kindly. 'I'm afraid mine must seem very dull in comparison.'

Puzzling over Hugh's last word, Jack asked, 'And does your watch play a tune?'

Hugh shook his head. 'Sadly no, but I expect yours does.'

Jack proceeded to demonstrate how his watch played a tune and reached for Hugh's hand as Sally walked behind with the buggy.

'You know it suits you – pushing a pushchair,' Hugh remarked kindly, waiting for her to catch up. 'Who would guess you were a Human Resources Manager?'

'Not for much longer,' she said acidly, 'or aren't you forgetting?'

'Sally! Stop being so dramatic. Look, is it okay for Jack to have an ice-cream or something? I mean, I don't want to cause problems – children accepting sweets from strangers and the like . . .'

Jack's ears pricked at the mention of sweets and he looked in anticipation towards his aunt. Sally nodded ruefully as Hugh gave Jack a one pound coin and nodded towards the kiosk by the park gates.

Hugh placed a hand on her arm. 'Listen,' he said reassuringly, 'and don't say a word until I've finished. As they said in that French sitcom; I shall say this only once! We haven't got time to discuss my feelings now, it's not going to take Jack long to spend that pound. I want you to be my mistress, Sally – yes or no?'

Sally shuddered at the mere connotation of the word mistress and looked Hugh straight in the eye. 'Don't you want to try the goods first, before you commit yourself?'

Disregarding the accerbic tone of her voice, Hugh enquired flatly, 'Shall I interpret that as a yes, then?'

She made no reply and held out her arms for Jack as he came running back to the pushchair.

'I got Smarties for me and Buttons for Sam and here's the change.' Jack turned in Hugh's direction.

'Change too, eh, what an astute shopper you are, Jack. Well, perhaps you could put the change in your money box . . .'

'No!' broke in Sally. 'Sweets are one thing, money's another.'

Hugh, visibly hurt by her sharpness, accepted the change Jack emptied from the inside of his striped mittens.

'Don't worry, Sally, I'm not trying to buy him – or you – for that matter, if that's what you're thinking?'

At that precise moment she didn't know what to think as she watched the immaculately dressed Hugh (with an obedient Stanley by his side) walking along holding Jack's hand. From their animated conversation, anyone would have thought man and boy had been friends for years. Sally felt tears prick her eyelids as they walked out of the park.

'Auntie Sally, are you crying?'

'No, Jack darling. It's just the wind stinging my eyes.'

'But there isn't any wind,' remonstrated Jack.

'I think there might be from up here, where we grown-ups are standing,' Hugh lied, glancing at Sally.

Puzzled, Jack stared at Hugh towering above him. 'Well p'raps it might be a bit windy,' he conceded, exchanging Hugh's hand for his aunt's.

'I think this is where we say goodbye, Jack,' said Hugh, stopping by the Range Rover. As if reading Sally's mind, he added, 'Serena's banned Stanley from the Jaguar.'

As Jack knelt and patted the dog goodbye, Hugh looked anxiously in Sally's direction.

'I just need time to think,' she answered in reply to his unspoken question, 'and then . . . I'll ring you.'

'Please do,' he whispered, 'anytime. You still have my number?'

She nodded and smiled weakly as his hand brushed gently against her cheek.

'Isn't Stanley a funny sort of name for a dog?' asked Jack on the journey home. 'I've never met a dog called Stanley before.'

Come to think of it, Sally hadn't either. She would add that to the increasing list of questions already forming in her head. Questions she needed Hugh to answer.

Jackie came running down the stairs to open the door to Jack's excited chatterings of events in the park. It didn't escape Sally's notice that her sister's face was flushed and her blouse undone. In the kitchen the pile of saucepans and greasy dishes remained untouched.

'We just sort of . . . after you left with the boys,' Jackie said, checking the zip of her skirt. 'I'll just take Dave a cup of tea and then get cracking on this.' She pointed to the sink and placed a kiss unceremoniously on Sally's cheek. 'Thanks for taking the boys out, Sal. You can't believe how lovely it was to have a couple of hours completely to ourselves.'

Sally felt herself colour with embarrassment. She'd pretended to ignore Jackie's state of *deshabillé* but her sister was making no secret of what had taken place in her absence. Busying herself with her nephews, she hurriedly changed the subject.

'I'll give you a hand with the boys' tea and then I must go home. You haven't forgotten I'm going to Roz and Donald's for supper?'

'Lucky you! Civilized suppers with civilized people. I've forgotten what it's like since we had the boys. Still,' she said smiling lovingly at her two rosy-cheeked offspring, waiting for their tea, 'we can't have it all, can we? You're the clever, sophisticated one and I'm the one that churns out the babies.'

'You're not pregnant again?' Sally asked in alarm.

'Lord, I hope not,' cried Jackie, thinking of the past two hours.

Driving to Roz and Donald's, Sally recalled Jackie's words. *You're the clever, sophisticated one.*

'I wonder what she'd think if she knew I might become Hugh Barrington's mistress,' Sally whispered to the confines of her car.

In her mind, her subconscious was niggling away. *Might?* it appeared to be saying. *You certainly didn't say no, did you?*

Pulling into Roz's drive, she suddenly panicked. Would Hugh be expecting her to share snatched afternoons in bed, just like Jackie and Dave? Only then it wouldn't be when they were free of Sam and Jack, but free of Serena!

'Gosh, you look flushed,' Roz remarked, taking her coat. 'You're not going down with 'flu or something, are you?'

'No,' Sally murmured. 'Perhaps it's just my age.'

'Well, I would have thought you were a bit too young for the menopause and haywire hormone bit . . . Still, I'm glad it's not 'flu. We can't have you missing your last few days at Barrington's!'

'Who's got haywire hormones?' enquired Donald, coming into the hall.

'No one, big ears!' said Roz, pinching his cheek. 'And we know there's nothing wrong with yours, don't we, Donald!'

Roz turned and winked deliberately at Sally. 'Right,' she said, 'come along in and meet the boring old farts we've gathered here this evening.'

Donald took Sally's arm in fatherly fashion. 'Just ignore her, Sally, she's been at the gin. Actually, I'm sure you'll get on well with Sheila and Gavin . . . and Bernard. His wife died about eighteen months ago. No, don't look so alarmed, we're not trying to match-make. It's just that Christmas can be such a lonely time – if you're on your own.'

Lying in bed later, Sally reflected on Donald's statement. He was right, Christmas could be such a lonely time. Okay, so she was luckier than poor Bernard who appeared to have no one. She had Jackie and Dave and the boys and numerous friends, of course. But it wasn't quite the same as having someone to share your deepest thoughts with

. . . or someone to snuggle up to on a cold night like tonight.

Sally closed her eyes but pictures of Jackie and Dave together and Roz and Donald – in each other's arms – flashed before her. She reached for a pillow and drew it close. Crying silent tears, she whispered softly, 'Oh, Hugh, I do want you, but I'm so frightened of letting it show.'

The following morning, after a night of troubled sleep, Sally rose to the sound of persistent drizzle on the window panes. She sighed deeply. The weather on the penultimate day of the Christmas holiday matched her mood. Usually with Christmas falling at a weekend, she welcomed the thought of two extra days at home. Today however, she couldn't wait to get back to Barrington's, finish her contract and put that chapter of her life behind her.

Her enthusiasm diminished rapidly when she contemplated the next chapter of Sally Palmer, aged thirty-three and a half. It wasn't 'Laura's Lair' that bothered her, but the association with Hugh. Gingerly, she picked up the phone and dialled his number. Almost immediately Hugh answered and she hung up. Terrified he might have realized who it was and call back, Sally dashed into bathroom, switched the radio to its highest volume and turned on the shower. Half an hour later when the doorbell rang, she froze.

'Richard! Won't you come in?'

Surprised not to have the door slammed in his face, Richard followed Sally down the hallway to the kitchen. His eyes took in her freshly showered appearance as the sweet fragrance of shower gel and dusting powder wafted behind her.

'Sorry to call at such an unearthly hour, only ..,'

'That's all right, I was just about to make so. coffee. Would you like a cup?'

Richard nodded and looked about the kitchen. 'Looks like you've been pretty busy. I see you've finished the decorating.'

'It's a question of having to, isn't it? When you rang with your good news and said you wanted the house sold . . .'

'Good news?'

'That Sharon's expecting again.'

'I don't know what's so good about that,' Richard groaned, watching Sally pour hot water into the cafetiere.

Seeing the disgruntled look on his face, she couldn't resist asking, 'Oh! It wasn't planned then?'

'No, it bloody wasn't!'

'Well, don't they say,' she continued cheerily, 'it's better to have your children close together, if you can. Sharon's still young and by the time the children are grown up, she'll be more like a sister than a mother.'

Sally turned her back, unable to suppress a giggle. She was enjoying watching Richard in his present predicament. She passed him his coffee.

'Still, I don't expect you've come to talk about babies, have you?'

'Too right I haven't. Jade kept us awake all last night – she's teething – and Sharon's got morning sickness. As a matter of fact, Sally, I wanted to see you . . . to see if you are okay.'

'Well, as you can see I'm fine and as I told you on the phone, the house is going on the market next week. I

just wanted to finish as many jobs as I could – to get a better price.'

'Did you do everything yourself?' Richard enquired, examining his 'halfway' projects newly completed.

Sally nodded. 'Of course. Didn't you think I was capable?'

'No, it's just that I thought your new man-friend might have helped.'

'What man-friend?'

Richard sensed the tone of indignation in her voice. 'Oh, I thought perhaps you might have . . . especially as I've been trying to get hold of you. You weren't here at Christmas and last night . . .'

'Last night, for your information, I was making up an odd number for supper. There I partnered an elderly widower, hardly a man-friend!'

Richard appeared to delight in this information and walked round the table towards her. Gently, he fingered her fringe where it lay still damp against her forehead and dropped his hands to encircle her waist. Stunned, she became aware of what was coming next and pushed him away.

'Come on, Sally,' he urged. 'You must be lonely if you haven't got anyone and it must be ages since you've . . . There's no harm in it, is there? Sharon's always tired these days.'

His voice was pleading as he grabbed her roughly by the shoulders.

'Sally, please . . . just for old time's sake. She won't find out.'

'What do you mean, she won't find out?' Sally asked coolly.

'Well, I'm hardly likely to tell her, am I . . .?' Richard hesitated.

'You mean you're hardly likely to tell your second wife who's pregnant with your second child, that you've been back to your ex-wife, begging for a screw!'

'Sally!' Desire in his face gave way to shock and indignation as Sally pulled away from his clutches.

'Don't look so shocked, Richard, it's clearly what you came for, isn't it? I was a fool not to recognize the signs earlier. In fact I can see it all now. What was it you said? "The baby's awake all night teething and Sharon's always tired." Don't you mean too tired for sex? Well, all I can say to that, Richard, is, you clearly still only think of yourself!'

Richard raised his hand as if to strike her, then stopped as if frozen in time and slumped onto a kitchen chair. Burying his head in his hands he remained motionless until he heard Sally open the back door.

'What have I done to us? What have I done to you, Sally? I've never heard you speak like that before.'

'Perhaps not, but there's always a first time, isn't there? As for what you've done to me, Richard – I think you've just brought me to my senses. Now, as I'm sure we don't have anything else to say to each other, I think you'd better go.'

'But . . .'

'Please go!'

Outside the backdoor, Richard pulled up his jacket collar against the continuing drizzle and shot one last, pleading look in her direction. Lashing out in frustration with his fist, the bay tree toppled over.

CHAPTER 6

Distraught and angry, Sally dialled Hugh's number. She had no idea what to say and only hoped he was alone and able to answer his phone.

'Dear God, please let him be there,' she whispered, keeping an anxious eye on the door in case Richard should return.

Her heart lurched as the monotonous ringing tone was silenced by Hugh's reassuring voice.

'Hugh . . . I . . . it's . . .'

'Sally, is that you?'

'Yes, I need to speak to you. Can we meet . . . now?'

'Now . . . but Sally, I'm . . .'

Sally ran her hands through her hair. 'I'm sorry, I should have realized it wouldn't be convenient . . . it doesn't matter.'

'Sally, stop! Look, don't hang up, of course we can meet, it's just that I'm in the middle of Campion Forest with Stanley, so I'm not exactly in the area. It will take me some time to get back to the car.'

'Perhaps I can come to you, meet you halfway?'

'What . . . yes that sounds like a good idea. Look, the

line's pretty bad and I can barely hear you. Do you know Campion Forest?'

'Not really, there're so many paths and . . . but I know Campion Church.'

'Right then, behind the church is the village hall and carpark. Wait for me there and I'll be as quick as I can. Sally, is everything all right? You sound upset.'

'I'm okay, it's just that Richard . . .'

Hugh's heart filled with dread at the mention of Richard's name and he remembered the night of Edith Hawtin's video show. 'Tell me about it when I see you, Sally. It's going to take me about half an hour to get out of here and . . . Sally . . .'

'Yes.'

'Drive carefully.'

'I will,' she whispered, hanging up the phone.

A noise at the back door made her jump but she realized it was just the bay tree rolling in its pot. 'Poor bay tree,' she murmured to herself. 'Picked on by Stanley and used by Richard as a punch bag!' Righting the upturned pot she went back indoors for her bag and car keys and caught sight of herself in the hall mirror. With no make-up and still wearing the jeans and sweatshirt she'd slipped on after her shower, she did a double-take.

'There's no time to change and beautify yourself, just go – and if he changes his mind when he sees you, well . . .'

With the windscreen wipers working full pelt, Sally drove out of Thornhampton and beyond to where the road forked for Campion Magna. Her sigh of relief at being in the vicinity was shortlived when she looked at her petrol gauge. It was at zero and the warning light was flashing. Why hadn't she seen it before? There was nothing for it but to keep going in the hope she reached Hugh before her car ground to a halt.

With row after row of dark coniferous plantation on either side of the road, she assumed she'd found Campion Forest and peered anxiously ahead for further road signs and the merest glimpse of a church spire. Perhaps if she opened the window, she might even hear the sound of a church bell, she thought but there was neither sight nor sound of church spire or bells, just the rain pouring through the window and the debilitating sound of an engine gasping for petrol. Sally banged her fists on the steering wheel in disbelief.

'Oh damn!' she cried. 'Damn! Damn! Damn! Now what do I do?'

Her immediate reaction was to wind up the window, lock the car and run. But run where and for what? There certainly wouldn't be any petrol stations here and she couldn't just run about blindly in the hope she would bump into Hugh. Besides, she was hardly dressed for trekking through mud-filled woodlands.

'Woodlands – more like wetlands,' she muttered wryly, watching the rain pour down the windscreen in rivulets. 'It's going to be like wading through peat bog in there.'

She studied her trainer-clad feet and peered once more into the forest. The view was still the same, apart from the fact the windscreen was becoming steamed up from the warmth of her body and the penetrating dampness. Rubbing at the condensation with a handful of tissues, she decided to open the window again.

For a brief moment the rain eased and in the distance she thought she heard – yes she did – a clock strike. Quickly she looked at her watch. It was a quarter to nine now, so at nine o'clock, it would be striking the hour. That meant she had a quarter of an hour to collect her thoughts, concentrate her hearing and be prepared to run like mad in the direction of the chimes.

The first ten minutes passed quickly enough as she searched in her handbag for a comb and the chance of finding some make-up.

'Wild plum,' she announced looking at the base of a lipstick. 'How appropriate; the wild certainly applies in more ways than one. Not only do you look like the wild man of Borneo, Sally Palmer, but this is a totally wild and plum-stupid situation you've got yourself into. For someone who used to go to summer camp, you're anything but prepared. Wait a minute!' A flash of inspiration caused her to discard lipstick and comb. 'But you're not totally unprepared, are you? In the boot, your winter emergency bag!'

Hurrying to the boot, Sally cast aside assorted debris from pre-Christmas shopping trips and visits to the tip and found the holdall she was looking for. Inside was a small shovel, a torch, some assorted polythene bags held in a roll with elastic bands, an old travel rug, an ancient plastic raincoat and a misshapen bar of chocolate.

When the church clock struck nine, Sally was ready. Newly attired in an assortment of tartan, polythene and plastic, she ran as fast as her legs would carry her, with the rain driving full into her face.

On seeing the church spire, the rain mingled with salty tears on her cheeks and she found herself running

straight into Hugh's arms as he emerged from the
Range Rover. In an instant she felt his lips on hers
and he held her in a firm embrace, to stop her from
shaking.

'Thank God, Sally! You don't know how worried
I've been . . . I thought I'd missed you.'

'I ran out of petrol,' she sobbed, 'then I got lost and
then . . .'

Hugh went to stroke her hair and found a handful of
plastic. Sally's shoulders shook once more. 'There's no
need to cry,' he murmured, 'you're here now and I'll
take care of you.'

'I'm not crying, I'm laughing,' she said, looking up
into his face through a veil of laughter and tears. 'I mean
just look at me, Hugh, is this how you visualized your
first assignation with your future mistress?'

For the first time since she'd arrived, Hugh studied
her appearance and roared with laughter. 'Well,
Mrs Palmer, I've always credited you with being a
stylish dresser and without doubt there's a certain *je
ne sais quoi* about your present attire. Ralph Lauren it
definitely isn't!'

Pulling back the hood of the raincoat – repaired with
cellotape – Sally looked away. 'Do you,' she hesitated,
'do you still want me, Hugh?'

'Want you! Oh, my darling Sally, if only you knew.
Of course I want you, more than I think you realize.' He
tilted her face towards him and kissed her tenderly
before leading her to the car.

'There's just one thing,' he said, with a glint in his eye
as he helped her into the Range Rover, 'I would
appreciate you toning down your style of dress some-

90

what when we're out together . . . I mean tartan rugs round your waist and polythene bags on your feet, held in place with colour co-ordinated elastic bands, are hardly conducive to . . .'

'You mean to say you intend to be seen in public with me? But that's impossible, what if Serena should . . .?'

'She won't. We'll be very discreet in Thornhampton and away from it, but that's another matter.'

Sally felt herself colour and bit her lip. Perhaps she should ask the long list of questions that had caused her troubled sleep last night.

He sensed her unease and put a hand on her arm. 'Don't look so worried.'

'I'm not worried, I'm just . . .'

'Not happy with the word mistress? It bothers you, Sally, doesn't it?'

She nodded. 'It's just the connotation of the word. It sounds so . . . so sordid and cheap and conjures up . . .'

'Go on, what does it conjure up?'

Sally fingered a frayed corner of the tartan rug, unable to look Hugh in the eye. 'Peroxide blondes with scarlet mouths and false fingernails, wearing nylon, see-through negligees . . . trimmed with maribou.'

'Good grief!' said Hugh, 'what a ghastly thought. I'd rather you kept your plastic bags and elastic bands in that case!' He reached for her hand. 'Gracious, you're cold. Come on, let's get going so I can switch the heaters on in here and get you warm. Have you had any breakfast?'

'No, only a cup of coffee and a few squares of chocolate I keep in the car for emergencies. Would you like some?' She held out the remains of the mangled chocolate.

'Thank you – no.' Hugh shook his head and smiled. 'Remind me never to get stranded with you in winter, Sally, if that's all you take with you by way of emergency supplies.' He reached for a hip flask in the pocket of his Barbour. 'Have a sip of this.'

Sally sipped reluctantly and felt the liquid burn her throat. She grimaced but it had the desired effect and before long she felt herself not only warmed by the brandy and enveloping heat of the car, but also by Hugh's presence.

'We'll get your car later,' he said, aware of her anxious look in its direction as they drove past. 'Let's get our priorities right. First of all you need a change of clothing and some breakfast.'

Hugh looked about the kitchen and his gaze fell on the two coffee cups. 'Richard must have called early. Do you want to tell me about it?'

Sally gestured to her wet clothes. 'I'd rather . . .'

'Of course you would. Right, upstairs with you and have a hot bath and I'll give you a call when I'm ready for you.'

A look of panic filled her face. Had it come to 'that moment' already? Hugh certainly didn't believe in wasting time, did he? Yet in the car he'd spoken of them having a weekend away – 'to get to know each other', as he'd so tactfully put it.

Hugh reached for her hand. 'Don't look so worried – perhaps I'd better rephrase that. What I should have said was: I'll call you when your breakfast is ready. Now if you'll just show me where you keep the eggs.'

Sally breathed a sigh of relief, pointed to the cupboard and contemplated the events of the morning as she went upstairs. So far, she'd had a shower followed by a confrontation with her ex-husband, a drenching in the woods and an assignation with her boss. Now here she was, barely two hours later, about to have another soaking and downstairs, Hugh was making her breakfast!

'Feeling better?' Hugh enquired, placing scrambled eggs and toast on the table.

Sally nodded. 'I feel it should be the other way round, me getting breakfast for you.'

'There'll be time for that, another day . . . I hope.'

Sally blushed. 'Hugh, there's so much I need to know.'

He bent and kissed her cheek. 'Eat first,' he whispered, 'and then we'll talk.'

Later, watching her put away the last of the breakfast dishes, Hugh studied the kitchen thoughtfully. No longer were there tins of paint and brushes adorning the work surfaces.

'You've been very busy since I was last here.'

'Yes, I've been trying to finish Richard's "halfway" projects, I'm putting the house on the market.'

'A good idea too, if I may say so. I thought one of those flats at Elmsmarsh would be ideal for you. I want you to have somewhere nice.'

Sally spun round to face him. 'Elmsmarsh?'

'What's wrong, don't you like the idea of Elmsmarsh?'

'It's not that. I was planning to live in the flat above Laura's Lair.'

Hugh seemed taken aback. 'You mean, you've already told Laura about us and our arrangement?'

'Of course not. Until an hour ago, I didn't know myself that you and I were going to be . . . "us". As for arrangements, I'm still not sure what you have in mind.'

Relieved, Hugh led her by the hand to sitting room.

'Right,' he said, joining her on the settee, 'the way I see it is this. You sell your house and work for Laura as planned. That way you've still an excuse to come into Barrington's . . .'

'How?'

'I want to open a picture department on a small scale and you can advise me on prints and the like. Don't worry, Sally, we shan't be taking business away from Laura.'

She stared at Hugh in disbelief as he continued.

'However, I'm really not keen on you living above Laura's Lair and would prefer you to take the Elmsmarsh flat. I'm getting the key the day after tomorrow.'

Sally was dumbstruck. 'You've obviously thought of everything. How long have you been planning this?'

'Not planning, Sally – just hoping, since the night I took you and Roz home. I would never have suggested anything if you and Richard were still married. I don't believe in relationships with other men's wives.'

'But it doesn't matter if I have a relationship with another woman's husband!'

'Oh, dear! Do I detect a distinct note of sarcasm there?'

'Well, you are still married, aren't you?'

'Yes,' said Hugh thoughtfully, 'but things are slightly different between Serena and myself . . .'

Sally's mind was on the conversation she'd had with Roz, the night of Edith Hawtin's gathering. She already knew of Hugh and Serena's arrangement, yet the thought of coming face to face with Serena now terrified her.

'Won't Serena become suspicious?'

Hugh laughed wryly. 'When Serena is at home, she barely has time to think of anyone apart from herself and as we've no children –' Hugh's face took on a pained expression – 'Well, we don't have to worry about causing them distress, do we?'

Sally remained pensive and solemn. Hugh reached for her and drew her into his arms. 'Sally,' he said, tilting her face towards his, 'I'm not going to make promises I can't keep. So I won't promise to leave Serena – but I will promise to care for you. I thought as you'd decided to sell this house, you'd already made your mind up . . . about us.'

'I didn't decide to sell because of your proposal, Hugh. I did it because of Richard.' Her voice trailed away almost to a whisper.

'Richard! Of course I was forgetting, you never told me what happened this morning. Is he forcing you to sell the house?'

Tears welled in Sally's eyes as the words tumbled from her lips.

'Not exactly. He came because his wife had rejected his advances and he thought I might be lonely. Well, not lonely but . . . he thought I might be desperate for . . . he wanted to . . .'

The reason for Richard's visit became all too clear. Hugh banged his fist on the arm of the settee. 'The bloody cheek of it, and did you – I mean did he?'

Sally shook her head and whispered an almost inaudible 'no' as Hugh took her in his arms once more.

'Then the sooner I get you out of here the better,' he said. 'So will you come and look at the Elmsmarsh flat when I have the key?'

'I don't have much choice, do I! I'm sorry, I didn't mean that to sound quite so abrupt.'

In a quiet, concerned tone, Hugh replied. 'Sally, you have every choice. Richard can't force you out of this house, he'd have to take you to court first. And I can't force you to become my mistress. So perhaps you'd be right in thinking we are just two very selfish, pigheaded males wanting you, each in our own way. At the end of the day however, the decision is entirely yours.'

'Do I have to wait until the end of the day,' she whispered, looking towards the clock on the mantelpiece. 'I think I'd like to decide now.'

Hugh waited in anticipation for her answer but the pregnant pause was broken by the ringing of his phone. Gently he put his finger to Sally's lips as he answered.

'Serena! What? Oh no, not too wet. I managed to take shelter from the worst of it. Stanley got a bit muddy though. Forgotten what? Oh, gracious so I have. No, don't worry I'll be with you as soon as I can. Bye.'

He turned to Sally. 'Damn! I had quite forgotten, we're supposed to be going to friends for lunch. My darling Sally, it looks as if I'm going to have to leave you. I'm sorry. It's going to take me ages to get Stanley cleaned up before Serena even lets him near the house.'

'Don't you want to know what I've decided?' she asked, handing him his Barbour as he walked to the door.

'Not unless it's in my favour,' he teased.

'Shall I ring you later then?'

'That's probably not a good idea as I shall be surrounded by people for the rest of the day. I could meet you this evening, when I take Stanley for his walk. It would probably be safer than phoning. We don't want to end up like the Royals, do we, with people listening in.'

Sally smiled and lifted her face to be kissed. 'Enjoy your lunch,' she whispered, 'and if I go for a run about nine o'clock perhaps I might just happen to bump in to you.'

'I hope you do,' he said warmly, 'I sincerely hope you do.'

Eating a solitary lunch, Sally thought of Hugh and Serena and wondered what they were doing, or more to the point what Hugh was doing. Making smalltalk with friends perhaps, or discussing business matters. Apart from seeing Hugh in a professional capacity, she realized she didn't know much about him at all.

'But then do you need to?' a small voice asked within her head. 'You've already made your mind up and you're already in danger of losing your heart.'

Sally stirred her soup absentmindedly, aware of the croutons disappearing beneath the creamy surface, only to reappear seconds later. What was it someone had written? *I'm not waving but drowning.* It was as if the croutons were drowning. Would she be in danger of drowning too, if she fell in love with Hugh?

The trouble was – not *if* but *how.* How not to let the feeling that lurked in the pit of her stomach take over and consume her whole being. Hugh had already said he had no intentions of leaving Serena, so it was up to her to remain level-headed and in control at all times.

Even at this early stage of their relationship, she knew it wasn't going to be easy. There would be days, perhaps weeks even, when she wouldn't see Hugh at all. Times when business and family – such as it was – came first. Not forgetting too, birthdays and Christmasses – just like today – when at the mere ringing of a phone he would just get up and go.

'Hey! Hang on a minute, Sally Palmer,' she scolded, looking at her distorted reflection in the bowl of the soup spoon. 'Aren't you just getting the teeniest bit carried away? This Christmas isn't quite finished yet – and you're already talking about the next one! Hugh Barrington might not even be interested in you next Christmas.'

Finishing the soup, she promised herself not to get carried away again by such thoughts. She knew the arrangement she was about to enter into would be best treated as her divorce had been – one day at a time.

Stanley recognized Sally's approach long before his master. He pricked up his ears and wagged his tail furiously. Sally stopped to catch her breath.

'When you said you were going for a run this evening, I thought you meant going for a gentle jog round the park. You look as if you've just finished the marathon.'

'I feel as if I have,' she panted. 'Tell me, Hugh, is there a sadistic streak in you that likes to see me looking my worst?'

She was smiling and the significance of her comment was lost on him.

'You've obviously forgotten . . . I don't have my car. It's still in Campion Forest!'

Hugh clasped his hand to his mouth. 'My God! So it is; we never went back for it. Sally, my love, I'm so sorry. Why didn't you ring me or get a taxi?'

'A, because you told me not to and B, because my handbag was in the car too. If you remember when you took me home this morning, we went in the back way and I used the spare key from under the flower pot.'

Hugh held her in his arms and kissed her warmly. 'You know,' he laughed, 'this isn't exactly fulfilling your picture of me waiting for you in a bordello, while you swathe yourself in see-through nylon and maribou.'

'Hardly,' she murmured, bending to stroke Stanley.

'Right then,' he said, 'we'd better not hang around here any longer. Let's go and get some petrol and rescue your car.'

'It's so quiet,' Sally whispered, as Hugh poured petrol into the tank.

'Yes, thank goodness. At least I've got you all to myself for a bit.'

'You've forgotten my chaperone.'

Hugh studied Stanley's soulful eyes gazing down at them from the back of the Range Rover.

'Mmmn,' he added thoughtfully, 'well, I shall just have to leave him behind when I take you away to my castle hideaway.'

'That sounds intriguing, I can't wait.'

'You think I'm joking, don't you?'

'Well . . .' she said uneasily.

Putting down the can and replacing the petrol cap Hugh stood up.

'Actually I lied about the castle. I don't own it and it's a hotel.'

Sally hesitated. 'What if someone recognizes us, or, more to the point, *you*?'

'I doubt it. The weekend after next is bound to be quiet. Next weekend – in case you've already forgotten – is the build up to New Year. Serena and I . . .' Hugh stopped himself, he didn't want to talk of Serena and their New Year plans. He continued: 'I'll book us a suite and let you know the arrangements during the week. This is, after all, to be your last few days at Barrington's, so it won't appear out of place if I take you out for a farewell lunch . . .'

Sally wasn't listening. The imposing, almost magical, presence of the fir trees, still damp from the morning's downpour, seemed to envelop her very soul. Cocooned in their gentle whisperings, she felt safe and protected from the outside world. But once she left them – and Barrington's too – what would fate have in store?

'I suppose I'm going to have to let you go now,' Hugh whispered as he stroked her hair. 'Still, I shall see you at the office.'

Moving her head from his chest and the slight prickliness of his sweater against her cheek, Sally sighed. Where Hugh had been holding her, there now remained the lingering fragrance of his after-shave, combined with the waxy smell of his Barbour jacket and even the faintest hint of petrol. Reluctantly she opened the door of the Range Rover.

'No! Don't get out! I can manage. If you'll just wait to see if my car starts.'

'I'll do more than that. I'll follow you home, just in case . . .'

By that she assumed he referred to Richard, and the earlier magic was broken, though she was pleased to see that he cared.

CHAPTER 7

Melanie entered the office carrying two bouquets, one of yellow roses and the other of mixed flowers.

'These have just arrived for you, Sally. Gracious! The office is looking more and more like a florist's shop every minute.'

Sally looked up from her desk, which was covered with assorted plants, flowers and good luck cards. 'Oh dear,' she sighed, 'this is so overwhelming. I never expected all this.'

'Well, as you wouldn't agree to an Edith Hawtin type of leaving do, I suppose everyone wanted to show you just how sorry they are to lose you.'

Sally opened the cards to her bouquets. Melanie was watching and waiting.

'Well,' she enquired, 'who are they from?'

'This one's from Roz and Donald and the yellow roses are from H –' quickly she changed what very nearly came out as Hugh into a cough – '– Mr Barrington,' and she coughed again feebly.

'How kind,' said Melanie, peering over her shoulder to look at the inscriptions on the cards. 'Roz is certainly going to miss you. You know she always terrifies the life out of me, but I gather people come back year after year to be measured by her. I understand she's on to a third generation of bosoms now!'

Sally wasn't listening, she was reading Hugh's card. 'Barrington's won't be the same without you. With every good wish for the future, Hugh Barrington.' She breathed a sigh of relief; for one awful moment she thought Hugh might have written something more personal.

'I gather he's taking you out to lunch,' Melanie continued.

'Yes, but it's all above board,' Sally added a trifle too quickly, 'Gareth, his nephew, is joining us too. Apparently he wants to pick my brains and tie up a few loose ends before he takes over in earnest.'

'Well, tell him from me, he can pick my brains and tie up my loose ends anytime he likes!' Melanie giggled.

'You can tell him yourself next week, when you start working for him.'

'I wouldn't dare!'

'Wouldn't dare what?' came a voice. The two women looked up in alarm to find Hugh standing in the doorway. 'Mrs Palmer, I assume you are ready for our lunch date.'

Sally nodded lamely as Melanie passed her her jacket. 'I was just admiring the lovely roses you sent Sally,' Melanie said.

'Oh yes,' said Hugh boldly. 'I thought yellow would be best. If I'd sent red roses, we really would have set the tongues wagging, wouldn't we, Mrs Palmer?' Hugh turned and winked at Melanie, whilst Sally's face turned a delicate shade of pink.

Reaching the corridor, Hugh turned back. 'Oh! by the way,' he called to Melanie, 'my nephew's just telephoned. Gareth won't be joining us for lunch after all. He was wondering therefore if you wouldn't mind working late a few evenings next week . . . to help him get the hang of things? Paid overtime of course.'

Melanie was ecstatic; she didn't mind at all. Her mind was already working overtime!

Subdued, Sally contemplated the menu, unable to meet Hugh's gaze.

'Have I said something wrong?' he enquired.

'It was your comment about the roses and setting tongues wagging. Do you think it was wise?'

'Of course! In the circumstances I couldn't have said anything better. Didn't you see the way Melanie reacted? She thought it was a huge joke, only you and I know otherwise don't we? Sally?'

'Perhaps,' she whispered. Her fingers played with the tassel on the menu, which was yellow like the roses.

'Does that mean you've changed your mind about us?' Hugh's tone was full of concern.

'No – it's just that I wish you hadn't said it.' She sighed. 'I'm sorry, this past week has been a bit of a strain. I hadn't realized how much I was going to miss everyone.'

'But you'll be coming back into the store to see them from time to time and when you do, I promise no more cryptic comments. Does that make you feel better?'

Sally nodded and smiled weakly.

'Good, then perhaps you'd care to order, if you've finished shredding that tassel on the menu to pieces.'

Hugh was studying her carefully. 'Because,' he said kindly, 'if we are away from the store for too long, people really will start becoming suspicious.'

'I expect you think I'm becoming paranoid.'

'No, I think you're lovely and I'd give anything to reach across the table and kiss you, but it's far too risky. There are people here I recognize.' Hugh nodded to an elderly couple in the corner.

With her final hours at Barrington's drawing to a close Sally breathed a sigh of relief. She had given Hugh strict instructions not to come to her office again and even refused his offer of help with all her flowers and gifts. Roz had volunteered Donald, and reliable as ever, he was there to organize the removal of what appeared to be a market garden, into the staff lift and out to the carpark.

'Thank you both so much for the flowers,' Sally said as she watched Roz and Donald set off up her garden path laden with blooms. 'You shouldn't have done it, you know.'

'Of course we should,' Roz cried, peering through a cluster of cream and gold spider chrysanthemums. 'Just think of all the years you've put up with my acid tongue and sick sense of humour.' She placed the flowers unceremoniously on the kitchen table and reached for her handkerchief.

'Christ, Sally! What am I going to do without your company during lunch? When I think back to Edith Hawtin's farewell do, I was convinced it would be me leaving next and not you.'

Sally watched sympathetically as tears welled behind the huge tortoiseshell glasses. She put a comforting hand on Roz's shoulder, 'Well it's not as if I won't be coming back. Mr Barrington's very keen to get this new art and picture project off the ground.'

Roz gave her a brittle smile and blew hard into her handkerchief. 'Well, just you make sure you do come back!'

'And don't forget, you're coming to the New Year concert with us,' Donald interrupted. 'Bernard's looking forward to seeing you again.'

'Yes, but I'm not so sure Sally wants to see *him*, Donald!'

Donald turned to face his wife. 'There's no harm in it, you know, Roz.'

'Maybe not,' said Roz, screwing her handkerchief into a ball and tucking it up her sleeve. 'As long as you make sure Bernard knows Sally isn't looking for a husband. God knows Richard was bad enough and Bernard . . .'

'I'm sure he means well,' Donald added lamely. 'Anyway, I think we'd better go, Sally looks all in. It will probably take her the rest of the evening to arrange all these flowers.'

At the door Donald turned and whispered, 'Don't mind Roz, she's just so upset you're leaving and I have absolutely no intention of marrying you off to Bernard.' He patted her on the arm and kissed her cheek.

She had just finished arranging Hugh's flowers when the phone rang.

'Sally, are you alone?'

'Yes – in fact I was just arranging your roses.'

'Good, because I'm ringing to let you know I have the key.'

106

'The key?'

'The key to the Elmsmarsh flat. You haven't forgotten I said I was getting it this week. I thought we could go and look at it tomorrow evening.'

'Tomorrow?'

'Isn't that convenient?'

Sally felt the familiar panic rise in her breast. If Hugh genuinely intended to set her up in a flat, then it was something she was going to have to come to terms with. She took a deep breath.

'Tomorrow will be fine, Hugh.'

'Shall I call for you or would you prefer to meet me somewhere?'

'If you've got to walk Stanley, I could meet you by the lake.'

The road to Elmsmarsh was thinly populated with the odd cottage and pub. Hugh studied the mileometer.

'It's quite amazing, we've done these twenty five miles in less time than it takes me to get into Thornhampton in the morning.'

Sally stared out of the window, her eyes catching sight of a filling station. 'Well, there'll be no excuses for running out of petrol here.'

Hugh laughed, remembering the day in Campion Forest and the confusion over her car. He reached across and squeezed her hand. 'And you certainly won't starve,' he said, nodding to a group of olde worlde shops. 'I did a reconnoitre of the area a few days ago, bakers, grocers, post office and a pretty decent fruit and veg shop by the looks of it. Right, here we go then, next turning on the left and we're almost there.'

Sally was entranced. Hugh's face was like a child's, transfixed with anticipation on Christmas morning, as he slipped the key into the lock, opened the door, switched on the light and waited for her reaction.

'Don't look so worried,' he said, 'there's no one in there. Shall I wait here in the hall while you have a look round on your own?'

Gingerly she left his side and switching on the lights as she went, surveyed the flat. The door immediately in front of her led into a galley kitchen whilst the archway to her right led to a lounge/diner. Beyond was a corridor with fitted cupboards on one side and bathroom on the other. At the far end was a door leading to what she assumed was the bedroom.

Sally hesitated with her hand on the door handle and looked back at Hugh. 'I take it this is the bedroom.'

Hugh waited for her to open the door and go inside. Slowly he walked down the corridor and found her peering from the bedroom window.

'Well, what do you think. Do you like it?'

'It's amazing, not another house in sight for miles.'

Hugh laughed at her face pressed up against the glass to study the rural landscape. 'Yes,' he whispered, 'you'll find the view quite enchanting – when you can see it – but what about the flat, Sally?'

Feeling her face colour, she turned to face him. 'I think it's very nice . . . if you're really sure, Hugh.'

'Of course I am.' He held her face in his hands. 'You don't think it's too small then and you won't mind the stairs? I know the flats round the corner are bigger and they have a lift but I thought you'd prefer this block because of the view.'

She smiled. 'I think I can manage one flight of stairs and to be honest, I'd prefer not to sleep on the ground floor. It's going to be strange not having a garden though.'

'Ah! But there's a balcony,' said Hugh, taking her hand and leading her to the far end of the lounge. A glass door led onto a small balcony.

'That's why the kitchen's so small,' Hugh explained, 'but I thought you'd want somewhere to put your bay tree.' He grinned at the memory of Stanley and the bay tree. 'I thought perhaps you could have a few window boxes and, who knows, there might even be room for Stanley's basket too.'

'Definitely not!' remonstrated Sally. 'I'm not having Stanley banished to the balcony, I want him indoors with us.'

Hugh put his hands on her waist and drew her towards him. 'No wonder Stanley and I both adore you,' he whispered. 'I can't wait for you to move in. Speaking of which, I'd better get a move on too.'

Locking the door, they heard muted voices and the sound of soft music coming from the neighbouring flat.

'I haven't had a chance to vet them,' Hugh whispered, 'but the agent assures me they're a very nice couple.'

Sally patted Stanley as she got into the Range Rover. 'Well, old chap, you can be my first dinner guest.'

'Oh really!' said Hugh in mock horror, 'and what about me?'

'Well, I might invite you too,' she said playfully.

'That's better. You seem more relaxed now. You had me worried for a moment when we first arrived. Look, I won't drop you by the park. It's too late and it's not safe. I'll drop you on the corner, okay?'

She nodded and, studying his profile in the semi-gloom, wondered what it would be like to spend more than a few snatched moments with him.

'Penny for them?' Hugh said softly.

'Sorry, they're not for sale – not tonight anyway.'

Sally watched his comforting silhouette as the Range Rover disappeared into the night and hurried indoors clutching the brown envelope Hugh had taken from the glove compartment. Carpet samples he'd said.

She studied her own threadbare carpet as she sat in front of the gas fire with a mug of hot chocolate, feeling the warmth penetrate the stoneware until it was almost too hot to hold. Then cupping her warmed hands to her face she sighed. New carpets, a brand new flat, with not a hint of stripped pine or Richard's efforts at DIY and yes . . . even a new man, she thought. The New Year she'd been dreading might not be too bad after all. Draining the remains of the chocolate she remembered she'd forgotten to wish Hugh a Happy New Year.

In the foyer of the concert hall Roz, Donald and Sally waited anxiously for Bernard to arrive.

'I'm giving him another five minutes, Donald,' Roz said angrily, 'and if he hasn't arrived by then, I'm going in without him. I can already hear the orchestra tuning up in there!'

Roz nodded in the direction of the door to the stalls, where the few remaining latecomers dribbled through to their seats. An usherette stood in the open doorway, her supply of programmes severely depleted.

'Here he is!' Donald added cheerily and waved his hand in greeting as Bernard arrived completely out of breath and dishevelled.

'So sorry I'm late, I couldn't find a parking space. I've been driving around for ages.'

'And you've been driving us mad for ages,' hissed Roz under her breath to Sally. She studied Bernard critically over the rim of her glasses. His dinner suit was obviously a relic from the seventies, with its wide lapels, enormous velvet bow-tie and flares!

Sally watched Roz's look of disbelief as she scanned Bernard from top to toe, like a probe. 'Please God, don't say anything, Roz,' Sally's inner self was pleading, willing Roz to look in her direction. When she did, Sally held a finger to her mouth and shook her head.

'Hmph!' was all Roz said as she gave Bernard a look that would kill. She turned on her heels in a swish of taffeta, snatched a programme from the startled usherette and left Donald fumbling in his pocket for money.

'Don't mind Roz,' Sally said sympathetically, watching Bernard struggle to adjust his bow-tie, 'she's a stickler for punctuality. She'll be okay by the interval.'

But for once Sally was wrong. By the interval, Roz was still fuming. It had been bad enough making their entrance just before curtain up, but the fact that their seats were in the middle of the row only made the situation worse. Disgruntled concert-goers – comfortably installed in their seats – shuffled to their feet angrily, their eyes full of contempt and their mutterings painfully audible.

To make matters worse Bernard had trodden quite heavily on the feet of a scantily shod female and added insult to injury by passing round a bag of peppermint toffees before the conductor even had a chance to warm his baton. Roz was seething.

'Remind me, never again, Sally! Donald can plead, "poor bloody Bernard" 'til the cows come home, but I absolutely refuse.'

'I'm sure he means well,' Sally said, trying to placate her. 'He's obviously not used to this sort of occasion.'

'Hmph! He's made that perfectly clear by that suit. My God! The last time I saw one like that was on some would-be Frank Sinatra at a talent concert, when Donald and I had that ghastly weekend away. Don't you remember me telling you about it? The geriatric medallion man, complete with chest wig, toupé, gold chains and the like, attempting to croon his way through an excrutiatingly painful rendition of *Strangers in the Night*.'

Roz laughed loudly, causing heads to turn in her direction.

'What's so funny?' asked Donald, returning from the bar with their drinks. 'Bernard's just bringing yours, Sally.'

'I was just telling Sally about that chap at that dreadful holiday camp, remember? The one with the appalling "dooby dooby do's".'

Roz giggled and winked at Sally as Bernard struggled through the crowd, clutching Sally's gin and tonic. In his other hand he carried a pint of lager.

'I wonder what *his* dooby do's are like, Sally. Let's hope he never gives you the opportunity to find out!'

Sally suppressed a smile and turned away. Lifting her glass to her mouth, familiar eyes met hers across the crowded bar. Hugh Barrington!

Sipping her drink nervously, Sally watched as Hugh turned to Serena, elegantly clad in black velvet, whispered something in her ear and made his way towards Roz and Donald.

'Crikey! If it isn't the boss man,' hissed Roz. 'Fancy seeing him here!'

'Roz, Donald . . . and Mrs Palmer too. What a pleasant surprise.'

Hugh turned to face Sally. His look, as he glimpsed Bernard by her side, was cold and questioning.

'This is Bernard,' Sally said nervously, 'he's an old friend of Donald's.'

Hugh extended his hand in Bernard's direction. 'Hugh Barrington,' he said, accepting Bernard's limp and clammy handshake.

'Hugh darling. Come along now, they'll be ringing the bell soon and you haven't even finished your champagne. Charles was going to order another bottle but there's no time now.' Serena put her arm on Hugh's and looked back towards her sister and brother-in-law and the rest of their party. She waved and turned quickly to Roz and Sally.

'How lovely to see you both, but you don't mind if I drag Hugh away, do you? Poor thing, it appears Barrington's follows him wherever he goes.'

Sally watched as Serena bent forward to proffer the perfunctory mid-air kiss of the cheek. She searched desperately for something to say.

'How's Stanley?' she asked feebly.

'Oh, my dear, don't ask! Unfortunately he's frightfully hale and hearty . . . almost with a new lease of life.'

113

'Well, don't forget I'll take him any time you like.'

'I wish you would, Sally,' Serena whispered in her ear, 'I wish you would take him – period!'

Sally was aware of Serena suddenly spotting Bernard by Donald's side. Unlike Roz, who had voiced her critique of Bernard's attire, Serena's face said it all. Her left eyebrow shot up and reaching for Hugh's arm, she wished them all a Happy New Year and hurried back to her sister. Hearing Serena's cruel shrieks of laughter, Sally was in no doubt it was Bernard who was on the receiving end of her vitriolic attack.

Feeling uncomfortable and dispirited, Sally reached for Bernard's arm.

'Come along, Bernard,' she said kindly, 'let's get back to our seats before everyone else, shall we?'

Bernard looked down at the remains of his pint glass. Still half full, he hesitated and looked to see if Roz and Donald had finished their drinks. Roz was chewing on the flesh of her lemon slice. Drawing in her mouth at its sourness, she deftly dropped the remaining peel into Bernard's lager and smiled sweetly.

'Yes, come along, Bernard, there's no time to finish that now!'

Cheered by Roz's change of humour, Donald duly obliged by putting down his glass and following Sally through the door. As the lights dimmed Roz's voice was heard to echo, 'And no more bloody peppermints please!'

Sally stirred sleepily and reached for the phone. It had to be a mistake; no one would ring her at this time of the morning, unless . . . Jackie or the children? Panic gave way to relief as she recognized Hugh's voice.

114

'Hugh!' Her eyes peered in the darkness towards the clock, 'It's a quarter to three in the morning!'

'I just wanted to wish you Happy New Year and . . .'

'Where are you?'

'I'm at home . . .'

'But won't Serena be suspicious?'

'No.' Hugh laughed wryly. 'She's only halfway through her beauty routine and I'm in the garden.'

'Then that will make it even more suspicious,' said Sally, rubbing her eyes.

'No it won't. I'm waiting for Stanley to do the necessary. I'm sorry. I obviously woke you up.'

'Yes, you did, I've been in bed for ages.'

'Alone?'

'Of course alone! Hugh, what are you getting at?'

'I just wondered . . . your escort at the concert.'

'Oh, you mean Bernard – but he's just a friend of Donald's, a widower. Hugh, you didn't honestly think he and I were . . .?'

Hugh recognized the early signs of anger in Sally's voice.

'No,' he said quietly. 'I just didn't like seeing you together, it made me feel terribly jealous. Why didn't you tell me you were going to the concert with . . .?'

'Because I didn't think it was important. Do you realize I don't even know Bernard's surname? That's why I couldn't introduce him properly. Besides, I didn't know you and Serena were going to the concert; perhaps *you* should have warned *me*!'

'Oh, dear, Sally, are we having our first row?'

'No, not row,' she said sleepily, 'more a misunderstanding. Anyway I thought it probably did us a favour.'

'Meaning?'

'It would probably be a good idea to be seen in another man's company. Like you trying to put Melanie off the scent with your comment about the red roses.'

'Touché! said Hugh in response to her tetchiness.

'I'm sorry, I'm afraid I'm not at my best when I'm tired.'

'Well, I'd better let you get back to sleep then.' Hugh looked towards his bedroom window. Serena had just switched off her bedside light. Only the dim glow of his own remained in an otherwise dark and starless night. He whistled for Stanley.

'Hugh, are you still there?' Sally whispered, feeling her eyes close.

'Yes, I'm still here, I'm just waiting for Stanley.'

'Wish him Happy New Year from me then.'

'I will, and Sally . . .'

'Yes?'

'Make sure you get plenty of sleep between now and next Saturday.'

'Why?'

'Because you and I are going to be spending next Saturday night together.'

The significance of Hugh's statement, prompted by his overindulgence of champagne to celebrate the New Year, was lost on Sally. She was already fast asleep. It was only in the morning, when she made the comparison between Hugh in his equisitely cut dinner suit and Bernard in his flares, that the memories came flooding back. What *was* it Hugh had whispered before she'd hung up the phone?

CHAPTER 8

As dusk fell on the wintry January afternoon, Hugh swung the Jaguar into the tree-lined driveway of Cedar Court. Sally felt her stomach churn; there was no turning back now. She bit her lip and flicked an imaginary piece of fluff from her skirt.

'Nervous?' Hugh enquired softly.

Sally nodded. 'Does it show that much?'

'Afraid so. Try and relax, Sally. We're no longer in the age of dirty weekends and the staff of Cedar Court are extremely discreet.'

'Oh! You've been here before then?'

'Yes.' Hugh watched her face fill with disappointment. He reached for her hand. 'Yes, I have been here before but not as an overnight guest. I was here for a golfing tournament – there's a superb course on the periphery – with Charles, my brother-in-law.'

'How do you know the staff are discreet then?'

'Just something Charles said in passing.'

'Has he stayed here with another woman?'

'Good Lord no! What is this? The third degree?' Hugh joked.

Sally smiled weakly. 'No, I'm just curious, that's all.'

'Well,' said Hugh, squeezing her hand reassuringly. 'How about becoming curious about the interior of Cedar Court? They serve wonderful teas in the library and their dinner menu is amazing.'

Helping her from the car he whispered, 'It's going to be wonderful . . . I promise.'

She braced herself and walked with Hugh to the main entrance.

Unable to look the receptionist in the eye, Sally studied her immediate surroundings. Beyond the oak-panelled hallway she glimpsed an enormous log fire burning in what appeared to be the library. Wasn't that where Hugh said they served afternoon tea? Gingerly she stepped sideways to view the interior. Row upon row of books lined the walls and comfortable armchairs and what Jack described as 'squidgy settees' were placed in welcoming groups.

'Will you be requiring afternoon tea, sir?' The receptionist was handing Hugh a key.

'Sally, shall we have tea or would you prefer to go to our room first?'

Sally turned abruptly, aware of two pairs of questioning eyes. She'd heard the words 'tea' and 'our room'. 'Oh, I think I'd prefer tea first please.'

'Coward!' the voice in her head murmured. 'You can't put it off forever, you know. You're going to have to walk up those stairs sooner or later.'

And what a staircase it was. Quite the baronial hall, with its sweeping oak panels and intricately carved banisters. Sally stared in wonderment at the ornate carving, galleried landing and walls adorned with oil paintings so vast that just one would have covered her entire bedroom wall.

As if from nowhere a young man in livery appeared at the foot of the stairs. 'Oh, he's got a suitcase just like mine,' she mused, then suddenly realized it was indeed her own suitcase that he was carrying. He was also carrying Hugh's. Sally felt a hand on her arm.

'Shall we go through for tea then?'

Watching the reflection of twisting, red, yellow and gold flames from the fire, dancing on the silver teapot and hot-water jug, Sally became aware of Hugh's questioning gaze. She smiled.

'I was thinking, it's not quite like my old brown earthenware, is it?'

'Not exactly, but shall we see if it tastes quite as good?'

Surprised by the weight of the teapot, she felt her hand drop.

'Careful,' said Hugh, steadying her wrist. 'Now you know why women were so well-built years ago.' He gestured to a portrait of a grand dame, of ample bosom, swathed in yards of gold brocade.

'It looks as if she could do with Roz's assistance,' Sally added with a knowing look.

'Most definitely,' agreed Hugh as Sally passed him his tea.

She studied the plates of neatly sliced finger sandwiches and cream cakes. 'I don't know if I could,' she whispered.

'Try,' urged Hugh. 'Look, I'll tell you what. If we hurry with the tea, we might be able to have a quick walk in the grounds before dinner. The fresh air will do wonders for your appetite.'

Appetite for *what* or for *whom*, Sally found herself thinking. Finishing a smoked salmon sandwich her eyes alighted on a dainty finger éclair and she immediately thought of Stanley.

Hugh's eyes met hers across the table. 'Stanley's favourite.'

'Will he be all right with Serena . . . She won't mind looking after him tonight?'

Hugh gave a brittle smile. 'Oh, she minds all right, but as she's going away for two weeks on a skiing trip, she can hardly begrudge me one night away from home, can she?'

'Did she ask where you were going? What did you tell her?'

Hugh leaned across the table and with the tip of his little finger wiped away the tiniest crumb of meringue from Sally's upper lip. 'Shhh,' he whispered. 'Finish your meringue. We didn't come to this wonderful place to talk about Serena – did we?'

Sally felt herself colour and placing the silver pastry fork onto white porcelain, dabbed at her mouth with a pink linen napkin. Hugh, having decided to try the éclair, popped the rest of it in his mouth and grinned.

'I'll tell Stanley how delicious it was. Now how about that walk?'

Reaching for her coat, Sally's eyes rested on their room key with it's elaborate key fob in royal blue and gold. Hugh's long, fine fingers deftly swept it away and into his pocket, but not before she read the bold gold-leaf on leather inscription – 'King Charles II Suite'.

Thoughts of Roz immediately sprang to mind. Had *she* been here no doubt there would be some reference made to Nell Gwyn. Tying the belt of her coat Sally followed Hugh back into the panelled hallway. On seeing them, the receptionist called from her inner office. 'Excuse me, sir, will you be dining with us this evening?'

'Most definitely. We're just popping out for some fresh air to give us an appetite.' Hugh looked thoughtful. 'Are you expecting to be busy this evening?'

The receptionist smiled warmly and shook her head. 'Not like last week. You couldn't move in here for haggis and bagpipes. Fortunately it's calmed down a bit during the past few days.' She studied the open book on her desk. 'We've a party of ten booked for nine thirty but before then it's –'

Hugh didn't even wait for her to finish her sentence. Looking in Sally's direction he announced confidently, 'Oh, we don't like to eat late, do we, darling? I think we'd prefer seven thirty.'

Sally nodded lamely, and watched as the receptionist wrote down their booking for dinner.

Outside in the dampness of late afternoon Sally shivered and breathed in the faint smell of woodsmoke, spiralling above the fluted chimney pots. Taking Hugh's arm a smile crept across her face.

'What's so funny?' he murmured.

'Oh, we don't like to eat late, do we, darling?' she mimmicked.

'We don't, do we?' he asked, bending to kiss her forehead.

'No,' she sighed. 'I don't believe we do.'

'Well, at least you nodded in the right place, Sally! Now then, as it was a unanimous decision to eat early,

121

let's have a quick walk around the block – or in this case the gravelled walk – as like most women I'm sure you prefer plenty of time to dress for dinner.'

At the foot of the stairs Sally stared up at the galleried landing with trepidation. Flickering candle-bulbs, in sconces, illuminated the stained-glass windows, casting delicate hues across the deep pile carpet and oak carving. She felt Hugh take her hand and guide her gently forward.

Logs the size of tree stumps had been placed on the fire below and for that she was grateful. It meant the thumping of her heart was drowned out by the crackle and spit of wood as fresh flames licked their way noisily and greedily up the chimney.

With her feet sinking into the deep pile of smokey-blue carpet, Sally was aware of Hugh closing the door behind her.

'Mmmn,' he murmured apreciatively. 'Yes, I think even "Old Rowley" would have approved of this setting.'

'Old Rowley?'

'Charles II's nickname,' Hugh enlightened her. 'After a stallion of the time, renowned for its prowess at stud.'

Sally wished she hadn't asked; she was only glad Hugh was a Hugh and not a Charles! Moving to a corner of the room she studied three miniatures on the wall. Hugh joined her.

'Charles II, Catherine of Braganza – his wife – and of course dear Nell,' he announced.

Sally recognized Nell Gwyn instantly, one of Charles' favourite mistresses. She was less familiar however with Catherine of Braganza, his Portugese wife. Strange that all three should be hanging side by side. Would Hugh consider hanging his own photo between those of Serena and herself, she wondered. Keeping her thoughts private, she turned and whispered. 'It is a magnificent room, isn't it?'

Hugh followed her gaze as it encompassed the four-poster bed with its heavy blue brocade hangings and bedspread. Taking her hand he led her to a settee by the window. It was squidgy, like those in the library.

Sitting down, he motioned her to join him, patting the peach chintz by his side. 'Five minutes,' he said softly, drawing her into his arms, 'then we must get ready for dinner.'

Sally closed her eyes dreamily as his lips met hers.

Released from his embrace, she looked at her watch. Hugh glanced at her wrist as she did so and announced, 'We've got just over an hour. Do you want to unpack and use the bathroom first?'

Unzipping the tapestry suitcase, Sally carefully removed layers of tissue to reveal the simple, navy-blue crêpe dress she'd bought specially for this evening. She smoothed out the long sleeves and went to the wardrobe for a hanger. Selecting one in peach chintz – the same material as the settee – she smiled. Her own wardrobe at home contained a selection of wood, plastic and wire.

Hugh, she noticed, was feeding the trousers of his lounge suit into the trouser press, pulling levers and setting dials with well-practised dexterity. She recalled Richard's first attempt with a similar contraption, only to discover, on waking the following morning, the creases in his best suit ran not vertically but diagonally.

123

Sally suppressed a smile. It was strange; this past week she'd hardly thought of Richard at all. Yet she supposed she should be grateful to him now. If it wasn't for Richard, she wouldn't be here – showering and dressing for dinner.

Hugh adjusted his silk tie and fingered his left lapel. 'No red rose?' Sally enquired, looking towards the floral displays distributed across the room. The arrangements were all creamy-white and peach.

Smiling, Hugh shook his head. 'No, that's just for Barrington's.' And with eyes that reflected warmth and approval, he walked slowly towards her. 'Sally, you look perfectly lovely.'

For a brief moment she thought he was going to brush his fingers through her hair. Instead he stopped and stroked her left shoulder gently with his right hand.

'Fluff?' she enquired. 'I did use the clothes brush.'

'No,' he said softly. 'I just wanted to touch you, but I didn't think you'd thank me for spoiling your hairstyle. Now, are you ready to eat?'

Finishing her aperitif, Sally watched Hugh nod discreetly in the direction of the maitre d' and they made their way from the bar to the restaurant. There, at Hugh's request, they were shown to a corner table by the window and although it was dark, they were able to look across the formal floodlit gardens.

'Of course they switch off the fountains and waterfall in the winter months,' Hugh announced, 'so we'll have to come back again in the summer.'

There was something comforting about those last words. The mere thought that Hugh was thinking of them sharing a summer together filled Sally's heart with hope. She smiled at him across the table and watched his eyes sweep unobtrusively in the direction of other diners. Seeing no one he recognized, he gave her his attention once more.

Sally sipped at her white wine thoughtfully, oblivious to the candlelight dancing on fluted crystal as it cast golden glints in her hair.

'Do you approve of my choice?' Hugh asked and watched her nod appreciatively. 'I have to confess,' he whispered, squeezing lemon juice on his seafood ravioli, 'I must admit, I've dreamt of sharing my favourite foods and wines with you.' He looked in the direction of the maitre d'. He was being discreet and remaining out of earshot.

Dismissing the wine waiter once the main course was finished, Hugh turned to Sally. 'You're sure you don't want any more red wine then?'

She shook her head. 'Thank you, no. If I drink more than one glass it gives me a headache.'

'We can't have that then, can we? Not tonight of all nights.'

Even in the subdued lighting of the restaurant, Hugh discerned the gentlest glow brush Sally's cheeks. Tenderly he reached for her hand. 'Sorry, would you rather I hadn't said that? I hope that look doesn't mean I've put you off choosing one of Cedar Court's irresistible puddings.'

She glanced at the dessert menu and smiled. 'It would take more than that. I'm afraid I have a very sweet tooth when it comes to anything made with chocolate.'

With the confection of white and dark chocolate placed before her, Sally watched wide-eyed as the waiter presented Hugh with his pear and stilton strudel. He grinned at the look of sheer disbelief on her face.

'Fruit and cheese course in one –' he smiled – 'and not, thank God, a hint of raspberry coulis anywhere! It's very nice, I can assure you. Would you like to try some?'

Looking round surreptitiously, Sally leaned forward and allowed Hugh to feed her just the smallest amount of filo pastry and filling.

'Well?' he enquired as her tongue savoured the unusual combination of flavours and textures.

'I'm afraid I don't much care for it, I think I'll stick with the chocolate.'

'You don't have to be afraid for that', Hugh said. 'Oh look, the party of ten has arrived. In that case, shall we have coffee in the library?'

Sitting by the fire, Sally allowed herself to relax in the deep cushions of the armchair. She sighed contentedly. 'It was a wonderful meal, Hugh, just perfect and just the right amount. I do so hate it when food is piled sky-high, to the extent it looks almost obscene.'

Hugh was looking towards the library door, where he was smiling at someone. 'Well, I hope you've just a little more room left, especially as you like chocolate.'

Sally watched as the waiter placed a tray of coffee on the delicate lace cloth and turned the silver salver of *petits fours* towards her. The first thing she noticed were tiny chocolate cups filled with fresh strawberries.

'Enjoy, Madame,' he said softly.

'You've obviously had these before,' she grinned, reaching forward.

Hugh nodded. 'Yes, the summer I was here. I wasn't sure they would have them in winter though. I expect they have the strawberries flown in from exotic parts.'

'Mmmn, summer in January.' Sally sighed as she popped the strawberry into her mouth.

'I prefer the physalis myself,' Hugh added, reaching across for the golden orb of caramelized fruit.

'After that superb white wine – not to mention the red – I don't think I'd even attempt that pronounciation!'

Hugh laughed quietly and fingered the papery petals of the fruit.

'I remember Gareth giving his mother quite a shock when he came home once from boarding school. Poor Vivienne, she thought she'd heard him say he'd got syphilis, when in fact he was talking about physalis! You see, he'd never tasted them before.'

Hugh placed the remaining stalk in his saucer and looked thoughtfully across at Sally. She looked contented and relaxed and the flickering flames from the fire glinted in her eyes.

'Are you ready to go up?' she heard him whisper.

Slowly her eyes met his and with a sudden surge of butterflies in the pit of her stomach she swallowed hard.

'Come,' Hugh urged gently, reaching for her hand. Feeling her nails digging into his palm, he led her to the foot of the stairs and whispered reassuringly, 'It's going to be all right.'

In the bedroom, the drapes had been drawn and the bedspread turned down to reveal ivory damask sheets. Sensing her unease, Hugh switched on lamps, turned

127

off the main light, reached for a magazine and sat down on the settee.

'I can read while you're getting ready for bed,' he announced tactfully. 'Or would you prefer me to go for a walk for ten minutes?'

Joining him on the settee, Sally hugged her knees and stared down at the toes of her navy suede shoes. 'I'm sorry, I don't appear to be much good at this game, Hugh.'

'Sally, darling,' he whispered softly, laying down the magazine and placing his hand gently under her chin he tilted it towards him, 'this is no game . . . this is serious.'

She felt his lips brush her eyelids and her cheeks before his mouth found hers. A few moments later, Sally straightened her shoulders, rose from the settee, strode purposefully towards her suitcase and announced, 'There's no need to go for a walk. I'll just get my nightdress. If I could just use the bathroom fir – Oh!'

'What's wrong?' Hugh looked up in alarm.

Sally was peering into the depths of her suitcase, pushing aside sheets of tissue paper, panties, shoes and tights.

'I can't find my nightdress!'

'Are you sure you packed it?'

'Yes, I can remember laying it on the bed just before the estate agent rang at least I think I did.'

Sally cast her mind back to the morning when she was packing. The unexpected phonecall from the estate agent had taken her by surprise. A young couple had been to look at the house the previous evening and wanted to come back for a second look before they headed back to Milton Keynes.

It was a company move, the agent had said and as they were first-time buyers they were every vendor's dream. Sally remembered now what she'd done with the nightdress. Taking the couple upstairs for a second look at the house, she'd seen it – a confection of cream satin and lace – lying on the bed with her undies.

Aware that the young husband was directly behind her as she'd opened the bedroom door she'd hurriedly hidden everything under the duvet. She'd later removed the sets of underclothes but forgotten all about the nightdress. In embarrassment, she turned to face Hugh and shrugged her shoulders.

'No problem at all,' he announced, putting down the magazine for a second time as he headed for a chest of drawers. 'We can share these!'

In his hand he held a pair of navy-blue silk pyjamas piped with red. 'You can have the top and I'll take the bottoms, how about that?'

He was going to add, jokingly, unless you'd prefer the other way round, but felt in the circumstances it wasn't appropriate. Sally stepped forward and accepted the top gracefully. Even in its folded state it was quite clear Hugh's pyjama jacket – with its long sleeves – was going to cover considerably more of her than her own mere slip of lace and satin.

In the bathroom she ran her fingers over the fine silk and lifted one of the sleeves to her cheek. She closed her eyes and sighed; it felt sensuously smooth and smelt of Hugh's aftershave.

'Well, Sally Palmer,' she murmured, opening her eyes again to face her reflection in the large mirror, 'this is where you join the ranks of Nell Gwyn and Lily Langtry!'

Stepping out of her dress she hung it back on the chintz hanger and slowly removed her bra, holding it to her modestly as she unfastened the hooks. Quite why she did so, she wasn't sure. Perhaps it was just that there were so many mirrors in the bathroom, she felt exposed from every angle. Yet there was no one to see and Hugh was hardly likely to come bursting through the door.

All the signs so far indicated he was the perfect gentleman and she had no doubt in her mind they would remain that way. He'd even gone so far as to offer to go for a walk while she got undressed! Sally smiled nervously and put on the jacket, counting each button as she drew the two edges together. There were four.

As expected the sleeves of the jacket were far too long, so she pulled them back to her elbows, as she did with her casual cotton shirts in the summer. The effect was pleasing and she ran her hands over the silky fabric, downwards over her breasts and on to where the silk met the less smooth fabric of her tights. Quickly she stepped out of those and felt the cold marble of the floor against the soles of her feet.

With only her panties left, it was decision time. Once more she turned to the myriad of mirrors and Hamlet style, asked of her reflection. 'To wear or not to wear?'

Whilst deliberating, she brushed her hair and fingered her fringe into place, sprayed a fresh mist of perfume onto her throat and wrists and reached for the door.

Hugh stood up and smiled appreciatively.

'Do you know, I've always heard tell that men's pyjamas look better on a woman and you've certainly proved that.'

He bent and kissed the top of her head, breathing in her delicate scent and only briefly thought of Serena. Her taste in perfumes of late had begun to annoy him. They were sickly and cloying.

In art and beauty, inanimate and human, Hugh had always preferred a more subtle approach to things beautiful. Serena was beautiful right enough, but her mere presence in a room in recent months was about as subtle as a London doubledecker in the desert!

Sally on the other hand, well, Sally was . . . Aware of his hand stroking her hair, and the gentle warmth of her body pressed against his, Hugh whispered softly, 'I won't keep you long.'

For the first time since they'd arrived, Sally sat on the bed and ran her hands along the folds of the damask sheets. She'd only once before heard of damask sheets. They had them on the Orient Express apparently. Roz had told her that one lunchtime ages ago and they'd sighed enviously, thinking of their own poly-cotton.

'Still, just think of all that bloody ironing!' Roz had announced at the time, trying to make them feel better.

I don't think I'd mind the ironing, Sally thought, slipping between the sheets. She could hear discreet movement in the bathroom and thought of Hugh minus his pyjama top. Feeling her pulse race, she decided perhaps she was already warm enough and decided to open the window.

On the far wall her attention was caught once more by the trio of miniatures. Charles, Catherine and Nell; all appeared to be looking at her – and Nell even more so than the others. It was as if she knew why Sally was here – waiting to be seduced by her lover!

'Don't look so smug,' she hissed under her breath to the king's paramour, just as she reached up to unfasten the window. At that moment, Hugh opened the bathroom door and caught a glimpse of Sally's thirty-six-inch bottom clad in navy satin and lace panties. For a brief moment Sally froze and her hand moved down fleetingly. Thankfully she had kept them on but Nell appeared to be grinning at her nonetheless!

'Contemplating the lasciviousness of the seventeenth century, Sally?'

With beating heart, she turned to face Hugh where he stood, tall, tanned and handsome in the doorway. Charles II's father had lost his head, now Sally had lost hers. As Hugh crossed the deep pile carpet towards her, she noticed a bowl of oranges on the table and smiled. How very appropriate!

CHAPTER 9

Being woken early next morning by the cooing of doves outside their bedroom window also seemed appropriate. Sally stirred sleepily. Vaguely aware of unfamiliar surroundings, she felt her hand brush accidentally against Hugh's naked torso. Alarmed that she may have woken him, she hugged her arms to her breasts and lay quiet and still, almost without breathing, every muscle taut.

The room was silent and full of shadows. There were shadows on the walls from the pictures, shadows on the canopy above her head, shadows from the heavy folds of fabric – enveloping each of the four carved posts of the bed – and the shadow of the man lying by her side. The man who, last night, had taken her in his arms and made love to her so gently and so lovingly that she'd wanted to cry.

Feeling tears from such contentment prick her eyelids, Sally lay with eyes closed and thought of Hugh. What was it he'd said, helping her from the car when they arrived? 'It will be wonderful . . . I promise.'

How had he known? How could he tell? When last night could have been a complete disaster. But it wasn't a complete disaster, was it? Hugh was right, it was wonderful. She smiled to herself. Well, it was, once she'd got over her initial nerves and shyness.

Turning to face the sidetable, she opened her eyes slowly and reached out with one finger to touch the cool, smooth stem of the now empty crystal champagne flute.

'A perfect cure for nerves,' Hugh had announced, opening the mini-bar, having first carried her to the bed.

Her initial reaction had been no more alcohol. An aperitif, followed by white and red wine had been more than enough but Hugh had insisted.

'It's good for headaches too,' he said, watching her reaction as the bubbles burst in her mouth and made her nose tingle.

'But I haven't got a headache!'

'Just goes to show how good it is then!'

She'd laughed and passed Hugh her empty glass before he slipped into bed beside her. Drawing her close, she felt his hands slide down her silk-covered arms and across her breasts whilst her own bare legs curved against his silken trousers.

'Sally,' he'd murmured softly, 'my own beautiful Sally,' and she counted in her head, one – two – three – four – as he found each of the four buttons and edged the jacket gently from her shoulders.

Feeling his lips on her mouth, throat and breasts, Sally fingered the tiny hairs on the nape of his neck and sighed. Hugh was right, champagne was definitely good for nerves and headaches!

Later – much later in fact – in a tangle of silk sleeves and pyjama legs, Hugh released her briefly, reached to the sidetable for the small lime-green envelope and switched off the bedside lamp.

'Something tells me you'd prefer the light off,' he'd whispered in her ear, stroking her hair as he did so.

In the darkness he was aware of the gentle nodding of her head and her softly murmured, 'yes,' – silenced by his mouth on hers – which was followed by the giving of herself . . . completely.

Sally stirred dreamily and felt Hugh's hand reach for hers.

'I take it you're awake,' he said. 'I hope you weren't disturbed by the doves.'

'No, I think they sound lovely. They remind me of a carol I once sang at infants' school.'

'Sing it to me then.'

'No,' she replied shyly. 'Besides I can't remember all the words. It was something about bowing and curtsey-ing and jubilation.'

'Do doves bow and curtsey then?'

'They did in the carol. They flew around too, and made pigeon and dove noises, like coo-coo and croo-croo.'

Hugh laughed softly and taking her in his arms said, 'Did they indeed! Well, fancy that!'

'I think you're teasing me,' she said, pulling away.

'No, I'm not. I'm just interested to have learnt something new this weekend. We certainly never had that carol at my school.'

Returning to his embrace, Sally remained silent. There was no way she was going to tell Hugh what *she'd* learned, this weekend.

She sighed. 'What time do we have to leave?'

Hugh reached for his watch. 'Oh, not for ages yet. Do you realize it's only six o'clock? Tell me, Mrs Palmer, do you always wake this early in the morning?'

'Mostly, especially when I'm going into Barrington's.'

'Well, you won't be doing that for a while.'

Sally was thoughtful. No, she wouldn't, she'd mostly be going into Laura's Lair.

'I hope you're not too hungry,' Hugh continued. 'If you remember we've ordered breakfast for seven thirty which means we've got another hour and a half, unless I ring downstairs . . .'

'We could always go for a walk,' she added brightly. 'I'm sure I can wait that long, especially when I think about last night and all that wonderful food.'

Hugh stroked his hand gently down her arm and lifted her fingers to his lips. 'I hope the food wasn't the only wonderful thing about last night,' he murmured.

Sally felt herself blush and her mouth go quite dry. Hugh's hand caressed her thigh and when at last she found her voice, she heard herself saying softly, 'Well, I suppose we could always go for a walk – after breakfast!'

Hand in hand, Hugh led Sally through the formal gardens and beyond to the woodland walk. On the periphery a magnificent cedar of Lebanon stood defiantly, its sweeping branches held out proudly. It was almost as if it was saying to the distant avenue of oak and ash – now stripped naked of their leaves – 'look at me; aren't I a fine specimen?'

'The cedar of Cedar Court, no doubt,' Sally remarked.

Hugh nodded and scanned the distant hedgerows, where a few remaining berries stood out brightly against bare twigs. There had been a slight frost during the night and a dampness hung eerily above the ground.

'Wonderful,' said Hugh, breathing in the chill morning air. 'Just look at it, not a soul for miles. You won't have quite the same view from the flat but at least you won't be plagued by people and cars.'

'I can't wait to see it in daylight,' Sally announced, turning to face him.

'By the way, did you decide on a colour for the carpet?'

'I hadn't until this morning and then I thought . . .'

'Go on,' he urged.

'Smokey-blue like the colour of our suite. I know the Elmsmarsh flat isn't exactly Cedar Court but the colour seems right somehow.'

Silhouetted against the skyline, Hugh took Sally in his arms and kissed her tenderly. 'You know something . . . you seem right too, somehow. What isn't however, is the fact that we have to leave this place now.'

The disappointment was all too clear in her face and swallowing hard she turned for one last look across the fields before they headed back to the car.

'We could perhaps stay for lunch and go home later,' Hugh suggested.

Sally shook her head. 'No we must stick to your original plan. Didn't you say you and Serena were going to have drinks with friends this evening? Besides if we go back inside Cedar Court I shall only . . .'

'Only what Sally?'

'. . . want to stay.' She sighed.

Hugh took her hand and in silence they walked back slowly to the carpark. There was no need to go in again. Hugh had already paid the bill and handed in their key but he nevertheless left her waiting in the car and ran back into reception. Returning moments later, he placed a green and gold box on her lap. 'No chocolate strawberries, I'm afraid, but they do have their own chocolate mints.'

Sally studied the dark green box with its golden cedar emblem in relief on the lid and smiled. 'I'll keep them until you come to dinner.'

For the rest of the journey conversation was subdued. Sally studied the set of Hugh's jaw in profile. Unlike last night and this morning, there was no hint of a smile. Pulling into the lesser used corner of Thornhampton Station carpark, he said sharply, 'Why won't you let me drive you home?'

Her reply was calm and precise. 'For the simple reason, Hugh, my car is parked here. If someone sees it or me, they will assume I've been away on a train. But if anyone were to see you dropping me off outside my house, then . . . I think you know the answer to that, just as well as I do.'

Hugh's face was pensive and his knuckles white against the steering wheel. 'It doesn't seem right, Sally . . . just leaving you here.'

'Oh, Hugh,' she whispered gently, 'it's hardly "Brief Encounter". At least I know when I'm going to see you again. Besides, it won't be long before I move into the flat. Then you won't have to leave me at stations or meet me in the park.'

Hugh's face brightened at the prospect. He opened the passenger door and then took her suitcase from the boot. Fleetingly their hands touched against the suit-case handle.

It was their only physical contact before their eyes said their sad farewells and in her rearview mirror – and through misted eyes – Sally watched Hugh drive away. He had one more call to make, before returning to his wife.

Serena looked up lazily, from where she had been compiling her holiday list. 'Hello, Darling! How was Uncle Bertram?'

'Much the same as ever. We had our usual game of chess and he still insists I'm his favourite nephew.'

'I'm not surprised, as you're the only one in the family who bothers about the old fool. Everyone else steers well clear of him – smelly old man!'

Hugh cast Serena a look of disapproval. 'For your information, Serena, Uncle Bertram does not smell! His generation were not into using colognes and after-shaves, that's all!'

'Considering you insist Stanley doesn't smell either, that's exactly the sort of comment I'd expect from you, Hugh.'

'By the way, how is Stanley? Where is . . .?'

'In the laundry-room! I didn't bother to take him for a walk as I knew you'd be back soon.'

'I'll take him now then.'

'But Hugh! You've only just got in! Don't forget we're going . . .'

'Don't worry Serena, I haven't forgotten!' Hugh strode grimly from the room, glad to escape the un-necessary and excessive heat of the room and the heavy scent of Serena's perfume.

From the other side of the laundry-room door, Stanley stood whining.

'Hello, old boy, has it really been that grim?'

The dog nuzzled his master eagerly and watched as the familiar leather lead was taken from its hook on the wall. Feeling in his pocket for car keys, Hugh realized they were for the Jaguar and not the Range Rover.

'Oh well, what the hell!' he announced to Stanley. 'Why shouldn't you go in the Jag, too? It's Sunday!'

Serena flung down her pen and pad in disgust. 'Bloody dog! And bloody Uncle Bertram! They're both long past their sell-by date and should have been put down years ago!'

Turning to the holiday brochure, Serena's imagination got the better of her. In her mind's eye, she saw herself strapping both Uncle Bertram and Stanley into a cable car and taking them to the highest mountain. From there it would be perfectly simple . . . all she had to do was push them both off! She gave a sardonic laugh.

'It would be just my luck for them both to land in a fresh fall of snow, brush themselves off and get up and walk away unscathed! Still,' she said smugly, focusing once more on chocolate-box style chalets, 'two more weeks and Vivienne and I will be in Gstaad.' She poured herself a whisky from the decanter and went upstairs to get changed.

Sally poured hot water onto the solitary Earl Grey teabag and put the lid on the brown earthenware pot. 'Back to earth with a bump, Sally,' she mused.

Taking her tray into the sitting room, she switched on the gas fire and sighed deeply. As the pungent smell of bergamot wafted into the air she bit her lip until it hurt.

'I mustn't, I mustn't, I mustn't.' She whispered over and over again. 'You knew it wasn't going to be easy! You said you'd be able to cope with goodbyes but you can't, can you? In fact you can't cope at all!'

The shrill ringing of the telephone caused her heart to leap and she ran frantically to the phone. Out of breath she called, 'Hugh!'

'Er no,' the male voice replied. 'It's Jason . . . from the estate agents. Look, I'm sorry to bother you on a Sunday . . . I did try ringing yesterday afternoon but . . .'

'I was away,' Sally said, disappointed that it wasn't Hugh's voice she heard.

'Well, it's good news. The Taylors . . . they like your house. They want to make you an offer! The only problem is they want a quick completion.'

'That's no problem.'

'It isn't? But I didn't think when I first spoke to you that you had anywhere to live.'

'I have now,' Sally replied flatly.

'That's great then. Shall I tell them you accept? I mean you haven't got to consult your ex-hus –?'

'No, I haven't,' she broke in. 'I haven't got to consult him at all anymore.' Her words trailed away. The house was sold. There were the usual things like surveyors and mortgage arrangements, but that was for the Taylors to sort out. Hadn't what-was-his-name? – Jason – said it was a company move?

Suddenly Sally's spirits lifted. 'Jason,' she enquired sagaciously, 'if, as you say, the Taylors are on a company move . . . and they've not actually offered the full asking price, do you think I could possibly ask an extra thousand?'

'Can't see why not. I'll put it to them and give you a buzz.'

Sally already had a buzz. A buzz from the glow inside her, when she thought of Hugh and the wonderful weekend they'd spent together, and a buzz from the deep satisfaction she'd get telling Richard she'd sold the house!

It didn't matter now that it wasn't Hugh who'd rung. She would be seeing him soon anyway. Just like the song, this weekend they'd taken their first steps along life's highway. Her next steps would be to Laura's Lair!

Laura Maitland carried a tray with two steaming mugs of coffee and a plate of biscuits from the tiny kitchenette of Laura's Lair into the front gallery. She passed Sally a cobalt-blue mug decorated with a question mark.

'What's the question mark for. In case I've forgotten who I am?' Sally enquired.

'Oh that!' Laughed Laura. 'They were a new line I got in for Christmas. You always get mugs with initials on but the question mark covers a whole gamut of things. Useful for the unexpected guest; when you can't remember someone's name, or –' she grinned wickedly – 'on those rare moments when you'd love to hand someone a mug with something really sarcastic printed on it. On such occasions my imagination runs riot and that simple question mark becomes an array of expletives.'

'Not in my case I hope.'

'Definitely not, Sally. In your case it was the first one I grabbed hold of!'

Laura peered from the bow window, watching large flakes of snow fall and settle. She turned and reached for a biscuit. 'The weather's just as I thought, which is why I'm glad I decided not to open for another week. I never do much business after Christmas.'

'Are you sure you really need me then?' Sally asked, running her index finger along the curve of the question mark.

'Good Lord yes! You're the answer to a maiden's prayer.' Laura brushed biscuit crumbs from her ample bosom and laughed hoarsely, setting a mass of apricot curls a quiver. 'Mind you, it's quite some time since I was a maiden!'

Sally smiled warmly and munched on a biscuit.

'However,' continued Laura. 'I have to confess I was delighted when you said you wouldn't be needing the flat after all. At least it means I'll be able to give Marion a roof over her head.'

'What did you say happened to her husband?'

'Clive? Oh, cancer, I'm afraid. It went through him like the proverbial dose of salts. Poor chap, never really knew what hit him. Which was just as well in a way . . .'

Sally shot Laura a questioning look.

'Well, he'd run up a load of debts, the house was in danger of being repossessed . . . In fact, I suppose you could say everything happened for the best.' Laura's green eyes misted with tears and she dabbed at them with a blue spotted handkerchief before reaching for another biscuit.

Through a fine spray of crumbs she murmured, 'When I told Marion she could have the flat, she simply handed her keys back to the building society. Now she can't wait to start painting again.'

Laura nodded to where a series of wild-flower miniatures hung in rows. Delicate snowdrops, miniature daffodils, crocuses, scillas and golden aconites blossomed from the oval frames, filling the shaded corner of the gallery with a breath of spring.

Sally put down her coffee and walked towards them. 'These are Marion's? But they are absolutely beautiful. Why on earth did she stop painting in the first place?'

'To help Clive with all his mad-cap ideas and the children . . .'

'She's not entirely on her own then, if she's got children?'

'She might just as well be,' Laura said wryly. 'Mind you, it's Marion's fault really. She always encouraged them to be free spirits and do their own thing. So they did, all five of them.'

'Five! No wonder the poor woman never had time to paint. And just where are these free spirits?'

'Oh, scattered, my dear. Scattered everywhere. Australia, Canada, Oxfam projects in Africa and the last I heard of Fern, she was living in a tree, trying to stop the Newbury bypass going through.'

Laura reached for a third biscuit and unsure as to whether Sally's eyebrow was raised in concern over the depleted biscuits or the movements of Marion's offspring, she left the biscuit perched precariously on the edge of the plate and picked up a feather duster.

'I know,' she said tapping her wide girth with a plume of feathers. I'm getting fat. That's why I'm glad you're going to be here instead of me. When I'm on the lookout for new artists, it means I do a lot more walking. I just wish they didn't produce such scrumptious biscuits.'

Laura reached for the wavering biscuit, held it in front of Sally then paused thoughtfully, before snapping it in two and offering half.

'What's a few more calories?' she laughed. 'It's jolly cold out and we're going to need extra fuel for our bodies. I'll diet when I'm on the road next week. Finish your coffee and then I'll explain all the stock to you.'

Sally took one last look at the miniatures and recalled those hanging on the wall at Cedar Court. She thought of Hugh and felt the now familiar tingle in the pit of her stomach. Only a few more days to wait and Serena would be going away skiing and she and Hugh would be together. She sighed and finished her coffee.

'I have to say,' she mused, 'your friend Marion's got the right idea.'

'Meaning?'

'Meaning, by starting with early spring flowers she can then progress through the seasons; violets, primroses, auriculas, sweet peas and so on. They'd all be suitable subjects, and you know what people are for collecting things. Just think how "The Country Diary of an Edwardian Lady" took off. And next Christmas if she produced a series with holly, mistletoe, cyclamen and Christmas roses, I bet you'd be on to a winner.'

Laura tapped Sally gently on the shoulders with the feather duster as if she was bestowing a knighthood.

'What's that for?' Sally asked, bemused.

'That, my dear Sally, is for being a genius. In this game you have to think months ahead and with you here to encourage Marion out of the doldrums that's one thing less for me to worry about.'

For the rest of the morning the two women discussed the existing stock, deliveries and banking arrangements and in the afternoon went to the upstairs flat to prepare for Marion Le Sage's arrival.

Surveying the dust, dingy paintwork and faded wallpaper, Sally was secretly pleased she wasn't going to be living here. Although prior to Hugh's offer of the new flat she would have lived anywhere just to get away from Richard's unwelcome visits. Now at least she'd been able to tell him the good news about the Taylors.

True to his word, Jason had 'invited' them to increase their offer, which they'd agreed to on condition Sally left all the carpets. She wiped at a mildewed window frame with a damp J-cloth and smiled. They could have the carpets willingly. Hugh was buying her new ones and the extra thousand offered by the Taylors could be used for new curtains. She could already picture them, smoky-blue with peach-lined swags and tails. She was sure Hugh would approve.

'Sally, you're dripping!'

Sally looked up, startled, as a pool of dirty water dripped from the bright yellow rubber gloves onto the windowsill.

'Sorry, I was miles away, thinking about decorating the flat.'

'Well if you've got any more ideas I'd like to hear them. We'll have to do something to brighten this place up before Marion comes. What exactly did you have in mind?'

Sally didn't have the heart to say it wasn't Marion's flat she was thinking of. It was bad enough wondering how she was going to cope with questions about her new role as Hugh's mistress. She dabbed at the sleeve of her blue sweatshirt where the drips were creeping from the rubber gloves and said without thinking, 'How about blue and yellow?'

'What fun,' replied Laura. 'That should cheer her up, blue sky and sunshine all day long.'

'I can get some paint and start tomorrow if you like,' Sally suggested.

Laura nodded enthusiastically. 'I was forgetting you're a dab hand at DIY, what with Richard and all his unfinished projects. I thought you'd be glad to get away from painting for a while.'

'Put it down to withdrawal symptoms. Besides, I won't have to do any at the new flat. Everything's brand-spanking-new. There's not a hint of lead piping or old wiring anywhere.'

Laura put a comforting hand on Sally's shoulder. 'You know I was quite worried about you a few months ago. Now you look a different person. It must be not having to worry about the financial burden of the house and mortgage. I know it's a wrench leaving it and the garden but at least with your share of the house, keeping the flat going will be a damned sight easier.'

Sally toyed with the fingers of the rubber gloves and the J-cloth. There hadn't been any awkward questions about the flat after all. If Laura wanted to believe she was buying it, then so might everyone else. There would be no need to discuss it further. Her only worry was that she might receive unexpected visitors when Hugh was with her.

CHAPTER 10

Pasting the last piece of peach and blue border and fixing it into place, Sally stepped back with a sigh of satisfaction.

'There, what do you think of it, Hugh?'

'Very nice. I just wish you'd let me send George Fry round to see to these finishing touches.'

Wiping a blob of paste from her fingers, Sally climbed down from the steps and stood on tiptoe to kiss Hugh on the cheek.

'It's sweet of you to offer but I don't think it's a good idea.'

'But why? After all, George could finish things in no time at all.'

'I admit it's a tempting prospect, but have you thought what people would say? I mean, are you usually in the habit of sending Barrington's maintenance staff to help ex-employees?'

'No, I suppose not,' Hugh added thoughtfully. 'However, it just doesn't seem right, coming here to find you doing all this when you've spent all week decorating Laura's flat for . . . what's her name?'

'Marion – Marion Le Sage. And by the way, you're just going to love some of her pictures. Laura will sell the originals of course and I was thinking perhaps you could try selling the prints at Barrington's.'

'Whilst on the subject of painting –' Hugh gestured to the decorating brushes '– do I take it you've finished for the day?'

Sally nodded and gathering up her tools took them through to the kitchen. 'Of course,' she added cheekily, 'you could help me finish hanging the curtains, while the casserole is cooking.'

Hugh smiled and took her in his arms. 'Actually, I had something else in mind. I was going to suggest going to bed.'

His face dropped when Sally passed him a packet of curtain hooks.

'Don't look so forlorn; if you can just put these hooks in here – like so – I'll go and have a quick shower and get rid of the smell of Eau de Polycell.'

Wedged together in her single bed, Hugh murmured, 'You know, you surprised me. I was beginning to think I was never going to drag you away from your paste brushes.'

'And I thought you were never going to ask!'

'Why, Sally Palmer! If I didn't know you better I would think that an extremely brazen statement,' Hugh teased.

'Funny you should mention that. That's a word Roz said she'd never use to describe me. If only she knew . . .'

'She doesn't though, does she?'

Sensing the concern in his voice, Sally said reassuringly, 'No, nobody knows. There's no need, is there?

But Laura thinks I've changed and as Roz is so perceptive, she might think I've changed too.'

'No, Sally, you haven't changed, you've just woken up to life.'

Hugh reached for her and drew her close, until their lips met. As he switched off the bedside light, she heard him mutter jokingly, 'Why didn't you tell me you had a single bed?'

'Because that was one thing you didn't ask me!'

Stroking her hair and caressing her bare shoulders, he sighed. 'Well, much as I love being close to you like this, I intend to get us a double bed as soon as possible.'

The next morning after breakfast, when Hugh announced he had to leave, Sally found herself staring down at the bowl of diminishing soapsuds with unfocused eyes. It was as if her bubble had burst too. Hugh put a comforting hand on her shoulder.

'I shan't be long, I'm only going to see Uncle Bertram.'

'Oh, you mean you're not going to the airport to fetch Serena.'

'Well, yes. I still have to go to the airport but that's not until this evening. I just thought if I saw Uncle Bertram now, it would still give me time to come back later . . . that is if you want me to?'

The shuttered look lifted from her face as she emptied the bowl of soapy water and rinsed the breakfast dishes. 'Who is Uncle Bertram? I've never heard you mention him before.'

'Uncle Bertram was my alibi for Cedar Court. I try to see him most weekends and as Serena loathes him – as do most of the family, come to that – it can be quite convenient. Sometimes I take him out to lunch or we have a game of chess and on occasions – if his asthma is bad – I've even stopped over with him. So as you can see, Uncle Bertram has his uses. Actually . . . I think you'd quite like him.'

'Why should I like him, if no one else does?'

'Ah!' smiled Hugh, 'because he's quite a character. If Uncle Bertram decides he doesn't like a person in the first place, he makes sure they don't like him in return!'

Sally was puzzled; her questioning eyes sought explanation.

'He's a crafty old devil is Uncle B. I suppose you could say he was the black sheep of the family; he was my father's eldest brother – Uncle Stanley being the youngest.'

At the mention of the name, Stanley looked up from his basket in the corner. Hugh continued: 'When he was a young man he had a bitter row with his father (my grandfather) and he left home. Grandfather cut him off without a penny but, just to spite him, Uncle Bertram made a fortune anyway.'

'And Uncle Stanley, what about him?'

'Oh, Uncle Stanley was the complete opposite. The dutiful younger son and the epitome of respectability. The only trouble was, he always looked a picture of abject misery. That's why Stanley here got his name.'

The dog's ears twitched and Hugh patted him affectionately.

Sally protested. 'But Stanley doesn't look a picture of abject misery!'

'Not now maybe, but he certainly did when he was a puppy.' Hugh looked at his watch. 'Look, I really ought to go. If you're sure about me coming back later, is it all right if I leave Stanley with you?'

She nodded. 'Of course, and why shouldn't it be all right for you to come back?'

Hugh shrugged his shoulders. 'I thought you might want to have some friends round or perhaps go and see your sister.'

Sally lowered her eyes and whispered, 'When I know you're free, I only want to see you. I can see Jackie and the others when you have to be with . . . Serena.

'Oh, Sally!' Hugh murmured. 'Things between Serena and myself – well, let's just say they're different from when you and I are together. For a start we have single beds and . . .'

Sally placed a finger on Hugh's lips and looked up into his face. 'Please, Hugh . . . I think I'd rather not know.'

'I was only going to say it's a totally different relationship. We're very fond of each other – after all, we've been married for almost twenty-five years – yet deep down, I know I'm not in love with her.'

Hugh's deeply expressive eyes gazed down at Sally. 'I expect you'll find that pathetic and hard to understand, like all those letters sent to agony aunts in which men protest their wives don't understand them.'

Managing a weak smile, Sally asked softly, 'And does Serena understand you?'

Taking her in his arms, Hugh kissed her tenderly before replying. 'Let's just say, I think Serena and I understand each other perfectly.'

Returning from a walk with the dog, Sally was surprised to find an enormous basket of fruit outside her

152

door. Puzzled, she carried it through to the kitchen to examine the gift card wedged between a pineapple and a bunch of black grapes. She certainly hadn't been expecting visitors and who would deliver fruit on a Sunday?

The card read simply, 'Welcome to Elmsmarsh. We hope you'll be very happy in your new home. Terry and Julie.' In a different hand someone had scribbled in brackets: 'Your neighbours across the landing, come and have a drink with us sometime.'

Her immediate reaction was to call straightaway, just to say thank you – but she'd heard no sounds from their flat as she'd climbed the stairs with Stanley and Hugh had said he would be coming back.

'Gracious! It looks like Covent Garden market in here. What happened while I was away?'

Sally handed Hugh the card from the basket of fruit. 'How kind . . . and have you met Terry and Julie yet?'

'No, I think they must have gone out. I thought I'd pop in and say thank you one evening when you are busy.'

Hugh read her thoughts and nodded in understanding. 'If I recall, the agent told me they were a nice couple. It's always useful to have one set of decent neighbours you can turn to in an emergency.'

'Let's just hope I don't have too many emergencies, even if the neighbours are nice. Now, can I tempt you with some of this wonderful fruit while you tell me all about your wicked Uncle Bertram.'

'Sally, you can tempt me with anything you like – but first of all I want you to come here.' Hugh reached in his pocket and brought out a tiny sprig of mistletoe and held it above his head.

'But where did you get that – it isn't Christmas!'

'Uncle Bertram's garden. He has an old apple tree with a wonderful clump of mistletoe and I thought as I didn't get the opportunity to kiss you under the mistletoe before . . .'

Sally struggled for comprehension.

'. . . when Roz had that ridiculous tinsel in her hair and mistletoe wedged in her glasses . . .'

'Oh yes, I remember. Do you know, you quite made her day.'

'Well, come here and make my day,' said Hugh, reaching for her hand.

At the airport Hugh studied the arrivals board only to discover Serena's plane wasn't expected for another three-quarters of an hour. Annoyed at having to wait unnecessarily when he could have been at the flat with Sally, he set off on a tour of the airport. It could be useful to study other people's merchandise, and airport shops were invariably up to date with all the latest trends.

After half an hour he was about to head back towards the arrival lounge when a silver box in a display case caught his eye. Smiling, he went inside. It was just what he'd been looking for. Putting the small gift-wrapped box in his pocket, Hugh hurried to find Serena and Vivienne.

He noticed Vivienne almost immediately but was unable to attract her attention. She appeared worried and kept looking anxiously behind her. Of Serena there was no sign until . . .

Hugh saw her companion first. At least to anyone else, the tall movie star lookalike by Serena's side would have passed as her companion. Hugh, however, knew otherwise. No wonder Vivienne was looking furtive. Deliberately averting his gaze away from his wife, Hugh called to his sister-in-law.

'Vivienne! Over here.'

Vivienne looked flushed as Hugh relieved her of her trolley and swung it away from the crowds.

'I expect Serena's having the usual problem with her luggage?'

Vivienne only nodded, relieved that Hugh had his back to her. Quickly she turned and gesticulated to her sister. Serena and her companion parted company instantly but not before an exchange of whisperings and knowing looks.

'Sorry we're so late, Hugh,' Serena said, catching up. 'There was a heavy fall of snow and it took simply ages to clear the runway. You must be bored stiff, darling. I know how much you hate airports. Still, I expect you found time for a drink or something.'

Taking his hand briefly from the handle of the trolley, Hugh touched his pocket reassuringly. Yes, he thought to himself, he had been able to find something!

With Vivienne safely home, Serena studied the newly springcleaned sitting room. The smell of beeswax and lavender mingled with her perfume. Hugh sighed as the cloying smell met his nostrils and he thought longingly of Sally.

'You look tired, Hugh. I expect you've been busy with pre- and post-Christmas sales figures and by the

155

immaculate state of the house, no doubt banished by Mrs Burt, if the smell of polish is anything to go by.'

'Exactly,' acknowledged Hugh. 'You know what Mrs Burt is like for early springcleaning the minute you're away. Anyway, it wasn't too bad, I stayed over with Uncle Bertram a couple of times to keep out of her way.'

'And how is Uncle Bertram and Stanley too, are they well?'

Biting his lip, Hugh struggled to keep his tone casual. Serena's sudden contrived concern for Uncle Bertram was always a sure-fire giveaway of her infidelity.

'Oh, they're fine, Serena. Bertram's asthma hasn't been helped by the damp weather and Stanley . . .'

But Serena wasn't listening. She was already crossing the floor, and pausing at the door, she blew Hugh a kiss. 'You don't mind if I go up, darling? Only I'm simply exhausted,' she sighed.

Relieved, Hugh watched her go, then taking a deep breath walked through to his study. He switched on the green desk lamp and opened a file. Yes, Serena had been partly correct; he had been studying pre- and post-Christmas figures but at this precise moment, would far rather be studying Sally's.

Before preparing for bed, Sally fixed the small sprig of mistletoe to the top of her dressing-table mirror. Hugh had given her strict instructions to do so. Smiling, she tied it in place with a piece of peach ribbon, from the peach roses he'd brought with him yesterday afternoon.

Hugh's words came back to her. 'You must put it somewhere high and not let it fall.'

When she had turned to him with questioning eyes, he'd smiled and whispered softly, 'It's Norse legend. When Freya, the goddess of love, cried for her lover, it is said the tears that dropped to the ground turned to pearls, just like the berries on mistletoe. A sprig of pearls was then given to her for safekeeping and . . .'

'And . . . what happened then?'

Hugh continued: '. . . and then she hung them between heaven and earth, promising never to let them fall to the ground.'

Tying the ribbon securely, Sally promised herself she wouldn't let the mistletoe fall.

'How peculiar,' she murmured softly to her reflection. 'That's probably why mother used to say "pearls for tears". If only she were still alive, I could tell her about Freya and the legend.'

Pearls of a different kind filled Sally's eyes as she thought of her mother. Had she really been dead for five years? It was amazing how time flew. At least she'd lived to see her first grandchild born to her youngest daughter and mercifully been saved the demise of her eldest daughter's marriage.

Sally sighed and reached for Hugh's silk pyjamas. She'd kept them ever since their first weekend together at Cedar Court. He had smiled kindly at her request to keep them and conceded to her plea without question.

When he wasn't with her she wore the jacket, which lingered with the smell of his cologne, and wrapped the silk arms around her body, but when he returned, they were always freshly laundered and neatly ironed. Wiping tears from her eyes, she slipped on the pyjama jacket, counting as she did so the four pearlized buttons.

'Pearls,' she murmured to herself, looking towards the mistletoe. Just like the buttons, there were four berries. Thinking of Freya, Sally decided she mustn't let the buttons fall from Hugh's jacket either and hurrying to her sewing case, reached for a needle and thread.

Making the buttons secure, Sally tried hard to stop herself thinking of Hugh at home with Serena, and closing her eyes, pictured him in her mind's eye saying over and over again, 'We have single beds . . .'

She looked at her own single bed where only hours earlier they'd lain together, locked in each other's arms. Swallowing hard, she forced herself to put Hugh and Serena out of her mind and think of Marion Le Sage instead. She'd promised Laura she would look after Marion while she was away. She must also remember to thank Julie and Terry for the fruit.

The next day Sally watched Marion squeeze yellow paint from a tube onto her palette, add the merest touch of green and apply it to the petal of a primrose.

'Are you sure you don't mind me watching you?' she enquired over Marion's shoulder, 'but I'm absolutely fascinated.'

'Not at all, I was always used to one of the children hovering behind me or playing at my feet. Besides, it's nice to have company for a bit.'

Transfixed, Sally gazed in awe as Marion's large hands, holding such delicate brushes, deftly filled in petals and leaves with the minutest details. Wasn't it

Redouté, she thought, who'd painted all those wonderful pictures of roses and flowers? Yet he too, like Marion, gave the appearance of being large and clumsy.

Her long salt and pepper hair, worn in a thick plait, held flat against her head with two brown plastic hairslides, only served to accentuate her angular face and the body beneath the flowing kaftan could have been anything from a size eighteen to a size twenty-four. Behind her Sally seemed positively dwarfed in comparison.

Rinsing her brushes, Marion sat back to scrutinize her work with a critical eye. 'What do you think, Sally?'

'I think it's beautiful. I expect Laura's already told you the earlier ones have been a great success and we've people placing orders for summer already.'

Marion laughed cynically. 'So I gather. She also tells me a store in Thornhampton might be interested in producing prints. What was it she said . . . Bravington's?'

'Actually, it's Barrington's. It's where I used to work and, yes, I think they will be interested.'

'Oh,' said Marion, turning to look at Sally. 'You know the buyer at Barrington's then?'

'Not exactly, because they don't have a particular buyer but it's something the MD is hoping to set up.'

'And this MD, is he a decent sort of chap, I mean he wouldn't cheat me, would he? Only I fell foul of an unscrupulous dealer years ago and vowed never again.'

Sally tried desperately to remain nonchalant as she heard herself saying, 'Oh, Mr Barrington. Yes, I think you'll find he is a decent sort of chap.'

Anxious to escape further questioning about Hugh, his character or Barrington's, Sally made an excuse to return to the gallery.

That night, returning home, she heard music and voices coming from the neighbouring flat. With Hugh not expected for another four days, now seemed the ideal time to introduce herself.

'Hello,' she said, extending her hand, 'I'm Sally Palmer. I've come to thank you for the fruit.'

'Well, hello at last. Come in, Sally. I'm Terry. Look, we're just about to eat, so why don't you join us? That is if you haven't eaten already?'

'No, I've only just come home from work but won't Julie . . .'

A mouthwatering aroma wafted into the hall from the kitchen, reminding Sally how hungry she was.

Terry was offering to take her coat. 'Don't worry, Julie always makes far too much and I'm in danger of getting a paunch.'

Terry patted his stomach with his short pudgy fingers, gestured to Sally to take a seat and, opening the kitchen door, called through, 'Julie, it's Sally, our new neighbour, I've invited her to dinner.'

'Smashing,' came the reply. 'I'll be with you in a minute.' And through the steam of bubbling saucepans, Sally caught the rear view of slim hips in blue denims, check shirt and a shock of curly blonde hair.

Terry poured Sally a glass of red wine. 'Italian,' he said, 'like the meal. Julie's a dab hand at Italian. Hence this –' and he pointed to his stomach yet again. 'Mind you, we make up for all the pasta with the fruit.'

Sally noticed a large Mediterranean terracotta dish at the end of the dining table brimming with fruit of every description. 'Well,' she said thinking of her own table full of fruit, 'you've certainly guaranteed me my dose of vitamin C for days.'

Raising her glass to her lips she studied the immaculate setting of the room, with its blue and green tartan upholstery and rosewood furniture, and made a mental note of the relaxed atmosphere created by numerous lamps. Next time she went into Barrington's, she promised herself, she would buy some.

'Terry,' a pleading voice called from the kitchen, 'can you give me a hand with the casserole dish; you know my wrists aren't strong enough.'

Terry stood up. 'I don't know,' he laughed. 'I get pestered to buy him a set of cast-iron cookware and then when I do, he complains he can't lift them.'

Sally took a long gulp of wine. Terry had referred to his flatmate as male and thankfully that hint had helped disguise the shock when Julie came through the door.

With the steaming chicken dish set upon the table, Julie removed his bulky oven gloves and held out a delicate white hand.

'Hi, Sally,' he said nervously. 'Nice to meet you. I'm Julian but as you've probably gathered, everyone calls me Julie.'

Pale blue eyes in a fine-boned face searched Sally's for signs of disapproval. There were none. Sally took the hand, which appeared smaller than her own, warmly.

'I'm not surprised you can't lift those dishes. I can't either. In fact I gave mine away to the charity shop only

161

last year.' She watched as Terry placed a large round casserole, brimming with tagliatelle, onto a heat proof mat in the centre of the table. 'You obviously need biceps like Terry's,' she continued.

The two men glanced fleetingly at each other and smiled knowingly.

Helping Sally to a chair, Terry placed three plates and serving spoons in front of her. 'Would you mind being mother?' he asked.

Towards the end of the meal, with the dishes soaking in the kitchen sink, Sally studied the enticing array of fruit.

'No wonder you have such a wonderful selection. I had no idea the greengrocer's shop in Elmsmarsh belonged to you. I have to confess I haven't been in yet, I've been so busy sorting out my flat and helping a friend with hers. Now that I know it's you I'll pop in and see you.'

'You can always leave us an order, if you don't want to carry it,' Julie insisted, 'and we can always drop it off on our way home.'

'Who thought of the name, Pots and Posies?' Sally asked.

'Originally we were going to call it Potatoes and Posies, but Julie thought that sounded a bit too earthy.'

Julie smiled. 'Well, you were the one who wanted to get away from the image of the market stall.'

'Too right!' acknowledged Terry, 'I've had enough of standing on market squares in all weathers. I need a bit of comfort in my old age.'

Sally perceived Terry to be about thirty-five and Julie possibly in his early twenties. 'I think Pots and Posies is a super name,' she said.

Terry nodded proudly at a dried arrangement of flowers, fruit and seed heads, standing in the bay window. 'The posies also refer to Julie's decorations. We started doing them just before Christmas. Not only is he clever in the kitchen, he's a dab hand with oasis and flowers too.'

'Your mother doesn't seem to think so,' Julie replied acidly. 'She threw the one I gave her at Christmas in the bin!'

'Oh, don't take any notice of my old mother. She just doesn't understand.' Terry turned towards Sally and smiled.

'We'd better eat some of this up, before it goes off.' Julie pushed the dish in Sally's direction.

She reached for the familiar golden-orbed fruits that all evening had reminded her of Hugh and Cedar Court. Now too many glasses of wine later, she wondered if she could remember. 'I think I'd like some physalis.'

'Try saying that on a tube of wine gums,' grinned Terry, reaching for a fig.

Outside on the landing, with Julie busying himself with the clearing up, Terry watched Sally open her front door.

'Thanks, Sally,' he said softly.

Her face took on a puzzled expression. 'For what, Terry?'

'For being so understanding about Julian. He gets a bit – well, you know – when he meets people for the first time. This being his first relationship and all . . .'

'That's okay, I quite understand. Anyway, it should be me thanking you. It's been a lovely evening and the meal was superb. You must let me have the recipe . . . I'll try it out on Hugh.'

'Who's Hugh . . . your husband . . . or partner?'

Sally sighed deeply. 'I suppose the best way to respond to that, Terry, is to say I'm Hugh's mistress – he's married, you see.'

'Oh!' was all Terry replied. But she could tell from the expression on his face that he thought being mistress to a married man, was perhaps even more difficult than having a gay relationship.

'If you ever want a shoulder to cry on then . . .' he whispered, watching her go into her flat.

'Ditto,' she said and sighed, closing the door behind her.

CHAPTER 11

With the memory of grey winter months fading into spring, Sally found her relationship with Hugh blossoming like early spring flowers. Her earlier uncertainties about their arrangement disappeared as rapidly as the morning mists. The flat – now complete with double bed – was exactly as she wanted, Terry and Julie were the perfect neighbours and at Laura's Lair, Marion Le Sage's miniatures proved to be a great success.

'All's well with the world,' Sally sighed contentedly, drawing back the bedroom curtains on a brilliant spring morning, 'and it's going to be a wonderful day.'

Jack thrust a bunch of daffodils into Sally's hand as Jackie wheeled Sam into the flat in his buggy.

'I must say, you've got this place looking really nice, Sally. I have to admit I had my doubts at first. Somehow I just never imagined you living in a flat. You being the gardener in the family.'

Sally filled a Poole pottery vase with water and quickly arranged the daffodils, before pointing to some seed packets on the work surface.

'I haven't completely given up gardening, you know. Those are for my tubs and hanging baskets on the balcony. I thought Jack could help me this afternoon, when Sam has his nap.'

'Rather you than me,' Jackie quipped. 'You know my thoughts on gardening. If I had my way I'd have Dave concrete the lot! Anyway, thanks for offering to have the boys. I suppose I'd better get a move on, if we're to get to the matinée on time.'

Spreading the seed packets after his parents had left Jack enquired, 'What seeds are they?'

'The red, orange and yellow ones are nasturtiums and the trailing yellow one in that packet is Creeping Jenny.'

'Why is it called that?'

'Because it creeps everywhere – like a spider!' Sally ran her fingers up Jack's arm and onto his shoulder.

He giggled, then added thoughtfully, 'I don't think I want to plant the creepy one . . . so can I plant the 'sturtiums instead?'

After lunch Sally took Jack onto the balcony where she spread out sheets of newspaper and filled the baskets with soil.

'Mummy has seeds but she told Daddy she didn't want them watered,' Jack announced solemnly.

'I'm not surprised,' Sally replied, pressing seeds firmly into moist compost, 'your mummy has never liked gardening. Now how about you planting these nasturtiums?'

For a moment Jack looked confused, shrugged his shoulders and peered into the packet of seeds. They didn't look at all like his mother's; in fact, apart from the colour, they looked more like the shrivelled peas she invariably forgot to sweep up from under the fridge.

166

'Are you sure they will grow,' he asked, wide-eyed.

'Yes, but only if they're watered.' Fixing the baskets into place, Sally sighed. 'There's only one problem, I shall need a special watering can to reach right up there.

'P'raps we can go and buy one.'

'What a good idea; we'll go when Sam wakes up.'

Jack skipped along the hallway, carrying Sally's handbag.

'Got it,' he cried waving it in the air. 'It was on the table by the bed.'

'Right then,' she replied swinging the pushchair onto the landing, 'let's go on a watering can hunt and . . . who knows, we might even find some Smarties too.'

Deciding on the long route home, Sally led the way across the fields at the back of the flat, pointing out as she did so the frenetic gatherings of nesting birds. Stopping to pick some sprigs of pussywillow she was surprised to find Terry coming in the opposite direction.

'Make the most of it while you can, Sally, it won't be here for much longer.'

'Sorry, Terry, what won't be here?'

'This lot.' And Terry turned and waved his arm to encompass the fields beyond.

'You're not serious?'

'Well,' Terry drawled, running his hand through his closely cropped hair and designer stubble, 'let's just say I heard a rumour.'

'What sort of rumour?'

'One of our customers – her husband works in the planning office – tells me there's going to be a new housing development.'

167

Sally's heart sank; her lovely view and all these beautiful fields may soon be gone. 'I suppose it's inevitable, isn't it?' she sighed. 'It all gets built on in the end.'

Terry gave a sardonic laugh. 'Yes and they call it progress. Anyway, if I was you I'd ask Hu –'

Before he had time to finish, Sally shook her head and darted a glance in Jack's direction. Terry got the message and changed the subject before they went their separate ways.

'Auntie Sally, is that man a pirate?'

'A pirate? Why, did you think he was?'

'He had an earring and pirates have earrings, don't they?'

Sally smiled. 'Sorry to disappoint you Jack, Terry's a greengrocer, not a pirate.'

There was a resounding, 'Oh well, never mind.' And Jack felt in his pocket just to make sure his tube of Smarties and his other treasures were still there.

On the Monday before Easter, Sally received a phone-call at the gallery from Muriel Baxter.

'Mrs Palmer, Mr Barrington has asked me to call you. He was wondering if you could bring in the latest set of Marion Le Sage's prints. He said Thursday afternoon, if that's convenient with you?'

Confused, Sally replaced the receiver. If Hugh wanted to see her, he usually rang himself. What on earth had prompted him to get Muriel to call her instead? And more to the point, why Thursday, when he knew she normally worked on Thursdays? Early closing at the gallery was Wednesday afternoons.

There just had to be a reason and as far as Sally was concerned, Thursday afternoon couldn't come quickly enough.

Entering Barrington's, Sally avoided the escalator and lifts and climbed the lesser used stairs with trepidation. She had already decided Hugh was summoning her to the store to end their relationship and now wished Thursday hadn't arrived quite so quickly. At the top of the stairs she heard a familiar voice.

'Sally! What on earth are you doing here?'

'Roz! You're late back from lunch! Have you been drinking?'

Roz held a finger to her lips and emitted a loud, 'Sshhh . . . not a word. Everything's under control, Sally dear. My junior's in charge of bums and boobs this afternoon and I've just been for a little drink with Doreen.'

'Mrs Hughes, have you been drinking?' Hugh's voice boomed. Roz looked up at him from where she clung unsteadily to the banister. 'And, Mrs Palmer, I thought we had an appointment!'

Sally reached sheepishly for her portfolio containing Marion's pictures, unable to look Hugh in the eye. His tone was ominous as he told Roz to take the rest of the afternoon off and ordered Sally to follow him to his office. Muriel Baxter welcomed them with a smile.

'Will you be requiring tea, Mr Barrington?'

'No, Miss Baxter, I will not. In fact I would suggest you take an extended teabreak. I want to talk to Mrs Palmer in private!'

Sally watched as Muriel's obsequious smile turned to a scarlet gash in an otherwise ghostly face.

'And, Mrs Baxter,' Hugh called after her, 'absolutely no interruptions and you may bring my letters for signing at half past four!'

With panic rising inexorably inside her, Sally followed Hugh through to his office, where, instead of sitting behind the desk, he strode to the doors of his private sitting room. Motioning her inside, she stood with baited breath and closed eyes until she heard the door slam shut.

'Right,' he announced. 'Now that we're alone, you can get undressed!'

Whirling round to face him, Sally saw that he was smiling.

'But I don't understand . . .'

'Don't you,' whispered Hugh, walking towards her. 'Well, I had to get rid of Muriel somehow, didn't I?'

'And Roz . . . what about Roz?'

'That,' remarked Hugh, 'just happened to be pure coincidence!'

Taking comfort from the look on Hugh's face, Sally fell into his arms. 'Oh, Hugh, you had me so worried. I thought you'd called me here to end our relationship.'

'Far from it,' he murmured, leading her to one of the settees. 'I just couldn't face the thought of not seeing you until next week.'

'But we are supposed to be seeing each other this weekend.'

'I know,' Hugh said glumly, 'but I can't make it, I'm afraid.'

'I suppose Serena's made other plans for . . .'

'No, it's nothing to do with Serena. It's Uncle Bertram. He's become dreadfully frail of late – so much so that he thinks he's dying. I don't think he is, mind you, but nonetheless he's asked me to take him to Harrogate to visit an old army friend for Easter.'

Reaching reassuringly for Hugh's hand, Sally sighed. 'We'd better make the most of the time we've got then.'

Heading for the customer cloakroom, Sally came face to face with Muriel Baxter. Her face was still ashen and she approached Sally cautiously. Muriel acknowledged Sally's flushed appearance and shook her head sadly.

'Oh, my dear! I'm so sorry, he's been in such a terrible mood, ever since he heard about his Uncle Bertram. I expect he gave you quite a dressing down.'

Suppressing a smile, Sally bit her lip and reached for her handkerchief. Holding it across her mouth she feigned distress and murmured through the delicate folds of fabric, 'Yes, Miss Baxter – he did – quite a dressing down.'

Jackie shifted uneasily in the chair, watching Sally pour the coffee.

'I mustn't stay long, Sal, as I've left Dave with the boys. It's just that I've got a confession to make. Well, not me exactly but Jack . . . the Saturday you had the boys, so Dave and I could go to the matinée . . .?'

Bewildered, Sally looked up. 'I'm sorry, I don't understand. Jack was perfectly well behaved, in fact no bother at all. We had lunch, I put Sam down for his nap, then Jack and I planted some seeds before we . . .'

'Yes – but Jack went into your bedroom . . .'

'Did he? Oh, well, that's not unusual, I probably asked him to fetch my handbag. Anyway, nothing's

171

been broken or damaged, so I can't understand what all the fuss is about.'

'Sally . . . Jack took these from your bedroom. He said they were in a silver box.' Jackie opened her bag and removed the familiar lime green condom packets – used by Hugh – and placed them on the table.

Sally's mouth gaped open. 'Oh! How stupid of me!'

'What do you mean, how stupid of you? Of course it wasn't stupid. I expect you forgot you had them; after all, it's been so long since Richard left. Besides Jack had no business . . .'

'Well, I suppose there's no harm done,' Sally said, eyeing the sealed packets. 'At least he didn't open them and he won't know what they're for.'

'Oh, but he does! We told him ages ago.'

'You did what!'

'We told him what condoms are for.'

Sally stared at her sister in disbelief. 'But why, for heaven's sake, he's only a child! Whatever happened to innocence?'

'He found a packet of Dave's,' Jackie announced, struggling to keep her tone casual, 'one Sunday morning when he came into our bedroom.'

Sally sipped her coffee in silence, waiting for her sister to continue.

'Do you know, when I was on teacher training, one little lad wrote in his school diary, "I went into mum and dad's bedroom but they were having a honeymoon!" Honestly, Sal, you'd be amazed at what we teachers read and hear . . .'

'And is that what you told Jack?' Sally whispered.

'No! Because quite simply "having a honeymoon" didn't suit our particular situation. Jack already knew I had seeds in my tummy to make babies – we had to tell him something when I became pregnant with Sam.'

Sally nodded for Jackie to go on with her version of the facts of life.

'Actually,' she added brightly, 'the whole thing couldn't have gone better when I think of it. We told Jack, mummies' seeds are only watered by daddies when people want babies . . . and when they don't – daddies wear condoms!'

'And did Jack accept that?'

'Of course he did, Sally, he's only a child! He didn't expect the full biology lesson; in fact . . .'

'In fact what?'

Jackie's face creased into a broad grin. 'Jack now refers to condoms as "wellingtons for Daddy".'

Sally found herself smiling too as she remembered the conversation she'd had with Jack when they'd planted the seeds. No wonder the poor child had appeared so confused. Refilling the coffee cups however, there was still something that niggled at the back of her mind. She gestured to the telltale packets on the table and enquired nonchalantly, 'Didn't Jack think it strange to find those in my bedroom?'

'Not at all. We told him Richard must have left them – mind you, it's a pity he didn't have them with him when he met Sharon! Still it's not so surprising you forgot all about them; how long is it since he left?'

Sally didn't reply. She was relieved to be saved the embarrassment of having to explain why she had a box of condoms in her bedroom, yet at the same time felt angry that Jackie should assume she was no longer interested in sexual relationships.

'Don't look so hurt, Sally. After all, Richard's got his comeuppance, hasn't he?' Jackie popped the black and green box back into her handbag with a wink. 'You don't mind, do you? Especially as you don't need them? I have to confess we've tried a couple already.' Jackie's eyes took on a dream-like trance.

Lost for words, Sally followed her sister to the door, where she turned and reached into her pocket.

'Oh yes! These are from Jack, by way of an apology. He's saved you all the orange ones. As you know, they're his favourite.'

Taking the Smartie tube, Sally noticed Jackie snap the catch firmly on her handbag.

'Tell him thank you very much,' she said lamely, 'and that I'm not at all cross.'

'Will do,' came the cheery reply. 'And in the meantime, why don't you ring that widower friend of Roz's, if you're lonely?'

Later that night, Sally tipped the Smarties onto the table and counted them. There were ten. Poor Jack, she mused, it must have been quite a sacrifice giving up all his orange Smarties.

'Willy wellingtons,' she chuckled, 'oh well, out of the mouths of babes as they say and after all, the packets were green!' She considered Jackie's parting comment, 'if you're lonely' and sat down on the settee.

'I'm not lonely,' she sniffed. 'I'm just missing Hugh and I've absolutely no intention of ringing Bernard.'

Bernard had rung a couple of times after Roz and Donald's Boxing Day gathering and Roz had even mentioned on more than one occasion that Bernard was keen to see her again. Luckily however, Roz also knew that Sally wasn't interested and didn't force the issue. Grateful for Roz's intervention, Sally wanted desperately to tell her about Hugh. Keeping quiet about their relationship was such a strain. It was strange really; only Terry and Julie shared her secret.

In Harrogate, driving past The Stray, resplendent with its spring blooms, Hugh headed back towards the Ripon Road and Uncle Bertram. On the front passenger seat of the Range Rover lay Uncle Bertram's prescription. Stopping for traffic, Hugh drummed his fingers thoughtfully on the steering wheel.

Bertram wasn't going to die but the young doctor who had been called out in the night said it had been a particularly bad asthma attack. So much so that, for the moment, it would be foolish to attempt the journey back to Thornhampton. Besides, Cyril, Bertram's old army colleague, and his sister Rose appeared to be giving the old chap the best attention possible.

It wasn't staying away from Barrington's that bothered Hugh. A couple of phonecalls to Muriel Baxter and his nephew Gareth had resolved that problem. It was not seeing Sally and having to cancel their plans yet again that irked him. There was also the problem of Stanley.

Serena was far from happy having to look after Stanley, it completely cramped her style. Hugh had left her the Jaguar but she refused to take the 'wretched dog' out in that and her sporty hatchback was hardly conducive for what she loosely described as Stanley's 'walks'.

Seeing a young mother pushing a baby in a pushchair, with a toddler on one side and a black labrador on the other, Hugh thought longingly of Sally and remembered how he and Stanley had come across her with her two nephews, last Christmas in the park.

'Oh, Sally my love,' he sighed, 'how I miss you,' he thought as he pulled into Cyril's driveway.

'Hugh old chap,' wheezed Bertram from his bed, 'so sorry to put you to all this bother.' He placed the nebuliser in his mouth, pressed the container down and breathed in as deeply as he could.

'Don't worry about it, Bertram. Things appear to be running smoothly at Barrington's. You know what Muriel Baxter's like and Gareth's running around, I expect, like a dog with two tails.'

'Speaking of dogs, Serena rang when you were out fetching my prescription. Rose took the call – something about Stanley and the vets?'

'Oh, God! I forgot, Stanley's due to have one of his injections. I'd better ring Serena right away.'

'Hugh darling!' Serena said with relief when she heard his voice. 'So you got my message, I wasn't sure. You know I couldn't understand a word that Rose – or whatever her name is – was saying! Yes, that's right. I just happened to look on your desk in the study and saw Stanley's appointment card for the vets. No, don't worry I'll take him . . .'

Returning to Bertram, Hugh shook his head.

'Everything OK?' Bertram enquired.

'Yes, surprisingly. Serena's offered to take Stanley for his injection, so that's one thing less to worry about. Funny, I was expecting her to read the riot act.'

'Well, I expect she'll be wanting something in return,' Bertram said, sardonically. 'Serena always was a cynical bitch!'

Hugh raised an eyebrow in his uncle's direction and smiled wryly.

'I always sensed there was no love lost between the pair of you, but you're right, she's asked me to try and locate a piece of Moorcroft Pottery for her collection.'

Bertram chuckled wheezily from his frilly pillows. 'I always was a great judge of character, my boy. Oh, I'll admit Serena's a stunner but has she made you happy? Has she, Hugh – has she really made you happy?' Bertram's voice held that inflection which usually meant he had no intention of giving up on the subject.

Hugh toyed with the fringe of the antimacassar on the bedside chair. For once he felt strangely vulnerable. Here he was in his mid-forties, being interrogated about the state of his marriage as if he was an errant schoolboy.

'Serena and I have a good relationship . . . I mean, we've been married for almost twenty-five years. We understand each other.'

'Bah,' said Bertram angrily, sending his medication flying. 'Good relationships and understanding, my foot! Hugh, as my dearest nephew, I'll tell you something. You are a Barrington through and through and we Barringtons need more than just good relationships and understanding. Know what I mean, my boy?'

Hugh slanted a curious sideways look at the old man, cocooned beneath layers of pink woollen blankets and floral print eiderdown.

'Well, put like that, Uncle, I don't quite know what to say.'

'Don't you, Hugh? Well I do. I'd be prepared to bet that young filly of yours that you've got hidden away somewhere is a damn sight better for you than Serena!'

'Whew!' Hugh whistled. 'That's quite a broadside you've fired.'

'I'm right though, aren't I? You can't keep much from me, Hugh.'

Bertram turned his rheumy old eyes in his nephew's direction. Hugh merely nodded, before saying softly, 'Yes . . . but I've told Sally I'd never leave Serena.'

' "Never" is a word I'd never use,' replied Bertram solemnly.

Hugh roared with laughter and patted his uncle's hand.

'What's so funny?'

'You are. Don't you realize what you've just said?'

With a sibilant splutter the old man's face creased into a grin and patting the eiderdown in rhythm with his laughter, he sent a fine cloud of dust into the air.

Through his renewed coughing, Hugh heard him beg to be taken away from all the 'damned lace, flowers, feathers and frills!'

CHAPTER 12

Scooping Jack's offering of orange Smarties into a Susie Cooper dish, Sally placed them in the middle of the coffee table and went to answer the phone. The distant male voice seemed strained yet vaguely familiar.

'Sally . . .'

'Bernard . . .?'

'No, it's not Bernard, it's Hugh.'

'Hugh, you're back! But you sound so different. Where are you?'

'I'm in a lay-by, on my way from the vets. Look, are you alone, is it okay for me to come . . .?'

'Of course, but why have you been to the vets? Stanley, is he –?'

She detected a choking sound in Hugh's voice. 'Yes, it's Stanley – I can't explain now. I'll tell you when I see you. I'll be with you as soon as I can.'

After he'd arrived Sally cradled the distraught and ashen-faced Hugh in her arms. It was obvious from his dishevelled and unshaven appearance that something dreadful had happened.

'I can't believe Serena could do such a thing,' she whispered.

'Oh, she could all right!' Hugh said bitterly. 'You don't know Serena like I do Sally.' Hugh buried his head in his hands.

'But why? You don't mean she did it deliberately . . . that she'd planned it before you went away?'

'Perhaps not before I went away – more like when I rang and asked her to take Stanley to the vets for me. I can still hear her voice now, all sweetness and benevolence, insisting I stay with Bertram.'

Hugh shuddered. 'How the hell was I to know Serena's idea of "taking good care of Stanley" was taking him to the vets and having him put down the minute my back was turned!'

'Oh, Hugh – my poor darling come here.'

Hugh fell into Sally's arms like a baby. 'I know he was old, Sally, but the vet said he'd be good for a while yet. And heaven knows, I wouldn't have let him suffer. I would have considered having him put down myself if the vet had advised it but he didn't.'

Sally stroked Hugh's head as he stared numbly into her eyes.

'You know what hurts the most,' he continued, 'is that I wasn't even there to say . . . goodbye.'

Sally felt her own eyes filling with tears at the thought. Poor dear Stanley, bundled off to the vets by Serena, no doubt thinking he was going on an outing or maybe even going to see his beloved master.

Pulling away from her embrace Hugh banged his fist on the table, sending the dish of Smarties scattering across its shiny polished surface. His face was a suffusion of hurt and anger and his eyes, flint-hard.

'And do you know what the bitch had the gall to say, in an attempt to appease the situation?'

Sally shook her head.

'She told me that at least he'd travelled in style . . . she took him in the Jaguar!'

In response to Sally's audible gasp, Hugh added sardonically, 'Oh, that's not all . . . when she arranged for Stanley to be cremated, she also asked for his ashes to be placed in an urn fit for a king. And that, Serena assumes, makes everything okay.'

Sally bit her lip and swallowing hard, reached for Hugh's hand. 'Come along,' she whispered, 'come to bed.'

Resisting, Hugh said lamely, 'Sally, my dear, I don't really feel in the mood. I'm sorry.'

'I don't mean for that, I just want to hold you in my arms and make the hurt go away; besides . . .' She chose not to finish her sentence. Now seemed not the time to tell Hugh they couldn't make love because, thanks to Jack, they were out of condoms. In silence, Hugh allowed himself to be led to the bedroom.

In the stillness of early morning, Sally stared into the blackness, aware of Hugh lying awake in her arms. Stroking his bare shoulders she asked, 'Hugh, what about the vet?'

'What do you mean?'

'Well, I presume you told him it was all a mistake. Stanley should never have . . .' She stopped herself, unable to finish the sentence.

'The poor fellow was mortified when I told him. Said he thought Serena had taken Stanley because I was too upset to take him myself. Apparently she put on quite a convincing act.'

Hugh held Sally's arm in a vice-like grip. 'You know,' he whispered, his voice cold, 'I shall never forgive Serena for this . . . never!'

Releasing her, Sally felt the blood rushing back through her arm and became aware of Hugh slowly and deliberately unbuttoning her nightdress. Moments later, when he reached for the silver box, she faltered, 'I'm afraid it's empty – Jack took them.'

In the fervour of the moment, she realized, was not the time to explain Jack and the missing condoms. Besides, Hugh wasn't listening. Instead she heard him murmur as the lid snapped shut on the delicate chased-silver box.

'What the hell! It doesn't matter now anyway!'

Sally made no reply and at that moment, needing her more than ever before, Hugh took her completely as his own.

Feeling him slip inside her, she heard him sigh and whisper.

'No, it really doesn't matter at all anymore.'

In the morning, surveying the scattered sweets on the table, Hugh remarked, 'What's this, the morning-after pill?'

Sally laughed and collecting the Smarties, popped one into her mouth. 'Just in case,' she joked.

Hugh laughed wryly. 'Well, you know you're quite safe from that – and other things. I've always been careful . . . and you know, there haven't been that many women in my life.'

'Won't Serena wonder where you are, or be worried about you?' Sally had to ask.

At the mention of Serena's name, Hugh's countenance took on its earlier thunderous appearance. 'If she is,' he snapped, 'then it's too damned late! I'm sorry, I don't mean to snap, it's just . . .'

'I know,' she whispered, smoothing the discreet silver hairs at his temples. 'I understand. I loved Stanley too.'

Taking comfort from the love he saw reflected in Sally's eyes, Hugh drew her into his arms. 'Thank God I have you, Sally. Uncle Bertram was right. You are good for me.'

'Uncle Bertram! You mean you told him about me?'

'I didn't have to. The old chap is so perceptive, he already guessed.'

'In that case, you don't think Serena knows too?'

'Lord no! She's much too interested in herself and her cronies to bother about us.'

Hugh stood up reluctantly. 'Speaking of which, I suppose I ought to be going back, though God knows I'm dreading coming face to face with her. But I've some paperwork to catch up on before I go into the office again.'

A slightly guarded look came into Sally's eyes. 'You won't do anything rash will you, Hugh?'

'No,' he smiled, 'I won't do anything rash, although –' the familiar twinkle came back into his warm brown eyes – 'I might just take you to see Uncle Bertam one of these days! You know, I think the pair of you would get on like a house on fire.'

'What makes you say that?'

'Because he absolutely loathes Serena'

Put like that, Sally felt it was better not to respond. Instead she watched Hugh's retreating figure as he braced himself for a confrontation with his wife.

One look at Hugh's rigorously solemn face warned Serena to take care. Panic rose inexorably in her throat and her mouth went dry.

'Hugh darling, you look all in. All that driving for Uncle Bertram – how is the poor man? Come and sit down and I'll get you something to eat. You must be quite ravenous.'

'I'm not hungry, Serena!' Hugh snapped.

'Well, a drink then, let me fix you a drink. I expect you could probably do with one, Hugh.'

'Could I, Serena? Could I really? And why pray, do you think I could do with a drink?'

Serena's eyes darted nervously in Hugh's direction. With trembling fingers she picked up the decanter and poured two large whiskys. Offering one to her husband she said feebly, 'Well, it might help numb the pain. I mean I know you must be absolutely devastated about losing Stanley, but it was all for the best, Hugh; the poor dog was in so much agony, he could barely walk from his basket to the back door . . .'

Hugh took a deep gulp of his drink. Feeling it burn as he swallowed hard, he enquired acidly, 'And did you give Stanley a shot of whisky before you took him to the vets?'

Serena slanted a puzzled look in his direction. 'I don't understand.'

'Don't you, Serena? Oh, I see, well let me rephrase that then.' Hugh stood up purposefully and placing his

184

glass on the mantlepiece, faced his wife with cold assessing eyes. 'I just wondered if you'd offered Stanley a shot of whisky, before you took him away . . . to ease his pain?'

Anxious to change the subject Serena made for the door.

'If you're sure you don't want anything to eat, Hugh, I think I'll go and have a bath and an early night. No doubt you'll want to check your mail. It's all on your desk in the study. Don't be too late yourself, darling.'

Sifting absentmindedly through the piles of letters, circulars and bills, Hugh found his attention drawn time and time again to the photos of Stanley. What was it Serena had said? 'The poor dog could barely walk from his basket to the front door.' Surely not – the vet hadn't said anything about such difficulties. Slumped at his desk, Hugh put his head in his hands and wept.

Upstairs in their bedroom, Serena paid particular attention to her regular beauty routine, only tonight having removed all her make-up, she reapplied the merest touch of blusher, lipstick and mascara. Then brushing her hair until it shone like burnished gold, she admired her reflection in the mirror.

Addressing a photo of Hugh on the dressing table, she whispered, 'I'll soon make you forget Stanley, my dearest,' and she reached down and opened the bottom drawer.

Casting aside silks and satins in stained-glass colours, Serena brought out a tissue-wrapped package and laid it on the bed. Although not bought for Hugh's benefit, Serena was desperate to make amends for Stanley's demise in the only way she knew how. Discarding the tissue, she slipped into the wisp of black lace, sprayed herself liberally with perfume, switched off all the lights except, the one on Hugh's sidetable and waited anxiously for her husband.

Hugh woke with a start, sending papers tumbling to the floor. The green desk lamp cast an eery glow about the study and he looked at his watch. It was almost one o'clock and he must have dropped off. Hardly surprising, he thought, as he got up to check the house for the night.

In the utility room, he automatically opened the back door, as if to let Stanley out for his last stroll round the garden. But there was no Stanley, only an empty basket and the familiar lead hanging on its hook. Feeling a lump in his throat, Hugh bent down to pick up the dog's water bowl.

It was still half full of water but the dust of the past few days had collected on the surface. Tipping the water away, Hugh rinsed out the bowl and wiped it clean with kitchen paper. Then refilling it, he placed it back on the floor by Stanley's basket.

'Just in case,' he told himself. 'Perhaps it's all just a bad dream and in the morning he'll be there.'

Opening the bedroom door, Serena's presence was enough to remind Hugh it was no bad dream after all. He watched as she got out of her own bed and slipped unceremoniously into his own.

'You don't mind, do you, darling,' she whispered huskily, with a deep languished sigh.

Hugh's reply when it came, shocked her beyond belief. 'Sleep in any damn bed you please, Serena, only don't expect me to share it with you!'

Removing his toilet bag from the still unpacked suitcase he'd taken with him to Harrogate, Hugh turned his back on Serena and strode towards the bedroom door. From now on the guest bedroom would suit him just fine.

'You're just over-reacting, Hugh!' Serena called after him. 'Stanley was only a dog. Besides, I'm sure if you really want another dog, we'll be able to find one just like him . . .' Her voice trailed away as Hugh slammed shut the guest-room door.

'Over-reacting, am I? We'll soon see about that. As for finding another dog like Stanley . . .' Hugh sat on the bed and began to undress. Then, just to be on the safe side, he got up and locked the bedroom door. Sally had told him not to do anything rash, but if Serena had come through the door at that precise moment, Hugh doubted if he could be held responsible for his actions.

'God knows I've never hit a woman,' he sighed, 'and I've no intention of starting now.'

Thumping his pillows in anguish, Hugh thought of Serena lying alone in his bed. What a pathetic figure she'd made in that ridiculous nightdress, if you could call it a nightdress. He'd never seen her wear anything quite like that before.

Hugh thought longingly of Sally. She had no need to get herself done up in strips of black lace, and just wearing his silk pyjama jacket she was the loveliest . . .

'Well, Serena,' Hugh said wryly to himself, turning down the covers, 'at least I shall keep to my part of the bargain. I once gave you my word I would never come to your bed if I had unprotected sex and

187

you know, my dear, I would never break my promise!'

With a glance at the ominous thunderclouds forming across the fields, Sally closed the bedroom window and went in search of a damp cloth. There were thunder flies all over the windowsill and the white painted surface looked as if it had been flecked with minute speckles of black paint. Rinsing out the cloth, the first clap of thunder echoed overhead at the same time as the ringing of the doorbell.

'Terry -- won't you come in?'

'No thanks, Sally, I was just calling to see if you're okay.'

'Yes, fine thank you. Why did you think there was a problem?'

Terry rubbed his stubbled chin. 'I didn't but Julie was wondering if you wanted to come in and sit with us – he thought you might be frightened of the storm.'

Sally smiled kindly. 'That's very sweet of him but tell him no, I'm not at all afraid of thunder; in fact, I quite enjoy a jolly good storm. At least it will clear the air.' She hesitated. 'Do I take it Julie doesn't like it then?'

Terry nodded. 'Yeah, he's absolutely terrified, poor thing. It's just as well I haven't got to go out just yet.'

'When you do, tell Julie from me just to ring my doorbell. He can help me do battle with these wretched thunder flies.'

Sally held up the cloth, impregnated with tiny black spots.

'Little buggars,' said Terry, 'they get everywhere, don't they?'

'Just one of the joys of living in the countryside, I expect. Oh, I told Hugh about the rumours they're going to build across the fields and he's going to look into it for us.'

'Cheers, Sally. How is he by the way? I don't suppose he'll ever get over Stanley, will he? I won't tell you what my old mum said when I told her about Hugh's wife putting the poor old thing down.'

A slightly guarded look came into Sally's eyes; she knew Terry's mother lived in Thornhampton. 'You didn't actually mention Hugh and Serena by name?'

'No way, Sally! Mum's the word in every way. I just said a friend of a friend. Don't worry, your secret's perfectly safe with Julie and myself.'

Sally gave a deep sigh of relief. 'Thanks, you don't realize how much it means to me to be able to talk to you both about Hugh.'

'I think I do,' Terry said, as another clap of thunder sounded overhead and a flash of lightning streaked through the curtains. 'Only too well in fact.' He nodded to where Julie was now peering into the hall-way with terrified eyes. 'Believe me, I had a pretty rough time keeping Julie a secret, but now I don't give a damn! People can think what they like.'

'I wish it was as easy as that for Hugh and myself. Oh well, I suppose I'd better get back to dealing with the dreaded creepy-crawlies.'

Closing the door, Sally went back to her bedroom and decided to tackle every surface. Beginning by the bed, she wiped the sidetable and lifted the chased-silver box. She smiled at the memory of Hugh presenting her with the small gift-wrapped parcel and its contents.

'Go on open it,' Hugh had teased, 'you'll never guess what it's for!'

No, she wouldn't, not in a million years! Blushing, she'd asked, 'You mean to say they sell these boxes with condoms inside?'

'Definitely not! In fact I think the Sloane Ranger type who served me would have had a fit if she'd known its intended purpose.' Smiling, Hugh had mimicked the young woman saying how she hoped Madam would enjoy her trinket box.

'Some trinkets!' Sally had remarked.

'Well,' Hugh explained, 'as I've noticed you've no drawers in your sidetables, we've got to keep them somewhere. It's not much fun rummaging about in the dark at the crucial moment, is it?'

It was a very pretty box, Sally thought, placing it back on the newly dusted surface. But after Hugh's last visit, would he bother to refill it?

'Talk about "Flaming June",' Laura sighed. 'If it gets any hotter I shall melt! I know,' she said, looking at Sally, 'I'd probably feel a lot better if I lost some weight. Marion's already told me!'

Helping Laura lift the box containing the latest stock delivery onto a table, Sally replied, 'Marion's not exactly sylph-like though, is she?'

'No, but considering she's nearly six foot tall and I'm a mere five foot three, I feel twice as wide!'

Laura studied Sally's trim figure in navy floral print calf-length skirt and white silk blouse. 'It's quite sickening, Sally; you eat like a horse and never put on an ounce. What's your secret?'

'Probably all the masses of fruit and veg I eat, courtesy of my neighbours.'

'Oh, you mean the two darling homosexuals?'

Sally shot Laura a disapproving look.

'Sorry Sally, I was forgetting you don't like them being mocked. The trouble is I don't like the word "gay". I was at school with a girl called Gay and she was such a pretty thing, so it doesn't seem right somehow.'

'Do people have to be categorized?' Sally snapped. 'Why can't adults just have friends, partners or lovers, whatever their sexual preference?'

Laura studied Sally thoughtfully. 'What about *your* lover, Sally?'

Sally looked up in alarm. 'I . . . I . . . don't know what you mean.'

Laura put a comforting hand on Sally's shoulder. 'Shall I assume from that that you don't want to talk about him then?'

Sally shook her head. 'If you don't mind, Laura, I'd rather not. It's not that I don't trust you. It's just that the situation is a bit complicated, that's all.'

'Well, as long as he's not spinning you along, telling you that his wife doesn't understand him and he can't bear to leave his children.'

'It isn't like that at all!' Sally replied, somewhat too quickly.

'So, I'm right then, he is married . . .'

Sally looked at Laura and nodded. 'Yes . . . but he doesn't have any children.'

'Then why doesn't he leave his . . .'

'Laura, please! I've already said I'd rather not discuss it.'

'Okay, okay. I'll say no more. I just don't want to see you hurt that's all. I apologize for prying.'

'And I apologize for biting your head off! I expect it's the heat or my hormones. Roz is forever warning me about the approach of middle age.'

'How is Roz?' Laura enquired.

'Oh, just as outrageous as ever. She wants me to go in and have lunch with her one of these days. I must admit I do miss her company, she's such a character.'

'Not like Marion and me then. We must seem a right pair of boring old farts in comparison!' Laura laughed and dabbed at the tiny beads of perspiration on her top lip. 'I'll tell you what, next early closing, why don't we all go into Thornhampton and have lunch with Roz? Heaven knows, if this heat continues I'm going to have to find some thinner dresses. And Marion says Barrington's summer stuff is lovely.'

Sally froze momentarily at the mention of Barrington's. If she thought Hugh was spending time at the store, she always tried to avoid going in. And she already knew Hugh was going to be there all next week!

The problem was, if she now tried to dissuade Laura from going into Thornhampton, she could also quite easily arouse suspicion. There was nothing for it but to go along with the plan. Anxious to avoid further discussion on Terry and Julie, Barrington's and her mystery lover, Sally changed the subject.

'Right then,' she said with a determined expression on her face, 'let's get this box unpacked, or before we know where we are, they'll be delivering the stock for Christmas!'

Clutching their acquisitions, Sally, Laura and Marion met up with Roz and made their way outside to the market square. The sticky heat of the oppressively hot June day hit them full in the face. Laura ran her fingers through her thick apricot curls and sighed, envious of Sally's new-look, shorter hairstyle.

Sally watched as beads of perspiration collected on the bridge of Roz's nose, causing her glasses to slip forward. Pushing them upwards, Roz looked about the market square for a spot of shade. Where to eat, that was the problem. The decision to avoid Barrington's restaurant had been unanimous and it was not so much a question of dying from hunger but wilting from thirst.

'This is a spot of luck,' Roz said, sitting down under a red, green and white striped parasol. 'I'd forgotten all about this place opening.'

Four bank clerks, with their identity cards bobbing, came scurrying round the corner and stopped abruptly, their faces crestfallen.

'Looks like we were here just in time then,' Marion agreed, 'we appear to have found the last free table.'

'They're young,' Roz announced. 'They've got more stamina than us, it won't hurt them to walk a bit further to find somewhere. Now you three, are you going to show me what you've all been buying?'

Taking out their purchases Roz gave a wicked grin and winked at Sally. 'If I didn't know otherwise, I'd think you were all going on a camping holiday. At least I'll know where to come if Donald and I ever need a tent.'

'Take no notice of Roz,' Sally said, 'she's only jealous because she has to wear that uniform all day long.'

'Too right I am, duckie.' Roz pulled at the waistband of her skirt. 'The last thing you want to wear in this heat, even with Barrington's air conditioning, is fitted clothing.'

Marion toyed with her spritzer, watching large cubes of ice melt without trace. 'I don't suppose this heat is exactly helping business though.'

Roz shrugged her shoulders. 'I don't know. I gather from Muriel Baxter, sales figures are up. At least with summer starting early, people are rushing out to buy summer clothes, not like the year before last when we were in winter woollies practically all year long.'

Roz gulped thirstily at her drink and crunched on the remains of an ice-cube. 'That's something to please the boss man anyway. I suppose you heard about him losing his dog – the poor chap looked gutted. That's the trouble with having pets . . .'

Watching the waiter place the tempting dish of antipasto on the table, Roz enquired, 'Whilst on the subject of things exotic and tasty . . .'

'I didn't know we were,' Laura said with a smile, following Roz's gaze as the young Italian flashed a brilliant white-toothed smile in her direction. 'Sorry, Roz, do continue.'

'I was just going to ask where you are all going for your holidays?'

Sally shook her head. 'At the moment, nowhere, but Laura's doing the Shirley Valentine thing and going off to Greece and Marion . . .'

'I'm going to Cornwall,' Marion announced, 'to stay with friends, so I shall probably come back bigger than ever, which is why I need my "tent".' She patted her dress in its Barrington's bag. 'You see, I have a terrible weakness for Cornish cream teas.'

CHAPTER 13

Sally stood looking dejectedly from the bedroom window across the fields of scarlet poppies. At any other time, she supposed, their bright silky blooms would have lifted her spirits, but with Hugh away, it was like being in the slough of despond. Feeling tears prick her eyelids she recalled his last visit.

'I'm sorry, Sally. I knew nothing about it, Serena arranged it all with Charles and Vivienne behind my back. According to Serena it's a belated birthday surprise but I know it's just another of her schemes to put things right since Stanley. And by involving her sister and brother-in-law, she knows damn well it's going to make it difficult for me to refuse.'

Hugh paced the floor in despair, his dark eyes filled with anger. 'Look, I'll make it up to you when I get back, I promise.'

'You don't have to make it up to me, Hugh. I have no claim on you and Serena is still your wife after all.'

'In name only,' Hugh said bitterly, 'and she needn't think this outrageous suggestion of hers is going to put us back in the same bed!'

Sally said nothing and fixed her gaze numbly on the dried flower arrangement Julie had given her at Easter. Reaching for her hand, Hugh drew her into his arms and whispered, 'That wasn't very tactful of me, was it? I'm sorry. But it's true, Sally. Serena and I will not be sleeping together; I've made that perfectly clear and she knows it.'

'But it might not be that easy with Charles and Vivienne . . .'

'Oh, it will be very easy. The villa sleeps eight and I intend to get up early and play as much tennis and golf as I can. Serena's a late riser. My excuse will be separate bedrooms so I don't disturb her.'

Stroking her hair, Hugh continued. 'Anyway, enough about that, I've got some good news for you.'

'Good news?'

'The proposed building plans Terry mentioned – they won't be affecting you after all. There's a new development right enough but it won't encroach on your view. Actually, it all sounds quite tasteful, a type of mews setting in keeping with the local stone.'

Now, forcing thoughts of Hugh and Serena out of her mind Sally was suitably mollified. Hugh had been correct. The bright yellow JCB's, lying in wait with their gaping jaws ready to sink their teeth into virgin meadows had trundled off in convoy in the opposite direction. She could at least go to work in better spirits.

Sorting through the post at Laura's Lair, Sally found the postcard signed 'S.V.II'. She laughed and handed it to Marion.

'I suppose by that she means Shirley Valentine the second and has no doubt met her Costas or Dimitri?'

196

'Heaven help us when she returns then, you know what Laura is like for holiday romances.' Marion sighed. 'Dear Laura, she hasn't changed in all the years I've known her.'

'People don't though, do they – despite their promises.'

'That sounds a very deep statement, Sally. Is it prompted by anything in particular?'

'Not really but I was sorting through some photographs at the weekend and came across some early photos of Richard. Looking back, I suppose I must have been really naïve when I met him.'

'Meaning?'

'Meaning, I thought I could change the little things that annoyed me about him, after we were married.'

'Oh, Sally! And pigs might fly, my dear!'

Sighing, Sally fixed Laura's postcard onto the gallery's kitchen door. 'Whoever he is, Laura, make the most of him and all that lovely sunshine.'

Marion studied Sally carefully. 'Are you beginning to wish you'd gone with her? You could have, you know. She's closed the gallery for a fortnight anyway, so there was really no need for you to come in.'

'I know.' Sally shrugged. 'I suppose I was feeling restless and I wanted to ask you something.'

'Ask away then.'

'I was wondering if you could paint a miniature of a dog . . . that is if I gave you a photo to copy?' Sally reached into her pocket and brought out some photos of Stanley. 'It's for a friend, you see, and it is, at least it was, a very special dog.'

Marion took the photos and laid them on the table where she could see them better. As she did so, her thick

197

plait fell over her shoulder. Standing up, she pushed it to one side and remarked thoughtfully, 'It's not something I usually do. I much prefer flowers to animals, but as it's you, I'll do it.'

Sally hugged Marion warmly. 'Oh, Marion that's wonderful, thank you. Thank you so much.'

'I wouldn't get too excited Sally; you haven't seen the end result yet and it might be far from perfect.'

'I doubt it,' she replied. 'There's no hurry, of course, but how long do you think it will take?'

Marion unclipped and refastened her two brown hairslides. 'It's difficult to say really. The flowers don't normally take too long but as it's a dog . . . Tell you what,' Marion added brightly, 'if I take these photos on holiday with me I could do it while I'm away. It will make a change from flowers.'

Despite Sally's protestations that Marion was supposed to be going on holiday, she was unable to dissuade her and the photos of Stanley were placed in a sturdy brown envelope and put with Marion's luggage.

Emerging naked from the shower, Hugh was surprised to find Serena standing in his bathroom. She was holding two glasses of chilled white wine.

'I thought you might like a drink, darling. Charles said it was a pretty exhausting tournament.'

Hugh nodded and murmured an almost inaudible thank you, before reaching for the towel that he tied round his waist.

Struggling to keep her tone casual, Serena whispered softly, 'Hugh, don't you think we could . . .' But she stopped abruptly when she recognized the now-familiar look in his eyes.

Setting one of the glasses on the bathroom shelf, Serena choked back a sob. 'Shall I go away for a while and come back when you're dressed?'

'That won't be necessary, Serena,' Hugh replied coldly. 'Just tell Charles and Vivienne I'll be out in ten minutes!'

Hugh heard the champagne cork before he reached the terrace.

'Hugh, old chap! Here, have a glass of champagne. After all, it's your birthday we're supposed to be celebrating and perhaps you can pass a glass to your good lady wife.'

Hugh turned to face Serena, who stood draped in a fuschia-pink and purple sarong, with matching bougainvillaea blossoms entwined in her hair. What was it Uncle Betram had said in Harrogate? 'Oh, I'll admit she's a stunner but has she made you happy – really happy?'

Holding out the champagne glass, Hugh saw not his beautiful and glamorous suntanned wife standing against the exotic backdrop of Moorish arches and blue Mediterranean Sea, but Sally, dressed in his navy-blue silk pyjama jacket, nervously sipping champagne.

Seeing Hugh smile warmly in her direction, a glimmer of hope stirred in Serena's breast but it was extremely shortlived. When Hugh heard the clink of glasses and the resounding 'Happy Birthday Hugh!' he was immediately transported back from Cedar Court and Sally to the villa in Spain with Serena. As she raised her glass in her husband's direction, only Hugh noticed how her sculptured mouth twisted with displeasure.

'Right everyone, let's eat,' announced Vivienne, coming in with an enormous plate of paella. 'And while we tackle this little lot, you two must tell us how you plan to celebrate your silver wedding anniversary. I trust you're really going to celebrate in style!'

Hugh and Serena faced each other in stony silence. Neither had spoken of the fact that in a few months' time, they would have been married for twenty-five years.

While Marion scooped the contents of a pot of clotted cream into a glass bowl, Laura cut squares of halva and placed them on a dish in the middle of the table. Sally looked at them and smiled.

'It looks as if my offering is the healthiest of the lot. Mind you, if I eat many more of these I shall end up *looking* like a strawberry!'

'Another contribution from the neighbours?' Marion enquired.

Sally nodded. 'Yes, they spoil me. All these wonderful summer fruits. I had thought of making some jam but it's too hot to stand over boiling jam pans, so we might as well make pigs of ourselves.'

'It looks like Laura already has,' Marion retorted playfully.

On her plate Laura had a heap of caster sugar and a generous dollop of clotted cream. Sally and Marion watched as she dipped a large strawberry first into the sugar and then into the cream before popping it into her mouth. 'Mmmn,' she sighed. 'Wonderful. It reminds me of . . .'

'We don't want to know!' Marion interrupted with a grin. 'You already look like the cat that got the cream.'

'Yes – and you're becoming almost as bad as Roz!' Sally teased.

'Not for much longer, I've too much work to do. Before we know where we are, the kids will have gone back to school and Christmas will be upon us.'

Sally groaned. 'Don't remind me. In last week's Thornhampton Gazette they even had a feature on this year's Christmas pantomime!'

'Well, I shall love you and leave you two to finish the rest of this.' Laura's tanned and beringed hand motioned to the remains on the table. 'I shan't be back until late, Sally, so if you can lock up . . .'

The two women watched her go and shook their heads.

'Whoever he was, it certainly looks as if he did her the power of good. That will keep her going until Christmas anyway.'

Sally got up from the table with Laura's empty plate. 'Mmmn – and she looks absolutely wonderful in that colour.'

Marion watched as a flash of green walked past the window. She sighed enviously. 'Not everyone can wear that acid green. You know it always makes me think of spurge and those wonderful lime-green tobacco plants. Which reminds me, I must paint some, one of these days.'

'Oh, you mean Euphorbia and Nicotiana.'

Marion laughed. 'Of course, I was forgetting you were the gardener in our midst. How are the hanging baskets and the tubs by the way?'

'Coming along nicely, I'm really pleased with them. I must take some photos.'

'And how about you, Sally . . . are you coming along nicely . . .?'

Sally looked up, bewildered, unsure of what Marion was implying. Her thoughts had been elsewhere. Laura's dress hadn't reminded her of summer flowers – but of lime-green condom packets instead!

'I'm not sure I'm with you, Marion.'

Toying with a strawberry stalk in the remains of her caster sugar, Marion said softly, 'Well, you are pregnant, aren't you?'

'No! Of course I'm not! What made you think that?'

'You just look it, that's all. Having had five of my own, I thought I'd recognized all the symptoms . . . Obviously I was mistaken – sorry.'

'But I haven't been sick,' Sally replied weakly, 'isn't that the first sign . . . morning sickness, I mean?'

'Definitely not! The first sign is missed periods . . .'

'Oh, well I haven't actually missed any, they're just a bit irregular that's all.'

'You can tell me it's none of my business, Sally, but, when exactly was your last period? Can you actually remember?'

'Why, yes of course I can, even though they're usually a bit erratic. It was at Easter and I can remember thinking what a stroke of luck, because . . .' Sally stopped herself. She was going to say, it was a stroke of luck because it was when Hugh was in Harrogate with Uncle Bertram.

'You were saying,' Marion said gently.

'Oh, nothing, it doesn't matter.'

202

Sally stroked her hand over her breasts and down onto her abdomen. Through the folds of the loose summer frock she'd bought at Barrington's there was only the gentlest curve. She looked up at Marion with questioning eyes.

'And you really think I am pregnant?' she whispered.

Marion nodded and pulled her chair closer to Sally's. 'Accidents do happen, you know. I can tell you that from experience – even if you are taking precautions. I take it you were . . .?'

'Yes, of course but since . . .' Sally wanted to say, since Stanley died we haven't . . . But she couldn't risk mention of Hugh. Instead she continued: 'We haven't recently because he told me he was infertile.'

'Oh, Sally!' Marion cried ruefully. 'Don't tell me you fell for that one! I admit it's novel, my dear, as usually it's "Oh, I've had a vasectomy so I'm OK!" But if you want my advice, you'll get yourself a pregnancy kit!'

'But it's true, even Roz told me he . . .'

Marion patted Sally's hand. 'Take my advice, Sally, it's best not to believe everything people say.'

Sally sat in numbed silence, unable to comprehend the conversation that had just taken place. Slowly she got up from the table and looked about her. 'I'll just clear these things away and then go back to the gallery.'

'If I was you, I'd go home and rest,' Marion urged. 'Don't worry about this place. I'll keep an eye on the gallery as I'm reasonably up to date with my painting. Speaking of which . . .' Marion reached into her folder and brought out not one miniature of Stanley but two. Placing them on the table she said, 'I hope they'll be all right. I did that one first – just the dog on his own – but

203

I couldn't resist having a go at copying one of the other photos you gave me.'

'But that's me!' Sally cried through misted eyes. 'You've painted me as well. Oh, Marion, they're beautiful, thank you.'

Marion smiled modestly. 'I'm glad you like them. I have to confess even I was pleased with my efforts. So much so, that after painting the first one, I thought why not try you and the dog together. Perhaps your friend might like that one too?' She studied Sally with questioning eyes.

'Yes . . . Yes . . .' came the murmured reply. 'Perhaps he will. I'll get them framed as soon as possible.'

Wrapping the miniatures in tissue paper, Sally placed them carefully in her bag and headed for the door. 'If you're sure about me going?'

'Positive,' said Marion.

Sally waited anxiously for Hugh's arrival, wondering quite how to tackle what she had to tell him. Taking Marion's advice she'd gone into the chemists and bought a pregnancy testing kit, which as Marion had predicted was positive. The problem was, what to do now?

Thinking back to her sister's pregnancies and the arrivals of the two boys, the prospect of motherhood quite appealed to her. And the thought of holding Hugh's child in her arms had even brought tears of joy to her eyes. But would Hugh share her enthusiasm?

He'd told her ages ago that he'd never leave Serena and she didn't expect him to – but would they be able to keep the baby a secret from Serena? Sally remembered one of her friends from university. She'd had a baby by a married man and somehow they managed to keep the child a secret for five whole years! It was only when the child went to school and he began asking awkward questions about his daddy that the secret came out.

'A lot can happen in five years,' Sally sighed. 'I've got to get through the next five months first!'

She studied the calendar and counted back to that fateful morning when she presumed she had conceived Hugh's child. Four months, she was four months' pregnant! Gracious, she must get a book or something and even make an appointment to see the doctor!

Holding both hands across her gently swollen stomach, she suddenly felt the urge to know just what this tiny being growing miraculously inside her looked like. Jackie had referred to her embryos in stages, like, spot, blob and tadpole, yet this didn't feel right to Sally. Her gaze wandered to the two neatly wrapped packages, waiting for Hugh.

'There's only one thing I can call you,' she sighed patting her stomach, before running her index finger along the blue foil wrapping of the miniatures. 'I shall call you Stanley.'

Walking to the bathroom door, she announced brightly, 'Right, Stanley, this is where you and I go and have a refreshing shower before your daddy comes and we tell him the good news!'

At the mention of breakfast, Hugh stretched lazily and watched as Sally drew back the bedroom curtains to let in the early morning sunshine.

'That was a wonderful meal you cooked last night, Sally. I don't think I could manage breakfast just yet. Can I suggest you come back to bed instead?'

Slipping back between the sheets and into his arms Sally sighed. 'And I thought you were an early riser.'

'Oh, but I am,' he teased, 'or hadn't you noticed!'

'I've noticed how tanned you are,' she said, blushing, looking down the entire length of his naked body. 'And I'm pleased to see that at least you didn't go in for nude sunbathing while you were in Spain.'

'Apart from tennis and golf and a spot of swimming, I didn't go in for anything else, either,' Hugh said, expressively. 'Which is why I missed you and want you so much now.' Turning on his side, Hugh reached out to caress Sally's breasts. She flinched visibly. 'Are you all right,' he murmured. 'Did I hurt you.'

'No,' she lied, turning on her back, ready to receive him. 'It was nothing . . . nothing at all.'

Later, running her hands down the fine hairs on his chest, bleached by the sun, she whispered, 'Do you know what I think we look like?'

'No,' he murmured, 'tell me.'

'I think we look like that wonderful chocolate dessert I had at Cedar Court. The one with the white, milk and dark chocolate . . . remember?'

Hugh laughed gently. 'Why, so we do. Me with my deep suntan and you with your pale-golden arms and smooth, white body.'

Thinking back to Cedar Court, Hugh let his right hand stray absentmindedly to the silver box on the sidetable.

206

'We really must go back to Cedar Court sometime, but that's one thing we won't need to take with us.' The silver lid clinked shut on the empty box. 'You'll have to think of another use for that from now on.'

'Not now perhaps, Hugh, but maybe in five months' time.'

Hugh was frowning at her. 'I'm sorry, Sally, you've quite lost me.'

'In five months' time,' she whispered softly, 'I could use it for the contraceptive pill. You see, Hugh, I'm . . . four months' pregnant.'

'You're what!' gasped Hugh, moving away from her.

Sally saw his eyes go cold and felt the muscles in his body go rigid.

'I know it must be a shock . . . and I know you won't leave Serena but I thought you might have been remotely pleased . . . Hugh . . .?'

Hugh's dark eyes flashed, deep with anger. 'Pleased! Pleased, Sally! Why should I be pleased that while I've been keeping you, you've got yourself pregnant by another man!' Hugh moved to the side of the bed and reached for his clothes.

'But, Hugh,' Sally pleaded, 'it isn't another man's child, it's yours, I swear. Apart from Richard and until I met you, I'd never even slept with another man.'

'Hmph!' Hugh muttered, 'and since you met me, by the sound of it, you've certainly made up for it.'

'Whatever do you mean?'

'Look at the time I came here and found . . . whats-his-name from next door in your arms.'

'You mean Julie? But he was only here because he and Terry had had a row and he was upset.'

'And you expect me to believe that? What were they rowing about then?'

'I don't know,' Sally said in an exasperated voice. 'What do gay couples row about?'

'Certainly not about being pregnant, that's for sure!'

'Well, just because they are gay, doesn't mean to say they don't have rows either!' she replied angrily.

Hugh was putting on his trousers; his mind was in turmoil. Something else was niggling away – but what was it? His gaze fell on the miniatures Sally had given him last night before they went to bed. Marion Le Sage's delightful paintings of Stanley on his own and Stanley and Sally together.

That was it! Hugh had suddenly remembered. The day he came from the vets and he'd telephoned Sally . . . When she'd answered the phone, she'd said not his name but . . . Bernard's! Bernard – the fellow from the New Year's Concert – surely not!

'Well, one thing's for certain, Sally, the child you're expecting definitely isn't mine – or had you forgotten I'm infertile!' Picking up his jacket, Hugh strode angrily to the bedroom door.

'And if it isn't Julie or Terry's – then why not try your ex-husband?'

'Richard! But that's preposterous; you know that as well as I do.'

'Do I? Well he seems to be making quite a name for himself as a stud, by all accounts. And of course we mustn't forget Bernard!'

'Hugh,' Sally sobbed, 'please!'

Hugh turned and glared at the tear-filled eyes, shadowed in her pale face. 'I'm sorry, Sally,' he said curtly, 'as far as I'm concerned, we've nothing more to say.'

Covering her nakedness with the lace-trimmed ivory sheet, Sally held out the two miniatures. Slowly and deliberately Hugh picked them both up. The one of Stanley on his own he placed in his pocket, the other of Stanley and Sally together, he placed face-down on the sidetable. Without pausing to even look at her again, Hugh walked down the hallway and let himself out of the flat for what he determined to be the very last time.

Hearing the door slam shut and wrapped in the tangled mass of sheet, Sally ran to the window. With tears streaming down her face, she was in time only to see the midnight blue Jaguar speeding away from the carpark in a cloud of dust.

In a daze, she righted the miniature of herself and Stanley and placed it lovingly by her bed. Then when she was showered and dressed, she went to the balcony and picked a sprig of bay leaves, which she placed like a laurel leaf on top of the silver frame.

'Oh, Stanley,' she cried, as tears welled in her eyes once more. 'What on earth are we going to do?'

Crushing a solitary, stray bay leaf in her fingers, Sally reached for her address book and searching through the pages, one at a time, realized there was no one she could phone and confide in, unless . . .

Terry stood at the door, bleary-eyed and in his dressing gown.

'Oh, I'm sorry,' Sally whispered. 'I forgot, you don't get up 'til late on a Sunday. Perhaps I can come back later.'

'No, you don't!' called Terry, pulling her inside. 'You'll come in now. What's the trouble, Sally, you look absolutely awful.'

'Thanks,' she said with a brittle smile, watching him close the door behind her. 'Terry . . . remember the time you said if I ever needed a shoulder to cry on . . . Well I need it now,' she sniffed. 'The trouble is I'm pregnant and Hugh doesn't want to know!'

'The bastard! And there was me thinking what a decent chap he was.'

'Oh, he's decent, all right,' Sally continued lamely. 'It's just that he won't accept the baby is his. I have to confess, even I can't understand how it happened.'

Terry fixed Sally with a peculiar look in his eyes and his fingers rubbed rasp-like against his chin. 'Well, if you sleep together, which you do, then it's obvious how it happened, isn't it? Or is there something my old mum didn't tell me about the birds and the bees?'

She smiled weakly in his direction.

'Come on, Sally,' Terry urged, taking her by the hand, 'come and sit down and tell your Uncle Terry all about it . . .'

At that moment Julie emerged sleepily from the bedroom. With his pale blue eyes, mass of golden curls and dressed in a pristine white bathrobe, Sally thought he looked like an angel.

If he was surprised to see her sitting on the sofa with Terry's arms comfortingly around her shoulders, he didn't show it. Terry answered his unspoken question. 'Sally's going to have a baby.'

'Oh, how lovely! Shall I make us all a coffee then and put some champagne in the fridge for later – when Hugh comes round.'

'Hugh won't be coming round, Julie.' Terry said softly. 'But if you could just make us the coffee . . .'

CHAPTER 14

During the following weeks, an air of gloom and despondency descended on Laura's Lair. Marion and Laura exchanged knowing looks when Sally was there and when she wasn't, their conversations were of acute concern for her welfare and wellbeing.

'Has she been to see a doctor yet?' Laura enquired.

Marion shook her head sadly. 'No, I keep telling her to go but it's as if she's on another planet. She seems in a daze most of the time.'

'Perhaps she wishes she was,' Laura said.

Marion looked up, puzzled.

'On another planet I mean . . . as far away from the bastard as possible.'

'You'd better not let Sally hear you call him that!'

'Well, he is! A complete and utter bastard! If I knew who he was, I'd certainly go along there and tell him!'

Marion was relieved that, Laura didn't know; the situation was bad enough as it was. Sally was clearly still madly in love with him, yet the pain and anguish so visible in her face was enough to make anyone weep.

No, Marion decided, Sally didn't need anyone to go and bully the man responsible for her present predicament, she needed someone to guide her gently through her pregnancy. For it was becoming clear she was probably too late to have an abortion, though Marion knew Sally would never have contemplated having one anyway.

'Look, you go off and do your rounds or whatever it is you do, Laura, and leave me to worry about Sally and the baby.'

Laura fingered her curls into an apricot froth round her still-suntanned face and nodded thoughtfully in Marion's direction.

'Okay, I take the hint. I've probably too fiery a temperament to deal with the situation and you're much calmer than me.'

'I've also had five babies of my own.'

'Crikey, so you have. You know I find it impossible to think of your brood as ever having been babies. I always visualized them being born carrying knapsacks and Greenpeace banners. I just wish . . .'

'Yes?'

'I just wish I knew who the bastard was, that's all – are you sure Sally didn't tell you?'

'Positive, and don't look at me like that either, Laura! In fact, when I see you all set to do battle, I'm glad you don't know!' Marion sighed. 'All I do know is that he must be a friend of Roz's. When talking about you-know-who, Roz's name slipped out.'

'Oh,' said Laura picking up her car keys, 'perhaps I could always go and see Roz then.'

'Laura, if you do!' Marion threatened.

* * *

213

Charles and Hugh picked up their tennis racquets and walked back to the pavilion and its changing rooms.

'Whew, that was a good game, Hugh, I enjoyed that.'

'You mean you enjoyed beating me?'

'Have to admit, I did, 6:2–6:4–6:1. Why, I feel just like what's his name when he beat that Spanish chappie for the gold medal at the Olympics.'

Charles studied his brother-in-law's dark countenance and patted his shoulder genially. 'Don't look so glum, old chap. After all, it's ages since I've beaten you. Usually it's the other way round.'

'I'm sorry, Charles, I was miles away.'

'Now, don't go and spoil my victory by saying you weren't concentrating on your game.'

Hugh smiled weakly. 'No, of course not, that wouldn't be very gentlemanly of me, would it?'

Standing in the shower, Hugh recalled the painful parting with Sally. That hadn't been very gentlemanly either. But how else did she expect him to behave, faced with such a shock announcement. Surely she wasn't that naïve to think she could tell him that the problem of his infertility had been resolved overnight. Hugh groaned audibly.

Charles' voice called out from the neighbouring shower; 'Hugh, old chap, are you okay?'

'Yes,' replied Hugh, 'nothing to worry about,' and he turned the shower to its coldest setting in the hope the icy needles of water would numb the pain and the desire he still felt for Sally.

There was also the problem of Serena. For days she'd been pestering him, not about returning to their bedroom – she'd conceded on that point weeks ago – but about this wretched business of their silver wedding anniversary. Egged on by Vivienne, Serena was desperate to make it a pretty spectacular occasion. Left to Hugh, he would have preferred to forget it. He had other things on his mind!

Back in the lounge Serena sat with a drink in one hand and pen in the other. 'Hugh darling! Just the man I need. I've been making some lists.'

'Lists?'

'Lists of guests, menus and likely venues.'

'Guests and menus I can understand, Serena, but why venues?'

'Well, this house isn't really big enough, is it?'

Hugh raised an eyebrow and looked about the expansive lounge and beyond to the dining room. Serena continued with her reasoning.

'And of course, being January, we can't really have a marquee in the garden.'

Hugh walked to the patio doors and stared thoughtfully across the expanse of manicured lawn, borders and shrubbery. A clouded blue butterfly hovered near the buddleia. Dipping and closing its wings, the colour reminded him of something. The carpet at Sally's flat. They'd even made love on that carpet – just after it had been laid and before the furniture had arrived.

'That makes two of us then,' Sally had whispered.

'Two of us?'

'Yes, me and the carpet, we've both been laid today!'

He'd smiled and taken her in his arms, caressing her body as he did so.

Hugh sighed deeply and shivered and was aware of Serena standing by his side. She placed a concerned hand on his arm.

'Are you all right, darling? Is there something bothering you?'

Hugh shook his head. 'No, I'm fine, thank you. Someone's just walked over my grave. Isn't that what they say, when you shiver for no reason at all?'

Serena gave a wry laugh and linked her arm in his. 'I would say you're just feeling cold. There seems to be a definite chill in the air this evening. When Mr Burt cut back all the dead stuff from the herbaceous borders and had a bonfire, there was a distinct smell of autumn in the air.'

Taking hold of Hugh's hand, Serena led her husband to the settee and her piles of lists and brochures. 'We can't have you talking about graves yet, we've a guest list to sort through!'

Hugh perused the lists of names while Serena scribbled down this menu and that menu, had conversations with herself about vegetarians and people with special dietary needs, until he could stand it no longer. When she began a tirade on colour schemes, he placed pen and paper on the table in front of him and stood up purposefully.

'Serena, by the looks of it, our wedding anniversary is in danger of turning into a fiasco. There are people on this list we haven't seen in years! In fact, I thought half of them were dead! If you want to have a celebration, fine, but let's at least keep it simple.'

Seeing the crestfallen look on her face, Hugh felt a pang of guilt and sat down again by her side. 'Look,' he said gently, 'I'm only suggesting we cut down the numbers a bit, that's all. Why don't we restrict it to twenty-five couples and have it here?'

'Why twenty-five couples?'

'Well, we've been married twenty-five years, isn't that reason enough? One couple for each year . . . and if you pick our dearest and closest friends and/or relations, what could be nicer?'

'Oh, Hugh,' Serena sighed, 'darling, what a wonderful idea.'

She turned to kiss him and he shivered again.

'I think you're getting a chill,' she announced, feeling his forehead and stroking her hand gently down his cheek. Nuzzling against him, Serena whispered seductively, 'You know we could always go to bed to keep warm if you're cold. Do you remember how freezing it was on our wedding night, how we went to bed early and your fingers were so numb with cold you could hardly manage the zip on my wedding dress?'

She sighed deeply. 'My lovely wedding dress, all those yards of wonderful white velvet and the cape and its hood, all edged with maribou. Perhaps I should wear velvet for our anniversary, not white of course, but black perhaps. What do you think, Hugh?' Serena placed a hand on Hugh's knee. 'Shall we go to bed?'

At the mention of bed, Hugh stood up abruptly. There was only one person he wanted to go to bed with! With a perfunctory look at his watch he strode to the door. Stunned, Serena ran after him.

'Hugh, where are you going? I thought we were . . .'

'Sorry, Serena, I promised Charles a drink as he completely slaughtered me in tennis this afternoon.'

'Well, I must say that's pretty decent of you old chap,' Charles replied in response to Hugh's invitation as he opened the front door.

'You're sure Vivienne won't mind me dragging you away?'

'Good Lord, no! But I'd better just check to see if she's got her box of tissues.'

'Why? Does she have a cold?'

Charles chuckled warmly. 'No, she's watching one of those *Heart Surprise* thingies and it always ends up with her in tears.'

Hugh frowned. 'What's a *Heart Surprise* thingy then, when it's at home?'

'Oh, just one of those programmes where they find long-lost relations you haven't seen since the year dot.' Charles gave a cynical laugh and lowering his voice added, 'Mind you, half the time they probably hate each other and don't want to be reunited . . . yet they all end up crying in each other's arms.'

Charles motioned to the door. 'You'd better just pop in and say hello to Vivienne while I go and fetch my jacket. Won't be a tick.'

'Hello Vivienne, how are you?'

Vivienne turned a tear-stained face in Hugh's direction.

'Good programme, is it?' Hugh enquired.

'Oh, wonderful,' Vivienne sighed ecstatically. 'You see that poor woman there? Well, she was deserted by a GI just after the war and –'

'Let me guess,' broke in Hugh, remembering Charles earlier brief description of the programme, 'they've just been reunited.'

'Oh, no, Hugh!' Vivienne said emphatically. 'Far from it! He must have been horrible anyway, so I doubt she'd want to be reunited with him. No, he deserted her when she was pregnant and she had to give the baby up for adoption. You know what it was like after the war. And they've just reunited her with her long-lost son. Isn't that wonderful?'

Vivienne's eyes filled with tears once more. As she reached for her box of tissues, Hugh turned his attention to the screen, where an elderly woman was crying on the shoulders of an athletic middle-aged man.

Leaving the room, even Hugh felt a lump in his throat. When Charles reappeared in the hallway, he called goodbye to his wife and followed Hugh to his car.

'What's it to be, the golf club or the Fox and Dog, Hugh?'

'The Fox and Dog, if you don't mind, Charles. I don't think I'm in the mood for the golf-club set tonight.'

'Problems at home with the good lady?'

'Not exactly what you'd call problems. It's just that Serena's got a bee in her bonnet about our anniversary. I mean it's not exactly a Royal Wedding, is it?'

Charles gave a laconic laugh. 'If you care to think about it, as far as the royals are concerned, a silver wedding is quite an occasion. I mean not many of the young ones look like reaching that goal, do they?'

'I suppose not,' Hugh replied, swinging the car into the pub carpark.

Handing Charles a beer once they were inside, Hugh raised his own glass saying, 'Here's to Thornhampton's answer to Andre Agassi. And thanks again for the match, Charles, you played well.'

Heartened by his brother-in-law's praise, Charles replied, 'And here's to your anniversary plans.'

'Don't remind me,' Hugh joked. 'No doubt Serena will have covered the entire sitting-room floor with her lists by the time I get home.'

'I take it she doesn't watch *Heart Surprise* then?'

'*Serena*? You've got to be joking, Charles! You know Serena; she's not at all like Vivienne and definitely not a sentimentalist.'

Charles sipped his beer thoughtfully and wiped a fine layer of froth from his moustache.

'You know,' he said, turning in Hugh's direction, 'it's peculiar really – Serena and Vivienne, I mean. There they are, two sisters, complete opposites in every way, yet they're the best of friends and always have been, according to Vivienne.'

Hugh was studying his reflection in his glass, his face looked sallow and distorted.

'Mind you,' Charles added brightly, 'that's probably why they get on, because they're so different. Although, I have to confess when Serena –'

'When Serena did what, Charles?'

Charles shifted uneasily. 'When Serena had poor old Stanley put down, I don't mind saying Vivienne was pretty cut up about it. She told Serena to wait until you got back but you know Serena.'

Hugh nodded. He did, only too well.

When Roz met Sally for lunch, it was too cold to sit under gaily striped umbrellas so they sat in the aromatic warmth of the trattoria instead. Roz faced Sally across the table and a look of concern spread across her face. Sally looked different somehow, yet she couldn't quite pinpoint why. Tiredness perhaps – she certainly had deep circles under

220

her eyes – or was it just the thought of autumn and the dreary months of winter that followed on?

'Right, tell me about everyone at the Lair then. Has Laura trapped anyone recently?'

'No.' Sally smiled. 'Not since Costas when she was on holiday.'

Roz's eyes scanned the restaurant for the young waiter who had served them on their last visit. 'I was wondering if she'd scared off our handsome Luigi, he doesn't appear to be here, does he?'

'Pardon?'

'Luigi, the gorgeous young thing who served us before. Laura kept giving him the come-on. Don't you remember?'

Sally shook her head. Shrugging her shoulders, Roz announced, 'Well if you've finished playing with that plate of lasagne, how about coming with me to buy some shoes?'

Leaving the shoe shop, Roz grabbed Sally's arm. 'Why didn't you try that pair on? They would have suited your feet, you know. You're lucky you can wear styles like that. Unlike me, with my feet I need shoes the size of kipper boxes!'

Sally turned to Roz with a forlorn look in her eye. 'There's no point in me buying shoes, Roz, when I won't be able to see my feet for much longer. You see, I'm pregnant.'

Dropping her shopping, Roz flung her arms around Sally and in the middle of the market square cried enthusiastically, 'Sally, how wonderful!'

As astonished shoppers passed by, Sally's eyes filled with tears and she clung onto Roz's shoulders.

'Hey!' Roz cried. 'What's all this? You're going to have a baby and you're crying. Surely you must be over the moon? Oh, Sally, just think, we can go shopping together, Barrington's has some beautiful baby clothes and Donald and I can come and babysit so you and . . . can go out.'

Roz's sudden enthusiasm diminished rapidly when she saw Sally's crestfallen face. 'Oh dear! Me and my big mouth again. I take it this wasn't planned and there are problems?'

'You could say that.'

'Do you want to talk about it?'

'Not really, but I just wanted to tell you . . .'

'And I'm jolly glad you did, after all, we've been friends for so long.' Roz grabbed hold of Sally's arm and tucking it in hers led her towards the covered shopping precinct.

'Where are we going?'

'To Barrington's to buy something for the baby.'

'No!'

'No? But why?'

Sally wracked her brain for an excuse. 'Because,' she said hurriedly, 'I know too many people there . . . and I don't want them to know just yet.'

'Point taken, but there's nothing to stop us going over here.' She led Sally to the nearby exclusive baby boutique and pushed her gently through the door. 'Now what do you need,' she whispered as the assistant approached.

'What do you mean, what do I need?'

'Well, what have you bought already?'

'Nothing'

'Nothing! Sally Palmer!'

Armed with bags from Les Enfants Sally found herself being led into Barrington's after all.

'Don't worry,' Roz said, feeling Sally's muscles tense within her grasp. 'We're not going to Babyware, we're going to my department as the one thing you really are going to need is a good maternity bra!'

In the confines of the changing room and the purchases from Les Enfants concealed in a Barrington's bag, Sally found herself relaxing.

'Tell me,' Roz whispered, reaching for her tape measure, 'aren't you just the teeniest bit happy about all this?'

'Oh, yes . . .' Sally rubbed her bump lovingly. 'I am honestly, it's just that . . .'

'Just what?' said Roz, taking the first set of measurements.

'Just that I wish the father was happy too.'

'No doubt he'll come round. I expect he was a bit shocked when you told him.'

In her mind's eye, Sally relived Hugh's outburst when she told him about the baby. 'A bit shocked' is hardly how she would have described it!

Coming out of the changing room, Sally was mortified to see Hugh coming in her direction. For a brief moment he looked as if he was going to ignore her and walk the other way, but seeing Roz nod in greeting, he had little choice but to approach.

'Mrs Palmer, how nice to see you and are you well?'

'Yes, thank you, Mr Barrington.' Sally felt her throat go dry. What else could she say?

Hugh stared at her momentarily with flint-hard eyes, before turning abruptly to Roz. 'Mrs Hughes, I understand you have a complaint about one of our suppliers. Perhaps when you've finished serving Mrs Palmer, you'd come and see me. Ladies, if you'll excuse me.'

Watching him nod and turn away, Sally choked back a sob.

'Whew!' whispered Roz. 'What's got into him?'

Regaining her composure, Sally gathered up her shopping. 'I'd better get going and you'd better not keep him waiting.'

'Suppose not. Muriel says he's been extremely irrascible of late. It's probably his hormones, male menopause or something.'

'Or something,' Sally whispered to herself as she said goodbye and headed for the escalator.

She breathed a sigh of relief as she left the store. That was one hurdle over. Roz had been absolutely marvellous, a real tower of strength. Next on her list was her sister!

'Right then. Leave it with me, Mrs Hughes. If they can't guarantee their supplies, we'll tell them we'll find another supplier. I shall expect a reply from them in forty-eight hours.'

Roz was impressed with Hugh's forthrightness at dealing with her complaint. For months she'd been trying to get Daisy Cup to improve their delivery times. They were an old established family firm but even firms like Daisy Cup had to move with the times. Long-standing customers were beginning to lose patience and some, Roz knew, had even deserted her for the High Street chainstores.

'I've told them to fax me,' Hugh announced sharply.

'I doubt whether Daisy Cup even know what a fax is. They probably burn up all their discontinued stock of brassieres and corsets and send smoke signals!'

A brief glimmer of a smile flickered across Hugh's face. Roz breathed a sigh of relief. She stood up to go.

'You didn't have any trouble serving Mrs Palmer, I take it?' he asked.

'No, thankfully. Daisy Cup are for the more mature woman and fuller figure. Sally's far too young. Besides . . .'

'Besides . . .?' Hugh stood up to escort Roz to the door.

'Well,' she whispered, 'perhaps I shouldn't tell you this but I'm sure you'll be as thrilled as I was, when Sally told me.'

Hugh stood with baited breath. 'Go on . . .'

'Sally is pregnant; isn't that wonderful?'

'Yes, wonderful,' Hugh responded weakly, 'and what is the – er father's reaction to the good news?'

'Oh, not very favourable at the moment, I'm afraid. I don't know who he is, mind you, but I'm sure he'll come round in time.'

'Really, Mrs Hughes, and what makes you think that?'

'Well, it stands to reason, doesn't it, Mr Barrington. What man doesn't want a son to dandle on his knee, or to take to cricket or golf?'

Roz stopped herself abruptly. Spying the photos on the wall of Hugh Barrington playing golf and tennis, she suddenly realized her *faux pas*. The poor chap could only fire blanks! Hurrying to the door, all she wanted to do was beat a hasty retreat back to the safety of ladies lingerie but H.B. was barring her way.

'And how does Mrs Palmer know it's a boy? Have the doctors told her?'

'Not exactly, because she still hasn't been to the doctor yet. I tried to persuade her but I think she's frightened of doctors in general, though she really ought to go, you know. I mean, having a baby at her age, there could be problems.'

Watching Roz hurry away, Hugh closed the door of his office and returning to his desk, buried his head in his hands.

'You're *what*!' Jackie spun round from where she was standing at the sink, peeling potatoes.

'I'm pregnant.'

'But how?'

'Jackie, I hardly need tell you *how*!'

'Okay, *who* then?'

'I'm not prepared to say.'

Angrily, Jackie threw a peeled potato into a bowl of water, where it bounced up and splashed her face. At that moment Jack came running into the kitchen. Seeing the water dripping down his mother's face, he enquired anxiously, 'Mummy, why are you crying?'

'I'm not crying, the potato splashed me when I dropped it in the water. Although, heaven knows, I've plenty to cry about.'

'Why?' Jack's voice pleaded.

'Your Auntie Sally is pregnant. She's going to have a baby!'

226

Jack left his mother's side and walked over to Sally. He peered at her inquisitively and placed a tiny hand, stained with felt-tip pen, on her tummy. Turning his head to one side he said, 'Oh dear. What happened?'

'What makes you say that, Jack?' Sally asked kindly.

Jack twisted his mouth from side to side thoughtfully, before replying, 'Well, you don't have a daddy to water your seeds, do you?'

Sally and Jackie's eyes met in horror across the kitchen table.

Bending down to Jack's level, Sally stroked his hair away from his face.

'Well, Jack, it's like this. I did have a "daddy", but he just sort of disappeared!'

There was a gasp from the kitchen sink as the knife slipped and Jackie cut her hand. She turned to Jack, urging him to go and wash his hands before tea.

'What are we having?' he cried, running to the cloakroom.

'Sausages, mash and spaghetti.'

'Is it 'ghetti from a tin or a packet?'

'A tin.'

'Oh,' came the voice, muffled by running water. 'I don't like 'ghetti from a tin, I prefer Auntie Sally's 'ghetti. She puts leaves in hers.'

Jackie raised her eyebrows in despair towards her sister.

'He means bay leaves in spaghetti bolognese,' Sally enlightened her.

Later, with the boys in bed, Jackie turned to face Sally apologetically. 'From what you said earlier, do I take it because Jack took those condoms . . .?'

Sally nodded.

'Oh, Sally, I'm so sorry. Why on earth didn't you say when I put them back in my handbag?'

'I didn't like to. It seemed mean somehow and I was also a bit cross with you for assuming I was past having a sexual relationship.'

'Well, you've certainly proved me wrong on that score, haven't you? And what have you decided to do about the baby – will you keep it?'

'Of course!' Sally said in alarm. 'I don't intend to have an abortion if that's what *you're* implying. This baby is very special to me.'

CHAPTER 15

Returning from her sister's, Sally decided to put her car away in the garage block behind the flats, rather than wait until later. She was tired. It had been a pretty exhausting afternoon off and a warm bath and early night wouldn't go amiss. Locking the garage door she was startled by a figure hovering in the shadows.

'Hugh! What are you doing here?'

'I came to see how you were.'

'You've already asked me that once today and my answer's still the same. Like I told you – I'm fine.'

Hugh's eyes scanned the discreet swelling of her tummy, showing through the folds of her dress. 'You're still pregnant then?' he asked clumsily.

'Yes! Why? Were you hoping I wouldn't be?'

'No, it's just that I understand you haven't seen a doctor yet.'

'What makes you say that?'

'Mrs Hughes told me.'

'Well, you don't have to worry, I didn't tell her anything else!'

'Sally! Please, why won't you see a doctor?'

'It's none of your business why.'

'Isn't it? Oh, I thought it was, from what you led me to believe.'

Objecting to the inference in his voice, Sally responded angrily. 'In that case, do I take it you're offering to come with me? Perhaps we could ask Richard and Bernard – not forgetting Terry and Julie – to come along as well. Then we could put all your names in a hat and the first one I pull out could be the lucky father!'

'I don't think this conversation is getting us very far, do you?'

'I never expected it to!' she said acidly.

Hugh put out his hand to touch her but seeing her flinch, put his hand to his head instead. Running his fingers through his hair, he murmured softly, 'I get the distinct impression I'm unwelcome here.'

'How positively astute of you. I thought you of all people would realize that I entertain my male friends in my bedroom and not in a draughty garage block!'

Though her tone was acerbic, in her heart she was longing to reach out and touch him – feel his lips on hers and be warmed by his embrace. Instead, from the sombre look on his face, she sensed only recrimination. There was no warmth, just his cold, icy voice saying, 'Regardless of what you think of me and what's been said this evening, I am concerned and would suggest you go and see a doctor.'

Choking back tears, she nodded and watched him walk away, only to run blindly after him, just as he reached the Jaguar.

'Hugh!' she called breathlessly.

Opening the car door, he looked up, wondering what else she could possibly have left to say.

'Hugh . . . I know you'll probably think it's none of my business but your . . . inability to have children . . . how did you find out? I mean, did you ever have a test?'

'Isn't the fact that Serena had a child test enough?' Sally watched him shake his head ruefully as if completely nonplussed by such a foolish question. It seemed there was nothing more to be said between them.

Serena studied her morning post critically. She was waiting for revised menus from the caterers. On reflection, Hugh's suggestion for close friends and family at home was proving to be a far better idea than she'd initially thought.

She would be able to decorate their feature staircase with garlands of flowers of her own choosing, have a horseshoe table, draped with more garlands, set up in the dining room and after dinner people could drift in and out, chatting about old times. She sighed, it would be wonderful.

Hugh, who was reading the morning paper, spied yet another list being thrust in his direction. Carefully, he removed it from where it was in danger of being stuck in the dish of ginger marmalade.

'Serena, please!'

'Sorry, darling, I just wanted you to have that one, it's the menus.'

'What do I want with menus? I thought that was your department.'

'It is. But I'm sure you'd rather see to the wine. And to do that, Hugh, you'll need to know what we're eating. And when you've finished your breakfast, I'd appreciate it if you called to see James before going in to the store.'

'James? James who?' Hugh enquired, folding the newspaper. It was obvious Serena had no intention of letting him read it.

'James, from the wine merchants, of course!'

With an air of impatience, Serena began loading breakfast dishes onto a tray. Watching her stack the dishwasher, Hugh enquired thoughtfully, 'Serena, have you never wondered what happened to your James?'

'*My* James? Whatever do you mean?' Serena's mind clicked away like a computer, searching for a relevant programme. In all of her 'little arrangements', there'd never been a James.

'James – your baby. Wasn't that what you said you called him, before he was handed over for adoption?'

With a resounding crash, the plate Serena was holding dropped to the floor. Her face was ashen.

'I'm sorry,' said Hugh, 'I should have realized what a shock it must be, having his name mentioned after all this time.'

Clinging onto the dishwasher Serena whispered, 'Yes, yes, it is, but why? I mean, what made you mention him now?'

'It's just that you mentioned the name James and it got me thinking about something Vivienne was watching on television the night I called for Charles.'

Unable to see the significance, Serena waited for Hugh to explain.

'There was this programme, where a woman was reunited with the son she'd given up for adoption years ago and I just got to thinking.'

'Thinking what, Hugh?'

'Thinking how nice it might be to try and find James for you, a sort of anniversary celebration, if you like.'

Keeping her back to her husband, Serena whispered quietly, 'No, Hugh, I really don't think that would be a good idea. Just think how distressing it would be for him after all this time. Anyway, he's probably perfectly happy with his adoptive parents – and it wouldn't be fair to rake up the past.' As an afterthought she added, 'Besides, how would we find him?'

'I would have thought quite easily. Apparently they do it on these television programmes all the time.'

'Hugh, stop please! It was a long time ago and much too painful to remember. I handed James over for adoption and that was that, and I really don't think we should start interfering in his life now.'

Hugh sighed. 'Okay, if that's what you want. It just seems a shame, that's all, especially when you think we've no children of our own and there's a great deal to inherit. Perhaps the boy could do with some financial help.'

'Hardly a boy!' Serena snapped. 'As we're about to celebrate our silver wedding, he must be nearly thirty and should have made his own way in the world by now!'

Taking the menus, Hugh left the breakfast table and walked towards the door. Serena followed him nervously.

'Hugh, darling, I'm sorry, I shouldn't have bitten your head off like that. It was a wonderful gesture on your part – truly – but I think we should leave James where he belongs, in the past, don't you?'

233

In a rare moment of compassion, Hugh bent and kissed Serena's ashen face and stroked her hair. 'Perhaps you're right, I promise I won't mention it again.'

In trepidation Sally got up from her seat in the waiting room and walked towards the door marked Dr Jeremy X. Mason and knocked timidly.

'Mrs Palmer, do come in and sit down.' Motioning her to a seat by the side of his desk, Dr Mason studied his computer screen.

'I see you're a new patient to Elmsmarsh. Have you lived here long?'

'About eight months.'

'And you've only just registered? Well, you've obviously had a healthy start to life in Elmsmarsh. Now then, what appears to be the problem.'

'The problem,' said Sally, staring into kindly grey-green eyes, 'is that I'm pregnant. Well, it's not exactly a problem in that I don't want the baby but . . .'

'But what . . .?' a voice urged gently.

'The baby's father says he can't be the father because he's infertile and because his wife's already had a baby by another man and . . .'

'Just one moment, Mrs Palmer, I'm afraid you've lost me. Can we go through that again but a little bit slower please?'

Explaining the situation Sally watched Dr Mason scratch his head and jot some notes on the file in front of him.

'I take it then that, the father of the baby is not your husband?'

'No – I'm divorced.'

'And there are no children from your marriage?'

Sally shook her head and said nothing. There seemed little point in relating why she and Richard were divorced and had no children.

'Right then and when was the date of your last period?'

'Good Friday, April the fifth.'

Doctor Mason's rainbow-shaped eyebrows shot up. They were copper-coloured and wiry like his hair and reminded Sally of the sisal front doormats they'd had at home when she was a child.

'April fifth! And why haven't you been to see me before?'

'I don't like doctors and hospitals. When my father was dying . . .' Sally's eyes filled with tears. 'My mother couldn't cope, you see, and my sister was too young . . .'

'I understand. Well, as we're dealing with birth here and not death, the situation should be greatly improved. Now let's see, you are how old, Mrs Palmer?'

'Thirty-four.'

'And as a point of interest, how old is the father?'

'Forty-six.'

The sisal matting arches shot skywards again. Dr Mason stroked his chin. 'And this is your first pregnancy, no miscarriages . . .' Getting up from his chair he motioned to the examination couch. 'If you'd like to go behind the screen, take off your pants and tights, I'll come and examine you.'

Concentrating on Dr Mason's head as he probed and prodded gently, Sally decided his shape resembled the copper urn Jackie had standing in her hearth . . . broad at neck and shoulders and narrow at the hips. Strange she mused, even his eyes she associated with copper; they were the colour of verdigris.

Dressed and back in the chair, Sally waited anxiously.

'EDD January tenth,' said Dr Mason, studying a printed chart.

'Pardon?'

'Oh, I'm sorry, I was forgetting this is your first baby. EDD – estimated delivery date. In your case January tenth. Does mid-April ring a bell?'

'Why – should it?'

'That's when you possibly conceived.'

'Oh!' was all Sally replied. She hadn't been aware of bells ringing the first time they'd not used condoms but at the same time she remembered mid-April very well. How could she forget seeing Hugh in such a distressed state when he'd just returned from the vets? She touched where her own Stanley lay curled up inside her and felt a warm rosy glow surge through her body.

Watching her, Dr Mason said, 'I take it you are pleased to be pregnant but what was it you were saying earlier about the father claiming to be infertile?'

Sally told him all she could remember. When she'd finished, the verdigris eyes sparkled mischievously.

'Mrs Palmer, much as I'd like to believe in miracles, take it from me we're not contemplating another immaculate conception here. If your -er- partner is interested, tell him I can arrange for a routine seminological analysis, or if he wants to come with you next time . . .'

'No!' Sally said determinedly. 'I don't think he'd want that at all.'

'Very well then.' Dr Mason was tapping away at his keyboard. 'As you've left things a little late we really ought to arrange for triple-testing or AFP.'

'What's that?'

'It determines the risk of spina bifida or Down's syndrome.'

Sally's face fell; a friend at school had a Down's syndrome brother. He was lovely and so affectionate but somehow very sad.

'Don't look so worried,' a kindly voice was saying, 'it's just a precaution and you don't have to have the tests if you don't want to. Older mothers can be more susceptible, that's all, which is why it would have been better if you'd come to see me earlier. You should have been taking folic acid for the first twelve weeks of your pregnancy.'

'Isn't that found in fruit and vegetables?'

'Amongst other things.'

A broad grin crept over Sally's face. Thinking of the regular contributions of wonderful fruit and vegetables from Julie and Terry she was in no doubt she'd had her fair share of folic acid!

Dr Mason reached into a drawer and produced a booklet. 'The midwife would normally give you this when your pregnancy is first confirmed. I suggest you take it now and read it.'

Taking it from him, Sally saw he was smiling at her.

'Don't worry, Mrs Palmer. You look a perfectly healthy specimen to me and I'm sure baby is too. Just go home and put your feet up.' He nodded to the booklet. 'You've got plenty of reading to catch up on.'

Pausing by his open door, Sally turned back and looked at him, a puzzled expression upon her face.

'Was there anything else troubling you?'

Gingerly she enquired, 'It's rude of me I know, but what's the "X" for in your middle name?'

The verdigris eyes creased at the corners and he laughed warmly. 'Xavier – so what do you think of that?'

'I think it's very unusual. I've never heard of any Xaviers before.'

'Neither had I. My parents both gave me conflicting stories. The first was that whilst my mother was expecting me. She was obsessed with the music of an American bandleader – an Xavier Cugat or something . . .'

'And the second?'

'My father was greatly impressed by a British chap working for the French Resistance during the war. His codename was Xavier. Personally I prefer the latter. I don't much see myself as a bandleader somehow. It's bad enough listening to that lot when they're playing their recorders and violins!'

Sally watched his gaze fall on a photo where a trio of freckle-faced, copper-haired youngsters beamed out with toothy grins.

'Perhaps they could call themselves the Xavier Mason Trio,' she suggested. 'It sounds very impressive.'

'So it does,' he replied, pressing the buzzer for his next patient. 'And don't forget, Mrs Palmer, if baby's father wants to come and have a chat . . .'

Sally nodded, and clutching her baby book and appointment card, left the surgery full of renewed hope. It was short-lived however, when arriving at her car, she recognized the Jaguar parked alongside.

'Hello, Sally. How was your appointment with Dr Mason?'

'Hugh! How on earth did you know I . . . have you been spying on me?'

'No, I did some detective work . . . I rang the surgery and told them I was your husband and you'd forgotten what time you'd made your appointment.'

'You did *what*? How dare you!'

'I was worried about you, Sally. Is . . . is everything all right with you and the baby?'

'Yes,' she replied curtly, 'Stanley and I are just fine.'

'Stanley?'

'Oh, didn't you know that's what I've decided to call the baby? You see, the doctor asked if mid-April rang any bells with me? That's when it was conceived apparently and I thought Stanley seemed appropriate. Perhaps you'd like to look back in your diary and see what you were doing in mid-April.'

For one normally so composed, Hugh looked decidedly unsure of himself. He found Sally's abrasive manner so alien to the sweet-natured woman he remembered. With a sudden determined set of jaw he drew himself up and announced, 'Well, I'd better be going. I'm so pleased everything is all right. Take care.'

Walking into his office the last person Hugh expected to find was his sister-in-law.

'Vivienne! What are you doing here? Is anything wrong?'

Vivienne cast an anxious look in Muriel Baxter's direction.

'Mrs Baxter, perhaps you could get us some coffee.'

Relieved to see Muriel busying herself with Hugh's instructions, Vivienne followed Hugh to his private sitting room.

'I get the feeling you'd prefer to be somewhere out of earshot. Rest assured these walls don't have ears.'

Vivienne forced a brittle smile, unbuttoned her suit jacket and rubbed her hands nervously together. 'You're not expecting Serena, are you?'

'No, why, should I be?'

'No, but it's because of Serena I'm here.' Vivienne looked furtively about her.

'You're quite safe you know –' Hugh smiled – 'now, what is all this?'

'Oh dear! It's all very difficult, Hugh, and I'm not very good at this sort of thing, so I suppose I'd better come straight to the point. Serena confided in me that you'd mentioned trying to find the – er – baby she had adopted.'

'You mean James?'

'Yes – James, that's right. Well, she doesn't want you to.'

'I know.'

'You do?'

'Yes, and as she got quite upset about it, I told her I wouldn't.'

'Wouldn't what?'

'Why, try to find him of course!'

Vivienne breathed an enormous sigh of relief and unclasped her hands.

'Is that it then?' Hugh enquired.

'What? Oh, yes – that's it.'

240

'Right then, I'll see if the coffee is ready.'

Later, ushering her to the door, Hugh said softly, 'I know Serena didn't think it was a good idea to contact James but I can't help feeling it's such a shame. After all, he can't be that much older than Gareth. And with Gareth an only child too, they could have been great company for each other.'

Vivienne thought fondly of her only son, now happily installed at Barrington's and glad to be away from his father's law practice.

She sighed. 'Gareth's very happy with you here.'

'I know,' Hugh replied wistfully, 'and I can't help but wonder, if James was that way way inclined too, who knows – perhaps I could have retired by now!'

Vivienne stood on tiptoe to kiss Hugh's cheek. 'You know you're so sweet and thoughtful, Hugh, and I know Serena's my sister, but sometimes I don't think she realizes how lucky she is to have you.'

Vivienne wiped a tear from her eye and Hugh, embarrassed by her sudden outburst of sentimentality, remarked good-naturedly, 'Very kind of you to say so, Vivienne, but I'd be the first to admit I'm not perfect.'

'I know dear,' she said kindly, remembering earlier days, when with Serena's permission, Hugh had . . . But then she also knew her sister! 'Anyway, I must be off, I'm meeting Serena for lunch. At least I can put her mind at rest.'

Sitting at his desk, Hugh turned back the pages of his diary to April. In bold letters he found 'HARROGATE WITH UNCLE BERTRAM'. On his return nothing much else had been pencilled in, but the thick black

241

circle around April the eighteenth was a grim reminder of Stanley's passing.

What was it Sally had said about mid-April ringing any bells? To Hugh, at that moment, in a particularly melancholy state of mind, it could only be the mourning bell that was tolling for Stanley. As for Sally, what then? Taking a tiny key from his pocket Hugh walked to a mahogany cabinet and turned the lock.

Inside, wrapped in tissue, he found the miniature Sally had given him. Lovingly, he ran his index finger round the rim of the frame and regretted bitterly the fact he'd left its partner – the one of Sally and Stanley together – on the sidetable in Sally's bedroom.

'Oh, Sally!' he whispered softly, 'and to think I don't even have a photo of you.'

Wrapping the miniature back in tissue paper, Hugh placed it in the drawer, where it rested against a box. The box that contained the urn of Stanley's ashes. Hugh shuddered and felt a lump rise in his throat. What did you do with a dog's ashes?

It didn't seem right to have them on display like some tennis or golfing trophy and he certainly didn't want them scattered in the garden at home, where Mr Burt was constantly digging, raking and hoeing. Closing the cabinet, Hugh realized the only person who would know of a sensitive solution was Sally, yet he could hardly ring and ask her advice.

Replacing the key in his jacket pocket, Hugh brightened. There was someone he could ring and the sooner he did that the better! Feeling suitably mollified, he scribbled some notes in his diary and was searching in the telephone directory for another number when Muriel Baxter called through.

'Mr Barrington, your brother-in-law's on the other line, will you take his call?'

'What? Oh, yes, all right. I was in fact just going out but . . .'

'Hugh, old chap. It's Charles. Look I need to speak to you urgently. Any chance of meeting for a spot of lunch?'

'Lunch? Well, I was just on my way out, I have something important to attend to . . .'

There was a note of urgency in Charles' voice as he broke in, 'Can't it wait, Hugh? This is very important.'

'What is?'

'Well, I'd prefer not to discuss it on the phone if you don't mind. It's a bit sensitive – you know.'

Hugh didn't know, yet supposed he ought to find out. Perhaps Charles was in financial difficulties; he had come unstuck once over the Lloyds affair after all.

'Okay, Charles. Where do you want me to meet you? At the club or . . .'

'Thornhampton Park . . . by the boating lake,' came the strained reply.

'Good God, Charles! What is all this? Have you committed a murder?'

'No. Let's just say it's to do with a miscarriage of justice.'

Puzzled, Hugh hung up the phone; his other appointment would definitely have to wait.

CHAPTER 16

With children still home for the school summer holidays, there was a hive of activity by the boating lake. It wasn't quite how Hugh remembered from last January. Then, he'd watched Sally and her nephews feed the ducks and Jack had proudly shown him the new watch, while Stanley . . .

Lost in thought, Hugh looked up to find Charles standing in front of him. He was carrying two brown paper bags and extended one in Hugh's direction.

'What's this, the evidence?' Hugh joked.

'No,' replied Charles without a glimmer of a smile. 'Lunch. It's a cheeseburger and fries, at least, I think that's what I ordered. I also got one coffee and one tea. I wasn't sure which you'd prefer.'

Hugh peered surrepticiously into a polystyrene carton and grimaced.

'It's only for effect,' Charles explained, 'just in case anyone sees us.'

'And I suppose all that's missing are the dirty old raincoats!'

Hugh studied his brother-in-law and himself. Each attired in Savile Row tailoring, they looked ridiculously out of place sitting in Thornhampton Park where half-naked children and their equally scantily-clad parents played and sunbathed.

'Look, Charles, what is this all about? I mean, we look so conspicuous here. I really can't see why we couldn't have had a proper lunch elsewhere.'

'Can't, old chap,' came the reply, 'far too risky. Vivienne's meeting Serena for lunch and as I don't know where, I thought this would be safer.'

'Would it really matter then if we bumped into our wives over lunch?'

'Yes, it would . . . especially today.'

Slightly exasperated, Hugh wrenched open the polystyrene container and took a mouthful of cheeseburger. It was quite disgusting and didn't make him feel any happier. He watched Charles chew thoughtfully on a chip.

'Well, if I can possibly tear you away from this gastronomic delight, perhaps you can tell me why I'm here. I do have a busy schedule this afternoon, Charles.' He refrained from saying he'd already had a meeting with Vivienne, not to mention the brief encounter outside the surgery with Sally.

'It's about Vivienne.'

'Why, what's she done?'

'Nothing. That's just the problem.' Charles shifted uneasily.

'Look, Charles, if this has anything to do with my idea of contacting Serena's adopted baby, you can forget all about it and tuck into your burger. Vivienne's already been to see me today. In fact, I'm now beginning to wish I'd never thought of the idea in the first place. First Serena putting me off, then Vivienne and now you!'

'I haven't exactly come to put you off, Hugh.'

'You haven't?'

'No, I've come to tell you the truth. Vivienne wanted to, but couldn't bring herself to do so because Serena made her promise.'

'Tell me *what*, Charles? You know, this is becoming more like Columbo with every minute.'

'I wish I could see the funny side of it, old chap, but I'm afraid I can't. What I have to say is no laughing matter.'

'Is Serena in trouble?' Hugh enquired, anxiously trying to remember Serena's behaviour of late. Apart from the fact they no longer shared the same bedroom, nothing else was untoward. In fact Serena seemed positively glowing with enthusiasm for their anniversary celebrations.

'No, Serena's not in trouble, Hugh, not now anyway. But she was before she met you . . . when she became pregnant.'

'But that was years ago, Charles. It didn't bother me at the time, when Serena told me she'd had the baby adopted, and it doesn't really bother me now. It was just the television programme Vivienne was watching that started me thinking about tracing James.'

'Hugh, I don't quite know how to say this . . . but there was no baby and there is no James to trace.'

'But that's preposterous! If there was no baby in the first place, why on earth would Serena pretend otherwise? I mean, why confess to your husband-to-be that another man had made you pregnant when in fact he hadn't?'

'Oh, Serena was pregnant all right, Vivienne will vouch for that.'

'Well in that case, what happened to the baby?' Hugh enquired lamely.

'First you say there was no baby and no James and in the next breath you talk about Serena being pregnant. Are you saying she lied to me?'

'Not exactly . . .'

'For Christ's sake, Charles! I think you'd better tell me once and for all. Quite frankly I'm getting tired of sitting here with a bag of plastic food on my lap trying to solve riddles! I do have a business to run, you know!'

In hushed tones Charles whispered simply, 'Serena had an abortion.'

As if waiting for further explanation, Hugh remained quiet and still. So what if Serena had had an abortion? Okay, so it was pretty commonplace today but twenty odd years ago, of course, things were different. Everything was different these days.

Today there was practically no stigma attached to being an unmarried mother. In fact, wasn't that what Sally was going to be, an unmarried mother? Strange he'd not seen it quite like that before. Hugh heard a woman's voice call to a child and half expected to see Jack running towards his aunt. But it wasn't Jack and it wasn't Sally. Slowly he turned to face Charles.

'So Serena had an abortion. Why all the pretence then? Was it just to appease her guilt at having got rid of the baby? If that's the case then no wonder she and Vivienne got so upset about me raking up the past. I shall have to try and make it up to her somehow and rest assured, Charles, I shan't mention James, fictional or otherwise, again.'

Charles shook his head sadly. 'Hugh, old chap, believe me I wish it was as simple as that but it's not. Serena's abortion – it was one of those back-street things, and it went horribly wrong. It left Serena unable to have children . . .'

Charles last words were barely audible amidst the laughter and cries of excited children and, like a film in slow motion, they moved their way in stilted fashion into Hugh's consciousness. Quite how long he sat in stony silence he couldn't remember. It was only when Charles placed a hand on his arm that he found a voice to his thoughts. His mouth was dry and his voice husky when he asked Charles to repeat what he thought he'd heard the first time.

In anguish Charles related how Serena, too frightened to tell her parents of her pregnancy, had confided in Vivienne and with the help of a 'so-called friend', had found herself in some dingy back street. When the abortion went horribly wrong and the family GP was called in, her parents had to know.

'Quite ironic when you think of it,' Charles was saying, 'because Gerald and Margot, anxious to keep things quiet had her whisked away to a private clinic immediately – but of course by then it was too late.'

'Too late?' Hugh added numbly.

'Yes, old chap.' Charles patted Hugh's shoulder. 'The doctor chappie told Margot that Serena would never be able to have any more children. In fact it was Margot's idea for Serena to tell you. She thought you might not want to marry Serena if you knew the truth and Gerald –'

'Stop!' cried Hugh, crushing the brown paper bag and its contents into a twisted mess. Angrily he got up and threw it into the nearest bin, whilst all the time Charles watched him nervously, relieved that his ordeal was over. For Hugh, however, his was just beginning.

Taking the remains of his own paper bag to the bin, Charles noticed Hugh's gaze drift from child to child, pushchair to pushchair. There was no doubt in his mind what Hugh was thinking.

'Of course you can't really blame Serena,' Charles said feebly, 'it was Margot after all who persuaded her to tell you a white lie.'

'A white lie! Christ, you call that a white lie, Charles! Well I bloody don't! The bitch! To think all these years Serena's led me to believe it's my fault – yes, *my fault*, do you hear – for not having children!'

'Hugh, old chap . . .'

'Don't *old chap* me, Charles! When I think of all the stick I took in the early days: poor Hugh Barrington, hasn't got it in him you know, can't even give the beautiful Serena a child!'

'Yes, but, Hugh, even you yourself said you didn't mind about not having children and Serena was madly in love with you . . . why she even condoned your . . .'

'Oh yes, she condoned those all right, providing I never had and I quote "unprotected sex". Too bloody right she didn't want me having unprotected sex and I can quite easily see the reason why; not forgetting the fact it eased her guilty conscience!'

'I suppose you could put it like that.'

All the time Hugh was talking, Charles was leading Hugh away from the main path, away from the crowds and out of earshot. It was probably best, he decided, to let Hugh vent his anger and hopefully lessen the verbal salvo when he returned home to Serena.

Finding himself back at the main gates and the sweet kiosk, Hugh remembered sending Jack off for his Smarties. There had been orange Smarties in the dish on Sally's coffee table. Sweets that Jack had given Sally as a peace offering for taking the condoms, sweets that Sally had jokingly popped into her mouth as . . .

'Oh God!' Charles heard Hugh moan. 'I just hope it's not too late to put things right.'

Completely on the wrong track, Charles added brightly, 'I'm sure you can, Hugh. Just think of the wonderful time we're all going to have at your anniversary.'

At that moment a black labrador puppy came bounding along the path from the park. He was heading towards the main gates and the road.

'Stop him, mister!' a voice yelled and Hugh deftly put out his foot and stood on the trailing lead.

'Cor thanks,' a breathless voice panted, taking the lead from Hugh's grasp.

Oblivious to the dusty pavement, Hugh knelt and patted the dog affectionately, whilst it wagged its tail and ignored the scoldings of his young master.

'What do you call him?' asked Hugh.

'Charlie,' came the reply, 'an' 'e is an' all, a proper Charlie.' The boy laughed and taking hold of his wayward charge, walked back through the park to join his friends.

Grateful for a diversion from their earlier conversation, Charles shook his head. 'I expect he reminds you of Stanley.'

'When he was a puppy, yes – but not when he got older.'

'I don't know,' said Charles. 'When you were in Harrogate and Serena was looking after Stanley, I remember saying to Vivienne how sprightly he seemed running about the garden.'

Dusting off the knees of his trousers, Hugh's hand hung as if suspended in mid-air. Then, avoiding Charles' gaze, he continued brushing nonchalantly. So according to Charles and Vivienne, over Easter, Stanley had been running about the garden, when in fact Serena had told him the dog could barely walk from his basket to the back door! Unaware of what he'd said, Charles waved goodbye and walked back to his office. Hugh, meanwhile, remained frozen to the spot and felt his blood run cold.

With a flourish, Roz drew back the fitting-room curtains and was surprised to find Marion Le Sage standing by a display of cotton nightdresses. She held up five fingers, indicating five minutes. Later, with yet another satisfied customer on her way, she joined Marion.

'Mrs Harrison – lovely woman, she's been coming here for years. Poor dear has a hiatus hernia so she has to find a bra that's just right.'

'And I'm trying to find a nightdress that's just right for Sally when she has the baby. I know it's not due for at least another three months but she's been a bit down lately and I wanted to buy her something to cheer her up.'

'There's nothing wrong, is there?'

'No – it's just that she's worried about the amnio-centesis test. Laura has taken her in for it today.'

'Oh God!' sighed Roz, 'I do hope everything is going to be all right. I don't suppose you're any the wiser about the father. If I knew who he was, the bastard!'

'You and Laura both. In fact I'm surprised she hasn't been in to see you. She keeps threatening to.'

'Why?'

'Something Sally said seemed to imply you knew the father.'

'You're joking!'

'No, I'm not.'

Roz curled one end of the tape measure that was hanging round her neck.

'Someone I know? Surely you don't mean Bernard?'

Marion shrugged her shoulders. 'I wouldn't know, my dear. Now what would you suggest for Sally by way of a nightdress?'

Unable to sit in his office, with the revelations of Serena and Stanley still fresh in his mind, Hugh took it in his head to patrol the entire store. Seeing Roz absentmind-edly winding and unwinding her tape measure, he was ready to pounce.

'Nothing to do, Mrs Hughes, no pricing or displays to rearrange?'

'As a matter of fact, Mr Barrington, I've just finished serving a customer – Marion Le Sage.'

'Oh, the wildflower artist. What a pity I missed her. How was she?'

'She was fine; she came in to buy Sally a nightdress for hospital.'

As calmly as he could, Hugh enquired, 'Mrs Palmer is in hospital?'

'Well, she is at the moment. Her friend Laura took her in. Poor Sally, it can't have been easy making the decision to have it done.' Roz looked at her watch. 'Anyway it should be over soon, they don't keep them in long, do they?'

Reaching for the red rose in his buttonhole, Hugh crushed it beneath his grasp. What was happening today? First Serena, then Stanley and now Sally. His whole world appeared to be crumbling apart. All he wanted to do was get in his car, go and find Sally and drive miles away where they could be alone together but Serena had arranged yet another of her pre-anniversary soirées. Still, he could make a detour and perhaps call at the flat on his way home.

Finding the flat in darkness, Hugh was filled with a deep sense of foreboding. Why wasn't Sally there? Remembering Roz's words, 'It should be over soon' he could only assume Sally's abortion, like Serena's, had also gone horribly wrong.

Tucked up in bed at her sister's, Sally contemplated the events of the past few days. She felt both physically and emotionally drained. Heaven knows, it had been bad enough having to make her mind up about the amnio-centesis test, let alone preparing herself mentally to cross the threshold of the hospital. Dr Mason's surgery had been one thing but Thornhampton Hospital was another.

Of course everyone had been kind and helpful, telling her to relax but how could she when she relived the nightmare of last night? Finishing the mug of Horlicks Jackie had insisted on making for her, Sally closed her eyes and once again saw Terry, waiting for her outside the flat.

'What is it, Terry, you look as if you've seen a ghost? It's not Julie, is it – there hasn't been an accident?'

'No, it's nothing to do with us, Sally, it's Hugh.'

'Hugh! Oh my God! Is he all right?'

'Oh, he's all right, Sally,' Terry said cynically. 'It's you I'm worried about.'

'But I don't understand. Why should you be worried about me?'

'Hugh's selling your flat, there's been an estate agent round.'

'I don't believe it,' Sally whispered incredulously. 'I mean he wouldn't, would he?'

'Fraid so. The agent knocked at ours by mistake – oh, here's his card by the way – Julie saw him first and I don't mind saying it put the wind up him. He thought it was me selling my place without telling him!'

In stunned silence, Sally hung onto the stair rail in utter disbelief.

'Careful,' Terry said in an attempt to steady her, 'we don't want you falling down the stairs, especially not in your condition.'

'My condition,' whispered Sally to herself now, hearing her sister lock the front door for the night and climb the stairs. It would probably have been better, in her condition, if she *had* fallen down the stairs. That way all her problems would be solved.

'Sally, are you asleep? Mind if I come in then?'

Sally made room for her sister to sit on the single bed, fitted with its Thomas the Tank Engine duvet and pillow case. It being Jack's favourite, it seemed only fitting that Auntie Sally should have it.

'How are you feeling, no aches or pains?'

'No, just tired, that's all, and looking forward to a decent night's sleep.'

'I don't suppose you got much last night, what with worrying about the test.'

And other things, like being forced to leave your flat, thought Sally to herself.

'Still,' Jackie continued, 'at least it's all over and I'm sure the results will be okay.'

'I hope so,' Sally whispered, clutching her hand on her tummy, 'I sincerely hope so, Jackie.'

'Well, you get a good night's sleep and tomorrow night when Dave comes back from his course I'll get him to drop round the bassinet and baby bath. I know it's still early days but you might as well try and sort a few bits and pieces out for the baby now, while you've still got the energy.'

'And I've still got a roof over my head,' Sally sighed as her sister left the room.

Hugh, she decided, had obviously intended to make things as difficult as he could. When she'd rung the estate agents to negotiate buying the flat for herself, she'd been told there was a couple already interested.

'But there can't be! Surely I should be allowed first refusal?'

'Sorry madam, Mr Barrington said nothing about offering you the flat; in fact, I quite distinctly remember him saying you wouldn't be interested!'

Crying silent tears, Sally felt Thomas smiling face become quite damp.

When Dave finished carrying the last of the baby items into the flat, Sally stared in amazement. 'I thought Jackie was only sending round a few bits and pieces, like the bassinet and the baby bath?'

Dave grinned cheekily. 'This *is* only a few bits and pieces. You wait, Sally, you're going to need a lot more than this, believe me! Mind you, I don't know where you're even going to put this lot. You've only got the one bedroom here, haven't you?'

Sally nodded and moved the bassinet away from the front door so Dave could leave and get back to her sister.

'Well, perhaps later you could look for somewhere else.'

'Looks like I'm going to have to,' Sally added cryptically.

Standing at the top of the stairs, Dave called back, 'What about those new places they're building round the corner, they look nice?'

'They are – very – but so is the price and they're way out of my league. Still, never mind, I'm sure I'll find something.'

When the bell rang, Sally assumed it was Dave having found yet more baby requisites in his car. Wedged behind the baby bath and the bassinet, she called out. 'The door's still open, come in, Dave.'

'As I'm not Dave, I don't know if I'm welcome,' a familiar voice murmured.

Sally looked up to find Hugh standing at the open doorway. He looked dreadful, almost as if like her, he hadn't slept for days.

'Sally, I need to speak to you,' he begged, 'so please don't tell me to leave.'

Her first feelings of compassion gave way to bitterness at the memory of her conversation with the estate agent.

'I suppose you'd better come in,' she snapped icily, 'just be careful you don't trip over the baby things, I don't want you suing me for broken limbs as well as evicting me.'

'What on earth do you mean?'

'Oh, please don't play the innocent, Hugh, as if you don't know what I'm talking about. I don't know how you could be so cruel. It's quite obvious why you're here and rest assured the estate agent has done your dirty work for you. I just think it's pretty despicable that you didn't have the guts to tell me yourself that you wanted me out of the flat!'

'But I don't want you out of the flat . . . well, not exactly.'

'And what's that supposed to mean?'

Struggling to reach her, Hugh caught his shin on the baby bath. Sending it skimming across the carpet he reached for her hand. 'Sally, please! Before you say anything else will you please answer me one question. Have you had an abortion?'

She looked coldly into his pleading eyes. 'No! I leave the killing of innocent creatures – like your dog – to Serena! And if you've come here to offer to pay for one, I've already told you, I want nothing from you, Hugh, absolutely *nothing*!'

Stunned, Hugh sank to the settee, still clinging grimly to her hand.

'Thank God!' he whispered, 'Oh, thank God!'

Feeling herself dragged to the settee by his side, Sally found herself thinking, Thank God for what? The fact that she hadn't had an abortion or the fact that she didn't want anything from him?

Hugh turned to face her. 'If you think I'm going to say your comment about Serena was uncalled for, then you're very much mistaken. It's Serena who has behaved badly and Serena who has been cruel. Sally, whatever else happens, promise me you'll have our baby . . .'

Sally's eyes filled with tears. 'But you said it's not your baby and you want me to leave the flat, when Terry and Julie have been so good to me . . . they want to look after me and . . .'

'Sally, *I* want to look after you! You and the baby – now please will you stop crying and listen to me.'

She allowed herself to be taken into his arms and through her sobs he heard her murmuring, 'I don't understand, I just don't understand.'

'Neither did I until yesterday and there's so much to tell you.' Reaching into his pocket, Hugh pulled out the now familiar white cotton monogrammed handkerchief. Passing it to her, he whispered softly, 'I seem to remember doing this somewhere before.'

Struggling to stretch his legs to the side of the bassinet, Hugh stood up and rubbed his shin. 'I think we could do with some fresh air; go and get your raincoat. It had stopped raining when I came in, but just in case it starts again . . .'

Slipping on her raincoat, Sally's eyes welled with tears once more. 'It doesn't do up,' she cried. 'Nothing fits me anymore. I'm getting fat.'

'Nonsense, of course you're not getting fat, you're just growing in all the right places and you look positively lovely.' Hugh tilted her chin upwards, wiped the tears from her eyes and kissed her full on the mouth.

'Forget about the buttons, we're not going far. Trust me – please.'

In a matter of moments after leaving the flat, she was surprised when he pulled onto a grass verge.

'But why have we stopped here, it's just a –?'

'Patience,' he urged, 'now just wait there for me to come and open the door, I don't want you tripping over. It's pretty dangerous out there.'

Gingerly she allowed herself to be helped from the car and led across shingle, planks, piles of bricks and scaffolding.

'Just make sure you keep hold of my hand, by day this is a hard hat area.'

'And by night,' she whispered, 'what then?'

'Ah,' he laughed softly, 'hopefully by night it becomes the answer to a maiden's prayer.'

'You're forgetting I'm no maiden!'

'Let's say you're the answer to my prayers then, now close your eyes.'

Sally felt Hugh's hands firmly on her shoulders as he turned her in the opposite direction. 'Okay you can open them now.'

'But I still don't know why you've brought me to a building site.'

'No, of course you wouldn't,' he said kindly. 'I suppose everything must seem confusing at the moment, so let me explain.' Pointing to the far corner of

259

the building site Hugh announced, '*That*, Sally, is why I want you to leave the flat. It might not look like much at the moment but that pile of bricks and scaffolding is to be your new home. A proper home for our baby, not a tiny one-bedroomed flat where you wouldn't be able to move.'

In the beam of security lighting from the site office, Sally studied Hugh's face critically. 'Why,' she whispered, 'why, after all this time, are you prepared to accept Stanley is yours?'

Hugh laughed ruefully. 'It's a very long story and one which I'd prefer to forget but I'll tell you on the way home. I only hope you can find it in your heart to forgive me.'

'I'll try,' she sighed, as their two silhouettes joined together as one.

Hearing footsteps on the stairs, Terry popped his head round the door of his flat. Seeing Sally and Hugh together he looked anxious.

'You okay, Sally?'

'Yes, I'm fine thanks, Terry, there's nothing to worry about.'

'Well, if you're sure?' He glared angrily at Hugh. 'Just call if you need me.'

'Gracious!' muttered Hugh, 'what's got into Terry?'

'He thinks you're a complete and utter bastard!'

'Along with everybody else, I suppose. No wonder my ears have been burning. I suppose I deserve it.'

'Mmmn,' Sally sighed, leaning against him. 'Roz, Laura and Marion are all of the same opinion. In fact if they were Macbeth's witches, you would have been turned into a toad weeks ago.'

'And they still don't know I'm the father?'

Sally shook her head.

'They'll have to know sometime I suppose – but for the moment if you could prevent me being turned into a toad or a frog for a little bit longer, I'd appreciate it.'

'I suppose a frog would be better really . . .'

Hugh looked perplexed.

'If you were a frog,' she enlightened him, 'then if I chose to let you sleep on my pillow and I kissed you . . . who knows, you might even turn into a prince!'

'That's highly unlikely!'

'What is?'

'Letting me sleep on your pillow after the appalling way I've behaved.'

'Oh, I don't know,' she teased, 'we'll have to wait and see – but not tonight as I'm tired and I've had enough excitement for one day. Besides you look all in too.'

'Sally, if only you knew. These past weeks I feel as if I've been to hell and back on a daily basis. In fact, I think you and I need some time away together. Give me a few days and I'll see what I can arrange.'

CHAPTER 17

Trying to prepare her shopping list, Sally found her thoughts drawn constantly to Hugh's revelations about Serena's abortion, her consequent lies and Stanley's untimely death. How anyone could be so cruel and deceitful was quite beyond her. No wonder Hugh had looked so dreadful. And how to deal with it too – that wasn't going to be easy. For the moment, Hugh told her, he had no intentions of raising the matter with Serena as now wasn't the right time. But when it was – what then? What exactly would Hugh say and how would Serena react?

Sally shrugged her shoulders and returned to her shopping list; she had more important things to think about. After weeks of planning, Hugh had decided they should go away for a long weekend. The Cotswolds, he suggested, not too far to drive and there was this wonderful cottage he'd heard about from a friend. It would mean self-catering but with plenty of eating places in the vicinity that shouldn't be a problem. If Sally could just shop for the basics for breakfast, she could leave everything else to him. They would get up when they liked, eat when they liked and above all, she was to rest, Hugh had insisted.

Standing by the delicatessen in Sainsbury's, Sally recognized a familiar figure. Richard! Quickly she turned her back, chose her selection of cheeses, paté and cooked meats and moved away to the bread counter. There, poised with tongs in her hands, ready to grip the first of the croissants, she felt a tap on her shoulder.

'Sally, it *is* you! I wasn't sure at first. How are you?'

'I'm very well, as you can see, Richard.'

Richard's eyes moved swiftly down from Sally's face to the now prominent curve of her stomach and registered complete and utter shock.

'You mean you're pregnant but . . .'

Unsure as to whether he was going to say 'but *how*' or 'but *who*', Sally said simply, 'I suppose it must be catching. How are Sharon and the children? She had a little boy I understand.'

Richard nodded numbly, still unable to believe his eyes.

'Yes – Damon,' he muttered. 'He's three months now and thank God is sleeping better than Jade did at that age.'

'And you're doing the shopping, I see,' Sally said, looking down at Richard's trolley, heavily laden with junk food.

'Yes, Sharon gets tired so she gives me a list.' He gestured to the list written in childish script on the page torn from an exercise book.

Sally's initial reaction had been to say something sarcastic but seeing Richard, who looked ridiculous in his jeans, T-shirt and a bomber jacket that was more suited to a man half his age, just smiled. Richard, she noticed, even had a chain round his neck; all that was missing was the lead!

Returning to the croissants Sally was surprised when he said, 'Perhaps I could call round and see you sometime. You're out at Elmsmarsh now, aren't you?'

'I don't think that would be a good idea, do you, Richard? Besides, I shall be moving again soon and I'm also going away for a few days.'

Richard's face dropped as he watched her knot the bag of croissants and turn away from him to continue down the aisle.

Humming to herself Sally swung her trolley into the carpark and narrowly missed hitting another shopper.

'Oh, I'm terribly sorry, I didn't see you. I was miles away.'

'Sally . . . Sally Palmer? I hardly recognized you. You look sort of different.'

'Hello, Bernard,' she beamed, 'that's probably because I'm going to have a baby. I thought Roz would have told you.'

'No . . . no,' came the stunned reply. 'I haven't seen Roz and Donald in ages. I was going to suggest going to another concert but I see you are . . .' Bernard nodded to Sally's hand. She had started wearing a plain gold wedding band. At least people would think she was married.

'Oh that! Yes,' she lied, crossing her fingers as she did so, just as she had when she was a child. Somehow she just couldn't bring herself to tell Bernard she was to be an unmarried mother.

'Perhaps I can help you with your shopping?'

'That would be very kind of you, Bernard, I'm parked just over there.'

With Bernard helping Sally load the carrier bags into the boot of her car, neither of them noticed Roz and Donald arriving for their Friday-night shopping.

'Donald, stop the car!'

'But, Roz, I can't, not here, I've already got some impatient idiot on my bumper. What's the panic anyway?'

'I don't believe it. I've just been Bernard loading shopping into Sally's car. Oh my God! You don't think – if he is I couldn't bear it!'

Finishing off her packing, Sally heard the frantic ringing of her doorbell. She looked at her watch; it was too early for Hugh.

'Roz, what on earth? You look as if you've seen a ghost.'

'I suppose you could almost call it that,' Roz panted. 'Goodness, I didn't realize how unfit I was, until I ran up those stairs.'

'What's the rush – why run up the stairs? The place isn't on fire is it?' Sally joked.

'Well, I'm pleased to see you in such good spirits. You look positively blooming, pregnancy is obviously suiting you.'

'Mmmn, I really think it is and –'

'Sally,' Roz interrupted, 'you can call me a nosy old cow if you like but can I ask you something?'

'It depends what it is.'

'We, Donald and I, saw you in Sainsbury's carpark. Bernard was helping you put shopping in the boot.' Roz pushed anxiously at her glasses, until they were practically embedded into her forehead. 'Oh blast! How am I going to put this? I mean, is Bernard the father of your baby and if he is, is he going to marry you?'

Sally shook her head. 'The answer to both questions, Roz, is no. Bernard is not the father and as for marriage that's out of the question too. You see the baby's father is already married.'

Without further ado, Roz's eyes filled with tears as she flung her arms round Sally's shoulders.

'Thank God for that,' she sighed, 'for one bloody awful moment I thought it was Bernard. You know I said to Donald . . . Hey, why are you laughing, what's so funny?'

'You are,' said Sally hugging her friend. 'If only you could see the look on your face. By the way, where is Donald?'

'Downstairs in the car I hope. Although he threatened to drive away and leave me stranded.'

'Why?'

'He said I had no right to ask you such an impertinent question and that it was none of my business. I suppose he's right really but when I saw you with Bernard, I just sort of flipped.'

'Well, flip no more, Roz, and rest assured, like I said, Bernard is not the father. In time no doubt you'll get to meet him but for the moment we have to be discreet, until the situation is resolved.'

'I suppose by that you mean his wife? Does she know about you and the baby?'

'I sincerely hope not. In fact he and I are supposed to be going away for the weekend, otherwise I would invite you and Donald to stay for supper.'

266

'Oh, really? Somewhere nice? What time are you leaving?'

Sally smiled, 'Oh, no you don't! You're not going to catch me out like that and just to be on the safe side, I shall come down to the car with you to make sure Donald takes you home!'

Waving goodbye to Sally, Roz turned to her husband. 'We could always drive round the block for five minutes, then come back, just in case her mystery man turns up.'

'We could quite easily,' announced Donald, 'but we won't. It wouldn't be fair. As Sally said, you'll find out soon enough. So, Roz, my dear, in the meantime you will just have to exercise a little patience.'

'Goodness, I thought they were never going to go!' Hugh gasped when she opened the door to his knock.

'Who?'

'Roz and Donald.'

Sally gasped. 'You mean you saw them! Did they see you?'

'No, luckily I parked round the back, as I thought it would be easier to load up the car. Then I just hid in the shadows until you called goodbye and I heard them drive off.'

'We'd better get a move on then; you take the food, I'll get my bag.'

'No, I'll take the food and your bag, the only thing I want you carrying is our baby.'

Sally gestured to the carrier bags. 'I got you some paté, stilton and *dolcelate* for your supper. There's a nice baguette too.'

'My supper! And what about you, what are you going to eat?'

'Oh, I'll probably have a bowl of cornflakes and a glass of milk.'

Hugh raised a quizzical eyebrow. 'Cornflakes!'

'Well, according to the midwife, I shouldn't eat soft cheeses and paté, it's not good for baby Stanley.'

Sally watched Hugh cut another wedge of stilton. 'You'll have nightmares,' she joked, 'or else you won't be able to sleep at all.'

'Who says I want to sleep?' Hugh said, reaching for her hand. 'Tell me, Sally, if the midwife says paté and soft cheeses are bad for the baby, did she tell you what's good for the mother-to-be?'

'She didn't have to, I already know.'

'Really . . . and what's that?'

'You are,' she sighed.

'In that case, shall we go to bed?'

Waiting for Hugh in bed, Sally studied the wallpaper and matching curtains. Everywhere was a profusion of roses, it was like being in a rose arbour.

'Have you any idea how old this place is?' she enquired.

'Parts of it date back to the sixteenth century, I've been told, and looking at the angles of some of the walls and doors, I would say that's probably about right. Even the bed looks ancient. Are you sure you're going to be comfortable?'

Sally stretched out fully in the bed until her feet almost reached the foot of the iron bedstead. 'Wonderfully comfortable. Do you know, I think it must be a feather mattress. I haven't slept in a feather bed since I was a child. Jackie and I shared one once, when we stayed with some friends in Norfolk.'

'And was that comfortable?'

She nodded. 'Mmmn, but for some reason I always ended up near the foot of the bed by morning.'

'If we're not careful then we shall probably end up on the opposite wall. Have you noticed how the floor slopes down?'

'That's what gives it so much character. I think it's perfect. It's a real chocolate-box cottage, isn't it? Roses round the door, log fires, herbaceous borders, a wonderful compost heap and space for an autumn bonfire.'

Hugh frowned. 'And there was me thinking the new house at Elmsmarsh was just what you'd prefer. Central heating, modern plumbing and en suite facilities. Perhaps I should have found you somewhere with a tin bath and a chemical loo!'

'Ah,' she sighed as he slipped into bed beside her. 'You're forgetting, there's romantic and there's practical. This is romantic but Elmsmarsh is practical and ideal for baby Stanley.'

'And how is baby Stanley?'

Sally reached for Hugh's hand and laid it gently across her stomach, where a tiny heel wriggled in her abdomen. 'Very active, as you can feel.'

Hugh swallowed hard. 'You know, I still can't quite believe it. To me it's like a miracle. To think after all those years of believing . . .'

Watching the familiar shuttered look creep across his face, she murmured, 'Sshh, that was then and this is now.'

269

'And you're sure it's all right . . . to make love, I mean?'

'Positive, the midwife said so and it says in all the books. In fact one woman at the clinic said her sex drive had increased so much it was a real case of Saturday night and Sunday morning and her husband was walking about with a grin on his face, just like the Cheshire cat!'

'I expect her husband was a lot younger than me,' Hugh added thoughtfully. 'You forget I'm getting on, I am after all forty-six.'

'Rubbish! You know for a fact you don't look it; you're also a lot fitter than most men half your age.'

Hugh stroked Sally's hair and looked earnestly into her eyes. 'And you've no regrets?' he whispered.

'None,' she murmured, turning on her side, 'and as for worrying about Saturday night and Sunday morning, let's deal with Friday night first, shall we?'

Hugh laughed and she felt his warm breath on the nape of her neck.

Driving back to Thornhampton through the magnificent Cotswold autumn, Sally reached into her handbag for her diary.

'Everything okay?' Hugh asked.

'Yes, I was just checking a few dates and counting how many weeks to Christmas.'

'As you've probably gathered, it's been Christmas at Barrington's virtually since the children went back to school in September.'

'I think it's all wrong. Did people really want to buy Christmas things in September?'

'According to our sales figures they did and speaking of buying things and at the risk of offending your sister, would you mind sending those baby items back?'

'But why? I know they're not exactly new . . .'

'That's exactly why, Sally. I would prefer baby Stanley to begin life with a new bassinet and bath. We have some super babyware products at the store, you know.'

'I know,' she sighed dreamily, 'Marion and I have positively drooled over them on many occasions; she even offered to buy a bassinet but I told her I'd already got Jackie's.'

'Send Jackie's back and get a new one.'

'But . . .'

'No buts about it. Pop into the store one day, make a list of what you need and let me have it.'

Sally slanted an anxious sideways look at him. 'I couldn't do that.'

'You can and you will,' Hugh replied, gently but firmly. 'This is my responsibility too you know. Make a note in your diary now.'

Pencilling in Hugh's instructions, she sighed wistfully. 'Do you realize, a year ago I was looking after Stanley for you, when you and Serena went to Devon. By the way, you never did say where Serena was going this weekend.'

Hugh gave a wry laugh. 'Oh, she's gone to London with Vivienne, to buy an outfit for our anniversary.'

'What's wrong with Barrington's?'

'You're joking! I expect it will be a designer outfit. I understand she's looking for something in black velvet.'

'That sounds very glamorous and I'm sure she'll look lovely,' Sally said, conjuring up a mental picture of Serena's elegant body caressed by black velvet.

Hugh pulled off the main road into a side street.

'Why have we stopped?'

'Because I just wanted to kiss you.'

'But, Hugh! People are looking, that woman in the florists' window, she's staring at us!'

'Let her! She doesn't know who we are.' Hugh turned to the woman who was placing buckets of roses in the window and smiled. Then he got out of the car.

'But where are you going?'

'To get you some roses, what colour do you want – red?'

'No!' Sally announced adamantly. 'Definitely not red!'

Puzzled Hugh got back into the car. 'Why not red?'

Sally shifted uneasily. 'I think red roses should only be bought for wives and fiancées. I mean, when people have really made commitments to each other. I'm sorry – you probably think I'm silly.'

'No, not at all. I think you're lovely. I mean who else would still find it in their hearts to say something complimentary about Serena, especially after that incident with the box of clotted cream fudge.'

'Heavens! You've got a good memory. Fancy you remembering that.'

'How could I forget . . . that's when I fell in love with you, Sally. The same afternoon I came through your back door to find you and Stanley asleep.' Taking her hand and holding it to his lips, Hugh said huskily, 'Black velvet may be glamorous, but believe me, you can look just as lovely in jeans and sweatshirt.'

'What about maternity dresses?'

'Those too,' he called as he walked to the door of the florists'.

Sally watched as the assistant went to the window and removed the entire bucket of white roses.

'Hugh, you must be mad!' she laughed when he returned. 'Where on earth am I going to put them all?'

'How about in your bedroom, then you'll think you're back at the cottage? Anyway, don't they say white roses for peace.'

'But we haven't had a row, or is this just in case we do?'

'No,' he smiled, 'it's just to reiterate how much I care and to remind you how bad I feel about not believing you when . . .'

Sally placed her finger to his lips. 'Sshh,' she whispered, 'remember what I said? That was then and this is now.' Ignoring the cheerful, bemused face of the florist, Sally took Hugh in her arms.

Four weeks later at breakfast, Serena asked casually, 'Hugh, have you been into Elmsmarsh recently?'

Masking his shock behind the morning paper, Hugh merely grunted. 'Not recently, why do you ask?'

'Mrs Burt tells me there's a super fruit and veg. shop there and they also do amazing floral displays. I thought perhaps I might use them for some of the anniversary flowers.'

Breathing an enormous sigh of relief, Hugh turned yet another unread page of his newspaper. 'I suppose you could always give them a ring first, if you didn't want to drive out that far.'

'Yes, I probably will. I'll get Mrs Burt to remind me of the name. I'm sure she said it was something like Pots and Pansies.'

'Never heard of it,' Hugh lied, reaching in his pocket to make sure he still had the list of baby items Sally had reluctantly compiled.

'By the way, Serena, don't make any plans for this weekend if you don't mind. I said I'd call in on Uncle Bertram. I take it, as usual, you won't want to come along?'

'Definitely not, Hugh, I shall be far too busy!'

In the baby department at Barrington's, Hugh handed Sally's list, now written in his own hand, to the departmental manageress, Mrs Murray.

'For a family friend,' Hugh explained. 'The baby's not due until January so I'll take some of the things for her before Christmas and I understand we keep things like the pram until after the delivery.'

Mrs Murray nodded and studied the list. 'Always a wise precaution, Mr Barrington . . . just in case.'

Hugh bit his lip; he knew what the 'just in case' implied and prayed with all his heart it wouldn't be used in relation to Sally and baby Stanley. Baby Stanley, he mused; was he really going to become a father in little more than eight weeks? Certainly Sally was blooming more each and every time he saw her. With the earlier anxiety of the amniocentesis test now behind her, she seemed perfectly content.

It was Hugh however, who had the problems. It wasn't easy keeping quiet about impending fatherhood and apart from Sally, he could only mention the baby to Julie and Terry. Although, even with them, there had been some earlier embarrassing silences. The situation having improved only when Hugh managed to convince Terry and Julie that his intentions were honourable – or as honourable as they could be in the circumstances – where Sally and the baby were concerned.

In the end as proof of their forgiveness, Julie had handed Hugh a 'Pots and Posies' business card, with the message scribbled on the back: 'Hugh, don't forget to ring if you need me, Julie.'

'It's in case you're ever worried about Sally,' Julie had said, running his fingers through his blonde curls. 'Only I'm at the flat more than Terry and I can always pop in and keep an eye on her, day or night.'

With Christmas looming, Hugh realized he may well have need of Terry and Julie. This Christmas it wouldn't be quite so easy to disappear with no dog to take for a walk, and Serena had already promised Vivienne and Charles that they would spend the time with them.

Sally stood nervously at Hugh's side as he pulled the brass handle by Uncle Bertram's front door. In the far distance she heard a series of bells jangling.

'It will take him quite a while to answer it,' Hugh explained. 'He always gets rid of Mrs Bailey if he knows I'm coming round.'

'Who's Mrs Bailey?' Sally whispered.

'The housekeeper – and there's no need to whisper, he won't bite you, you know.'

'I'm not so sure, from all the horrendous tales you've told me about him. I mean Serena never comes, does she?'

'No, but that's quite simply because they loathe each other. Something tells me however that you'll both get on like a house on fire.'

Sally reached for Hugh's hand and clung on grimly as she heard the sound of footsteps echoing down the long corridor.

'Oh, by the way,' Hugh said, 'just in case you're interested, the place used to be an old rectory.'

'Hugh, my boy! Why didn't you use your key? You might just as well, you know; after all this place will be yours as soon as I've departed this mortal coil.'

'Which won't be for a long while yet, Bertram, so in the meantime can I introduce you to Sally Palmer?'

'You can indeed,' said the old man, welcoming them in, 'but we'll have our introductions inside in the warm, if you don't mind. This special lady of yours should not be left standing on the doorstep.'

Sally looked up into kindly brown eyes, surrounded by a halo of frothy white hair. To her surprise she was no longer terrified and found herself being led into a flagstone porch and through to a large reception hall. She gazed about her in wonderment at the curved staircase and family portraits. Bertram followed her gaze.

'Well, what do you think of us, Sally, we're a rum lot, aren't we?'

'That's not really a fair question to ask, Uncle, considering I'm the only Barrington Sally knows.'

'And from her condition, Hugh, I would say she knows you pretty well!'

Aware of Sally's flustered appearance at his outspoken comment, Bertram held out his arm. 'You must forgive me, Sally, I've never been known for my tact and I suppose I'm too old to change now. If you'll just take my arm, my dear, we'll go through to the drawing room.'

Turning briefly to look at Hugh, who only nodded for her to go ahead, Sally was escorted to a comfortable settee, in an equally comfortable room. Motioning Hugh to sit by Sally's side, Bertram returned to his own upright armchair by the fire.

'Now, let me look at you both,' he announced, peering at them through rheumy eyes, as if he was studying a pair of teenagers. 'Yes, just as I thought,' he said, gleefully banging the arm of his chair, 'quite charming and a perfect match.'

Smiling, Hugh reached for Sally's hand. 'Well, Bertram, I'm glad you approve and before you ask, I can assure you the baby is mine.'

'Didn't doubt that for a minute, my boy!'

'You didn't?'

'Course not! All that earlier cock and bull stuff about you not being able to do the necessary in the man's department, didn't believe that for one minute!'

'But you never said . . .'

'None of my business, Hugh, to interfere in other people's marriages, even though I was pretty damned certain; just hoped and prayed – yes, even your wicked Uncle Bertram has been known to pray – that one day you'd find out for yourself. So tell me, when's Baby Barrington due?'

'January tenth,' Sally announced shyly.

'Is it, by jove! Well, I shall just have to get them to pump me full of pills and potions to keep me going until then. Just think, the next generation of Barringtons, what a delightful prospect.'

Warmed by his uncle's response, Hugh turned to the neatly laid teatray of Mrs Bailey's homemade scones and Victoria sandwich.

'Shall I put the kettle on, Uncle?'

Bertram was staring thoughtfully at Sally. 'What? Oh yes, Hugh, if you will, my boy.'

'Would you like me to make it?' Sally enquired. 'If Hugh can show me where the kitchen is . . . perhaps you'd like to talk . . .'

'Good Lord no!' Bertram's voice boomed. 'I've spent years talking to Hugh; now that he's brought a decent young woman to meet me – and a pretty one at that – I'd far rather talk to you. Perhaps I could even show you the garden. That is if you're interested.'

'I'd like that very much but first you must get your coat. It's getting quite damp out there.'

Returning with his coat, Bertram led Sally through the casement doors.

CHAPTER 18

While Sally and Bertram took a tranquil stroll around the garden, elsewhere Serena's mood was anything but tranquil. Angrily she kicked at her wheel with the toe of her Gucci loafer. It had no effect whatsoever on the flat tyre and did nothing to improve her temper. In disgust she slammed the garage door, breaking a finger nail as she did so, and stormed into the house. There was only one thing for it, she would have to take the Range Rover. The problem however, was where Hugh had left the keys.

With no one in the house to respond to her vocal outburst as she banged and slammed endless drawers and doors, Serena retired to the kitchen defeated and made herself a coffee.

'I suppose I could always ring Hugh at Bertram's,' she sighed, watching a swirl of cream whirlpool its way from the dainty porcelain jug into the strong, tar-black coffee. 'Only, I don't want to speak to that odious old man!'

Stirring her coffee, Serena tried to remember what jacket Hugh was wearing; the night before last when he'd gone out in the Range Rover and so she assumed the keys must be in the pockets of his Ralph Lauren tweed. Brightening, she ran upstairs to find it, checking the hall clock on the way.

The once familiar guest room now had Hugh's stamp all over it. Serena ran her fingers over citrus-smelling bottles that had once stood alongside those of her own heavily scented ones and sighed. Why hadn't Hugh returned to their bedroom? After all, it had been simply ages since they'd last . . .

Walking to the wardrobe door, Serena told herself the situation couldn't possibly last; Hugh was bound to come round sooner or later. It hadn't bothered her too much at first; she still had the memories from her wonderful skiing holiday and later there had been two heavenly weekends spent with Carlo.

Recently, however, Carlo was beginning to bore her; he wasn't the fun he used to be. He'd also been extremely rude, telling her she talked about nothing but her anniversary preparations, and he found that dull.

'Oh well, perhaps he's right,' she whispered, putting her hand in Hugh's jacket pocket. 'I don't suppose it was very tactful of me to discuss my . . .'

In stunned silence Serena withdrew her hand from the pocket of the Ralph Lauren. It contained not the Range Rover keys but the card from Pots and Posies at Elmsmarsh.

'But you told me you'd never heard of it, so why lie?' Turning over the card, Serena gasped when she read Julie's written message.

'Hugh please ring me if you need me – Julie.'

'So that's it, is it!' Serena said angrily, confronting one of Hugh's golfing photos. 'That's why you've decided to stay away from me – because of this Julie. Really, Hugh, I thought you'd better taste than to take up with a common greengrocer's assistant!'

Flicking the card against the jagged edge of her broken fingernail, Serena walked towards Hugh's bedside phone and dialled.

'Pots and Posies, can I help you?'

'I'd like to speak to Julie please.'

'Sorry, luv,' came the male voice, 'Julie's away for the weekend.'

Slowly Serena replaced the receiver and looked about Hugh's bedroom. Who was this Julie? Had he any photos of her and was there any other evidence lying hidden? Glaring distractedly at the inscription on the card, Serena struggled for comprehension. In all their previous 'little arrangements', she'd never once wanted to know about the other woman in Hugh's life, but this was different. In fact, looking back, Hugh was different and had been ever since . . . Stanley.

So she'd stepped way out of line over Stanley. She realized that now. On the other hand, however, who would have thought Hugh would still be sulking about it? Or *was* he still sulking about it? Perhaps that was all a front to disguise his relationship with this Julie, this trollop who served cabbage and onions to the people of Elmsmarsh. In her mind's eye, Serena pictured a woman with henna-coloured hair, heavily pencilled eyebrows and dirty fingernails, like the woman on the corner stall of Thornhampton Market.

Bracing herself, Serena did what she'd never done before and opened each and every one of Hugh's drawers. From there she moved to the wardrobe,

281

searching and reaching into every jacket and trouser pocket. Each time she drew a blank. Dejected, she was on the point of giving up her quest when she remembered the brass casket Hugh had been given years ago by Uncle Bertram.

Encrusted with semi-precious stones, it was a pretty garish object bought in some far-flung place known only to Bertram and his cronies. Not wanting to offend his uncle, Hugh had announced he'd use it for cufflinks and the like. Now with her heart pounding, Serena wasn't interested in cufflinks but she was interested in finding 'the like'!

Paying scant regard to the mess she was making, Serena returned to Hugh's wardrobe and rummaged on the top shelf until she found the box. Then with trembling fingers she lifted the lid and peered inside. At first it all appeared pretty ordinary with various boxes containing Hugh's selection of gold and platinum cufflinks and for some reason one of his white monogrammed handkerchiefs.

Replacing the handkerchief, she suddenly remembered the hidden compartment in the lid and pressing down on the tiger's eye stone, dislodged the thin cedar wood lining.

'Got you!' she cried. 'Now what have we here?'

Serena's earlier elation gave way to disappointment as she unwrapped the layers of tissue on what she assumed was going to be a photo of Julie. Instead she found herself staring at a miniature of Stanley. A miniature with *Le Sage* painted in small letters on the bottom right-hand curve.

'Infernal animal!' screamed Serena. 'This is all your bloody fault! Why couldn't you just have died years ago like most dogs, instead of hanging on. And as for being good, I don't know what was so good about being an incontinent dog – goodness knows why Hugh wanted that inscription written in French!'

Returning the miniature to its hidden compartment, Serena placed the box back on the shelf and closed the wardrobe door. It was much too late to go into Thornhampton now and the table napkins and candles she was looking for, to match the colours she'd chosen for their anniversary, seemed almost irrelevant. At six thirty on a dreary Saturday afternoon all that seemed relevant was Julie, from Pots and Posies.

Back in the kitchen, confronted by a cold cup of coffee, Serena shuddered and threw the contents into the sink with the force of a fast bowler.

'Damn!' she cried, watching dark splash marks seeping across her beige cashmere sweater. Angrily she jerked at the kettle, then, stopping midway between plug and tap, she muttered bitterly, 'I don't need a coffee, I need a drink and a cigarette!'

Hugh, she knew, frowned on people who smoked but Serena always kept some hidden for friends who did. In desperation she pulled out the tin that had once held Fortnum and Mason's Assam tea and lit a menthol cigarette with trembling fingers.

With a whisky in one hand and a cigarette in the other Serena paced the sitting-room floor, with the name Julie ringing over and over in her head. Why was Julie away, she wondered. In fact, where had she gone? Was she perhaps with Hugh? Had they gone away together? No, she decided they couldn't have done. Hugh had said he was going to his uncle's.

At that moment, Serena decided there was only one solution; odious or not, she must ring Bertram! Unceremoniously dumping her tumbler on the sideboard, she sent a jet of whisky swishing across the silver tray and dialled the old man's number. For a while there was just the endless ringing, while Serena chewed anxiously at her jagged nail.

'Come on, you stupid old man. Answer the bloody phone, won't you! Oh!'

'Hello, who is that?'

'Hello. Uncle Bertram, it's Serena, how are you?'

Serena heard a faint wheezing down the line and waited impatiently for the old man to reply. 'Oh, Serena, this is a surprise and it's kind of you to ask but . . .'

Not waiting for him to finish, Serena broke in impatiently. 'Look, I'm sorry to bother you but I've had a spot of bother with my car. I wondered if I could speak to Hugh.'

In all honesty Bertram replied, 'I'm very sorry, Serena, but Hugh's not here.'

'Are you sure? But he said he was coming to see you . . .'

'He did – but he's not here now.'

There was a lame, 'Oh!' and for one awful moment she thought Bertram was about to hang up the phone. Then with a shrill voice, full of uncertainty, she found herself asking, 'Uncle Bertram, was Hugh alone when he came to see you?'

'Er no,' began Bertram, 'he . . .'

'There's no need to continue!' she snapped and hung up the phone, leaving Bertram to study with quiet satisfaction the portrait of his own father gazing down at him from a lofty height.

'Well, father,' he chuckled, 'you always said I was a no-good scoundrel but even you would have to admit that that little episode might mean Serena's on her way out and if I've helped in the slightest bit, then I'm absolutely delighted.'

Bertram was still chuckling to himself when Hugh and Sally returned with steaming bags from the Chinese take-away.

'You look jolly pleased with yourself,' Hugh said, placing the foil containers on the ancient stripped pine table, 'what have you done, won the lottery?'

'No, better than that, I've just spoken to Serena.'

'You've done what!'

For a few anxious moments Hugh and Sally listened, while Bertram recounted the brief phonecall from Serena.

'First she asked if you were here, then when I said you weren't, she asked if you'd come alone . . . and I told her no.'

'Oh, Bertram, I wish you hadn't,' said Hugh, watching Sally slump onto a chair, her face full of anguish.

'Look, my boy, I only told her you weren't alone and if you want my opinion – although by the look on your face – you probably don't, Serena suspects something. I mean why else would she ring? Think, Hugh, Serena never rings here, she loathes me, always has and knows the feeling's mutual.'

Hugh placed a reassuring hand on Sally's shoulder. 'Don't worry, it will be all right.'

'But what if she knows about the baby? What if she comes to Laura's Lair or even knows I'm at Elmsmarsh?'

'Somehow I don't think that's likely,' Hugh replied. 'We've been so careful and apart from Uncle Bertram who knows about us?'

'Only Terry and Julie that I'm aware of,' Sally said thoughtfully, 'and you know they wouldn't say a word.'

Hugh rubbed his chin, trying to think if he'd left any incriminating evidence in his bedroom. Knowing there to be none, he added brightly, 'The best thing we can do is to pop in and see Terry and Julie when I take you back to the flat to see if Serena's called at Pots and Posies.'

'But why would she do that?'

'I'm sorry, Sally, I should have said before. Mrs Burt suggested to Serena that she go to Pots and Posies for the anniversary flowers.'

'I can see from your faces,' Bertram remarked, 'that you're in a bit of a dilemma but take it from me, I think things will turn out all for the best, you know – and if you don't mind my saying so – I'm jolly hungry. That walk in the garden gave me an enormous appetite and that Chinese smells damned good!'

Smiling and walking to the table, Hugh realized his uncle was probably right and opened up the steaming cartons.

Whilst Bertram ate with solid concentration, Sally – Hugh observed – chewed slowly and absentmindedly. 'Cheer up,' he said reaching for her hand, 'it might never happen.'

She gave a brittle laugh and patted her baby Stanley bump. 'You're forgetting,' she whispered softly, 'it already has and in two months' time . . .'

'In two months' time,' Hugh assured her, 'everything will be resolved. I promise.'

Studying Sally's troubled expression, Hugh turned to his uncle. 'I think it might be an idea if Sally has a rest. Is it okay to take her up to the room I use when I stay over?'

'Of course, my boy. You do that, then perhaps you and I could have a little chat. I've one or two suggestions to make that might be of interest to you.'

Covering Sally with the counterpane, Hugh stroked her hair and kissed her forehead. 'Look, just have a rest and I'll talk to Uncle B.; he might be a bit of a rogue but at least he talks a great deal of sense – most of the time.'

'You know,' Sally sighed sleepily, 'I really like him, we had a most interesting walk in the garden, he even showed me the old apple tree – the one with the mistletoe – and I told him what you'd said about Freya and the pearls . . .'

'Sshh,' murmured Hugh, caressing her hand and placing it beneath the covers, 'sleep now and we'll talk later.'

'How is she?' Bertram enquired when Hugh returned to the kitchen to clear away the remains of the meal.

'Tired. I think the rest will do her good. We'll let her sleep for a bit; so how about a game of chess?'

'Will you be able to concentrate on a game, Hugh?'

'Why ever not?'

'I'd be prepared to stick my neck out and say you've got an awful lot to think about. Sally and the baby – not to mention Serena.'

Following Bertram into the drawing room, Hugh watched the old man move the games table into position and motion his nephew to draw closer.

Some time later, Hugh asked, 'What would you do in my position, Uncle?'

Bertram replied, 'At the moment I'd worry about protecting my queen, I'm sure you don't want to lose her!'

Hugh studied the chess pieces and seeing the vulnerable position he'd got himself into, nodded ruefully. 'Actually, I didn't mean the game of chess, I meant in relation to Sally and Serena.'

Bertram chuckled. 'In that case, my boy, I'd still probably give you the same advice. What you have to decide is, who do you want to be your queen? Which one can you afford to lose?'

Conceding defeat, Hugh moved towards the fire. Running his hands through his hair he turned to face his uncle, whose face was full of anticipation.

'Well,' Bertram wheezed, 'aren't you going to put me out of my misery, or haven't you made your mind up yet?'

'Oh! My mind is made up; in fact, it was made up months ago. The problem is how to deal with everything in the best possible way. I haven't said too much to Sally of course but the silver wedding anniversary celebrations – which are a complete farce if you ask me – more or less coincide with the arrival of baby Stanley.'

'Good Lord! You're never going to call the baby after your dog!'

'No,' grinned Hugh. 'It's just that we think Sally must have conceived about the time Serena had Stanley put down. That's how we found out, quite by chance, that I wasn't infertile after all.'

'I always knew Serena was a bitch!' muttered Bertram. 'I also know she's not going to give you up easily.

Or, put another way, she won't want to give up her extravagant lifestyle.'

Hugh contemplated Bertram's remark. 'I suppose in the end, it all boils down to what you said a while ago. Who can I afford to lose? As I see it, financially I could lose considerably if Serena and I divorce, but . . .'

'But what?'

'But Sally said she never expected me to leave Serena.'

Bertram looked downcast and replaced the chess pieces in their original positions.

'Don't look so worried, Uncle, it's not what you think.'

'It's not?'

Hugh moved back to the games board and picked up the two queens. 'This,' he said, holding up the ebony queen, 'is Serena, and this is Sally.' Placing the ebony queen in his left hand and the ivory queen in his right, Hugh closed his fingers round both pieces.

'Now,' he whispered, gazing into his uncle's concerned face. 'If I say goodbye to the black queen, I lose a considerable fortune and no doubt my standing in the community, for a while at least. But if I say goodbye to the white, what I lose then is beyond price. A financial loss I can cope with but . . .'

'Hugh, my boy . . .'

'I hope you're not going to tell me I can have both.'

'No, at one time I have to confess I would have taken that option, but not anymore.' Bertram shook his head sadly. 'I'm older and wiser now and I've made my mistakes – too many of them in fact – and all I would ask is that you don't do the same.'

Laying the black queen face-down on the chessboard, Hugh reached for Bertram's wrinkled and trembling hand, turned it over until the palm was uppermost and placed the ivory queen in an upright position. 'Hold on to this one very carefully, Uncle, as I intend to do the same with Sally.'

When Sally opened the door some time later, she found Hugh sitting at the games table, watching his uncle carefully lower an ivory chess piece onto the board. In the fireglow, something about it seemed strangely magical, yet she told herself the two men were only playing chess. Hugh turned round and gazed at her lovingly, while Bertram, she was convinced, had tears in his eyes.

'Have you had a good game?' she enquired?

Returning Sally to the flat, a brief meeting with Terry gave Hugh the information he required with regard to Serena. No, there had been no tall blonde calling at Pots and Posies but a well-spoken woman had telephoned late in the afternoon asking for Julie. Terry remembered it clearly, because the woman had hung up so abruptly.

Taking Sally in his arms, Hugh ran his forefinger across her forehead. 'Don't frown,' he said, 'it doesn't suit you.'

'But she's probably been wondering where you are?'

'Well, if she has, wondering about it until morning isn't going to make that much difference now, is it?'

'You mean you're going to stay the night?'

'Don't you want me too?'

'No, it's not that, I just thought perhaps you ought to go home.'

'And I think I ought to stay here, so that's settled.'

Leading Sally through to the bedroom, Hugh noticed a book and a video lying on her bed. Picking up the book with its sexually explicit cover he grinned. 'What's this? I didn't know you were into women's pornography?'

'I'm not; Roz insisted I read it. She's just finished it and thought it might take my mind of being pregnant.' Sally laughed. 'But considering I'm finding it increasingly difficult to see my feet, I think it's going to take more than that! Before you say anything about the video, it's not a blue movie!'

'It's not?'

'No, it's a birth tape I've borrowed from the midwife.'

'What's a birth tape?'

'It shows you what to expect when the time comes. They showed it last week to the prospective mums-to-be but I didn't go,' Sally said softly.

'Can I ask why?'

'I didn't like the prospect of sitting there on my own whilst everyone else was sitting there with their husbands and partners for support.'

'Oh, Sally, I'm so sorry. This is all so new to me. I'd never even considered that. Is it so awful having to face things on your own?'

Sally shrugged. 'I suppose I'm getting used to it now – but then I never expected it to be anything different. I mean in the circumstances, it can't be, can it?'

Moving the book and the tape to one side, Hugh pulled Sally gently onto the bed and cradled her in his arms. 'It will be different, you'll see. For the moment I can't tell you exactly how – probably because I don't

291

know myself as yet – but I had a very interesting talk with Bertram while you were resting and between us I think we've found a solution.'

'That sounds very intriguing.'

'Mmmn – but perhaps not as intriguing as the plot of this book,' Hugh teased, perusing the back cover of the paperback.

'Would you like to read some of it while I have my bath?'

Hugh shook his head. 'How about if we watch the video instead.'

'You might not like what you see.'

'I'm prepared to risk that, if it means it might help us both discover what being parents is all about.'

Later, in the darkness, listening to Sally's peaceful and rhythmic breathing, Hugh sighed and laid a hand gently across her stomach. She was right, he hadn't liked what he'd seen. It was bad enough watching a complete stranger go through the ordeal of childbirth, but to think of Sally in a similar situation made him nervous.

Beneath his hand, Hugh felt a gentle movement. Sally had mentioned how the baby always seemed to move the minute she began to rest. Very gently Hugh stroked the tiny limbs and for a brief moment Sally stirred, murmuring softly. Soon mother and baby were still once more but for Hugh, sleep was not so simple.

Arriving home after breakfast, Hugh was greeted with a look of complete and utter disdain.

'And how was Uncle Bertram?' Serena asked sarcastically.

'He was very well, considering his age and before you say anything Serena, I gather you rang. Trouble with the car or something?'

Something was right, thought Serena. But how did Hugh know she'd rung, when Bertram had said . . .?

'I'm sorry I missed you. I'd only gone out to get us a Chinese; you know what Bertram is like for Chinese. He says it always makes a welcome change after Mrs Bailey's cooking.'

'I would think anything is a change after Mrs Bailey's cooking!'

Serena poured herself yet another strong black coffee. She'd overindulged on the whisky yesterday evening and her mouth tasted dreadful, full of stale tobacco and alcohol.

'What was the trouble with the car?' Hugh asked.

'A bloody flat tyre!'

'Why didn't you take the Range Rover?'

'Because I couldn't find the damned keys! I looked everywhere, the study and your bedroom.' The words slipped out unintentionally, and Hugh cast a suspicious look in her direction. So, Serena had gone through his belongings. Slowly he walked to the utility room.

'Why didn't you ring the garage or the recovery service?'

'Because I spent so long searching for the bloody keys in the first place and by the time I remembered the recovery service it was too late, the shops were shut and –'

'And you'd probably had too much to drink,' Hugh added, noting the empty whisky bottle on the floor of the utility room. As he turned to face Serena he held up a bunch of familiar keys.

'Where the hell were they?'

'On the same hook as Stanley's lead. I still do that sometimes, force of habit, I suppose.' Laying the keys on the table in front of her, Hugh left Serena muttering something about 'the bloody dog' under her breath and went to examine his bedroom.

A quick check on his drawers and wardrobe confirmed his suspicions. The Pots and Posies card had been tampered with. All along one edge were tiny jagged ridges and the minutest smear of red. No doubt from Serena's nail polish. She'd often remarked how her favourite brand frequently left tiny red marks if she caught her nails at a certain angle.

Pondering the situation, Hugh placed the card in his wallet for safekeeping. Having watched last night's birth video with Sally, he wanted to make sure he always had Julie's number handy.

'Julie,' he whispered softly, remembering the message on the card. 'That's why Serena is in such a foul mood. She's found the card and obviously thinks Julie is female! Oh, well – let her. For the moment at least, that could be quite convenient!'

CHAPTER 19

Helping Sally with yet another packing case, Hugh mopped his brow.

'Whew! I'm glad that's it and we're leaving the rest to the removal men.'

Sally handed him a coffee. 'I'm sorry, I know they would have seen to everything but I just wanted to pack those bits and pieces myself.'

'What time are they coming in the morning?'

'Eight o'clock.'

'Are you sure you'll be able to cope? You don't want me to be here?'

'Hugh darling, it's very sweet of you – but we've managed so far without drawing too much attention to ourselves. If you're here when the removal men arrive, it would be just our luck that someone recognizes you.'

'Promise me you won't attempt any lifting or do anything silly.'

'I've already done that by letting you persuade me to move two days before Christmas – and before you say anything – yes, in the circumstances it probably is better to move now, rather than wait until after the baby is born. Marion keeps telling me I won't have time for anything then.'

'Not even for me?'

Sitting by his side, Sally leant her head against his shoulder. 'I'll always have time for you,' she sighed.

Hugh kissed her cheek and murmured, 'I just wish Serena hadn't said we'd go to Charles and Vivienne's for Christmas.'

'You must, they'll be expecting you, besides they sound a nice couple and you've always got on well.'

'Yes,' mused Hugh, 'we have, but I expect it will be the last Christmas I spend with them. They'll probably give me the cold shoulder next year.'

'Do you think Serena's said anything to Vivienne?

'Definitely not! For the simple reason that she's determined we should go ahead with this ridiculous charade of a siver wedding anniversary.'

Sally's eyes were full of concern. 'Hugh, twenty-five years is a long time for a couple to be together and much as I want to be with you, I don't know if I could live with the knowledge that I've destroyed your marriage. A year ago when I agreed to become your mistress, I never envisaged . . .'

Reaching for her hand, Hugh interrupted. 'You haven't destroyed my marriage, Sally. Serena did that all by herself – both with Stanley and her lies.' He studied Sally's heavily pregnant state. 'As for being my mistress, that's not really how I would describe you now. You are, after all, going to be the mother of my child.'

Somewhat reassured, Sally eased herself from the settee with a smile. 'Well, the mother of this child had better get a move on, if she's going into Laura's Lair. And don't look so horrified, I shan't be doing anything silly there either. For a start Marion and Laura won't let me and secondly it will help pass the time, the days are beginning to drag.'

Hugh reached for his jacket and his car keys and kissed her goodbye. 'Promise me you'll take care then.'

'I promise.'

'And you'll ring if you need me?'

'Yes.' She smiled. 'I'll ring if I need you.'

On Christmas Eve morning, Serena decided to call at Barrington's for her last minute Christmas shopping. She'd already organized the main presents but remembered Vivienne liked everyone to open one small present after supper on Christmas Eve.

'Don't ask me why we do it. It's something Charles' family began years ago,' she'd told Serena, 'something to do with Scandinavian tradition, I believe.'

Standing on the escalator, Serena considered Vivienne's surname and supposed Anderson could quite easily have Scandinavian connections. It was strange how she'd never thought of it before. What she had to think of now however, was what to buy Vivienne. Charles and Gareth hadn't been a problem, and neither had Hugh. It had been a case of personalized golf balls all round.

Wandering from department to department, Serena found her attention drawn to some silver and gilt handbag mirrors. Their size was perfect but the problem was which one to choose. Selecting three, she held each one up in turn, admiring her reflection as she did so. At the same time she also saw, reflected, something that seemed vaguely familiar.

Placing the mirrors back on the display stand, Serena turned towards a selection of Marion Le Sage's miniatures. Now she remembered! The frames of these miniatures were identical to the one Hugh had hidden away of Stanley. Only these pictures – apart from two of robins in the snow – were of flowers, not animals. Had the person who painted these also painted the one of Stanley?

'They're quite charming, aren't they, Mrs Barrington?'

Serena looked up in surprise.

'I'm sorry, I don't expect you remember me. I'm Celia Foster, the new manageress of Babyware.'

'Oh, of course,' Serena lied. Never having to visit babyware, she didn't remember the woman at all.

'You're admiring Marion Le Sage's work I see. Of course these are only prints, the originals are to be found at that wonderful art and craft gallery out at –'

Serena wasn't listening; she was peering at the bottom right-hand corners of the miniatures. Le Sage – that was the artist's name. It hadn't implied that Stanley was good after all.

'Does she? I mean does this Marion Le Sage undertake commissions?'

'I'm afraid I wouldn't know,' replied Mrs Foster. 'I suppose you could always go to the gallery and ask Mrs Le Sage herself, or perhaps ask Mr Barrington. I understand setting up this department was his baby, so to speak.'

Serena nodded thoughtfully; perhaps if she went to see this Le Sage woman she might be able to discover if the miniature of Stanley had been commissioned by Hugh or his onion-selling friend Julie!

'By the way, speaking of babies,' Mrs Foster's shrill voice echoed, 'how's your friend? The one who's having the baby? I know Mr Barrington said she wants us to keep the pram until after baby is born and as I told him it is safer to do so, just in case . . .'

Bewildered, Serena faced Mrs Foster in silence. What was the woman prattling on about? They hadn't got any friend expecting a baby!

Biting her lip Serena thought hard. No! It wasn't possible was it? Julie couldn't possibly be pregnant! Hugh had promised. Feeling a knot in her stomach, all Serena wanted to do was get out of the store and with an abrupt goodbye, she left a puzzled Celia Foster deliberating over which of the two robins in the snow she should buy.

'Damn,' muttered Serena, slamming her car into gear, 'where did that stupid woman say the gallery was – Elmsmarsh? No,' she whispered with an ominous tone, 'it's not the gallery that's at Elmsmarsh, it's our friend Julie. Perhaps I should go there first!'

At Pots and Posies the early morning scramble for Christmas fruit and vegetables had eased and Terry despatched Julie to the kitchen to make them both a well-deserved cup of coffee. When Serena entered the shop there was only one other elderly customer.

'Hello, Mrs H! How's the old rheumatics?'

'Drivin' me up the wall, Terry, my dear, I just thank Gawd our Shane and Debbie are having me for Christmas dinner.'

Serena winced at the prospect of this wizened old woman being served up for Shane and Debbie's Christmas Dinner!

'Very nice too,' continued Terry, 'and I expect you'll have a jolly good knees-up in the evening.'

Trying to ignore the old woman's cackling, Serena peered surreptitiously for signs of Julie. She heard movement through the back of the shop and for a brief moment saw the rear of an exceptionally slim figure in denim jeans, with a mass of fine blonde curls.

So you've gone for a blonde again, Hugh, Serena thought, but if I'm not mistaken those hips don't belong to a heavily pregnant woman. Perhaps Mrs Foster has misled me after all. Relieved, Serena told herself perhaps Hugh was doing a favour for one of Muriel Baxter's nieces.

'Anyway,' began Mrs H., 'what about you two, what are the pair of you doin' this Christmas? I bet you 'aint goin' to your mum's.'

Terry shook his head. 'We're still undecided. I'd prefer to stay at home but I could go to Julie's sister if I wanted to. The thing is, as she's pregnant and suffering from morning sickness, I don't expect she'll really be up to having visitors.'

So, it was Julie's sister who was pregnant, Serena thought angrily. And no doubt, if this skinny blonde with the frothy curls had managed to twist Hugh round her little finger, he would then quite probably give her or her family anything they asked for!

'Well, whatever you do, if you go to Julie's sister's, don't take her one of those enormous melons.'

'Why ever not?' Terry enquired.

'Because,' the old woman laughed coarsely, 'they say havin' a baby is like tryin' to pass a melon!'

'Oh, I wouldn't dream of doing that, Mrs H.,' a voice broke in softly. 'She's frightened enough as it is.'

Serena turned in the direction of the voice, delaying for as long as possible the first glimpse of Hugh's Julie. Slowly her eyes moved upwards from the Nike trainers to the slim blue-denimed hips and Naf Naf sweatshirt – with no trace of a bust – until she reached the face surrounded in the froth of angelic golden curls.

Giving an audible gasp, Serena fled towards the door, causing the other three occupants of the shop to stare after her in bewilderment.

'I dunno,' said the old lady, 'some people can't wait five minutes to be served, can they?'

Watching the elegantly dressed blonde rush to her flashy hatchback, Terry nodded knowingly in Julie's direction. When Mrs H. had left the shop, he murmured, 'Something tells me we ought to ring Hugh.'

Driving with unfocused eyes from the shock of what she'd just seen, Serena drove aimlessly for miles, then realized she was hopelessly lost. In desperation she called at a service station for petrol and cigarettes and also asked the way back to Thornhampton. Following the attendant's instructions she passed one hamlet after another until, as predicted, she came to the first set of crossroads.

'Now,' she asked herself, 'is it left or right?'

To the left she noticed, was just another nondescript country road but halfway down on the right she saw a black and gold sign announcing Laura's Lair. With a violent screech of wheels and a smell of burning rubber, Serena turned right.

'Oh my God!' Sally gasped, glancing out of the window. 'I'm going to have to go!'

'You don't mean to say the baby's started!' enquired Marion, rushing from the kitchen.

'No, it's that woman. I don't want to speak to her. If she asks for me tell her I'm not here!'

'But, Sally . . .' Marion watched as Sally rushed to the loo and locked the door.

Walking through the door, Serena caught sight of Marion's paintings and was reminded she still hadn't bought anything for her sister. Vivienne's stipulation for Christmas Eve presents was for nothing wildly extravagant. The prints in Barrington's weren't wildly extravagant but the originals here at Laura's Lair were.

'I'd like the Christmas Rose, Winter Jasmine and Cyclamen.'

'You mean to take all three!' Marion asked in amazement.

'That's what I said,' Serena snapped. What did it matter how much she spent? It was only Hugh's money, after all, and how much had he been spending on that – his *boyfriend* from the greengrocers. Feeling a sickening sensation in her stomach, Serena put her hand to her mouth.

'Do you feel all right, you look quite pale,' Marion asked anxiously, 'perhaps I could get you a glass of water.'

302

'No! No thank you, I think it's the perfume from all these scented candles and pot-pourri in here that's all. If you could just wrap the paintings.'

Watching Serena drive away, Marion walked to the loo door and knocked gently. 'It's okay, Sally, you can come out now, she's gone.'

Ashen faced, Sally emerged and reached for a stool. 'What . . . what did she say?'

'Apart from asking to buy three of my pictures, she didn't say much at all.'

'You mean she didn't ask for me?'

Marion shook her head. 'No. Were you expecting her to?'

'Er, no, I just thought perhaps she . . .'

Marion studied Sally carefully. Why should she have panicked so much, unless the woman who had just left was connected in some way to the man who was the father of Sally's baby? Slowly Marion opened the till and drew out the credit card slip she'd just swiped through the Access machine. The signature was indistinguishable but the name on the card imprint was perfectly clear – S. BARRINGTON.

'Oh dear!' sighed Marion, holding up the Access slip. 'Could this explain everything? I do believe your secret is out, Sally my dear.'

Not moving from the stool, Sally said nothing as she watched Marion push the credit card slip to the back of the till and deliberately close the drawer.

'I think perhaps we should have a cup of tea,' Marion whispered, 'then if there's anything you want to talk about, I'm a very good listener.'

Numbed, Sally was aware of the mug with the question mark being placed before her.

Marion smiled warmly. 'I thought the question mark seemed appropriate; somehow I get the feeling you are very confused.'

'Oh, Marion!' Sally sighed. 'What on earth am I going to do? I mean what if Serena comes back, what if she knows?'

'If you mean, what if she knows about you and the baby, I would be prepared to say from her reaction when she came in here that she doesn't. Mind you, she seemed pretty upset about something. At one point I thought she was going to pass out. I even offered her a glass of water.'

Sally looked aghast. 'I'm glad she didn't accept. I was getting desperate in there. That loo is barely big enough for one person, let alone a heavily pregnant one and Stanley was beginning to complain.'

'Who's Stanley?'

'Oh, that's what I've called the baby until it arrives.'

'And wasn't that the name of the dog I painted?' a puzzled Marion enquired. 'Somehow, Sally, I think you've a lot of explaining to do.'

Half an hour later, when Marion unclipped and refastened the familiar brown hairslides, she emitted a low whistle. 'My goodness! By the sounds of it you and Hugh have had quite a year. How on earth have you managed to keep things so secret?'

'With great difficulty and this,' she said, pointing to her bump, 'has made things decidedly awkward of late. Naturally we've always tried to be discreet and most of the time Hugh came to the flat. Terry and Julie have been terrific and I shall miss them, although they're still only round the corner.'

'And, am I right in assuming, Hugh has bought your new house?'

Sally nodded. 'Yes – but I didn't ask him to, in fact I haven't asked him for anything; he insisted that's all.'

'And I should jolly well think so too.'

'You do? You don't think it makes me appear cheap and sordid, like a little bit on the side?'

Marion roared with laughter. 'Sally, my dear, from the state of you, I would say you look anything but a little bit on the side!'

Seeing the joke, even Sally managed a smile. 'Oh Marion,' she sighed, 'true to your name as ever and a real tonic.'

'Well, Mrs Barrington seems to think my paintings are good. Fancy buying three! Even though I suppose it will mean Hugh footing the bill. Laura, no doubt, will be delighted.'

'Speaking of Laura, I'd appreciate it if you didn't mention what I've just told you. I know she's going to find out about Hugh sooner or later but for the moment I'd prefer for us all to have a peaceful Christmas. I don't much relish the thought of Laura confronting Hugh on Christmas Day with a carving knife!'

'Then it's probably better if you go home. I'll tell Laura when she comes back that you were feeling tired after the move and everything. By the way, you're not lifting those heavy packing cases, are you?'

'No. In fact the removal men were terribly sweet and helpful and Hugh had already organized the new carpet, so it all went like a dream.'

Marion gave a wry smile. 'Some people have all the luck. My removal experiences have always been like nightmares, never dreams.'

'Ah, but you're forgetting,' Sally said, fetching her coat, 'I got rid of an awful lot of stuff when I left my old house, so there wasn't really that much to move.'

'And the nursery is all ready and waiting?'

Sally nodded and felt the colour rise in her cheeks. 'Yes, courtesy of Hugh. He brought it round last night.'

Placing a motherly arm around her shoulders, Marion whispered softly, 'You really do love him, don't you, Sally?'

'Yes, I do. I don't expect things are going to be easy for us but . . .'

'In that case, we'll all have to say a little prayer this evening when we go to midnight mass. You are still coming with us?'

'Mmmn, if it's still all right for you to come and fetch me. I don't fancy driving there on my own.'

Hugh stood in the doorway of the new house, half hidden by a large pink poinsettia.

'Hugh! What are you doing here? I thought you were supposed to be going to Charles and Vivienne's?'

'I am, but I just wanted you to have this. I thought the house looked a bit bare, and I needed to see you – if only for five minutes – not knowing when I'll be able to get away over Christmas.'

'It will have to be five minutes only I'm afraid. Roz telephoned and asked if she could call in on her way home. She wants to see the house and give me my Christmas present.' Sally placed the poinsettia in the middle of the dining table and turned towards Hugh. 'Come,' she said softly, 'I've got something to show you.'

Taking him by the hand she led him upstairs to the tiny nursery and opened the door. 'I came home from work early and thought I'd try and get a few things organized. What do you think?'

Hugh's gaze took in the basinet with its white broderie Anglaise trim, the new baby bath on its stand and white nursery furniture. Feeling a lump in his throat, he drew Sally into his arms and held her close.

'Sally, I . . .' He got no further as there was a sharp rapping at the door.

'Oh, no!' Sally cried. 'It can't be Roz already. What are we going to do?'

Releasing her from his grasp, Hugh said calmly, 'Don't panic, I'll pop into the downstairs cloakroom and you go down and open the door. Now don't rush, I don't want you falling downstairs – as for Roz, just leave everything to me.'

Nervously Sally approached the front door and braced herself.

'Merry Christmas, Sally!' came the voice from behind yet another poinsettia, only this time it was red. 'Housewarming present,' said Roz, holding forth the plant as she followed Sally into the dining room.

'Oh! You've got one already – well, never mind, you can stick mine in the kitchen, as it's not as impressive as the pink.'

'The pink one,' Sally said, trying to appear calm, 'is a housewarming present from Mr Barrington. In fact he's only just brought it.' She motioned towards the cloak-room door and from within came the flushing of the loo, followed by a running tap.

'Oh, I see,' Roz nodded. 'I'd better be on my best behaviour then.'

At that moment, the cloakroom door opened and Hugh, feigning surprise, reached for Roz's hand. 'Mrs Hughes, well I never! I take it we're both here on the same mission, to wish Mrs Palmer a Merry Christmas and every happiness in her new home. I must say it's a charming house and I can certainly vouch for the plumbing!'

Roz laughed, whilst Sally, with her back to them, reached for a bottle of sherry and some glasses. 'Can I offer you both of sherry?'

Hugh looked at his watch. 'No thank you, I must be going I'm afraid. We're spending Christmas with my sister-in-law and her family and if I don't get a move on I shall be late for supper. If you'll excuse me.'

Walking to the hallway, Hugh turned and addressed them. 'Are you both spending Christmas at home?'

Roz spoke first. 'You bet. You'll never get Donald and me away from home at Christmas. But what about you, Sally? You're not spending Christmas here on your own, are you?'

Directing her reply more at Hugh than at Roz, Sally replied, 'I'm spending Christmas Day and Boxing Day at Laura's. I was going tomorrow but I've decided to go this evening instead. We're going to midnight mass and Laura and Marion are calling for me at eleven o'clock.'

Hugh acknowledged Sally's information with a brief nod, while Roz removed her coat and sat down on the settee. Looking at her watch, she said brightly, 'Good, that means I've got time to join you in a sherry, Sally.'

Sipping her drink, Roz nodded in the direction of the pink poinsetia. 'That was kind of the boss man, wasn't it? I bet you were surprised to find him standing on your doorstep . . .'

'Yes I was,' Sally said in all honesty.

'After all, it must be almost a year since you left the store. Still, you know what, I reckon he always had a soft spot for you.'

Sally took a large gulp of sherry and stood up. 'Would you like to see the nursery, Roz? It's not completely finished yet . . .'

Without warning, Roz was on her feet and heading for the stairs. 'You bet. You know Donald and I can't wait for this baby to arrive.'

With Roz drooling over the nursery furniture and the contents of each and every drawer, Sally thought of Hugh's reaction when they had stood in the same room only ten minutes ago. What was Hugh going to say before Roz had arrived so abruptly? Had Serena said something about calling in at Laura's Lair? Marion had been convinced Serena was upset about something. Sally sighed, it was no use worrying about it now. It would have to wait until she saw Hugh again and that wouldn't be until after Christmas.

With the examination of the nursery completed, Sally took Roz to show her the master bedroom.

'I see you're reading the sexy book I lent you. How are you getting on with it?'

'At the moment I'm finding it hard to work out how they manage to get themselves into all those amazing positions.'

309

'Ah! But that's because you're pregnant. You wait until after you've had the baby. By the way, I shall have to let you borrow the book I'm reading at the moment. Whew! It's enough to make your hair curl! It's set in ancient Greece and they're at it day and night. I only wish Donald and I had half their energy.'

'Mmmn,' Sally murmured thoughtfully. 'But what always amazes me is quite how and why the characters never get pregnant.'

'Quite possibly,' said Roz, peering from the bedroom window, 'because they stuffed their vaginas full of vine leaves or something!'

Sally laughed and clutched at her stomach. 'Maybe that's what I should have used. Only if I remember correctly, there weren't any handy at the time.'

Roz followed Sally's gaze to the double bed. 'You mean to say you weren't using anything?'

Blushing, Sally turned to go downstairs. 'Let's just say we had been very careful until then, only . . .'

'Only?'

'We were out of vine leaves on that occasion!'

'Blimey Sally! That's some virile man you've got then. You'll have to watch yourself after the baby is born, you know.'

'Meaning?'

'Meaning, you could quite easily fall pregnant again.'

Running her hands over baby Stanley, Sally sighed anxiously. 'Let me just concentrate on this one first, Roz. I'm terrified enough as it is; besides I'm not sure what H . . . he, the baby's father . . .'

Sally turned to face Roz with panic in her eyes. Had Roz noticed her slip of the tongue? She'd almost said Hugh and changed it to he, at the last minute.

Roz placed a comforting hand on her shoulder. 'Christ, Sally, I'm sorry, here I am rabbiting on about ancient Greeks and virile men and you've got the whole birth thing ahead of you. No wonder you look scared.'

Sally was smiling. 'As ever, Roz, your choice of words is spot on.'

'Why, what did I say?'

'Rabbiting.'

'Well, you know what Donald would say . . . I've got a one-track mind and he's probably right.'

Back in the dining room and thinking of Hugh, Sally placed a finger on the potting compost of the pink poinsettia. Hugh had told her it would probably need watering. Following her into the kitchen, Roz watched as she filled a jug and watered both the red and the pink plant.

'What I can't understand,' said Roz, fingering one of the large pink leaves, 'is why he brought a pink one. I mean red are far more Christmassy, aren't they?'

Remembering the incident with the roses, Sally knew only too well why Hugh hadn't bought her a red poinsettia.

Saying goodbye, Roz hugged Sally warmly and patted her bump. 'Now, have a lovely Christmas with Laura and Marion and let's hope next year you'll be able to spend it with you-know-who.'

For a brief moment Sally panicked again, before she realized Roz meant *who* and not *Hugh*! She decided it was probably just as well Roz was leaving as she felt herself becoming more paranoid by the minute.

'And another thing,' Roz demanded, pushing her glasses back into place, 'I want you to promise you'll let me know the minute the baby arrives. I want to be your first visitor – that is – after the baby's father, of course. Is he . . . will he be with you for the birth?'

Sally shook her head sadly. 'I doubt it. You see, as yet his wife doesn't know about the baby and I can't really see . . .' Sally thought it safer not to coninue. So far she and Hugh had yet to decide how they were going to break the news to Serena. Somehow baby Stanley's anicipated arrival was hardly conducive to Serena's plans for her silver wedding anniversary!

CHAPTER 20

Struggling to behave as if there was nothing untoward, Serena waited for Hugh to open the car door. Then, deliberately avoiding his outstretched hand, she swept past him to her sister's front door.

'Hello you two,' beamed Charles, 'Vivienne was getting worried. She thought you weren't coming.'

'Hugh was late home!' Serena snapped icily.

Charles watched as Serena tossed her mane of golden hair and sauntered off in the direction of the kitchen. He turned raised eyebrows in Hugh's direction.

'Search me,' said Hugh, 'she's hardly spoken a word since I got in.'

'I shouldn't worry, old chap, she's probably over-wrought with all the plans for your anniversary. It's not long now, is it?'

'The actual anniversary is two weeks tomorrow but, as you know, we're having the celebrations three days later on the Saturday.'

'Going to be quite an occasion then. Vivienne hasn't stopped talking about it for weeks. I just hope she doesn't expect something similar for our Ruby Wedding.' Charles helped Hugh with the luggage and called to his wife from the hall, 'Vivienne, where are we putting these good people?'

'In the pink room, Charles,' a voice called from the kitchen.

Vivienne replaced the lid of a saucepan and turned to her sister, winking as she did so. 'That's what you wanted, wasn't it, Serena?'

'Pardon?'

'A few weeks ago, when you mentioned your little problem with Hugh, you asked if I'd put you in the pink room, the one with the double bed?'

A look of horror crept over Serena's face; she'd quite forgotten her original request for sleeping arrangements. Now it was the last thing she wanted. The mere thought of sharing a room with Hugh was bad enough, let alone the same bed.

'I'm sorry, Vivienne; if you don't mind I've changed my mind.'

'You mean you'd prefer single beds? Well, in that case I'll tell Charles to take your luggage to the blue room.'

'No!' Serena broke in. 'I'd rather Hugh and I were in different rooms.'

'But Serena! What on earth's the matter?'

'I don't want to talk about it – not now. Later when you and I are alone perhaps. Just put Hugh in a separate room from me. I don't care where, he can sleep on the sofa for all I care!'

Laying down the wooden spoon she was holding, Vivienne placed a comforting hand on her sister's shoulder. 'I'm sure things aren't that bad, are they? It's so near your anniversary.'

'Oh, they're bad, all right.' Serena looked towards the kitchen door and was aware of Charles hovering nervously.

'Vivienne my dear, could I have a word?'

Leaving her sister to watch the simmering sauce, Vivienne followed her husband into the hallway and closed the kitchen door.

Charles coughed discreetly. 'I think we have a problem. Hugh's not happy with the sleeping arrangements. You should have seen his face when I opened the door to the pink room and he saw the double bed. I suggested the blue room with the single beds, but you said Serena specifically requested the pink room and I don't know what to do.'

Vivienne sighed and shrugged her shoulders. 'I get the distinct feeling something is dreadfully wrong. Yet it can only have just happened as Serena's been on such a high with all her plans. Did Hugh give you any clues?'

'None at all, just said he and Serena preferred separate beds. I know they have separate beds at home but if I recall, when we went to Devon, they never complained about having the double room.'

Shaking her head, Vivienne said sadly, 'Yes – but that was over a year ago and so much can happen in a year.'

'You don't suppose it's got anything to do with Serena putting old Stanley down and that business over her abortion? Hugh was pretty cut up about it as I recall.'

'And quite rightly too,' Vivienne hissed under her breath. 'I told Serena years ago to . . . Oh! Anyway what's the use of going over that now? The important thing is to sort out where they're both going to sleep over Christmas, and if you ask me, this doesn't exactly bode well for a Merry Christmas!'

Deciding to leave Serena in the pink room, Charles took Hugh's luggage to the blue room, leaving Vivienne to explain the revised sleeping arrangements to her sister. Later, with Hugh and Serena unpacking, Charles poured two large sherries and took them through to the dining room. Vivienne was making a few last-minute adjustments to the seating arrangements.

'I thought in view of what's happened, they'd probably prefer not to sit next to each other either!'

Charles nodded approvingly and offered Vivienne her sherry. 'I was going to open a bottle of Moet but decided against it, do you mind?'

Vivienne shook her head. 'No, the only thing I mind is if the two of them keep up their stony silence throughout supper. It's going to be pretty embarrassing for Gareth and his new girlfriend if they do.'

Checking the table one last time, Vivienne picked up her drink and sighed. 'Thank goodness we've got a circular dining table that's all!'

With Charles and Vivienne facing each other and Hugh and Serena, Gareth and Debbie sitting diagonally opposite each other, the meal got off to a promising and genial start. It was only when the main course arrived on the table that the atmosphere deteriorated rapidly.

With the precision of a surgeon, Charles carved the clove-studded gammon into slices and passed the first plate to Debbie who sat nervously on his left. Vivienne meanwhile placed tureens of vegetables on the table. 'The dishes are very hot and quite heavy. So be careful everyone.'

'In that case,' said Hugh, turning to Debbie as he sensed her unease at eating amongst strangers, 'will you allow me to help you?'

Debbie looked anxiously at the dish Hugh was offering. 'I'm afraid I don't much like vegetables. I only eat potatoes and peas. I don't know what some of those are.'

Taking a large gulp of wine, Serena raised an eyebrow and looking in Debbie's direction, said sarcastically, 'Well, my dear, you're in luck, Hugh knows all about vegetables, don't you, darling!'

Completely nonplussed, Hugh ignored Serena's remark and described each vegetable in turn to his bewildered neighbour, who was beginning to wish she hadn't accepted Gareth's invitation. It wasn't so much sitting apart from Gareth that bothered her, or even having Gareth's father on one side and his uncle on the other – both men had been charming and attentive – the object of Debbie's discomfort was Serena.

During the first course, Debbie had noticed Serena drank more than her fair share of white wine and once again her glass was empty. Oh well, she supposed, it *was* Christmas and her own parents only ever opened a bottle of wine on high days and holidays. Toying with the haricot verts Hugh had persuaded her to try, Debbie felt Serena's penetrating gaze once more.

'Of course, Hugh's not only a gourmet when it comes to vegetables, he's pretty good with exotic fruits too!'

317

Ignoring Serena's remark, an embarrassed Charles refilled Serena's empty glass and looked towards his wife for support. In desperation she offered Hugh more vegetables. He declined gracefully and turning to Debbie, said kindly, 'Don't eat the beans if you don't like them; you can fill up on dessert. Vivienne makes the most wonderful chocolate roulade and *crème brulée*.'

Seeing the puzzled expression on the young girl's face, Serena broke in without warning and with a sardonic sneer announced, 'To you, Debbie, that's probably best described as chocolate swiss roll and custard with burnt sugar on the top!'

At that moment you could have heard a pin drop and laying down his napkin, Gareth turned towards his mother. 'If you don't mind, I think we'll give the puddings a miss. We said we'd meet up with some of the others at the wine bar. That okay with you, Debbie?'

Nodding in Gareth's direction, Debbie gave an anxious sigh of relief and smiled warmly when Hugh held her chair and helped her from the table.

'I hope you all have a Merry Christmas,' she whispered shyly.

Serena raised her glass and with a resounding, 'I'm sure we shall!' emptied yet another glass.

With the table cleared and Serena and Vivienne in the kitchen, Hugh watched Charles fetch brandy and four glasses.

'Not for me, Charles, thank you. I might go out later but not before I've had a word with Serena about her disgraceful behaviour. That poor girl. Goodness only knows what she must have thought.'

Charles frowned as he filled three of the glasses. 'Mmmn, I have to admit, old chap, Serena did go a bit over the top tonight. I know she's always been the feisty one and Vivienne's the big softy, but her comment about the swiss roll was a bit out of order.'

'What's out of order?' Serena demanded, coming in and reaching for a brandy.

'Your behaviour!' Hugh said tersely.

'That's choice coming from you, Hugh!' Serena snapped. 'You're a fine one to talk about behaving out of order.'

Attracted by the raised voices, Vivienne hurried in with the tray of coffee. 'Now you two! Don't forget it's Christmas and it will soon be your anniversary!'

'How could I forget!' Serena called, storming from the room.

Watching her go, Hugh turned in Vivienne's direction. 'Look, I'm sorry about all this. Leave it to me and I'll see if I can talk to her. If not, Serena and I might just as well pack up and go home as there's no point in spoiling everyone else's Christmas.'

Pacing the floor of the pink room, Serena drew heavily on the cigarette she held with trembling fingers. 'Out of order indeed! How dare he!'

Hugh knocked abruptly on the door and not waiting for Serena's response, opened it and went inside.

'I don't remember saying you could come in!'

'Don't worry, I'm not stopping and this will only take a moment. All I have to say Serena is that I think you should apologize not only to Charles and Vivienne but also, when you next see them, to Gareth and his young lady.'

319

'Young lady! You think Debbie is a young lady? Well, I don't! Goodness, she hardly knew what piece of cutlery to use, let alone recognized a vegetable!'

'In that case, instead of sneering at her, why the hell couldn't you have helped her? Surely you could see how nervous she was? Can't you ever remember being in a similar situation when you were young?'

'No! Because no doubt I was better educated than her. I always knew how to behave in public and what to do . . .'

'Of course!' Hugh said sarcastically. 'How stupid of me to forget, of course you did, Serena! Well, if ever Debbie needs a back-street abortionist – although from the look of her I very much doubt whether she will – you'll be able to tell her where to go!'

From where she had been pacing the floor, Serena stood motionless as if frozen to the spot and screamed, 'How dare . . .!'

'Yes . . . go ahead, Serena! How dare *what*?'

Watching Serena's sculptured mouth gape open, Hugh turned on his heels.

'Remember! It had better be an apology to everyone, Serena, otherwise we might just as well go home and if you've got anything else to say I suggest you say it now.'

For what seemed like an eternity, there was silence. Then seeing Hugh's hand on the door, Serena announced flatly, 'I want a divorce.'

'Really? Well that's fine by me – but tell me, Serena, would you prefer it before or after our wedding anniversary?'

Serena gave a brittle laugh. 'Oh, I'm not joking, Hugh. If you think I want to remain married to you after what I discovered today . . .'

Still with his hand on the door and his back to her, Hugh asked quietly, 'And what exactly did you discover today?'

With a voice full of certainty, Serena replied, 'I found out all about the lover you've been keeping from me, the reason for all your little visits to Uncle Bertram, your weekends away and your purchases from Barrington's babyware department. I never thought you could stoop so low.'

Puzzled by her last remark, Hugh rubbed his chin. Why should Serena accuse him of stooping so low over his relationship with Sally? Sally was an attractive and educated woman.

'We've both had other relationships during our marriage, Serena. You were the one who suggested it in the first place, remember? To compensate for my infertility, I think you said at the time.'

Sensing the scathing tone in his voice, Serena didn't know how to reply. Nervously she stubbed out her cigarette and waited for him to continue.

'You also said – and correct me if I'm wrong – you never wanted to know about "the other woman", so you've only yourself to blame if you didn't like what you found today.'

'Too right I didn't like what I found today, Hugh! Another woman I could cope with but to discover that you've been having an affair with that – that pretty blond boy in the fruit shop is enough to turn anyone's stomach!'

Hugh stared at Serena wide-eyed. 'What did you say?'

'Oh! You don't have to pretend, Hugh! I know all about dear Julie and his "please ring me if you need me, Hugh" messages.' Serena put on a simpering voice and reached for another cigarette. 'All I can say is, if he's now got you paying for his sister's nursery furniture as well, then it looks as if you're being properly screwed in every direction!'

With a face as black as thunder Hugh strode towards Serena until their faces were only inches apart. 'Very well, Serena, if a divorce is what you want, you can have it, but I would think very carefully if I were you, about making the same accusations in court.'

'Hah! Don't think you can threaten me, Hugh. Just wait 'til I tell them about all your clandestine meetings and those gifts, hidden away.'

'The gifts . . . whatever do you mean?'

'The picture of Stanley for a start. The picture you had hidden away. You should think yourself lucky I never burnt it.'

'Like you did with my dog and your baby I suppose!'

If, at that moment, he'd wanted to strike Serena where it hurt, Hugh's last verbal retort scored a bull's-eye. Defeated, Serena slumped onto the pink kingsize bed that only days ago she'd hoped to share with her husband.

Opening the bedroom door, Hugh announced coldy, 'I'm going out, and, in case you're wondering, I shall explain why to Vivienne and Charles. You can tell them what you wish of course.'

'In that case, if you're going out for a quick grope with your golden-haired Julie, why don't you ask him to do one of his dried flower arrangements for Debbie as a special favour. I'm sure you'll find him very obliging!'

Choosing to ignore her remark Hugh made his explanations to Charles and Vivienne and left the house.

'Whew! What do you make of that?' Charles said, finishing his brandy.

'I don't know, dear. I honestly don't know. But if Hugh's left to be with another woman on Christmas Eve, then it must be serious.'

'Another woman! Is that what he told you? My God, Vivienne, I always said you were far too gullible.' Serena stood in the doorway, her eyes flint-hard and assessing as she studied Charles' and Vivienne's reaction to Hugh's untimely departure.

'That's what he said,' Vivienne replied nervously. 'Hugh said they'd been seeing each other for about a year and that it's serious. He also said you've asked him for a divorce.'

With a voice distinctly lacking in warmth, Serena announced, 'Oh, it's serious all right and too right I want a bloody divorce. So would you, Vivienne, if you'd just discovered your husband was a homosexual!'

Easing herself from the front passenger seat of Laura's car, Sally breathed in the chill night air and listened to the sound of bells welcoming them to midnight mass.

'Isn't it perfect?' she sighed. 'A clear, crisp night, the sound of church bells and . . .'

'Three overweight women trying to extricate themselves from one tiny car,' broke in Laura.

'Sally's not overweight,' interjected Marion. 'She's just heavily pregnant, that's all.'

'Mmmn and by the looks of it, we could have our own real live baby to put in the manger tonight if we're not careful!' Laura shook her apricot curls and looked at Sally. 'Are you sure this is a good idea?'

'Positive,' announced Sally. 'There's only one birth we'll be celebrating tonight and that's baby Jesus'. Now are we going inside while we've still got a choice of pews?'

Pulling up her coat collar against the cold, Laura whispered to Marion, 'Just make sure we're near the door then – just in case!'

The scene inside the church was charming. All the electric lights had been switched off and every pillar was decorated with creamy white candles. They shone brightly and flickered each time the ancient wooden door was opened to let in more worshippers. To the side of the pulpit, near the central aisle, Sally noticed the newly decorated crib, with its layer of straw and baby Jesus wrapped in swaddling clothes. Feeling tears prick her eyelids, she thought lovingly of how, only hours ago, she'd taken Hugh by the hand and led him to baby Stanley's bassinet in the newly decorated nursery.

Touching Sally gently on the elbow, Marion whispered softly, 'Are you okay, Sally?'

'Yes, wonderful, thank you . . . just thinking.'

At half past eleven, the organ began to play and a side door opened. From within came the procession of choirboys with freshly scrubbed faces and neatly combed hair. Holding candles, they began to drift forward and a solitary clear voice sang the opening verse of *Once in Royal David's City*. Standing, the congregation joined in at the second verse, aware only now and then of the usual straggle of latecomers.

At midnight, with the clock striking twelve and the rest of the congregation kneeling, Sally sat with her head in her hands and offered up silent prayers. 'Dear God, you already know what I desire . . . and is it so very wrong, when I have so much already?'

Outside once more, with the bells heralding the birth of the Christ Child, Laura's jovial vicar greeted each departing parishioner with a smile and a warm shake of the hand. Face to face with Sally he grinned even more broadly, adding, 'I'm glad you made it through the service, my dear. For one moment I thought I was going to have to call on the expertise of my wife.'

'She's with the Red Cross,' Laura explained as they set off towards the lych gate, 'and once helped deliver a baby during the church fête! In fact, she's never stopped talking about it. I expect she would have welcomed the opportunity for a repeat performance.'

'Well, I'm sorry I couldn't oblige,' Sally said, stepping sideways through the gate. 'Oh!'

'Sally!' Marion grabbed at her arm, 'are you okay? Is it the baby?'

'No, it's not the baby. I've just seen Hugh. He's standing by Laura's car. What on earth shall I do, Marion?'

'Why, go over and talk to him, silly! After all, that's probably why he's here. There's no point in trying to hide things anymore is there?'

'But what about Laura?'

'Don't worry about Laura.' Marion turned to look back in Laura's direction. 'By the looks of it, she's been cornered by the vicar's wife. She probably wants to know where you'll be spending Christmas Day.'

'I'm hoping Sally will be spending Christmas Day with me,' Hugh murmured softly, stepping forward to take Sally's hand.

'Go on,' urged Marion, kissing Sally's cheek. 'Off you go, both of you. I'll explain to Laura.'

Struggling to get through the lych gate, Laura stared in amazement as she saw Sally being helped into the front passenger seat of a midnight-blue Jaguar. 'But where's Sally going?' she asked.

'She's going to spend Christmas with the father of her baby.'

'But wasn't that . . .?' Gasped Laura in amazement.

'That's right Laura, that was Hugh Barrington. Isn't it wonderful?' Marion cast her eyes skywards and whispered softly. 'Thank you, Lord; at least you answered my prayer.'

Nestled in Hugh's arms, Sally listened as he recounted the disastrous meal spent with Charles and Vivienne, followed by Serena's outburst and her eventual demand for a divorce.

'I just don't believe it.' She said softly. 'Are you sure she meant it?'

'Oh, she meant it all right.'

'But that's because she thinks you and Julie . . . well, you know.'

'Yes, I do. Only too well.'

'And yet you didn't tell her she'd made a mistake.'

'Sally,' Hugh laughed wryly, 'with Serena in that frame of mind, no one would be able to convince her she'd put two and two together and made five. Besides. . .'

'Besides what?'

'It makes it easier for us at the moment, doesn't it? Gives us more time to think about our future together . . . You do want us to have a future together, Sally?'

Looking up into Hugh's eyes, Sally realized he was in earnest. There was just time for a whispered, 'Oh yes,' before she felt his lips on hers.

Making two mugs of hot chocolate, Sally glanced at the kitchen clock; it was almost two o'clock in the morning.

'What do you intend to do now then, go back to Vivienne's?'

'No way! As I said in the church carpark, I intend to spend Christmas Day with you. Don't worry, I'll ring Charles first thing in the morning. I really don't want to disrupt their Christmas any further. Serena will no doubt stay with them and I will stay here – simple really.'

Sally grinned and handed Hugh a mug of chocolate. 'What's so funny?'

'Everything, when you come to think about it. A short while ago Roz was convinced Bernard was the father of my baby. Then when she arrived tonight I thought the cat was really out of the bag. But of course she still thinks you can't have children. So while I'm worrying about what Roz is thinking, you're in the middle of a row with Serena, who thinks you are gay, and there's poor Laura, gaping open-mouthed as I drive off into the night with you!'

Returning to the settee, Hugh sipped his hot chocolate thoughtfully. 'Put like that, I suppose it does seem amusing but I have to confess, at the time, confronted by Serena, I found the situation anything but funny.'

'I'll tell you what will be though. Our Christmas dinner! Do you realize that as I was going to be spending Christmas with Laura and Marion, I've hardly any food in the house! Unless you fancy a spaghetti bolognese. I made a couple of those for the freezer last week.'

'Spaghetti bolognese would be wonderful and we can pretend the poinsettia is the Christmas tree.'

'Speaking of your poinsettia, Roz was curious why you'd bought a pink one. Am I correct in assuming you remembered what I'd said about the roses?'

Nodding, Hugh helped Sally to her feet. 'Come along, let's go to bed, you look exhausted. We can discuss things in greater detail tomorrow.'

'You mean today.' She yawned sleepily.

Preparing their spaghetti bolognese hours later, Sally removed a stray bay leaf and her thoughts turned automatically to Stanley. 'Hugh, what did you do with Stanley's ashes?'

'For a while I kept them with the miniature you gave me. Then I decided to take the picture home, that's how Serena found it, but Stanley's ashes are still in the mahogony cabinet in my office. Why do you ask?'

'I was thinking, perhaps once the lawn is laid and I start planting out some shrubs, we could scatter

Stanley's ashes round the bay tree . . . that is if you'd
like to?'

Encircling his arms around her, Hugh thought fondly
of Stanley and replied, 'I'd like that very much and I'm
sure Stanley would have approved.'

CHAPTER 21

Watching a fine drizzle fall on the newly laid turf, Sally turned away from the window and absentmindedly switched on the video. The midwife had told her the baby's head was engaged, so it seemed as good a time as any to run through the birth tape just once more. It would also take her mind off the fact that at that precise moment Hugh was meeting Charles unofficially with regards to the divorce.

With the tape drawing to its conclusion and the rather dramatic birth sequence, Sally was relieved when the doorbell rang.

'Terry, what a lovely surprise. Is Julie with you?'

'No, he's out delivering flowers but he asked me to give you these.' Terry held out the first of the new season's daffodils and followed Sally through to the kitchen.

'Thank you, they're lovely and the perfect reminder that spring is just around the corner. Mind you, it doesn't look very spring-like out there. Just look at the mess. Hugh will be furious when he sees it.'

Terry peered from the kitchen window and whistled. 'Bloody hell! What happened there? It looks like the battlefield of the Somme!'

'The men picked today of all days to lay the new turf. I know January isn't exactly the best time of year for it, but I didn't think they were going to make quite so much mess. They even managed to knock over Stanley's bay tree and practically demolished it with the roller.'

'You mean the one where you were going to scatter Stanley's ashes?'

Sally nodded tearfully. 'Hugh's going to be dreadfully upset.'

Terry put a kindly hand on her shoulder and added brightly, 'Don't worry about the mess. Julie and I'll pop round one day when it's not quite so wet and clear up a bit. As for the bay tree, it doesn't look too healthy to me, but when I go to the wholesalers I'll see if I can find a replacement.'

'I'd appreciate that. Now, how about a cup of tea.'

Insisting on carrying the tray, Terry placed it on the coffee table just as the video began to rewind. 'Oh, I'm sorry, was I interrupting a film or something?'

'Or something is right, Terry! It's the birth tape I borrowed. Luckily you called at the right moment. They were just about to show the actual birth.'

'In that case, wind it back then so I can have a look!'

'Are you serious?'

'Yes, I've always wanted to see a baby born, but with things the way they are with Julie and me we're not likely to have any, are we?'

'No, I suppose not,' Sally said thoughtfully, rewinding the tape.

Terry stared in wonderment at the television screen where, with the final stages of labour, the baby's head

331

began to emerge. Feeling a lump in his throat he whispered, 'That is amazing, I never realized . . .' Turning to Sally he asked, 'Aren't you frightened? I know Julie's sister is.'

Sally nodded and placed a hand on her bump. 'I have to admit I am, just a little bit.'

Stirring his tea, Terry added, 'And will Hugh be with you at the birth?'

'I doubt it. Our timing wasn't very good I'm afraid. The baby's due about the same time as Hugh and Serena's wedding anniversary. Considering Serena still doesn't know about the baby, I can hardly ring her and ask her to send Hugh to the hospital for me!'

'You mean to say they're still going ahead with the anniversary celebrations? I thought Serena wanted a divorce.'

'She does, though she's still convinced Hugh is having an affair with Julie. I hope you don't mind us going along with that, by the way?'

Terry grinned and shook his head. 'Not at all. Julie and I think it's a scream. Anyway Serena deserves it, especially after poor old Stanley and the other business.'

Sally patted her stomach and shifted uncomfortably in the chair. 'The other business will quite possibly be making its presence felt soon if the past twenty-four hours have been anything to go by.'

'You mean to say you think you're in labour!'

'No, I've just been getting what they call Braxton Hicks contractions. They're not the real thing but nevertheless can be pretty uncomfortable.'

With a look of concern Terry patted Sally's hand. 'Don't forget, Sally, you know Julie and I said you've only got to ring us, when things start to happen.'

'I know,' she smiled. 'In fact I've got your numbers, both for the flat and Pots and Posies, stuck up in every room! And when things start, Terry, I'll expect you to come and hold my hand!'

'Right, you're on!' he said determinedly.

'But I was only joking . . .'

'Well, I'm not!' Terry concluded.

Sally contemplated the prospect of Terry being with her at the birth. Nobody could stop her having him there, could they? Besides, Hugh wouldn't be able to make it and Roz, Laura and Marion would quite possibly be working and even Jackie would find it difficult to drop everything and rush to the hospital with her.

'If you're really sure.'

'Positive!' said Terry, extending his hand with a smile. 'After all, I've seen it on the video, haven't I, so I know what to expect.'

Getting up to leave, he suddenly remembered something. 'By the way, you never finished telling me about Hugh and Serena's anniversary. Why on earth are they still going ahead with it?'

'Ah! That's quite a long story. Hugh and Serena both have their reasons for doing so and agreed that having gone to all the expense of arranging it, it would be foolish to cancel.'

'Meaning?'

'Meaning Serena, according to Hugh, who heard it from his sister-in-law, is planning to announce to all

333

their guests that Hugh is a homosexual, which is why she's divorcing him.'

'The bitch!' hissed Terry. 'And what about Hugh?'

'Oh, he's proposing to let her make a fool of herself, before he makes a speech to celebrate the twenty-five years of their marriage and its inevitable end.'

'And will he tell them about you and the baby?'

'At the moment he's undecided.'

'Well, all I can say to that, Sally, is, I wish I could be a fly on the wall!'

In Thornhampton, Charles welcomed Hugh to his office and motioned him to a chair. 'It was good of you to come, Hugh, I, er . . .'

'Look, Charles, before you begin, can I say that I fully appreciate how difficult this is for you. And if it will make things any easier, just try and pretend I'm not family.'

'Can't do that, old chap.'

'Why not?'

'Because as far as Vivienne and I are concerned, you are still family.'

'It's kind of you to say so, Charles, but if you are acting for Serena, you know we really shouldn't be meeting like this in the first place.'

Charles clicked the top of his ballpoint in and out. 'I know, and Serena's making the whole thing deuced awkward for me!'

'And you're still maintaining this is an off-the-record meeting?'

'You have my word, Hugh.'

'What exactly do you want to know then?'

Charles rubbed his moustache nervously. 'It's about this homosexual business though of course Vivienne and I don't believe it for a minute! But Serena – well,' Charles sighed, 'you know Serena.'

Hugh nodded ruefully. 'I most certainly do and much as I deplore her behaviour in recent months, I still don't want her making a complete and utter fool of herself.'

'You don't?'

'Of course not. I can't dismiss twenty-five years of married life with a mere flick of the fingers, you know.'

'But she's so adamant about you and this Julie person.'

Reaching into his jacket pocket for the Pots and Posies card, with Julie's written message on the back, Hugh placed it on the desk in front of him. '*That*, Charles, is the soul basis for Serena's accusations. So tell me, where on that small scrap of card does it say Hugh Barrington is a homosexual?'

'Nowhere.'

'Exactly and do you think a barrister would be prepared to stand up in a court of law using that as evidence?'

Charles shook his head. 'But Serena says you've spent the evening at this Julie's flat.'

'Of course I have! Julie and his partner Terry – and for your information *they* are homosexuals – invited us to dinner.'

'You mean you and Serena?'

'No, I mean me and the person I intend to marry when the divorce comes through. And shall I tell you why we were invited to dinner?'

Charles moved the Pots and Posies card back in Hugh's direction and smiled. 'Even if I said no, I still feel you'd go ahead and tell me, Hugh.'

'How well you know me, Charles.'

'Yes, known you an awful long time, old chap. In fact, I feel I know you almost as well as I know myself, which is why I didn't believe Serena.'

'That's where I made my mistake,' Hugh said bitterly.

'Afraid you've lost me there, Hugh.'

'I *did* believe Serena . . . when she told me about the so-called adopted baby. You then told me it was a lie – remember?'

'How could I forget?' Charles replied. 'The day I insisted meeting you in the park, when you stopped that young lad's dog from running into the road, the dog that looked like Stanley, I remember going home to Vivienne that night wondering how could two sisters be so close and yet so different. Vivienne would willingly give a home to every damned stray in the neighbourhood and Serena . . .' With an embarrassed look, Charles stopped himself from finishing his sentence. 'I'm sorry, Hugh, got a bit carried away there, I'm afraid, and if I remember correctly, I think I interrupted you.'

Hugh looked at his watch and stood up. 'I'm sorry too, Charles, I've actually got an appointment with my own solicitor in twenty minutes, so I must dash.'

Shaking Charles' hand warmly, Hugh said in a quiet tone of voice, 'The reason my future wife and I were having dinner with Terry and Julie was to celebrate the fact that I'm going to be a father.'

'You're *what*! But *how*, I mean *when*?'

Smiling, Hugh picked up the pen Charles had been fidgeting with and reaching for the desk calendar, drew a circle around January tenth.

'But that's –'

'Exactly. That's a week from today, so do advise Serena not to do anything silly in the meantime!'

Stunned and ashen-faced Charles stood at his window, watching Hugh run down the steps from his office and across the market square with the energy of a twenty-year-old.

'Well I never!' he murmured. 'Serena my dear, you are in for a rude awakening!'

On the actual morning of their wedding anniversary, Hugh placed a small box by Serena's breakfast plate.

'What's this, a peace offering?' she asked sarcastically. 'Because if you think it will make me change my mind about the divorce, you've got another think coming!'

'No, it's not a peace offering. Let's just say it's a joint anniversary and parting gift, shall we? I think you'll find it's the one you wanted.'

'You mean,' said Serena, tearing excitedly at the gift wrapping, 'the one I saw when I went to London with Vivienne?'

Hugh merely nodded, poured himself a coffee and picked up the morning paper, while Serena examined her ring. Five rows, each containing five diamonds, sparkled in the light of the angled spotlights suspended from the kitchen ceiling.

'If you've changed your mind about it, you can always sell it. After all, you know how much it's worth,' Hugh said, turning to the financial pages. 'It was no doubt one of the most expensive you could find!'

Serena said nothing, and only fingered the ring on her finger as she stared into the ghostly and deserted winter garden. Aware of Hugh folding the paper, she turned to face him.

'Thank you,' she said numbly, 'it is the right one.'

'That's good,' Hugh replied coldy, walking from the kitchen. 'And an appropriate choice, if I may say so. One diamond for each of the twenty-five years. It's just as well it's not our golden wedding!'

At any other time, Serena would have thrown both the ring and the box after him, but even she wasn't that stupid.

Later, getting ready to have lunch with her sister, Serena was surprised to see Mrs Burt walking up the drive to the front door.

'What is *she* doing here today! I told her not to come until tomorrow and why isn't she going to the back door?'

Angrily Serena walked downstairs and opening the door found her cleaner in her best coat and hat. In her hands was an exquisite dried flower arrangement.

'Mrs Burt, I wasn't expecting you.'

Holding forth the arrangement, Mrs Burt announced proudly, 'Happy Anniversary, I had it done special like, to match your colour scheme.'

Completely taken aback, Serena found herself opening the front door wide and inviting her cleaner into the house for a coffee.

'Only a quick cuppa then,' Mrs Burt insisted, 'because Mr Burt's coming for me in ten minutes. We're going in to Thornhampton 'cos the sales are on and it's also market day. I always prefer to get my fruit and veg on the market, the stuff in the greengrocers at the bottom of our road is dreadful. Not like where I got that.' Mrs Burt pointed to the arrangement she'd just brought.

'It's very beautiful, Mrs Burt. So exquisitely delicate and the colours are just perfect.'

'That's just what I said to Mr Burt; well, not in quite the same words, mind you. And he agreed with me, you'd never think that was done by that pretty young man would you?'

Serena felt her whole being go rigid. 'Whatever do you mean, Mrs Burt?'

'That Pots and Pansies place I told you about.'

'You mean Pots and Posies?'

'Well,' Mrs Burt laughed. 'It's the same difference, isn't it. In fact, come to think of it, you could say that about Julie and Terry.'

Remembering her brief visit to the shop, Serena asked, 'Do you know Julie and Terry, Mrs Burt?'

'Not really. I know Terry's mum better. She's had her stall on the market for years and quite cut up about it she was, when her Terry came out of the cupboard, or whatever they call it these days.'

'I think you mean closet,' Serena said softly.

'Oh, do I? Anyway as I was saying, Lily – that's Terry's mum – didn't like it at all, and when he moved Julie into his flat there were ructions. She refused to have anything to do with them.'

Pouring the coffee and keeping her tone casual, Serena enquired, 'And does she have anything to do with them now?'

'Apparently they all got together at New Year and buried the hammer, or is it hatchet? Anyway it's like Lily says, Julie and Terry have been together so long now and they're not causing no trouble to anyone else, so why not let bygones be bygones.'

'Why not indeed?' Serena heard herself saying.

Mrs Burt was still chattering away about Lily, her son and his flat, when Mr Burt tooted the horn of his car to announce his arrival.

'It's small but beautifully furnished and decorated, Lily said, and it just goes to show what a small world it is, 'cos she said she thought she saw Mr Barrington coming out of the flat opposite when she was there at New Year. She said she remembered him from the store.'

The moment Mr and Mrs Burt's car was out of sight, Serena grabbed her coat and car keys and headed for Elmsmarsh. Driving past the small row of shops she searched the neighbourhood for blocks of flats, which, with all Mrs Burt's detailed descriptions – courtesy of Lily – weren't too difficult to find.

Parking at the rear, Serena gazed up at the windows with their assortment of drapes, nets and blinds. The problem was, which one belonged to Terry and Julie? After a few moments she realized there would have to be names on the letterboxes, and, filled with renewed enthusiasm, she headed for the entrance hall.

'Julie and Terry,' she whispered loudly, 'Julie and Terry, where are you?'

'If you mean the couple from Pots and Posies,' a voice cut in, 'they are upstairs on the right, only you won't find them in. They'll be at the shop I expect. Why don't you try there?'

'Of course,' Serena replied lamely, pretending to leave. 'I will.'

Some time later, when the coast was clear, she ran up the stairs to Terry and Julie's flat. Standing outside their door, she then turned to face the flat opposite and rang the bell. There was no reply. Totally dejected and disillusioned, Serena walked slowly back down the stairs, but not before taking note of the name outside the door – A. and M. Lacey.

Returning home, Serena pulled the Thornhampton telephone directory from the drawer and frantically scanned the list of Laceys for an A. or M. Lacey at Elmsmarsh. Seeing there were none, she threw the directory to the floor in disgust and dialled directory enquiries. It was only then that she realized the time and remembered she was meeting Vivienne.

For the umpteenth time, Vivienne looked up as a cold draught from the doorway heralded the arrival of yet another diner. When at last she recognized Serena's flustered features she waved her arm and called out, 'Serena, over here!'

Walking to the table, Serena cast a sideways look at the other customers, hoping there would be no one she recognized. It was the last thing she wanted.

'I thought perhaps you'd forgotten,' Vivienne said, passing the menu across the table.

'No, I had to go to Elmsmarsh unexpectedly.'

At the mere mention of the name, Vivienne's eyebrows shot up. Charles had refused to tell her anything of his meeting with Hugh, yet she was convinced Hugh's so-called homosexual 'lover' lived at Elmsmarsh. Wasn't that what Serena had told them at Christmas?

'Oh, Serena! I hope that doesn't mean you've been trying to see . . .'

'If you mean the boyfriend, no I haven't. But I have been to where he lives – if you can call him a "he"?'

Vivienne shook her head sadly. 'But you really have no proof of Hugh and . . .'

'Julie!' broke in Serena. 'No, perhaps not, and *maybe* I jumped to the wrong conclusions, but I'm convinced there is a connection with Hugh and Julie one way or another. I mean, why else would Hugh have his card with that cryptic message on the back?'

'It needn't be cryptic at all,' Vivienne insisted. 'When you think about it, it could be a perfectly innocent message.'

'Hmph!' muttered Serena, after giving her order to the waiter. 'The way Hugh's been behaving recently, I would hardly think innocence has anything to do with it!'

Vivienne watched as Serena nervously drummed the fingers of her left hand on the table. 'And is that,' she nodded in the direction of the new ring, 'anything to do with Hugh's behaviour?'

Serena gave a wry smile and fingered the ring admiringly. 'Well, at least I got that out of him. It was the one we saw in London – remember?'

'Of course.' Vivienne sighed, thinking back to the day she and Serena had gone to London. By the time they'd left Harrods, Serena's plastic was practically red hot!

342

All that money spent on clothes, shoes and fripperies for their anniversary and now they were talking of a divorce.

Sipping at her spritzer, Vivienne took a deep breath and braced herself. 'It's a beautiful ring, Serena, and I'm sure Hugh wouldn't have bought it for you unless. . .'

'Unless what?'

'What I suppose I'm really trying to say is, does it all have to end in divorce?'

'According to Hugh it does,' Serena announced matter-of-factly. 'He gave me this as a parting present!'

Wide-eyed and almost choking on her drink, Vivienne gasped in astonishment. 'That is a *parting* gift!'

'Apparently so,' said Serena flashing the ring, sending a myriad of rainbows darting on the crystal glassware.

Saddened by the disclosure, Vivienne picked at her seafood pancake and watching Serena stab at a black olive in a bed of radiccio, whispered softly, 'Serena, I think you should consider the situation very carefully.'

'Why? What did Hugh tell Charles?'

'I can't tell you.'

'You mean you won't!' Serena snapped angrily.

'I mean I don't know, and even if I did, I wouldn't be at liberty to say.'

Reaching for her spritzer, Serena threw her sister a disapproving look.

Vivienne covered Serena's beringed hand with her own. 'Look, Serena, I'm your sister and I don't want to jeopardize our relationship but can't you see, it's your future we're discussing here.'

'So!'

343

'So, it could be a future without Hugh, have you thought about that?'

Serena shrugged her shoulders. 'Not really, but he'd have to pay me a pretty decent settlement. I'd certainly want my fair share of . . . Whatever's the matter, Vivienne? Why are you looking at me like that?'

As in their younger days, unable to cope with Serena's obdurate nature, Vivienne finished her meal in silence.

Uneasy at parting on such a discordant note, Serena returned home, picked up the telephone directory where it still lay on the floor and put it back in the drawer. Toying with the idea of returning to Elmsmarsh or trying directory enquiries, she decided on the latter.

'I'm sorry, madam,' came the clipped and precise tone of the operator, 'we have no one of that name listed in the directory at that address.'

'Could they be ex-directory?'

'If they are, I wouldn't be able to give you their number.'

'I know that . . . but could you just check anyway?'

'We have no A. or M. Laceys registered as ex-directory at that address either. I'm sorry.'

Sensing the operator was about to terminate their conversation, Serena said hurriedly, 'Wait a minute! What about a new listing? What if they've only just moved in? That would explain why the number isn't in the book, wouldn't it?'

'Yes madam, but today with everything being computerized –'

'Look! I don't give a damn about computers. Could you just check if the Laceys are under a new listing?'

344

With a deep sigh, the operator followed her instructions.

'Christ, it's like dealing with a bloody robot!' Serena announced when a number eventually echoed tonelessly down the line. Scribbling the six digit number, she dashed to her bedroom and picked up the phone. It was safer to ring from there, just in case Hugh arrived home unexpectedly. Moments later, to her delight, a young and confident male voice answered.

'Hi! This is Andy Lacey. I'm sorry Melanie and I aren't here to take your call. If you'd like to leave your name and number, we'll get back to you as soon as we can.'

'Damn!' hissed Serena, hanging up the phone.

Studying the telephone number on the square sheet of paper, torn from the pad in the hall, Serena whispered the two names she'd just heard. 'Andy and Melanie. Well, I've certainly not heard Hugh mention a Melanie before and we definitely don't know any Laceys.'

Lifting the lid of her jewellery box, Serena folded the paper with the telephone number into four and hid it beneath a saphire and diamond brooch. She would ring the Laceys again later. With two days to go before their anniversary celebrations, there was still time to surprise Hugh. Who knows, she might even be able to surprise Andy Lacey too, particularly if she was able to tell him that his wife had been having an affair with Hugh.

'If that is the case,' Serena considered with quiet satisfaction, 'then I doubt if Mr Andy Lacey will be sounding quite so confident in the future.'

CHAPTER 22

On the Saturday morning, with the caterers setting up tables in the dining room and Hugh discussing the wine and champagne, Serena took herself off to the tranquillity of her bedroom. There, she once more removed the square of paper, containing the Laceys' number and dialled.

She'd been dialling it persistently since having lunch with Vivienne but to no avail. Each time Andy Lacey's confident tones had emitted the same answerphone message. Concluding they were perhaps away on holiday, Serena was quite taken by surprise when a male voice answered sleepily.

'Hello, Andy Lacey here.'

'Oh! I'm sorry to bother you, Mr Lacey. You don't know me but I'm trying to trace the previous owner of your flat – a Mr Hugh Barrington.'

'Sorry, I think you must have the wrong flat. There was a woman living here before us but that wasn't her name.'

Serena heard Andy Lacey yawn noisily down the phone. 'Why don't you try directory enquiries,' he suggested.

'I have. That's how I got your number.' Serena was beginning to get desperate. Perhaps she should try and talk to Melanie Lacey instead. After all, if Melanie was having an affair with Hugh, her husband was hardly likely to know about it, was he? 'I wonder, is your wife there, Mr Lacey? Perhaps if I asked her?'

Andy Lacey, angry at being woken up within only hours of returning from an exhausting journey, studied the handset of his phone. 'Look, I don't know who you are, but take it from me neither myself nor my wife know a Hugh Wots-is-name! Like I said, there was a woman living in the flat before us, not a man!' Not knowing what to say, Serena was aware of a muffled voice calling in the background but was unable to distinguish what it was saying. 'Ugh! Oh, all right I'll tell her. If you hang on a minute, my wife says she might be able to help.'

Relieved, Serena listened for more murmured whisperings and then heard the thin piping voice of Melanie Lacey. 'Hello, can I help you?'

'I'm so sorry to trouble you, Mrs Lacey,' Serena simpered. 'But it is very important, I'm trying to contact a dear friend of the family – a Mr Hugh Barrington. I was told he used to live at your address. And he was seen coming out of your flat just after New Year.'

Melanie Lacey thought back to New Year; it was just before she and Andy left to spend a few days with relatives. 'Oh, you don't mean the man with the keys?'

'The man with the keys?' Serena asked puzzled.

'That's the only person I can think of. We'd only just moved in. Sally left just before Christmas and I remember the estate agent ringing to say a man would be calling round with the spare set of keys. To be honest, he did give his name, but what with trying to unpack the tea chests and then pack for our holiday, I didn't take too much notice. I only remember thinking at the time his name sounded similar to that mountaineering guy's.'

Clutching the receiver, Serena heard Melanie call to her husband.

'Andy! Who wrote that book *The Everest Years*?'

'Chris Bonnington,' came the muffled reply from beneath the duvet.

'That's it! Bonnington,' she replied chirpily. 'Was that the name you were asking about?'

Exasperated, Serena thought to herself, Bonnington – Barrington. Well, if you were completely thick, as the Laceys obviously were, you could be forgiven for confusing the two names. 'And this Mr Bonnington – I mean Barrington, was he tall and dark . . .?'

'Come to think of it he was. Yes, tall and dark and as my mother would say, distinguished looking. But not young, more like the chap she always drools over in South Pacific. The one with the nice voice singing *Some Enchanted Evening* only it wasn't him singing, was it? It was someone else.'

Hardly in the mood to discuss Rogers and Hammerstein, Serena had gleaned at least one snippet of information. Hugh had turned up at the Elmsmarsh flat with a spare set of keys. Why, however, should he have a spare set of keys? She couldn't expect Melanie Lacey to know but she could perhaps add yet another piece to the puzzle.

She'd already mentioned someone leaving the flat before Christmas. Someone who could have been a friend of the Laceys or better still a friend of Hugh's! Erring on the side of caution, Serena said casually, 'The person who left just before Christmas, do you think she might know where I could contact Mr Barrington? Did she leave a forwarding address?'

'She did,' Melanie replied, reaching for the pile of post they'd picked up from the hall floor on their return home, 'but her name wasn't Barrington, it was Palmer. In fact we've got some of her post here.'

In stunned silence, Serena heard Melanie chattering away about delayed Christmas post and mislaid addresses. 'I'll try and find it for you if you like, only Andy and I have just come back from holiday. Perhaps if you'd care to call round and collect Sally's post for her, I might be able to find her forwarding address. From what I gather she's still living in Elmsmarsh.'

Choking back a sob, Serena said huskily, 'Yes, why don't I do that. I'll call you before I come just to make sure you are in . . . and then I can give Sally a nice surprise.'

'What a good idea,' Melanie replied in all innocence.

'Good idea indeed!' Serena spat, hanging up the phone and stormed into her bathroom to find the supply of cigarettes she kept hidden. 'Sally Palmer, you've got to be joking! I just don't believe it. You bet I'll go round and collect her post – I'll . . . I'll give her a nice surprise. Good God! How long has this been going on?'

'About a year,' Hugh answered softly.

Startled, Serena spun round to face him. 'How long have you been there!'

'Long enough to hear you mention Sally's name and say something about giving her a nice surprise.'

'Too damned right I will! Just you wait until I tell her.'

'Tell her what, Serena?' Hugh asked calmly.

'Tell her that she's destroyed my marriage.'

Walking over to Serena, Hugh lit the cigarette she had wedged between her lips and taking her hand, led her back through to the bedroom. There he sat her on the bed, while he himself sat at the dressing-table stool.

'Serena, let's just get one thing straight, shall we, Sally didn't destroy our marriage – you did.'

'I did! How dare you! After all these years of letting you . . .'

'Letting me what?'

'Letting you do as you please with whomsoever you please . . .'

'And what about yourself, Serena, what have you done?'

Serena shrugged her shoulders and drew on her cigarette. 'Well, put like that . . . I suppose I've done the same.'

'Exactly,' replied Hugh. 'And whose idea was it that we should have that sort of arrangement?'

Serena hesitated. 'We both agreed to it, Hugh.'

'Yes, we might both have agreed to it, but you haven't answered my question. Whose idea was it in the first place?'

'Mine, but that was because you couldn't give me a baby,' Serena replied defensively, 'And when you felt guilty about it –'

'Oh yes! I felt guilty about it all right. Any man would, not being able to give his wife a child.'

'But I didn't want a child! You didn't either, Hugh, you said so.'

'Perhaps I did,' conceded Hugh, 'but that was only because it helped numb the pain of not being able to, and stopped people constantly asking when they were going to hear the patter of tiny Barrington feet.'

Studying the lengthening ash of her cigarette, Serena reached for a blue Wedgwood dish and flicked the ash onto the figure of a horse. Hugh turned away and went to open the window as she exhaled a thin column of smoke into the air. From below came the noise of excited voices unloading food and glasses.

'What I can't understand,' Serena said angrily, crushing the remains of her cigarette on the horse's head, 'is why you let me go along with all this – the anniversary and inviting our closest friends. Don't you realize what we've done? We haven't invited them to a silver wedding anniversary celebration at all. We've invited them to a Whitehall farce!'

Hugh nodded in agreement. 'It was, after all, what you wanted, Serena. You've known for months how things have been between us, ever since Stanley died, in fact.'

'Good God! You're never going to blame the break up of our marriage on the death of that bloody dog, are you?'

'No, let's just say having Stanley put to sleep unnecessarily was the final straw.'

'And who says it was unnecessary, your wonderful Sally? Well, if you hadn't been away sleeping with her,

351

your precious dog might still be alive. Perhaps you should have stayed at home that weekend!'

'Serena, that weekend I was with Uncle Bertram and well you know it! And for your information, it wasn't Sally who told me, it was . . .'

'Well?' Serena demanded, lighting yet another cigarette.

Anxious to protect both Charles and Vivienne, Hugh declined to be drawn further. 'Anyway I didn't come up here to discuss Sally or Stanley, I came up here to tell you the catering manageress wants to discuss the seating plan.'

'I don't give a damn about the seating plan!'

'And there was me thinking you wanted everyone sitting in the right place for the very moment you chose to stand up and tell them I'm having a homosexual affair with a local greengrocer!'

Studying the disturbingly inflexible set to Hugh's jaw, Serena felt her face redden. Nervously she fingered the new diamond ring, slipping it up and down her knuckle until she wedged it back into place next to her wedding ring.

'I'll go and see to the seating arrangements, but you haven't heard the last of this, Hugh.'

Standing up as she left the room, Hugh called after her, 'No, I don't suppose I have, Serena, and neither have you.'

Serena shot him a withering look and disappeared downstairs. There then followed the sound of raised voices and the grating of furniture as tables were moved about the dining room.

* * *

At Elmsmarsh, Sally stretched lazily in her bed. For once she'd not bothered to set her alarm. As it was the day of Hugh and Serena's anniversary celebrations, she knew that unlike other Saturdays Hugh would not be coming to see her.

He'd called in yesterday lunchtime and, smelling the ubiquitous lavender polish and spying fresh tell-tale tracks of the hoover in the carpet, had admonished her severely. 'You are supposed to be taking it easy, not leaping around like a mountain goat.'

'I would hardly put myself in the mountain-goat category. At the moment I feel more like a beached whale!'

Taking her in his arms Hugh whispered, 'Sally, you must be careful. After all, the baby is due today. I call in and expect to see you resting and what do I find?'

'I don't feel like resting, in fact I feel particularly energetic. I haven't felt this good for weeks. Besides, though today is my due date, you must know first babies are always late.'

'Always?' asked Hugh, his voice full of concern.

'Let's just say mostly.'

Now almost twenty-four hours later, she was beginning to regret the vigorous spell of early spring–cleaning, her back ached and she felt distinctly uncomfortable.

Running a warm bath Sally thought of Hugh and Serena and wondered what on earth was going on in the Barrington household. Hugh's vivid description of recent events made the whole business sound so utterly farcical, that Sally had described both husband and wife like hounds baying for the kill.

'Though I can feel the adrenalin rising –' Hugh had grinned – 'I can assure you, there won't be any killing. There might however be some bruised egos.'

Stepping carefully into the warm scented water, Sally studied her own bruise. The one on her right hip, which had resulted when an over-zealous push of the vacuum cleaner had practically impaled her against the sharp corner of the bedside table, throbbed painfully. Not only had she bruised her hip but she'd also sent the bedside lamp and the delicate chased-silver box cascading to the floor. Running her hands gently from her hip to the now more than prominent bulge of the baby, Sally pondered the events of the past nine months and of having this wondrous miracle growing inside her. Because as far as she and Hugh were concerned, it was still a miracle.

'It will be a blooming miracle if we ever get to lay the table let alone serve the bloody food!' the catering manageress muttered angrily to her assistant. 'First she wants a horseshoe table, with her and her husband sitting side by side. Now she wants one long table with her at one end like the lady bountiful and her husband at the other.'

'All I can say is, best let her have her own way then. She looks a pretty hard bitch if you ask me.'

'Yes – and quite possibly used to having her own way. Okay, lads, start shifting the tables and get the places laid as soon as possible, before she changes her mind again.'

When Hugh popped his head round the dining-room door, a sea of faces looked anxiously in his direction. 'What happened to the horseshoe?'

'Mrs Barrington changed her mind about it,' came the reply.

'Did she? Oh, fine, just so long as I know. Carry on then.'

Breathing a sigh of relief, nimble hands smoothed out starched white damask tablecloths and folded ice-blue napkins into fans.

Freshly bathed, Sally prepared herself some lunch, flicked through a magazine and settled down to watch *The Glen Miller Story* on the television. She'd watched it at least half a dozen times before, having first seen it with her mother when she was a girl. She'd cried then and no doubt would cry again this afternoon, it was all so dreadfully nostalgic. In preparation for the distressing ending, when June Allyson (playing the part of Glen Miller's wife) receives the terrible news, Sally went in search of a box of tissues and heard the phone ringing.

Three incoming phonecalls later, she got up and switched off the television. 'What's the point,' she sighed, putting her hand on her Stanley bump. 'I shan't have any peace until you arrive. Don't you realize all these people keep ringing to find out whether you've arrived yet? Perhaps we should leave them a message and go out for a walk instead.'

Slipping on her coat and reaching for her handbag, it was no surprise when the telephone rang for a fourth time. 'Well, who's it to be this time?' she asked her reflection in the hall mirror. 'We've already had Jackie, Roz and Laura. By the law of averages, it's got to be Marion.'

'Sally.'

'Hugh! What are you doing ringing me now? I thought you'd be busy with . . .'

'My darling, I am. But not too busy that I can't ring you.'

'But where are you ringing from, and what about Serena?'

'Don't panic! I'm ringing from the garden on my mobile and Serena doesn't even know I've left the house; she's far too busy giving the caterers hell.'

'Oh dear. It doesn't sound much like a celebratory occasion.'

'Don't you believe it! Everything's going swimmingly,' Hugh chuckled. 'In fact, it couldn't be better.'

'Hugh, have you been drinking?'

'No, I haven't touched a drop and I don't intend to either. I want to be sober when the fun and games start.'

Sally wasn't so sure whether or not she liked the sound of 'fun and games'. What had Hugh in mind? 'What exactly do you mean, Hugh?'

'Quite simply that I don't intend to drink as much as my guests so that when I tell them all about you, they'll all be completely pie-eyed and probably cheer me on my way.'

'Hugh, you must be mad! Why tell them about me, today of all days?'

Hugh's tone was matter-of-fact. 'Because, my dear sweet Sally, if I don't, Serena will!'

Recovering from the shock of his announcement, Sally lowered herself to the stairs. 'You mean you've told Serena about me?'

'No. I didn't have to. She found out quite by chance this morning. You've got to give it to her, Sally, her timing was perfect. In fact it's just what I've been waiting for.'

Unable to share Hugh's enthusiasm, Sally made no response and sat undoing and refastening the buttons on her coat.

'Anyway, my darling, as long as you and Stanley are okay, that's my main reason for ringing. You haven't been tearing about like a whirling dervish today, have you, I hope?'

'No, nor a mountain goat,' she said lamely.

'That's good. I'll ring you later tonight then, when they've all drunk me out of house and home. Take care, remember I love you.'

'I love you too,' she whispered as Hugh switched off his phone and returned to the house and Serena's ravings. Opening her front door, Sally was glad to be going for a walk. She needed some fresh air after Hugh's revelations.

Nodding to the new neighbours who were busily hanging their curtains, Sally walked past the row of unfinished houses in the direction of Elmsmarsh village and the shops. Then, remembering it would soon be Roz's birthday, she called at the newsagent's for a card.

Contemplating whether to send a pretty or humorous one, Sally found herself wondering whose name would be on it. Would it be just her own or hers and the baby's? But what name, that was the problem. As yet, she and Hugh were totally undecided over names. To them, the uncomfortable bulge now pressing on Sally's bladder was still baby Stanley.

Leaving the newsagent's and feeling the desperate need to spend a penny, Sally looked about her. It was too far to walk home and the only solution was to call in at Pots and Posies. There Terry was busy weighing out potatoes and Julie was taking some daffodils from a bucket on the floor.

'Do you think I could just use the loo?' she whispered to Julie.

'Sure, but mind how you go through, the floor's a bit wet from the sap of these daffodils.'

Manoeuvering herself past sacks of potatoes and onions, Sally reached the safety of the toilet. It was only when she went to close the door that her foot slipped on a piece of cabbage leaf and she found herself propelled clumsily onto the lavatory seat.

'Just in time,' she sighed, struggling with her panties and tights. Relieved to have the pressure taken off her bladder, Sally attempted the reverse struggle with her undies, only to be stopped short by an excrutiating pain shooting through her back.

'Damn,' she muttered, 'I must have strained a muscle when I slipped.'

Waiting for her to wash her hands, Julie held up the teapot.

'Fancy a cup of tea, Sally? Terry and I are just going to have one.'

Rubbing her back, Sally nodded and reached for a stool.

'Hey! Are you all right?' Julie asked, passing her a mug. 'Only you look a bit pale.'

'Mmmn, I'm fine. I think I overdid it with the cleaning yesterday and I must have twisted my back just now. I slipped on a piece of cabbage.'

'Who slipped on a piece of cabbage?' Terry asked, coming through to the back room for his tea.

'Sally did. She's also been overdoing it with the cleaning.'

'I know,' Terry replied. 'Hugh told me.'

'He did? But when did you see Hugh?' Sally enquired.

'Yesterday. He called here after he'd been to see you.'

Sipping her tea and wondering why Hugh should have gone to see Terry, Sally suddenly felt another surge of pain and clutched at the stool. Watching her place her tea on the ledge by her side, Terry cast an anxious look in Julie's direction.

'Sally – is anything the matter?'

'I don't know . . . I mean I'm not really sure. It can't be the baby, can it?'

Terry smiled kindly. 'And you're asking us . . .?'

Smiling weakly at the two of them, Sally said, 'Do you think one of you could walk home with me?'

'Walk home with you! You've got to be joking! Julie, shut the shop!'

'But you can't shut the shop just like that,' Sally remonstrated.

''Course we can!' announced Terry, throwing Julie a bunch of keys.

Helping Sally into the white van with its green Pots and Posies emblem, Julie turned to Terry and whispered nervously, 'What are we going to do?'

'First we're going to the flat to fetch my car, then I'll take Sally home so she can ring the hospital and get her bag.'

'And what about me?'

'You, Julie, can stay at Sally's in case Hugh calls.'

'No, Terry! I don't want you to tell Hugh,' Sally insisted. 'It's their anniversary.'

'Hmph! Wake, more like, from what Hugh was telling me yesterday. Anyway don't let's bother about that now. Let's just get you home.'

While Sally was on the phone to the hospital, Terry frantically scribbled some instructions onto an envelope and thrust them into Julie's hand, putting his finger to his lips as he did so.

'I understand,' Julie acknowledged. 'Mum's the word.'

'In more ways than one,' Terry replied, watching Sally walk uncomfortably into the sitting room. 'What did the hospital say?'

'They say I can go in if I want to, or I can stay at home until the contractions become more regular.'

Helping her to the settee, Terry asked kindly, 'And what would you prefer to do, Sally?'

'At the moment I don't really know. Hospitals terrify me, yet I don't want to leave it too late before I go in.'

'From what I remember of that tape and looking at you now, I would be prepared to say it's safe to stay at home a bit longer.'

Sally made a grab for Terry's hand as another contraction began. 'You will stay with me, won't you?'

'Of course. Like I told you, I'll stay with you now, then take you into hospital when you're ready and remain with you until the baby arrives, if you're sure that's what you want.'

Concentrating on timing her contractions, Sally nodded in relief.

Watching all this made Julie uneasy. He'd always been squeamish and it bothered him to see Sally in distress. Casting an anxious look in Terry's direction he motioned to the door.

'That's all right, Julie. You go and see to those last deliveries. Don't forget to take the mobile and I'll call you later.' Oblivious to the wink that, Terry gave Julie, Sally closed her eyes and breathed deeply.

CHAPTER 23

At approximately seven thirty on the Saturday evening, Serena was applying the finishing touches to her make-up as Terry collected Sally's bag from the nursery and helped her to his car.

'Are you sure you don't want me to ring Hugh?'

Feeling another contraction coming, Sally shook her head and held on to Terry's hand. 'No, they'll have barely started on the canapés and regardless of what Serena thinks of me, I don't want to spoil her evening.'

Terry sighed and opened the car door. 'I think Hugh would want to know, that's all.'

'Terry, I want you to promise me on no account will you ring Hugh.'

Grim faced, Terry found himself reluctantly agreeing to her request and switched on the ignition. 'I'll drive as carefully as I can but tell me if you want me to stop along the way.'

Outside the main doorway of the maternity unit, Sally stopped abruptly.

'Another contraction?' Terry enquired.

'No, it's just that I'm terrified of hospitals. I go to

pieces when I get that first smell of disinfectant or whatever else it is.'

Holding Sally's arm with one hand and carrying her bag in the other, Terry led her through the door. 'Take it from me,' he urged kindly, 'I have absolutely no intention of letting you go to pieces.'

'From the state of me, I feel as if I'm about to – but it's too late for me to change my mind about all this, isn't it?'

Watching her force a smile, Terry took a last deep gulp of crisp January night air before the same familiar smell that Sally dreaded so much hit his nostrils.

'Hello, Sally, so we're on our way at last then.' A chirpy voice greeted them and Sally breathed a sigh of relief at seeing the familiar smiling face, framed by wavy chestnut hair, of the woman in front of them.

'Terry, can I introduce you to Sue, my midwife.'

Terry nodded in greeting and was aware of a questioning gaze in his direction. Reading Sue's mind, Sally explained. 'Terry's not my partner, he's my neighbour, he's offered to stay with me. That's okay, isn't it?'

'If that's what you want, my dear, that's fine. Just don't go and pass out on us, Terry, at the crucial moment.'

'No way! I've watched the video, so I know what to expect. Before we left for the hospital I was even practising rubbing Sally's back, although she seems more comfortable walking than sitting. But some women are like that, aren't they?'

Sue smiled kindly. It seemed strange Sally should arrive with a neighbour – and a male one at that – but he seemed extremely conscientious about his forthcoming role. Hers was not to reason why the father of Sally's baby wasn't with her. These days mums-to-be turned up with a variety of friends and family for support during the birth. In fact, the young girl she'd delivered only that morning had arrived with her mother, who'd then sat and cursed the young lad who'd got her daughter in the family way. Somehow Sue didn't foresee the same problems with Terry.

'He seems very keen,' Sue murmured when she and Sally were alone.

'Oh, he is. He's really looking forward to the birth. I only wish I could share his enthusiasm.'

Examining her, Sue then laid her hands on Sally's stomach to gauge the strength of the contraction. 'Well, you've a while yet before the cervix is fully dilated. So if you do want to go for a walk . . . Just don't go charging about like a mountain goat.'

Sally laughed. 'That's what Hugh – the baby's father – said the other day. By the way, I haven't told him I'm in labour, because he's got a family celebration this evening – that's why Terry's with me.'

Puzzled, Sue shook her head and whispered to herself as she watched Terry help Sally down the corridor, 'And what's this then, if it's not a family celebration?'

Hugh tapped on Serena's bedroom door, which she opened almost immediately.

'I was wondering if you were ready, I can hear the sound of cars in the driveway,' he told her.

'No doubt Craig and Belinda!' Serena said curtly. 'They're always the first to arrive, the first to get drunk and the last to leave.'

Hugh was going to ask why she had invited them but instead kept his thoughts to himself and studied Serena's appearance. As Sally had predicted, swathed in sumptuous black velvet, she looked lovely.

Looking up with an expectant smile on her face, Serena waited for Hugh's reaction. 'Well,' she murmured, 'what do you think?'

Using Uncle Bertram's expression, he replied, 'I think you look stunning; now, are you ready to greet our guests?'

Hugh held out his arm to a slightly bewildered Serena. Yes, she did look stunning but at the same time he felt no familiar stirring as her hand clasped his arm. Any such feelings had long since disappeared.

Walking down the staircase, decorated with garlands, with Serena by his side, Hugh contemplated the past twenty-five years. They had shared some good times together but somewhere along the way – and at that precise moment he couldn't pinpoint exactly when – they had begun to drift apart. And, if they were to be entirely honest with one another it was probably even before Sally and Stanley.

Sweeping past the two waitresses standing in the hall with trays of Bucks Fizz, Serena fixed a smile on her face and greeted Belinda and Craig with open arms. 'Darlings! How wonderful to see you. So pleased you could come.'

'Just you try and keep us away, old thing,' Craig said, plonking a wet kiss on Serena's cheek.

'Less of the old, if you don't mind!'

Craig chuckled and standing back shot Serena an admiring glance. 'I stand corrected, Serena, you look even lovelier than ever, doesn't she, Belinda?'

Belinda cooed in Serena's direction and brushed her hand gently against Serena's shoulder. 'Lovely, darling, and the dress is simply divine. Velvet again I see, just like you had on your wedding day all those years ago. Hugh, my dear, how are you?'

'Very well as you can see, Belinda. Let me offer you both a drink.'

Hugh watched Craig gulp at his Bucks Fizz. 'You'd probably prefer it without the orange juice, but the night is still young and I'm relying on you to get the party going with a swing after dinner,' he said to Craig.

'Your wish is my command,' Craig replied, emptying his glass and watched Hugh and Serena step forward to meet the rest of their guests.

Studying the distress on Sally's face, Terry reached for the small triangular-shaped sponge, moistened it with water and applied it to her mouth and forehead. 'Keep going, Sally, it can't be much longer now.'

'I hope not,' she whimpered. 'To be honest I've already had enough. I don't think I can cope with much more of this!' Her eyes pleaded in Sue's direction.

'You're doing fine, Sally, how about trying with the gas and air again? Trust me, it will help, you know.'

'I think she's frightened of it,' Terry explained. 'It's all connected with her fear of hospitals.'

Sue turned aside to Terry. 'Try and persuade her if you can, just for a bit. She really is doing well, you

366

know. And in a while I'll be able to give her some pethidine which will help.'

At the mere mention of pethidine, Sally's face brightened as she reached for the mask Terry was holding. 'Thank goodness,' she sighed. 'That's the injection I was telling you about earlier.'

Terry's face went suddenly white. Injections! He hated injections, both having them himself or watching other people on the receiving end. Years ago, when he was at school and they'd all lined up for their BCG jabs, it hadn't been the ashen-faced girl in front that had passed out, but Terry!

'Would you mind if I went out while you had your injection, Sally? They do for me what the smell of hospitals does for you.'

Coping grimly with a contraction, Sally shook her head and in between her controlled panting, urged Terry to have a cup of tea while he was out of the room.

'No way, I'm not staying away longer than I have to.' Squeezing Sally's hand reassuringly, he added, 'I'll be back in a mo. Don't run away.'

'Fat chance of that!' Sally cried. 'Just wait 'til I get my hands on Jack, the little menace! It's all his fault I'm having to go through this!'

'Who's Jack? Her partner?' the young trainee nurse asked Terry, as he moved towards the door. Spying the needle in Sue's hand, Terry just shook his head and ran.

Smiling, the nurse watched him disappear down the corridor. At first she'd thought Terry was the father of Sally's baby, yet in his T-shirt and jeans, complete with designer stubble and earring, he'd seemed a most unlikely partner. And why should Sally be blaming someone called Jack for her predicament, if like Terry he wasn't the father either? Confused, the nurse took Terry's place by the bed, held Sally's hand and began rubbing her back.

Giving Hugh a hearty slap on the back, Craig returned to his seat at the table.

'A great meal, Hugh! Now what about your speech? We're all waiting and hoping you're going to put an end to all these rumours.'

'Rumours?' Hugh enquired, looking in Serena's direction, where she sat at the far end of the table.

'Oh, Craig means about you retiring from Barrington's,' Belinda explained.

From the bottom of the table, Serena commented icily, 'You'll never get Hugh to retire, he's just like Pa-in-law used to be – married to the wretched place!'

There was polite murmured laughter from the guests and Vivienne looked anxiously in her husband's direction. As she'd whispered to Charles, only moments earlier, the atmosphere between Hugh and Serena was becoming decidedly more strained as the evening wore on.

'Perceptive as ever, Vivienne,' Charles said, squeezing his wife's hand.

'But I shouldn't worry about it too much, if I were you. Some of the guests haven't seen Hugh and Serena for a while anyway, and the rest of them are too well oiled to sense otherwise.'

Vivienne's gaze rested on Craig as he banged noisily on the table in preparation for Hugh's long awaited speech.

'Order! Order!' he boomed in true headmaster fashion as all eyes turned in Hugh's direction.

'Be quiet!' Belinda hissed to her husband.

Adjusting his bow-tie and straightening the cuffs of his dress shirt, Hugh rose to his feet.

'Before I begin, let me just ask the delightful ladies who have served us this evening to top up your glasses again. Then at least if you think my speech is going on for too long, hopefully you'll be too polite to complain!'

Hugh nodded as the waitresses, dressed in black with white frilly aprons, stepped forward with the champagne, then good-naturedly dismissing them, he donned his reading glasses and began.

'Ladies and gentlemen, dear friends, as we've known each other for at least twenty-five years, I expect you'll be wanting me to begin my speech with what makes a happy marriage and to that end I don't intend to disappoint you. The secret to a happy marriage, as I see it, is lust!'

Ribald cries of, 'Good old, Hugh,' came from Craig's direction and the faces of some of the female guests filled with horror. Hugh tapped on the table to draw everyone's attention once more.

'Ah! Lust,' he sighed. 'And if I could just borrow a phrase from that well known television series *Star Trek*, lust but not as we know it!'

'Beam me up Scottie!' a voice echoed, amidst the laughter.

'LUST,' continued Hugh, 'as I interpret it, stands for Love, Understanding, Secrets and Trust. Actually I think a better order would be, Love, Understanding,

369

Trust and Shared Secrets, but that wouldn't have held your attention in quite the same way now, would it?'

Across the table, Hugh noticed people nodding in assent whilst others sipped at their champagne. So far so good, he thought; at least everyone seemed suitably mellow. Even Serena was smiling. Raising his glass in her direction he continued.

'Of the first three, love, understanding and trust, I'm sure most of us here have shared those qualities in our marriages, otherwise we wouldn't be here now. Let's face it, with one in three marriages ending in divorce, we've not done too badly between us, have we?'

Waiting for the cries of 'Hear, Hear!' to subside, Hugh fixed his eyes on Serena. 'Secrets,' he began said softly. 'Now who among us has not had secrets? Ladies, I expect you've all had the little black number hanging in the wardrobe, knowing full well it wasn't the amazing bargain you made it out to be and gentlemen, well let's just say it's strange how all those unexpected business meetings involved taking along the golf clubs.'

Draining her glass of champagne, Belinda said sarcastically, 'Or in Craig's case, a little blonde number and the golf clubs!'

There was an embarrassed silence which was broken when the head waitress came back into the room. She bent in Hugh's direction.

'Excuse me, Mr Barrington but someone's just arrived with a bouquet of flowers for you.'

Hugh looked at his watch. It was eleven o'clock. 'Flowers at this time, Mrs Evans, surely not?'

'Yes sir, they've just this minute arrived.'

'Then they must be for my wife – not me.'

'No, Mr Barrington. I distinctly heard the young man ask for you. The funny thing is I thought he said his name was Julie but he must have meant the flowers are from Julie . . .'

'Julie!' Hugh exclaimed.

To the rest of the guests it appeared Hugh was referring to Mrs Evans; only Serena, Vivienne and Charles knew otherwise.

Leaving the table, Serena followed Hugh into the hallway while Vivienne asked Mrs Evans to organize coffee and liqueurs and Charles amused the guests with a rendering of *The Lion and Albert*.

Hugh motioned the nervous Julie into his study.

'I'm sorry to disturb your evening, Hugh, only Terry's just rung from the hospital and insisted I came to see you.'

'The hospital! You mean Sally . . .?'

Julie nodded. 'Things started this afternoon when she called at the shop. Terry took her home and stayed with her until about sevenish, then he took her in . . .'

'But why didn't she ring me? Why didn't *you* ring me!'

'Because Sally made Terry promise. In the end he got desperate and rang me and suggested I came straight round here. I put a message in with the flowers just in case I didn't get to see you personally.'

Hugh moved towards the bouquet but Serena who had been hovering in the doorway was there before him. Snatching at the envelope with its rose decorated card and message she gave a loud gasp.

' "Sally in labour, can you come?" What the hell does this mean, Hugh!'

'Exactly what it says, Serena! Sally is in Thornhampton hospital about to give birth to my child, so if you'll excuse me I'd better go.'

'That's preposterous! I mean you can't have children!'

'Correction, Serena!' Hugh broke in tartly. '*You're* the one who can't have children, or had you forgotten?'

Reminded of her deception, Serena bit her lip and threw the card she was holding on the floor in disgust. 'But you can't just leave, Hugh! It's our wedding anniversary. What about our guests?'

'I'm fed up with *can't*, Serena, and as for our guests,' Hugh continued coolly, 'well, they've been wined and dined this evening at some considerable expense to myself and whether they want to celebrate the end of our marriage or the birth of my first child is up to them!'

'The end of our marriage?' Serena asked lamely.

'Exactly,' replied Hugh. 'Now if you'll just come with me, Serena, I'll bid our guests a fond farewell and leave them in your capable hands.'

In stunned silence, Serena allowed Hugh to lead her back to the dining room, where they were greeted by loud cheers of 'Hugh and Serena'.

Aware of Serena's nails digging into his left hand, Hugh raised his glass with his right. 'My dear friends, I'm afraid my speech was cut short. I won't dwell on the reasons why at the moment as I'm sure Serena will explain after I've gone.'

'Gone?' murmured Craig drunkenly, 'but you can't leave us yet, old thing, the night's still young.'

'I know, Craig, but I must. Still, I'm going to leave you in Serena's fair hands and no doubt if you twist her arm, I'm sure you'll be able to persuade her to entertain you at the piano. Don't forget, Serena and Vivienne do a wonderful rendition of *Sisters*.' Hugh cast a knowing look in his sister-in-law's direction.

Placing a glass of champagne in Serena's hand, Hugh announced to his guests, 'As I said earlier, most couples share the odd secret or two and in our case the one Serena and I have been keeping from you is that you were all brought here tonight under false pretences.'

Feeling twenty-five pairs of eyes turning in his direction, Hugh said matter-of-factly, 'You all think you were invited here to celebrate our silver wedding – which is after all partly correct – but at the same time Serena and I wish to announce the end of our marriage as well. As civilized beings, why not, we thought, have a double celebration? So if you'll all join me, I'd like to propose a toast, not only to our past but also to our future.'

Leaning forward Hugh kissed the ashen-face Serena on the cheek and raised his glass. 'To the past and the future – Serena.'

'The past and the future,' she whispered numbly as a sea of surprised voices rang out in unison.

Hurrying to the hall to join Julie, Hugh released his grasp on Serena's hand and gave her over to her sister's care.

'Take care of her, Vivienne. I'll ring tomorrow.' Climbing into the Pots and Posies van, Hugh was aware of someone running from the front door.

'Hugh!' Charles cried breathlessly. 'I take it the baby is on its way? Good luck, old chap!' Shaking Hugh firmly by the hand, Charles added, 'You will let us know, won't you?'

'Yes, Charles, I'll let you know, and thanks for everything.'

Watching the white van disappear down the gravelled driveway, Charles went back inside the house where he heard the opening bars of *Sisters* echoing into the hallway. Serena, once more the centre of attention, had begun to play.

Terry, feeling particularly smug with himself, walked back into the delivery room just as Sally burst forth with a string of expletives which included not only Terry's name but Jack's and Hugh's as well. The young nurse in attendance blushed bright red.

'Oh, it's quite usual,' the midwife explained. 'The quieter ones are often the worse. It's transition and a sure sign baby's almost here.'

'But it can't come yet!' Terry announced. 'Hugh's not here!'

'Terry!' Sally cried, between shallow breathing, 'you promised you wouldn't ring Hugh.'

'I didn't, I sent Julie round to fetch him!'

'You did what!' Sally called in disbelief. Then refraining from further obscenities called out, 'Oh my God! I think I want to push!'

At the same time there was a commotion in the corridor and Hugh's voice was heard to say, 'Terry's not the father, I am! So will you please let me through.'

As Sally started pushing, she and Terry looked towards the door and the trainee nurse, seeing Hugh – a picture of elegance – did a double – take. It was the man with the red rose in his lapel from Barrington's department store. Only tonight he wasn't wearing a lounge suit and a red rose, he was wearing a dinner suit and bow-tie!

'Sally!' Hugh cried. 'Why didn't you send for me?'

Unable to reply, Sally just clung to Hugh's hand and concentrated on Sue's instructions.

'That's fine, Sally, half the head is there, so stop pushing for the moment and just do as I say . . . gently now.'

Awestruck, Hugh and Terry gazed in wonderment as with a final groan, Sally pushed and Sue, guiding the baby's head and body, performed the perfect delivery.

'Oh! My God, its head's all blue,' Terry called, keeling over.

'All babies are like that until they take their first breath,' Sue called reassuringly.

With misted eyes Hugh kissed Sally and caressed the tiny, wrapped bundle lying peacefully in her arms.

Swallowing hard he whispered, 'I just can't believe it. I just can't believe it. Has this really happened, Sally?'

'Oh yes,' she said, 'I can assure you it has!'

'I'm just so sorry I wasn't with you all the way through.'

'You were here for the most important bit, Hugh, and that's all that matters and Terry was marvellous – by the way, where is he?'

'Being led round the carpark by Julie. I think it all got a bit much for him in the end and . . .' Hugh got no further as at that moment a tiny hand wriggled from the blanket and grasped his finger. Gazing adoringly, Hugh turned to Sally. 'I've been thinking, we're not really going to call him Stanley, are we? Shouldn't we think of something more suitable?'

Smiling, Sally carefully peeled back the blanket. 'Yes, I think we should – think of something more suitable, I mean – she's really not going to thank us for calling her Stanley, is she?'

'But I thought it was a boy! You mean it's a girl – but that's wonderful!'

'You mean you're not disappointed?'

'Gracious no! If she turns out to be anything like her mother, how could I be disappointed?'

Watching Sally cover up his baby daughter, Hugh sighed contentedly and looked at his watch. It was gone midnight. 'I suppose I'd better go and let you both get some sleep.'

'Will you be going back home to Ser –?'

Hugh shook his head. 'No, that's no longer my home. Serena will stay there of course and I'll probably go back tomorrow for a change of clothes. If it's all right with you I thought I'd go back to Elmsmarsh.'

'The keys are in my handbag, in case you don't have your set with you.'

Hugh reached in his pocket and jangled some keys. 'That's okay, I came prepared.'

'But not for delivering babies,' Sally announced. 'You've got a stain on your shirt.'

Hugh laughed and stroked her hand.

'What's so funny?' she asked.

'I seem to remember that's how all this began – with me getting make-up on my shirt . . . remember.'

Sally blushed at the memory . . . she in her bathrobe and Hugh in her kimono.

'My goodness, but it was worth it!' Hugh sighed, standing up. 'Who would have guessed?'

'Who indeed?' Sally asked, as Hugh kissed her good-night.

CHAPTER 24

Hugh woke early the next morning and driving past Terry and Julie's flat he noticed the curtains and blinds still drawn. Not to worry, he thought, he would call them later.

Pulling into the driveway of his house, he recognized the caterers vans and assumed they would be clearing up from yesterday's party. It also meant Serena wouldn't be alone in the house either, which in some ways came as a relief.

It had been one thing waking up with that wondrous sense of euphoria, knowing that overnight he had become the proud father of a beautiful baby daughter, but on the other hand he still had to face Serena. Inserting his house key into the lock, Hugh felt the door open without effort.

'Charles! I didn't expect to find you here.'

Charles put a finger to his lips and beckoned him inside. 'Vivienne and I thought we ought to stay over with Serena.'

'She's all right, isn't she?'

Charles smiled ruefully. 'Oh, yes. She's just a bit hung over, that's all.'

'I see, and where is she?'

'Still sleeping. So are you going to come and tell Vivienne and me the good news?' Charles looked at Hugh's dishevelled appearance. He was still wearing his dinner suit. 'It is good news, I hope?' he asked anxiously.

'Oh, yes!' sighed Hugh. 'Wonderful news, I have a daughter!'

Vivienne looked up from where she was reading the Sunday paper. Her eyes brightened when she saw him. 'Well?'

'A baby girl, quite tiny in fact, only six pounds but perfect.'

'Oh, Hugh, my dear, that's simply wonderful . . . and is the mother . . .?'

'Yes, Sally's fine, just very tired. It was all a bit of an ordeal as you are only too aware, Vivienne.'

Vivienne nodded in agreement, remembering back to all those years ago when she'd given birth to Gareth. Giving Hugh a warm hug, she whispered, 'And are we going to be able to see your beautiful daughter?'

Hugh looked warily towards the sitting-room door. 'Of course. But aren't you worried about what Serena will think?'

Shrugging her shoulders, Vivienne announced, 'Concerned, yes, but not worried. Still, we'll think of a solution, I'm sure, and from what Serena was saying last night, she's already got her future mapped out.'

'Yes,' broke in Charles, 'but don't forget, my dear, Serena was also very drunk.'

'So she was and perhaps I'd better go and make us some fresh coffee. Hugh, you will stay for a cup?'

'Vivienne, Hugh does live here you know.'

'I know, Charles, but I doubt very much if he's staying, are you, Hugh?'

Hugh shook his head. 'Not for long, I only came back for a change of clothes. I can't really go back to the hospital looking like this, but I would very much appreciate a cup of coffee, Vivienne.'

Packing a suitcase, Hugh became aware of the aroma of freshly ground coffee wafting up the stairs and the murmur of voices from further down the landing. Presently there was a gentle tap on his bedroom door.

'Hugh, I've brought you a tray as I didn't know how long you'd be. I thought I'd also let you know Serena is awake. I told her you were here and about the baby. I hope you don't mind.'

'No,' he said, taking the tray. 'She's got to find out sooner or later. Perhaps it was easier coming from you, Vivienne – who knows?'

'The old man of the mountain knows, that's who!'

Hugh looked up puzzled.

'I'm sorry, Hugh,' Vivienne explained. 'It's a line from one of the Sparky songs Serena and I used to listen to when we were girls. Uncle Mac on the radio and 78rpm records remember?'

'I remember Sparky and his magic piano . . .'

'Oh, this is another one when Sparky lost his echo. I suppose we might still have the record somewhere, I'll have to ask Charles. It's probably in the loft. Perhaps when your daughter is older . . . By the way, you never said, what are you going to call her?'

'To be honest, Vivienne, we haven't decided. We'd been calling her Stanley until she arrived.'

379

It was Vivienne's turn to look puzzled. Taking a pile of shirts from a drawer, Hugh coughed. 'She was . . . er . . . conceived the weekend Serena had Stanley put to sleep.'

'Oh!' Vivienne said knowingly and patting Hugh's arm continued. 'Well, thank heavens some good came out of such an unpleasant episode. I know Serena's my sister but she has behaved . . .'

At that moment Vivienne heard Serena's bedroom door open and close. Keeping a furtive eye on the door she whispered to Hugh, 'I'd better go down. Look, if we don't see you before you go, all the best. And if you think we're being anti-social when you come down, we're just doing it for Serena's benefit okay?'

'Okay.' Hugh nodded.

As expected, moments later Serena burst into Hugh's bedroom. Still in her bathrobe, with her hair uncombed and probably for the first time ever, with traces of smudged make-up around her eyes, she appeared strangely vulnerable. Any feelings of pity Hugh felt stirring in his breast rapidly diminished when Serena spat sarcastically, 'Well, well, our Mrs Palmer deceived us both all right. No doubt she had it planned right from the very start. She certainly knew how to wheedle her way into your affections. I can just see her now, plotting and scheming, with her "I'll look after Stanley for you."'

'Sally certainly looked after Stanley a damn sight better than you did, Serena! Unlike you, she never made the poor animal sleep in a utility room, she even allowed him to have his bed inside in the warm.'

'Hmph!' Serena snorted, 'no doubt encouraging you into her own bed at the same time and deliberately getting herself pregnant!'

'How could she, when practically half the world knew I was supposed to be impotent!'

'Don't exaggerate, Hugh, half the world indeed!'

'Considering you yourself, Serena, broadcast to most of our friends and even members of Barrington's staff, that I was incapable of . . .'

'Barrington's staff. Whatever do you mean?'

'Oh, don't come the innocent with me, Serena! And as for talking about deceiving people, I think you've got a bloody cheek!'

Nervously Serena stepped backwards to the door. 'I don't understand, I don't know what you . . .'

'Don't you? DON'T YOU! Well let me tell you!' Reaching out, Hugh grabbed hold of Serena's wrist and pushed her forcibly onto the bed.

'You're hurting my wrist.'

'Good! It's about time someone hurt you for a change as you're so good at hurting everyone else!'

Letting go of her wrist, Hugh reached for the bedroom chair and placed it directly in front of her. Unable to face his gaze, Serena sat with eyes lowered and fingered the sash on her bathrobe.

'Now,' Hugh sighed, sitting down, 'have you got anything at all to say for yourself?'

'I gather you've got a daughter – she couldn't even give you a son!'

Exasperated, Hugh reached for Serena's chin and tilted it until he was staring her straight in the eye. 'And what did you give me, Serena? As I recall you just fed me a pack of lies about adopted babies and suchlike. Good God! Thinking about it, you even tricked me into marrying you!'

Serena bit her lip. 'But you said it didn't matter, Hugh. You said you didn't mind not having children . . .'

'No, of course I didn't mind . . . not then, because I loved you and I thought you'd been honest with me. To think I actually trusted you and for all these years I'd thought . . .' Hugh shuddered.

'By that I take it you don't love me now, then?'

Standing up, Hugh snapped the lid shut on his suitcase. 'Don't be so pathetic, what do you think? As you're already aware, you will have the house and be well provided for. And doubtless it will be *your* story our friends hear first – but I can live with that. Just thank your lucky stars I didn't stick to my original speech last night.'

Serena looked up as Hugh reached for his sports jacket. 'And just what is that supposed to mean?'

'When I got to the bit about secrets, I felt sorely tempted to tell everyone the secret you'd been keeping from me for the past twenty-five years – but then I'm not as vindictive as you, Serena.'

Watching Hugh open the bedroom door, Serena called, 'Anyway you're the one who broke the rules. If you hadn't Sally would never have become pregnant.'

'Broke the rules? Broke the rules! Why, you bitch! You mean the rules you laid down to cover up your despicable deception! Have you any idea what it's been like, living with the knowledge that you actually had the gall to . . .'

Clasping her hands to her ears, Serena cried, 'Stop it! I don't want to know.'

'No, I don't suppose you do but sooner or later you're going to be reminded of it and when you are, I hope it hurts, just like you hurt me!'

'Well I hope you'll be very happy,' Serena said unconvincingly.

'Thank you. But you don't have to hope, Serena, as I already am, *extremely* happy in fact. And by the way, with regards to your earlier reference about my daughter, perhaps Sally and I will have a son next time!'

Walking briskly down the stairs, Hugh noticed the sitting-room door ajar. He glanced in briefly and nodded; no doubt Charles and Vivienne had heard everything.

'I'll call you.' Charles mouthed silently.

Still fuming from his encounter with Serena, Hugh stopped outside Sally's room. 'Put it all behind you,' a voice said from deep within himself. What was it Sally had said to comfort him months ago? 'That was then and this is now'. Exactly! Now, showered and changed, he was ready to greet his new daughter.

Spying the empty cot, Hugh turned towards the bed where the baby lay quietly sleeping against Sally's naked breast. Overcome with emotion, he found himself unable to move, as if trying to freeze-frame the delightful scene. Sally looked up and smiled. 'Aren't you coming in to see us?'

'Yes, yes, of course.'

Moving to the bed Hugh bent and kissed her, before stroking his index finger gently down the baby's cheek. 'How is she?' he whispered.

'Greedy!' came the reply.

Hugh grinned. 'And how are you, my darling?'

'A little bit sore but blissfully happy.'

Sitting on the bed Hugh reached for her free hand. 'I must say you're looking a lot better than when I last saw you.'

Taking the sleeping baby from her breast, Sally placed the baby in Hugh's arms. 'Stanley, I think you should get to know your daddy.'

Alarmed, Hugh asked, 'Are you sure? You mean it's all right?'

'Of course. After all, you only held her briefly last night, or should that be this morning?'

Watching Hugh tenderly cradle the sleeping baby, Sally asked, 'Speaking of this morning, how did it go with Serena?'

'Let's just say it wasn't particularly pleasant, but Charles and Vivienne were wonderful. Anyway, we don't have to discuss such things now, do we? More importantly, I think we should discuss the matter of this young lady's name. Uncle Bertram was most concerned to discover we're still calling her Stanley.'

'I'm glad you managed to ring Bertram and tell him.'

'I did more than that, I called in to see him before I came to the hospital. Oh, and by the way, he asked me to give you this.' Gingerly, so as not to wake his daughter, Hugh reached in his pocket and brought out a long thin box.

'Whatever is it?'

'Search me! But apparently he bought whatever it is years ago, for a very special lady only he left it too late to give it to her.'

Opening the dark green box, Sally lifted out a string of perfectly formed pearls and held them against her cheek.

'They're beautiful but why give them to me?'

'Possibly because he remembered the day when you walked in the garden together. Weren't you talking about Freya and the mistletoe?'

'Of course! Freya's pearls.'

'Speaking of pearls, this little one is about to dribble all over my shirt. Do you have a tissue or something?'

Dabbing at the pearl of milk forming on the baby's rosebud mouth, Sally added cheekily, 'And there was me thinking you were used to females ruining your shirts!'

Hugh looked thoughtful as his eyes met hers. 'You know that could be a possibility for a name.'

'What – ruined shirts!' She grinned.

'No! I mean Freya. What do you think?'

'I don't know. Freya Barrington,' Sally said softly. 'I shall have to think about it. I was thinking perhaps Rachel or Katherine. Perhaps I could ask Roz. She asked if she could come in and see us before we go home.'

'In that case, perhaps I'd better go. I take it she still doesn't know who your mystery lover is?'

'No, but I expect your time is running out, "mystery lover". Any day now, you and Roz are going to come face to face.'

'I shall look forward to it immensely,' Hugh said, carefully handing back the baby.

Roz stood by the side of Sally's bed and peered into the cot with tear-filled eyes. 'She's beautiful and so perfect, just look at her rosebud mouth, and she's even got hair!'

Removing her glasses to dab at her eyes with a handkerchief, she turned to face Sally. 'I hope you didn't mind me coming in, only I just had to see you, you clever girl.'

Roz grabbed hold of Sally's hand. 'Tell me,' she urged, 'was it truly awful? Donald said I wasn't to ask but I'm dying to know. Was he, I mean the father, was he with you for the birth?'

'Let's just say it wasn't a bed of roses, and yes, Roz, he was with me to hold my hand when she was born.'

Roz slumped on the bedside chair with a deep sigh. 'Thank God for that! I can't tell you how anxious I've been. By the way, speaking of roses, just as I was coming into the hospital I could have sworn I saw the boss man with an enormous bouquet of roses by one of the telephone booths. I didn't know Serena was in hospital! Still, if she is, I expect I'll get all the news when I go into work tomorrow.'

'Yes, I expect you will,' Sally said knowingly.

Moments later when the door opened and Hugh walked in, he called brightly, 'Hello Roz. How lovely to see you and what do you think of my beautiful daughter!'

Sally chuckled as Hugh helped her and the baby into the Jaguar.

'Poor Roz! If only I'd had a camera to record her reaction. It really wasn't fair of you, you know.'

'How else was I going to tell her?' Hugh grinned. 'To be honest I didn't think she'd stay with you that long, and at the time, it seemed the only way. Anyway, you have to admit my timing was perfect.'

'Yes,' Sally sighed, 'in fact, it always has been when you come to think of it.'

'Like finding you and Roz collapsed on the stairs in a fit of giggles that afternoon when she was drunk.'

'I wasn't actually thinking of that occasion.'

Drawing to a gradual halt outside the house, Sally was surprised to see Terry and Julie in her front garden. They were tying pink ribbons onto an avenue of clipped bay trees in pots.

'What on earth are they doing?' she cried.

'It was supposed to be a surprise,' Hugh announced. 'I wanted to make up for the ruined bay tree, where we were going to scatter Stanley's ashes. Then Terry had the idea to have a whole avenue of them and Julie got carried away and came up with the idea of blue ribbons.'

'But it's pink for a girl.'

'I know. But it was only this afternoon I realized Terry and Julie still thought you'd had a boy. That's why Roz saw me in the telephone booth. For once I didn't have my mobile and I had to get Terry to race back to Pots and Posies for some pink ribbon.

Sally watched as in a swirl of pink ribbon, Julie rushed to the last bay tree still tied with blue. She called out anxiously, 'Julie no! Don't!'

A confused Julie stepped aside as Sally, holding the baby, approached the blue beribboned bay tree. 'Can you leave it like that, please? I'd like to keep that bay tree for Stanley.'

Swallowing hard, Hugh walked back to the boot of the car and brought out the bouquet of roses Roz had mentioned earlier. Sally gave a gasp and clasped the baby tightly – Roz had never mentioned their colour. Through tear-filled eyes, she saw Hugh coming towards her, carrying a sea of red blooms. Putting his arm around her, he whispered lovingly, 'What was it you once said, about red roses for commitment?'

THE EXCITING NEW NAME IN WOMEN'S FICTION!

PLEASE HELP ME TO HELP YOU!

Dear *Scarlet* Reader,

Last month we began our super Prize Draw, which means that **you could win 6 months' worth of free Scarlets!** Just return your completed questionnaire to us (see addresses at end of questionnaire) before 31 July 1997 and you will automatically be entered in the draw that takes place on that day. If you are lucky enough to be one of the first two names out of the hat we will send you four new Scarlet romances every month for six months, and for each of twenty runners up there will be a sassy *Scarlet* T-shirt.

So don't delay – return your form straight away!*

Sally Cooper

Editor-in-Chief, *Scarlet*

*Prize draw offer available only in the UK, USA or Canada. Draw is not open to employees of Robinson Publishing, or of their agents, families or households. Winners will be informed by post, and details of winners can be obtained after 31 July 1997, by sending a stamped addressed envelope to address given at end of questionnaire.

Note: further offers which might be of interest may be sent to you by other, carefully selected, companies. If you do not want to receive them, please write to Robinson Publishing Ltd, 7 Kensington Church Court, London W8 4SP, UK.

QUESTIONNAIRE

Please tick the appropriate boxes to indicate your answers

1 Where did you get this Scarlet title?
Bought in supermarket ☐
Bought at my local bookstore ☐ Bought at chain bookstore ☐
Bought at book exchange or used bookstore ☐
Borrowed from a friend ☐
Other (please indicate) _____

2 Did you enjoy reading it?
A lot ☐   A little ☐   Not at all ☐

3 What did you particularly like about this book?
Believable characters ☐   Easy to read ☐
Good value for money ☐   Enjoyable locations ☐
Interesting story ☐   Modern setting ☐
Other _____

4 What did you particularly dislike about this book?
_____

5 Would you buy another Scarlet book?
Yes ☐   No ☐

6 What other kinds of book do you enjoy reading?
Horror ☐   Puzzle books ☐   Historical fiction ☐
General fiction ☐   Crime/Detective ☐   Cookery ☐
Other (please indicate) _____

7 Which magazines do you enjoy reading?
 1. _____
 2. _____
 3. _____

And now a little about you –
8 How old are you?
Under 25 ☐   25–34 ☐   35–44 ☐
45–54 ☐   55–64 ☐   over 65 ☐

cont.

9 What is your marital status?
   Single ☐   Married/living with partner ☐
   Widowed ☐   Separated/divorced ☐

10 What is your current occupation?
   Employed full-time ☐   Employed part-time ☐
   Student ☐   Housewife full-time ☐
   Unemployed ☐   Retired ☐

11 Do you have children? If so, how many and how old are they?
   _____
   _____

12 What is your annual household income?
   under $15,000 ☐ or £10,000   ☐
   $15–25,000   ☐ or £10–20,000   ☐
   $25–35,000   ☐ or £20–30,000   ☐
   $35–50,000   ☐ or £30–40,000   ☐
   over $50,000 ☐ or £40,000   ☐

Miss/Mrs/Ms _____
Address _____
_____
_____

Thank you for completing this questionnaire. Now tear it out – put
it in an envelope and send to:

Sally Cooper, Editor-in-Chief

USA/Can. address   *UK address/No stamp required*
SCARLET c/o London Bridge   SCARLET
85 River Rock Drive   FREEPOST LON 3335
Suite 202   LONDON W8 4BR
Buffalo   *Please use block capitals for*
NY 14207   *address*
USA

SALAC/4/97

Scarlet titles coming next month:

CAROUSEL   Michelle Reynolds
When Penny Farthing takes a job as housekeeper/nanny to
Ben Carmichael and his sons, she's looking for a quiet life.
Penny thinks she'll quite like living in the country and she
knows she'll love the little boys she's caring for . . . what she
doesn't expect is to fall in love with her boss!

BLACK VELVET   Patricia Wilson
Another SCARLET novel from this best-selling author!
Helen Stewart is *not* impressed when she meets Dan Forrest
– she's sure he's drunk, so she dumps him unceremoniously
at his hotel! Dan isn't drunk, he has flu, so their relationship
doesn't get off to the best start. Dan, though, soon wants
Helen more than he's ever wanted any other woman . . . but
is she involved in *murder?*

CHANGE OF HEART   Julie Garratt
Ten years ago headstrong Serena Corder was involved with
Holt Blackwood, but she left home because she resented her
father's attempts to control her life. Now a very different
Serena is back and the attraction she feels for Holt is as
strong as ever. But do they have a future together . . .
especially as she wears another man's ring!

A CIRCLE IN TIME   Jean Walton
Margie Seymour is about to lose her beloved ranch, when
she finds an injured man on her property. He tells her not
only that he is from the 1800s, but that *he*, not she, owns the
ranch! It's not long before feisty Margie Seymour is playing
havoc with Jake's good intentions of returning to his own
time as soon as he can!